"Betty Krawczyk's (... of wit and evocative ~~Southern~~ ... phrase make THIS DANGEROUS PLACE an immense pleasure to read. And like any cherished moment, the book is a delight to recall after inhaling its last pages. Krawczyk's personal, idiosyncratic story transcends the particularities of time and space and takes you to a deeper place within yourself, a place of new possibilities."

Shelley Wine, PhD Candidate, L.L.B, M.S.W, B.A.
FURY FOR THE SOUND: *The Women at Clayoquot*
(Producer/Director)

"A great read. With humour and compassion Krawczyk demonstrates the triumph of freedom over despair."

Bonnie Simpson, M.A.
Psychotherapist and Educator

Available for purchase on the FriesenPress Online Bookstore
at www.friesenpress.com/bookstore

This Dangerous Place

My Journey Between the Passions of the Living and the Dead

By Betty Krawczyk

SCHIVER RHODES PUBLISHING

Copyright © 2011 by Betty Krawczyk
First Edition – May 2011

Edited by Kyla Sentes

Photographs by Todd's Photos and
Dan Toulgoet

ISBN
978-1-77067-294-9 (Hardcover)
978-1-77067-295-6 (Paperback)
978-1-77067-296-3 (eBook)

All rights reserved.

No part of this publication may be reproduced in any form, or by any means, electronic or mechanical, including photocopying, recording, or any information browsing, storage, or retrieval system, without permission in writing from the publisher.

Some names have been changed to protect individual privacy.

Published by

Schiver Rhodes Publishing

in association with

FriesenPress
www.friesenpress.com

Distributed to the trade by The Ingram Book Company

Table of Contents

Preface	ix
Acknowledgments	xi

Chapter One
    The Crazy Lady Unit — 3

Chapter Two
    Moving into Laycott Place — 29

Chapter Three
    Courtroom and Ghost Talk — 65

Chapter Four
    The Lion Appears — 75

Chapter Five
    More Cousins Arrive — 99

Chapter Six
    Country Girls — 109

Chapter Seven
    The Horses — 119

Chapter Eight
    Becoming a Woman — 129

Chapter Nine
    The Mighty Will — 137

Chapter Ten
    Cousins Leave; Voodoo Arrives — 143

Chapter Eleven
    The Unraveling Begins — 161

Chapter Twelve
    The Contest is Over — 173

In memory of my father, William Jacob Schiver.

Preface

The use of court ordered injunctions in British Columbia to protect the right of logging companies to deforest public property is, in my opinion, indefensible. This court protection has allowed corporate international logging companies to largely decimate the old growth trees of British Columbian, to slash and burn large tracts of land, to ruin salmon streams, erode top soil, and spread poisonous chemical substances throughout the forests and all without the consent of many First Nations people. This has seriously eroded respect for the Supreme Court of British Columbia. This book is in part the story of what happens when protesters choose not to be sorry for trying to help save public forests, and instead, choose prison.

Within this context, THIS DANGEROUS PLACE is also an intense personal investigation into the mystery of the human will ... what it is, where it comes from, and the myriad ways humans develop and manage such enormous psychic responsibilities. It is also the story of what happens when passions of the dead apparently collide with those of the living. This is a true story.

Betty Schiver Krawczyk

Acknowledgments

First, I want to thank the members of Women in the Woods who stood together in solidarity on the blockades in the wilderness of the Walbran Valley during May through July of 2003. We were a motley crew of disparate women, both young and old, with one thing in common: a desire to halt or slow down the destruction of the public forests in British Columbia by industrial logging.

I also want to thank from the bottom of my heart all of our male and female supporters who came with us to the woods, who brought food, good cheer, and encouragement. There was a wonderful fund raising art auction at Sooke Harbour House to help with our legal fees. I want to express my appreciation to all of the artists who contributed to the auction with a special mention to the organizers; Jasmine Phillips, J Scott and Nancy the Blacksmith.

Cameron Ward gave his all in my defense in Court. It's like swimming upstream in black strap molasses to find a good, dedicated lawyer who works for the environment with his or her heart, often without adequate pay. Or any pay. Cameron Ward is one of a very select group in the legal profession in British Columbia. Very select.

I want to particularly acknowledge Ruth Masters, a well know elder environmental activist in British Columbia. As I was being carried to the police wagon in the wee hours of the morning on an isolated logging road in the Walbran Valley, Ruth whipped out her harmonica and started playing "Oh Canada." It was surreal. It melted my heart. I carried that image with me into prison. I also want to mention Ingmar Lee who helped keep good order in the protest camp and the young men busy in constructive pursuits. A large camp of people to be fed and kept dry in

the rainy season was a challenge. And later, while imprisoned, Monika Marcovici made sure my messages to the outside world were delivered uncensored as the prison censors whatever it pleases to censor. I am grateful to Monika for her care and concern.

At the end of my trial I received a six months sentence plus the four and a half months I had already served while waiting for trial. I could not have survived this period had it not been for the sweet and steady support I received from so many people who stood with me, who appeared in court, who wrote and visited and brought news.

Last, but not least, I want to thank my family. My daughters and my sons and their families are with me always, wherever I am.

Betty Schiver Krawczyk

SOME NAMES HAVE BEEN CHANGED TO PROTECT INDIVIDUAL PRIVACY.

An unexamined life is not worth living.

Socrates

Chapter One

The Crazy Lady Unit

This morning our entire unit seems somewhat more animated than usual. Unit A is the Medical Observation Unit in Barnaby Correctional Centre for Women in British Columbia. Janit and I have been told that we are being temporarily housed in this "Are You Crazy, Lady? Unit" until some bed spaces are found in another unit. Oh, yeah, sure. We have been in this unit since our arrest on July 7, 2003. It is now July 28 and my own special brand of paranoia is beginning to kick in. Wouldn't the Supreme Court judges and Weyerhaeuser Logging, and the RCMP who have to deal with us, be delighted if they could have some sort of official documentation that we were, as they knew all along, simply wacko? But I am trying to get grounded into the morning; to still the brain chatter in my head asking what a relatively normal law abiding grandmother is doing locked up with thieves, prostitutes, drug addicts, and murderers?

This is a small unit. There are only eight cells and one is empty. The women in here are emotionally ill, depressed, and despairing. One has HIV, and as Hepatitis C is rampant in the prison as a whole, the odds are most of our unit mates also have Hepatitis C, and God only knows what else. Most have been working on the street for greater or lesser lengths of time, and two wear the wrist bandages indicating the wearers have recently slashed.

As the women in this particular unit are somehow more thoroughly prisoners than in the rest of the compound I'll give them names of birds, sweet birds that could fly over the surrounding outside walls if they took a notion. The prisoner I'll call Robin was taken down to segregation last night. She had stolen one of the five-pound weights from the gym and hidden it in her room, which caused no end of trouble for the guards. They had to search the entire building before they the dumbbell in Robin's room.

"Aw, she just wanted to work out in her own room," Mocking Bird says from the next table in answer to my inquiry of why Robin might have done such a thing. Mocking Bird is tall, lanky, and darkly brooding. She speaks slowly, deliberately, searching for words. She appears to be heavily medicated, but her comments and responses always seem rational enough.

"She didn't plan to kill nobody with it," Robin continues.

Jay Bird, sitting across from Mocking Bird at the same table, pauses in the laborious job of buttering her toast without smearing the jam, which she habitually spreads on first. She is thin to the point of emaciation and moves about with curious waving arm motions that give the impression she is trying to swim through the air. She needs a haircut. Her thin, ratty bangs obscure the top part of her face. And her comments and responses are frequently angry and irrational.

"That's not the fucking point," Jay Bird snaps, emphasizing her words with a jab in the air with the white plastic fork. We all eat with plastic utensils and paper plates in this prison. "There was a lockdown. We were locked down for a fucking three hours until they found the fucking thing."

Lockdown means locked into our cells with no access to the common sitting room or the outside smoke pit. It is being separated from the smoke pit for undetermined amounts of time that causes the most concern because, except for Janit and me, all of the other inmates smoke when they have the tobacco. Next on our fellow inmates' panic list is being separated from the kitchen area, which holds the coffee pot and tea bags.

THIS DANGEROUS PLACE

Suddenly Sparrow, sitting at the table directly in front of us, begins to laugh. She is sitting alone and her laughter is high, raucous, and maniacal. Sparrow's laugh spooks me.

"What the fuck's so funny?" Mocking Bird demands, turning to face Sparrow.

"Cause those toilets in general population probably ain't stopped flushing yet," Sparrow answers, chortling into her coffee mug.

Mocking Bird parts her bangs with thin fingers and stares into space for a moment. And then, as if just getting the joke, smiles. It's the first time I've seen Mocking Bird smile since we've arrived in the unit.

Janit and I exchange glances. Janit, at forty-eight, is only a fledgling grandmother. At seventy-five, I'm a great grandmother, definitely an elder, and a recidivist in the criminal justice system. This is Janit's first incarceration, not counting the previous two weeks we spent together here recently, stemming from our first blockade in the Walbran.

As members of Women in the Woods, we are on an environmental mission to save the last remaining old growth public forests of British Columbia for future generations. We decided to start a campaign against Gordon Campbell's proposal entitled "The Working Forest" which meant that his government, simply by an order in council, could remove public forests from public protection laws and declare them private lands. Weyerhaeuser Tree Farm License Number 44 in the Walbran Valley on Vancouver Island seemed a good place to start our campaign. Janit and I both lived on Vancouver Island, but after we were arrested for refusing to move from the blockades we were sent to the women's prison on the mainland for incarceration until trial. Had we signed a promise not to return to the Walbran Valley we could have been released until then. At the time, neither of us would sign.

"So ... what's so funny about toilets flushing?" I ask, curious about the joke.

Jay Bird looks at us steadily for a long moment before answering. The prolonged gaze may simply be an effort to focus her bloodshot eyes. She is fair, with a mottled complexion and a missing front tooth. She is anywhere from 35 to 50 and wears one of the telltale wrist bands. She

also seems heavily medicated, but I think I detect a glint of pity in her loopy gaze as she stares at us.

"For Christ's sake. You ladies know there's dope in here, right? And brew, right?" she asks. While harsh and insistent before, her speech has suddenly adopted patient overtones, as if speaking to children.

I nod. Yes, I know from previous incarcerations that drugs find their way into the joint and that some of the inmates, from time to time, make, or try to make, some kind of alcoholic beverage by stashing away fruit and sugar.

"Well, in a lockdown the screws are either fucking looking for dope or brew. Or else somebody's tried to escape. Or slashed or some other fucking thing. Usually it's looking for dope and brew, so inmates flush whatever they've stashed. And they're going to be pissed when they find all the fucking fuss was over a fucking dumbbell … 'specially when they've been brewing for weeks. No, it's a fucking good thing Star is in the fucking protected unit right now. If she goes into general population later she can just fucking hope some of the mean ones have cooled down. Oh, Fucking Christ, yeah. I can still hear those toilets flushing. Call the plumbers, man …."

Robin laughs out loud.

"Well, at least," I say softly to Janit, "the unit is a little merrier this morning." Even Mocking Bird has a bit of colour in her cheeks.

After breakfast Janit and I help clean up the unit. All who live here, unless we have a health care notation on our record sheet, must perform a morning chore. I opt for sweeping and mopping the hallway and dining area of the unit. There's something soothing about mopping. It's the back and forth movements of the arms; I get a rhythm going, swoosh, swoosh, not too fast and not too slow, about one swoosh to every three heartbeats. I don't have to fight any of the other women for the mopping job. This is my fifth trip to this prison and I know for a fact that the vast majority of women incarcerated in here have bad backs.

What to make of the prevalence of bad backs among the prison population? It's true most live physically dangerous lives, and physical tussles occur when running from cops, from dope dealers trying to collect on

debts, pimps, bad dates, ripped off friends, and that's discounting the drunken car crashes. But even the non-users in here, such as the women who simply do bank fraud or women working as accountants who rip off their employers, or shoot or knife their mates in cold sober fury, all have back problems. My seventy-five-year-old back is fine. So I mop.

After our chores are done Janit and I head for our cells. I have a pile of correspondence to answer before I can even get to my epistle writing.

The epistles are what I call my letters to the world's editors that I habitually send out in great volume. Mostly I think the epistles go into the same black hole occupied by the majority of logging protesters who try to squeeze justice out of the Justices of the Supreme Court of British Columbia, but some of the letters and articles, actually bring back bright, knowledgeable, sympathetic replies. It's enough to keep me in the epistle writing business. I learned how to write short and pithy back in Louisiana when my husband John was going to Louisiana State University. I learned to write short stories for women's Confession magazines and if you couldn't tell a story in five to seven thousand words you weren't going to sell much.

But before I can get to my epistles I have to make some notes from sections of the book *Woman* by Natalie Angier along with Stephen Hawking's two books: *A Brief History of Time* and *Black Holes and Baby Universes*. These are the three books I brought into prison with me and I'm trying to synthesize these two writers.

Sometimes the projects I assign to myself are so outlandish I frighten myself. Are you crazy, lady? Yes, because I have no science background, in fact no academic background at all except for a year's study of Creative Writing through the University of Oklahoma. This was a graduate course but they let me take it because I had already sold three pieces of fiction. I was home schooled by my mother, married at sixteen, raised eight children with entirely satisfactory results, and four husbands with mixed results. This was a time consuming business, not to even mention the causes I got swept up in on the side that resulted in some serious relocations, including changing countries. And I was writing all the time.

My mother taught me to read and write and love literature. I have read and written my way through life at a non-stop pace, and I set great store by both these activities. I've also learned that if I can't put an issue or circumstance on paper, then I don't really understand the issue or circumstance. So while I am in this miserable place I will use my time not only to further the cause of trying to help save what's left of the public forests of British Columbia, but I will try to understand why I intuitively find Angier and Hawking to be talking about the same thing, even when they seem to be universes apart.

Pulitzer Prize science writer Natalie Angier describes the dazzling beauty of the human egg which is half the size of a pin head, while the renowned theoretical physicist and mathematician Stephen Hawking describes not only huge stars and planets that dwarf our own, but whole other universes that uncannily resembles Angier's egg. Both Hawking and Angier's publishers bill the authors as popular writers, that is, they suggest that these books are intended for a general audience.

Well, people will claim anything, especially publishers trying to sell books. I'm a general audience, for Pete's sake. Probably just a tad more well-read than most, and I don't understand much of Angier's book or most of Hawking's books.

However, what I do understand, or think I do, stuns me; it makes chills run up and down my spine. It's the Twilight Zone. In my opinion there's an eerie connection going on between Angier and Hawking. These two think in terms of opposite ends of space, time, beginnings, and evolution; they are the quintessential micro and macro duo. The glow of Angier's circular human egg resounds in the globalism of Hawking's imaginary time where there is no beginning and no end and the only analogy he uses is the circularity of the earth. It's all too much. My head spins with the breathless vision they invoke in my imagination, a vision of a design so vast it echoes in the teensiest particles ever discovered, outward to an unimaginable universe upon universe that has no boundaries.

Janit suddenly sticks her head into my doorway. "Are you going to write to the judge?" she asks.

I reflect for a moment. Our last Court appearance was before Mr. Justice Pitfield a few days before. I had yelled at Justice Pitfield in a very disrespectful manner. Since then I have been having second thoughts because later I remembered that Mr. Justice Pitfield was actually one of the judges who had expressed reservations about the way protesters are charged and arrested. He is one of the judges we should be trying to romance, so to speak.

"Yes, I'll do that now," I say, closing Angier's book. "And you write one too," I add. "Last night I reread some of Mr. Justice Pitfield's judgments on protesters and injunctions and you know what? I, in fact, used one of his oral reasons for judgment in my address to the Court in the Elaho trials."

"What should I say?" Janit asks, wrinkling her brow. Janit is short, plump, with glossy black hair and dark eyes. She is of Burmese descent.

"Whatever your heart tells you to say."

The guard appears on our tier. "Lockup, ladies," she says in a singsong voice. I like this guard. She's Chinese, and kind of funny. Sally Tan. That's her real name. She told me to be sure and use her real name in my writings. Some of the guards are not very funny or friendly, either. But most are just doing a job and are not out to get you.

A lockup is not the same as a lockdown. A lockup comes routinely half an hour after breakfast and half an hour after lunch. A lockdown means there's a fight in the unit or yard, or there's a serious search on for suspected contraband, or as the inmates say, some bad shit is coming down. Death. It happens in here. But not at the moment.

Janit disappears into her own cell and the heavy iron doors on our tier clang shut. I put aside my books and take out pen and paper. At home I write at least four hours a day. That's ingrained in me now. If I were shipwrecked on a desert island with no supplies I probably would write for four hours a day in the sand with a stick. But my computer is at home and what I have in this prison is a couple of pens and some paper. So my thumb and middle finger are feeling strained and sore along with my elbow and inner right arm between shoulder and elbow. It will get worse before I am out of this place, I am sure.

Is this judge the one? The one we have been waiting for? The one who will bring us at last out of the darkness of total judicial compliance with the logging companies? The judge who will lead us into the light of some sort of belated grand refusal on the part of British Columbian judges to do the dirty work of the Attorney General and the politicians who depend on corporate logging campaign funds? Probably not.

But the evils of each day are sufficient thereof, I remind myself, mentally echoing one of my mother's favorite Biblical phrases. Not that I'm keen on Christianity any more. Or ever was, really. But especially not after I found out what Christianity did to women. But Mama's calm reasonable voice is forever in my head, side by side with Daddy's fierce questioning. Daddy became an evangelistic preacher when I was in my early teens. This seemed very weird to me at the time and has remained so. And it didn't seem to answer for me, even as a child, at least not in a reasonable way, the question of where did we all come from? And how did we get here along with the chickens and pigs and frogs and lightening bugs? Because I was home schooled Mama taught me what she thought was important. Charles Darwin wasn't exactly absent from the curriculum but he wasn't squarely on it either. And God was huge. He was responsible for everything important. But I learned a little something about the theory of evolution as I grew older because Mama didn't forbid me reading whatever came into my hands from the library. Sometimes she would look at a book I had chosen, maybe even frown at it, but she would never make me take anything back, or take the frowned at book away. So I knew about evolution. Not how it worked, but that it existed.

In those early days I didn't think fundamentalist Christianity actually answered these questions for Daddy, either. It was just that it seemed to be the only answer in town to some very troubling questions that arose for him out of his contest with a ghost in a haunted house we lived in when I was a kid. I think Daddy was a preacher without faith, while Mama was a true believer. I believed in Mama without believing what she believed, so I began my own search for answers to life's fundamental questions early. The search goes on.

THIS DANGEROUS PLACE

I settle down on the thin plastic mattress that covers my bunk, with pen and pad in hand and start to compose a letter of at least a semi-apology to Judge Pitfield. Just as I am finishing the letter a bellowing scream cuts through the unit, the piercing sound bouncing off the walls of my cell. Startled, my hand slips and the pen makes a scribble mark on the bottom part of the letter I was so carefully composing. Damn. I get up and go to the door. And then the scream repeats itself, rising in crescendo. I can hear someone running through the common room, but from the narrow slit in my door I can't quite see who it is. I press my nose anxiously against the slit of glass, trying to get a better view.

Are the screams coming from our tier? Is that Janit screaming? No, thank the goddess, it isn't Janit. It's Humming Bird, the new inmate in the next tier. She's older, with long gray hair and wears her red institutional sweats pulled haphazardly over her lumpy body. She walks about carefully, with head down as though fearful she'll trip. But if you speak to her or ask a question she'll answer with a sweet, sad smile. A guard I don't know is hastily unlocking her door.

"Miss Humming Bird, what's wrong?" the guard asks anxiously.

"This room. I don't want to be in this room," Humming Bird wails in a loud, trembling voice. "It scares me." There is certainly enough panic in the woman's voice.

"What is there in the room that scares you?" Guard asks.

"The room ... it's the room!" Humming Bird wails again, her voice threatening to segue into a scream. And then it does. Another ear-splitting scream fills the unit.

"All right, Miss Humming Bird, try to calm down," the guard says. I don't see her press her guard panic button, but I know she's doing it. All the guards have this little panic button when there's trouble. "And you can come out. Come on out and sit on the couch and I'll see if there's any coffee."

I can see Humming Bird being coaxed by the guard to the couch, and then they are out of my line of vision and I can't hear what they're saying, either. But in just a few minutes two other guards appear and then I can

see all of the players again through the glass slot on my window as well as hear the conversation.

"It's that room, I don't want it." Humming Bird is reiterating, "I'm scared of it."

"And you don't have to go back to it," one of the senior guards is saying. Her voice is soothing, gently matter of fact. "We'll put you in another room. Would you like to see the nurse?"

Wild shaking of head, gray hair flying. "No. I don't want to see the nurse. I want another room."

"Well, I don't think there's any problem with that. Just stay here for a bit and rest. We'll see about getting you another room."

It's getting past our lock up time, the time we should be let out of our cells for exercise, or access to the common room. I know from experience that the rest of us will not be unlocked until the problem on the floor is resolved. And resolved it is. Another ten minutes and Humming Bird is smiling and nodding at the officers. After another five, the two extra officers leave. At eleven a.m. our unit guard comes and unlocks us. It's our time for the exercise yard.

Unit A takes exercise with Unit B. Unit B is the protected custody unit. Most of the women who reside in Unit B have been convicted of murdering children. They range in age from mid-twenties to ninety-six. Surprisingly enough, this group seems to me to be the most stable population in the prison. These inmates are not addicted, or if they were at the time of their crime, they are now so isolated from the other prisoners, the ones who do manage to get drugs in and sell them to the others, that these Unit B inmates have lost touch with their addictions.

They are in protected custody because the other women might harm them. Because of this threat of violence our women's prison seems to mimic the men's prisons. Which grieves me.

I read a study somewhere that showed that in cases where there is no sexual motive, men who kill their own children or step-children do so out of revenge in order to punish the children's' mothers for rejecting them or making them angry. When women kill their own children it is usually out of desperation and feelings of helplessness.

THIS DANGEROUS PLACE

It does seem to me that the women who are in the general population of the prison, many of whom have deserted their own children in one way or another for alcohol, or crack or heroin or any combination thereof, could be a tad more understanding of another woman's desperation, but they aren't. As a rule, they don't see that by choosing the dope over the kids they commit multiple murders: murders of themselves as mothers, of kids who deserve sober, attentive mothers and of the very notion of motherhood.

All they will admit to is that at least they didn't physically kill their kids. That puts them one up on the child murderers in their own minds. As long as the kids are alive the chance is always there, however slender, for a good outcome. The kids who were in the care of these women in Unit B didn't live. I try not to judge these women. I've had my own moments of desperation, brief perhaps, but real enough to experience a soul bleakness as black as night.

We must go down to the exercise yard in the elevator. A passenger I will call Pelican is Chinese and speaks no English. She is the elder, in her nineties. Flamingo, also in the elevator, is young and pretty and standing next to Pelican. After inmates have been here awhile they can exchange prison garb for their own clothes and wear jewelry. Flamingo is wearing a skimpy top that hangs off her shoulders and barely skims her pierced belly button. Pelican is displeased. She suddenly reaches over and tries to pull Flamingo's little top together across Flamingo's front while scolding in rapid Chinese. A brief scuffle ensues but is quickly subdued by the guard.

On the track grounds I am allowed to have a soccer ball to kick across the yard. Behind the high wire fence I can see the high rises of the city of Burnaby in the distance. Burnaby is part of greater Vancouver. I call these high rises the towers of Babylon. There are six of them. I like looking at them. They face west. On sunny days the sunlight reflects off their collective windows and creates a metallic glow.

In the evenings of such days, just when the sun has almost disappeared over the Fraser River and the sky is deep blue streaked with amber, all six of the buildings catch fire and send out shooting stars. Just

for a brief moment or two. I am now so familiar with the exercise yard that when the weather is just right, I can almost tell the exact moment the phenomenon will occur. At these times I stand transfixed, my breath caught in my throat.

The sun is shining today, and it's hot. Janit decided to stay in and work on her letter to the judge. One of the other inmates falls into step beside me and begins talking as I kick the ball around.

I kick the soccer ball hard as I can, then walk to it at a brisk pace, kick it again. The action is good for my legs. On the outside I tap dance and do the Bayou Bugaloo to stay flexible. In here I kick a soccer ball around the field and shoot baskets in the gym.

I don't particularly care for company while I'm doing either, but because I have a friendly grandmotherly demeanor and am not one of them, so to speak, the others seem to want to talk to me. I listen. That's my job. I didn't apply, but the job has claimed me. To listen.

At lunch I get into a discussion of feminism with Janit. Janit wants to get a feminist lawyer to represent us in Court, particularly one who is familiar with forestry issues and who will work pro bono.

"I don't think that's going to happen," I say, "as none have appeared on the scene so far. I don't even know a feminist lawyer who might be familiar with forest issues who has a private practice, much less one who has a private practice and will work pro bono. We've got Cameron Ward. He's committed to our issues and is willing to work for whatever we can scrape up. I say we stick with him."

"I wish I had a good lawyer," Owl says from the next table, evidently eavesdropping. Owl is in here for stabbing her man in the face for abusing her daughter. "That's what fucking happened to me," she continues, "a bad lawyer. You know, more than half the women in here were abused since they can remember by men who are supposed to protect them, and then when they get away from that there's just other men out there waiting who say, 'Oh, I love you, you pretty thing" but who are really pimps and suck all the juice out of them and addict them and then junk them. I got three years for stabbing this jerk in his sleep."

I take a bite out of my cold grilled cheese sandwich and chew thoughtfully. I could warm up the sandwich in the microwave, but I've always had a thing about microwaves leaking radiation, so I try to stay away from them as much as possible. It's the sleeping thing, I think, considering Owl's case, which would heavily influence a male judge. If one man can be stabbed while he sleeps, regardless of his crimes, then how can any man sleep peacefully at night?

"Yeah, sure, eh," Robin joins in. sitting across from Owl. "There was a woman right here in Vancouver who cut off her husband's dick and she didn't get any prison."

"I think they reattached it," Janit puts in, "didn't they?"

"Yeah, sure," Robin sneers. "Like it's ever going to work right again."

"Was the husband sleeping?" I ask, draining the last of the coffee in my cup. "When his penis was, you know, slashed."

Owl shrugs. "I don't know. But I fucking know I had plenty of reason to stab my old man. He raped my 16-year-old daughter."

I begin to peel the orange served with lunch. I love oranges. Prison fare is heavy on carbohydrates and light on protein – it's just shy of being criminally light on protein. So I buy canned salmon from the canteen. I usually save my oranges to eat with the salmon, but today the lunch was skimpy and the soup was watery.

Owl is elaborating on her family troubles. I listen with half an ear. As this is my fifth (or is it my sixth?) incarceration, I have heard variations of her story many times before. The men in these women's lives inflict deep wounds on daughters whose mothers can't or won't protect them. The daughters are taught to put up with their men's abuse. Then it is the daughter's turn, if they live long enough, to turn a blind or addicted eye to their daughter's abuse by successive husbands, lovers, or pimps. If a mother explodes at this monstrous activity and turns violent under the influence of alcohol or other drugs, the prison is awaiting her.

This kind of betrayal is the commonest story in this prison. Variations of it must be the most common story in this province, in this country, in this world: stories of the betrayal of daughters by fathers, step-fathers, uncles, brothers, other family members or friends of family members. Men

love stories of the betrayal of young females. It is the commonest theme of pornography and increasingly of mainstream entertainment. Someday, some day, I think, women will finally tire of this betrayal once and for all, and in spite of addictions to chemical substances and TV, and computer-induced shopping sickness, will rise up and demand reparation.

"You cannot betray your daughters," they will yell, "and not betray yourselves, your families, your society, your country, your human evolution, you could not lie and cheat and steal if you did not first give tacit permission for the portrayers of the violation of daughters to be part of mainstream media, of porn, of pop culture..."

Not that woman are impervious to lying and stealing. When it is the only game in town for some women, they may also be recruited to betray their daughters. Not just by direct sexual acts from their men, but by putting up with the sexualizing of children in videos and ads, by not resisting when women's rape crisis centres and safe houses and resource places are gutted by misogynist governments, by not yelling blue murder when a child is threatened by any man whether he wears a suit or a motorcycle jacket, by not equating the rape and molestation of native children as serious as that of white children, and by a million and one blind eye turnings that we all do every day, every week, every month, every year of our lives.

Yet how we all long for the good, wise father: the one who is kind and tolerant, who infuses his children, both boys and girls, with self-confidence and optimism. Maybe it isn't the average guy's fault that fatherhood is such a mess.

Maybe the confusion is that fatherhood as we know it just might be an artificially imposed concept, oscillating between *Father Knows Best* and *Mac the Knife*. Men are on their own too, just as women are. I think that trying to father growing kids in isolation in this culture of fast cars, drugs, gangs, violent electronics, massive corporate theft, and the cult of the ugly, is a tricky business. Growing kids are a major, major challenge under any conditions, and where we stand at this moment in the evolution of our society, parenthood is rapidly becoming so problematic that it's going completely out of style.

It's as difficult for boys as it is for girls to grow up and blossom in what I have essentially come to think of as a computer-loving, people-hating society. Boys grow up thinking, if they think about having kids at all, that they can depend on the kids' mothers to do the hard stuff that their big job is to shine in whatever that job they may have, to be a manly man, to be kind but not a sissy, and to be thoughtful, but not exactly sensitive. They can't afford sensitive. They should contain their emotions without being thought heartless, although maybe just a dash of heartlessness adds to their persona.

Men also have to be stronger physically than women, so while it's important to keep up with manly beer drinking and watching sports on TV, at the same time, they can't allow their muscles to deteriorate through too much beer drinking and couch potato watching sports. It's imperative to drive a really neat car because this man-car thing is a relationship, after all, right up there on par with a man's relationship with his wife. If push comes to shove, well maybe, after all, a man needs his car more than his wife. The list of conflicting messages goes on until it's enough to drive a good man mad.

So young men who are swimming through this morass of manly man stuff don't have time to get a realistic handle about what it might mean to be a father. Yet while they don't know the specifics, many sense the treacherous undertows. This is why so many men, like many women, are deciding to forego the entire parent thing and just let the violent videos, TV, stereos, chat rooms, CD disks, Game Boys, and multi-purpose sound systems raise the kids; they wash their hands of the whole messy bit.

After lunch Janit and I are told we are to be moved to another unit. Evidently, we are not crazy enough to take up the crazy space that is more needed by other crazier women. So we pack up our belongings, stuff it all into plastic bags and are trudged out of the crazy lady and protected side of the prison that includes sections A and B. We are on our way to Unit G, which is on the other side of the building, the more settled, workaday side.

This prison houses both provincial and federal prisoners. The federal prisoners are long-term, and a significant number are sent here from

other parts of Canada. They are privileged in this prison as the federal government pays for their clothes and programs, and best of all, because they are long-term they can't be bunked with other inmates. As they have already been sentenced, most work outside the unit in other parts of the prison, go to school upgrading, or attend programs.

If I'd had my druthers, I'd have stayed where we were. Although our new unit is more stable, it's twice as big, and compared to our secluded Unit A, it's noisy. There is another problem: neither Janit nor I want to work outside the unit because we have so much writing to do for our cause. But we are greeted warmly enough by some of the other inmates. Lifers. I know them from my previous stays. Some of them are convicted of murder or manslaughter.

But we are all women together, and I am happy enough to see friendly, familiar faces. I introduce Janit around. She is a little apprehensive of this unit because these mostly federal women seem louder, tougher, and are only lightly medicated if medicated at all. By dinnertime she is relaxing. We are sort of assigned by default a small table in front of the glassed-in office bubble that is roughly the same in all of the units. In addition to our regular prison meal there is an offering from the prison garden. The units take turns receiving the bounties from the prison garden and we just lucked into Unit G's day. There is lettuce, tomatoes, crisp Bok Choy, and long green onions. One of the lifers has given me an extremely delicious, fresh hot pepper.

By bedtime I realize that Janit and I are in a no man's land both figuratively and literally in this unit: we have a cash flow problem in here just as on the outside. We have almost no money left in our prison bank accounts. So I make an emergency phone call to Marya Nyland, the treasurer of our Women in the Woods group, for some operating funds.

That night I turn restlessly on the thin, plastic mattress on the floor, trying to get comfortable. We are double bunked in this unit. Janit offered me the bunk, but it's hot in this room and the only breath of air that seems to be stirring is from the vent close to the floor. Goddess only knows what is mixed in with the air that comes through the vent. One hears all kinds of stories: that the air is recycled over and over with no fresh air

intake; that the vents are never cleaned; that we are breathing dust mites continuously along with the germs of the respiratory illnesses of the other inmates, like tuberculosis.

Oh, God. But the vent sends out a little breeze along with its pathogens, real and imagined. Without the breeze the room is so hot and stuffy it's almost unbearable, even though our little window is pushed out as far as it will go.

Janit is sleeping peacefully in spite of the heat. I get up and wash my face with cold water, trying to make as little noise as possible, and then lie back down.

I wonder who our judge will be for trial. Will it be Mr. Justice Pitfield again, or some other judge? Janit and I have already been before six different judges who have shuffled us off onto the next one in line. Oh, please let our next one be a benevolent judge! This becomes a kind of prayer in my mind...

Oh Judge of the Moment
Bestow upon us, upon the forests and streams,
the lowly mosses and ferns,
The little scurrying furry animals that make their way through the
dense undergrowth, the mice, chipmunks, martens, raccoons, and
the large ones who take up more room on the forest paths,
The bears, richly brown, with a rolling gait, yes,
come bears, bring your cubs forth,
And the wolves, who send their yowling cries out upon
the night air while they hide themselves in the bush,
And the most unseen of all, the secretive cougar,
who watches from the treetops, waiting,
And all, all, that are seen from the sky by the seagulls, blue herons,
ducks, eagles, and even the smaller birds who head for the sky, the
crows, Stellar jays, robins, starlings, yes, even the tiny flashy hummingbirds that can hang in the air above the mountain streams,
The waters gurgling down to meet the mother,
the mother of all things, the sea,

> The sea, who gave up many of her creatures to the land,
> but still holds tightly to the most treasured, refusing to
> give up the whales and dolphins and sharks
> Along with all of the little crusty creatures that line the shores,
> flashing brilliant colours under the sun or digging down into the
> wet sand and who feed from sea water and are fed upon by other
> little water beings that in turn nourish the luscious fish that live
> in the top waters of the mother sea and the others who are iridescent and show their wonderful light only to each other down,
> down, down in the bottom of the sea ... Oh, yes, Judge of the
> Moment ,bestow upon us all your blessings and your mercy ...

Yes. Doggone it, we need a judge who might have something of a notion of life's systems that are out there, inside us, everywhere, encoded not in SLAPP suits or Court-ordered injunctions and Contempt of Court charges, but that are in our genes, the code tides of the sea in our veins, a spiraling, silvery connection to the universe, the spirit world ...

An old song from the southern musicians, The Meters, floats through my mind. This tune has been bugging me lately. I heard it many years ago; there is a story behind the lyrics. In the song a father, or big brother, is telling a child who is ill, but who has many times when well, accompanied the man on trips to the zoo, to the beach, to the outdoors, and when he was forced to go alone because the child was ill, he tells the child how the animals have missed him (or her)...

> *Oh, I wennon down to the Audu'mon Zoo*
> *And they all axt fuh' you*
> *The monkey's axt*
> *The tiger's axt*
> *And the elephant axt fuh'you, too*
> *Went on down to the deep blue sea*
> *And they all axt fuh' you,*
> *The sharks axt and the whales axt ...*

The singer's raspy blues voice is toying with my brain:

> *I wennon up to the big blue sky;*
> *And day all axt fuh'you;*
> *Duh crows axt, duh sea gulls axt;*
> *And duh eagles axt me too) ...*

Yeah, the animals are asking about us, the wild ones both in the prisons of zoos and out there in the pollutions of corporate industry. They are asking for us, all of us, including the human mothers. And where are we? Where? Well, some of us are in prison, I remind myself ruefully, trying to find a comfortable position on the thin, lumpy mattress on the floor. And the fathers? Where are the fathers in this?

Suddenly I am thinking about my own father. Daddy. My brother, sister, and I called him Daddy. Never Poppa as some Southern kids called their fathers. Not that any of us kids regarded our father as being the chum that the term Daddy might imply. We all kept our distance. We knew that while Daddy laughed a lot, he also had a mean streak. Not deliberately cruel perhaps, but dictatorial and uncompromising.

When he bit into an idea or plan of action the entire universe got swept along in his wake. At least it seemed that way to us kids. It must have seemed that way to Mama, too, I thought, at least some of the time. The problem was when Daddy's idea or plans of action was obviously not working, he didn't know when or how to give it up.

Like the time the authorities showed up in our yard after repeated warnings and told him if he didn't stop selling home-made medicines he would go to jail. Daddy kept on at it and it wasn't until Mama was packing her bags and ours to leave him that Daddy conceded defeat and got out of the medicine man business.

The only other time Mama got close to leaving Daddy was over the ghost in the old Laycott Place.

I was eleven years old then, almost twelve, the first time I saw Laycott Place. I let my mind wander, thinking of the old plantation house as I turn restlessly on my makeshift bed on the prison floor. I can still see the

winding gallery, or veranda, of the rambling, two story house that circled the entire circumference of the building. I can see the floorboards sagging badly on the left side of the gallery, leaving some of the railing unconnected to the gallery floor, and the enormous wisteria vine shading the right side of the two-story structure. It was a vine so lush and aggressive that it climbed all the way across the porch valance and then dropped, heavy with purple blossoms in full early summer's bloom, to the long-neglected weed-choked flower garden below.

That first day, even from where I was standing next to Daddy's car in the equally unweeded graveled lane, the vine generated a scent so overwhelming my entire body seemed to be bathed in perfume as I stood there trying to adjust to the sight of our new home.

I didn't know what to make of it. The house was drastically unlike our old place. This one was so huge, and weather-beaten. It had a copper roof in front that had turned green with time. The house originally, way back, over a hundred and ninety years way back, according to Daddy, had also claimed a thousand surrounding acres. There were other buildings, too. Down a ways, past the enormous Black Walnut Tree and two Paper Shell Pecan trees way on the other side of a small stream running past the house began a row of caved in shacks that had originally housed slaves (who never really stopped being slaves for many years after emancipation), but who had long since deserted the place. Beyond these shacks stood the decrepit remains of an old sugar cane mill on the far side of the stream that had been dedicated to extracting juice from the sugar cane. But Daddy cautioned that all of these ruined buildings were off limits to us kids.

Most of the vast acreage had been sold off. Only fifty acres were included in our lease. The house itself along with the fifty acres was hung up in court, Daddy explained, and couldn't be sold. It had been hung up in court for a long time. Some earlier relatives who had inherited from the original owners had left a covenant forbidding the sale of the house but it was occasionally leased. It had been awhile since it had been leased. Like years. Daddy didn't say how many years or why the last people had left.

I thought the entire scene was a bit spooky and weird that first day. It was not exactly scary, but it was nothing like the comfy little shotgun

THIS DANGEROUS PLACE

house with its two add-ons that sat jauntily on the five acres we had just left. But Daddy was happy and Mama was pleased that Daddy was happy, and that she would now have all the room she needed for her sewing and Daddy's business materials and there was lots of room for her piano. In fact, the house was so cavernous we were only moving into one side of it, leaving the west side and the upstairs closed off.

Oh, yes, Daddy was pleased with his farm deal. He dreamed of becoming a sugar cane farmer. And here was this huge house and lots of land and he had negotiated the lease down to something we could afford. Daddy was so excited that day of our moving in, his bright blue eyes fairly snapped and crackled with enthusiasm, his feet were almost dancing as he scurried about with Mama, discussing where our well-used furniture was to be placed in the house. Later we learned that Daddy had already heard about the ghost who also lived in or around the house, but he didn't even think it worth mentioning to Mama, even then. He didn't believe in ghosts. Oh Daddy was a stubborn man!

The images of our little family moving into the old dilapidated plantation house fade from my inner view; I am exhausted and must sleep. But when I sleep, I dream of Laycott Place and I can hear screaming. I wake suddenly, heart pounding. Had Humming Bird moved into our unit, too, or was it some other woman, or ... Was that Daddy screaming? Or me? I sit upright, looking wildly around. No, Janit was still sleeping. The screams have obviously come from inside my head. I lie back down, still thinking about Daddy and Laycott Place, and about the first time I saw the old plantation house, shabby, but still standing straight and proud with its green copper roof after almost two centuries of high winds, pelting rains, and sweltering summer heat.

Oh, yes, Laycott Place had been built to last. It was grey with age, but doggone it, you could tell by looking that this big ole house at one time had been an imposing sight in the back country and, even yet, stood enduring and proud against years of neglect.

But what were we, a poor country family, doing moving into such a place?

L to R: Me age 7, my brother Ray Allen age 10, and my little sister Doris age 3 – 1935.

L to R: Ray Allen age 12, Me age 9, and Doris age 5 – 1937.

L to R: Ray Allen age 15, Me age 12, and Doris age 8 – 1940.

My father, William Jacob Schiver "Uncle Jake", moving into Laycott Place – 1940.

My mother, Martha Winifred Rhodes Schiver "Aunt Bug", just before moving into Laycott Place – 1940.

Chapter Two

Moving into Laycott Place

I finally fall asleep out of sheer exhaustion, and morning in the prison comes soon enough. Today already has an air of busyness. It's Saturday. Cell inspection day. How to smarten up a cell with roughly a five by seven foot walking space that is housing two people? We do our best, and it is good enough. We pass.

I spend the rest of the day at the desk, writing. Janit must make do with writing on her bunk. As I am composing the address to the judge for both of us, my writing takes precedence. By the end of the day my butt is sore from sitting, but I have four handwritten copies of my address, one for the judge, one for the Crown, one for Cameron, and one for me to read.

I think I write with my butt as much as my head and fingers, and I write only as much as my butt can tolerate. I am reminded of Karl Marx and his carbuncles suffering in the Reading Room of the British Museum, and declaring that the capitalists would pay for every one of his carbuncles. Not that I think I could ever write anything that would either change or scare the heck out of half the world as Marx did. Or at least engage the entire world in argument and conversation as reflected by the tons of papers by others explaining or accepting or rejecting Marx's theories. I've struggled enough on occasion just trying to change the thinking of teenagers. Or provincial politicians. Don't even mention logging corporations.

Yet, while I don't have carbuncles, my butt is sensitive. And it wants to dance, not be sat on for hours on end.

There is a little misunderstanding that must be settled. One of the federal inmates I am acquainted with from previous incarcerations is told, and takes exception to the fact, that I'm sleeping on the floor while Janit takes the bunk. I assure her that I am on the floor because there I am closer to the vent. It is the month of July and I have a fan addiction, one that I have passed on to all five of my daughters; we cannot sleep unless the air is moving around us. Even if it is forty below and the air laden with frost crystals, it must move, dammit. My protector finally seems to understand that Janit is not mistreating her elderly friend and backs off.

Two weeks later Janit and I are back in Court. Mr. Justice Pitfield advises us that he will not be our trial judge. Then he does something very strange. At least strange to me. He changes the injunction order for Weyerhaeuser Tree Farm License Number 44 to read that if Janit and I should go out there again to blockade, we are not to be arrested under the charge of disobeying the Court injunction.

How would this even work if the only other way we could be arrested would be under the Criminal Code? This is one of the main points we have been pushing as an environmental organization; that all environmental protesters should be arrested under the Criminal Code rather than under an injunction. Court ordered injunctions lead to charges of Contempt of Court. There is no defense for Contempt of Court. But what if four of us went out there and were arrested, would Janit and I be arrested under the Criminal Code and the other two under the order of the injunction? What the heck is Judge Pitfield doing? Does he know? I'm sure he does but it is peculiar.

Still puzzled by Judge Pitfield's order, we are taken back to Burnaby Correctional Centre for Women in leg shackles and handcuffs with no further explanations. But once back at the BCCW ranch, life goes on.

A couple of days later Janit and I are just finishing eating dinner when the jokes start making the rounds about our evening's dessert, which is an enormous cookie —a particularly dry and tasteless one.

"It's wood. I swear to God it's just a fucking piece of wood," Jingle Pot declares from the next table, contemplating her tasted, but uneaten cookie. Jingle Pot is an addict and long-term prostitute. She smokes crack instead of injecting it, so she hasn't suffered some of the most terrible obvious degenerations, but she isn't well. Pushing fifty, she knows dozens of drinking songs in many foreign languages from partying with her customers. She's in this time for running a crack house, and she cracks endless jokes about her crack house and the people who frequent it. She glares in mock indignation at me.

"You brought these fucking pieces of wood in here from the fucking forest, didn't you?" she demands, and immediately bursts out laughing. Tweedle Dee, sitting to her right, joins in the merriment. Tweedle Dee is a thief. She can't help herself. She steals even when she has no need. She likes her liquor, but she's not a junkie.

"Hey, man ... just think, though. In her line of work she at least gets some wood ... you know, where it might do some good."

Tweedle Dee, doubling over with mirth at her own witticism, is gasping for air. Some of the other women join in. In their parlance a piece of wood is equated with a penis. I am used to being the butt of their sexual innuendoes. It isn't malicious, it's more curious, I think, than disrespectful. They toady around the question without actually asking me – does a fit, healthy woman in her seventies still do it? They always watch for my carefully measured response. I just play dumb. And my apparent dumbness about sexual matters tickles them. I pretend not to get the wood joke.

Later that evening as Janit and I sit over our late cup of tea just before lockup, a young native girl comes and sits at our table. This one talks about life on her reserve. The alcoholism and the drugs. The sexual abuse. She is in her late twenties but looks much older. She tells of her experience at the hands of the police in a remote BC town when she was first brought in, and that she thinks she was raped by the two officers right after she was booked and taken to a cell in the police station.

"Don't you remember?" I ask, astonished.

"Naw. I was drunk. Really drunk. But when I began to sober up a little bit later in the morning I was all wet down there and next day there were some bruises ... "

"Oh, God. Didn't you tell anybody?"

She shakes her head. "No. Who would I tell? There was only two other guys in the police station, no women, and then I was so drunk, I can't actually remember it happening ... except, you know, I just ... this guy's face pushed down into mine ...."

Her voice trails off. I feel sick. Is it true? Could it possibly be true? How could any police station anywhere in Canada not have a woman on the premises when women prisoners are brought in?

"What's your name?" I ask.

"Margaret."

My stomach lurches. "I have a daughter named Margaret," I say numbly, "Margaret Elizabeth."

As the words passed my lips, the images come of my Margaret as a baby, a quiet, sweet, achingly beautiful baby, and then as a little girl, grey-green eyes wide with questioning, too big for her anxious little face, such a perfectionist in her ways.

I had never understood her enough, never sought to make sure she was comforted and encouraged. She needed this more, perhaps, than the others. Then in my divorce from her father, she took the brunt of this separation because she was an introverted child, not gregarious like her older sister, so that when she was with her father she was more confined in the house. No, I had never done right by this child. I always managed to do the wrong thing with her. I was a rotten parent.

Suddenly, I am full to the bone with sadness, both for my own Margaret and this Margaret sitting beside me telling me unspeakable things in a soft voice. Oh, yes, I am a rotten parent. All of us are, we mothers of daughters. How could we be otherwise when we have our faces stuck so far up men's behinds trying to please them?

Oh stop it, I tell myself firmly, trying to get a grip. But I don't quite succeed. It is also because this young woman is native that my outrage is full of festering boils. These women are the expendable ones, almost

by definition. The prison is so full of them, anywhere from half to seventy percent of the prison population at any given time when they are less than one percent of the outside population.

Yet I am drawn to them. Where they go is where we all go; all expendable women— the elderly, the ill, the ugly, the poor, the uneducated. We are all First Nations women.

I feel something else when I am with them, especially those who were raised in the bush, and who know the bush. We are sisters under the skin, even though most know their native heritage less than I do. Even with my German father's ancestry written all over my face and body, his intense blue eyes and white blond hair unmistakably proclaiming our ancestry of European origin, my native heritage comes from my mother's Cajun side. It is my maternal grandmother's Indian blood flowing warmly through my own veins from some unknown, unvisited Cherokee band of long ago, that I feel this surge of wild, joyful familiarity when I saunter into the forest. I know without being taught how to go quietly, alert, and listening. There are animals here, danger, too, along with good things to eat and smell and touch, and all are wild. Wild like me ... oh yes, I love to play Indian.

But it is more than that. In the magnificent old-growth rainforests of British Columbia sometimes I feel this connection so strongly that it transports me to another plane of living altogether; to a land where the separations between my brain and body and the trees and the mosses and ferns and the wild animals become very thin and I can almost feel the beating heart of the little marten scurrying through the brush. If I stand still and breathe deeply I can feel the joyful pulse of the entire forest throbbing through my veins, my own heart, my head.

I become one with the sky and the land and the sea, and I know, oh yes, I know, I am part of this indescribable place. This parcel of earth was given to me personally to love, to revel in, and to protect, if need be.

Our table visitor breaks into my thoughts by asking Janit what band she's from. Janit explains her parents are Burmese, not First Nations. That sparks a discussion of Burma, where it is, and what is going on there politically. Too soon it's ten o'clock and lockdown time for the night.

The following morning there is a kafuffle because Janit refuses to do a morning chore. Janit had understood that you don't have to do a morning chore if you forfeit the dollar each inmate is paid for doing a chore. Chores consist of sweeping and mopping the unit, cleaning the bathroom or laundry room, vacuuming the common room, and so on. Those inmates who don't go out to work usually do a chore that helps the regular unit maintenance person. I always do a chore, not for the dollar, but because we all live in the joint and we should all lend a hand in keeping it clean.

However, if a prisoner is on remand, that is, not yet sentenced, then technically they don't have to do a chore. But then you also run the risk of being locked in your room. This was okay with Janit, but not with me because if she's locked in, then I'm locked out. I tell Janit this isn't okay with me. I need all of the court papers and writing materials in our room that is on what I have come to think of as my desk. And it definitely isn't okay with the particular staff on duty.

Sergeant, our present staff guard, is an old school soldier. She goes by the book and doesn't tolerate any back talk. First Janit is locked in. Then, Janit points out she doesn't have to do a chore and she wants to do some letter writing, that this is her priority and it is her right to have this priority. Sergeant calls her superiors and is told Janit is right; she doesn't have to do a chore. That then raises the issue of what are we doing being bunked on this side of the building where everyone else works. So Sergeant unlocks our door and lets Janit out, and tells me in no uncertain terms we will now be moved back to the other side. To the dark side. Where the Crazy Lady unit is, and the protective custody unit, and the segregation unit, and the two intake units.

Oh, hell's bells. I can't take all this moving around.

But in the evening after lockup I go outside to the exercise yard and hear the drumming. There are half a dozen native women sitting around a large drum in the middle of the track field drumming and singing native songs. Curiosity piqued, I mosey over.

The drumming and singing is being led by an attractive big-boned native woman with short, black curly hair. She is sitting in a chair and the

other women are sitting on the ground, grouped around the drum. They are all drumming. While I am given a few shy smiles at first, I get the idea that the drumming mustn't be interrupted by curious strangers.

I just sit there. It's a lovely evening, soft, a little breeze off the Fraser River making its way over to our pitiful palace. But the drum and drumming somehow lends an aura of dignity, of integrity to the brooding buildings and sad lives contained therein. I relax into the beat of the drum and the singing. After awhile it begins to appear obvious to the lady sitting in the chair that I'm not going to leave. She asks if I'd like to try to drum with them. That's what I am waiting for. I say, "Yes," and take the drum stick offered.

Tap shoes are a kind of percussion instrument, and I have tap danced forever, so I have a good sense of rhythm. There is no problem with the drumming. The singing, though, is something else. The words are in Cree, Ojibwa, West Coast Salish, Chippewa, and half a dozen other languages. I can tell right off this is going to take time. I try to join in quietly on the chant repetitions, but even these aren't easy either, as some of the repetitious chants within each song are atonal, with unfamiliar voice inflections. But I am fascinated. When I am invited to come back the next time I eagerly accept. When I wake up the following morning the fingers on my right hand are red and sore from the unfamiliar action of the drumstick.

Janit and I are told to move back to Unit A. I know in my gut this is not a good thing. However, this time we are advised we can go out to gym and track in the evening with the general population. I can at least continue with the drumming and singing.

Several days later, Janit and I have a big row at lunch over our lawyer, Cameron Ward. When Janit and I were arrested previously, she signed the undertaking and was released, but I refused to sign. Cameron was in the Courtroom that particular day of our appearance and he managed to get me released three days later without my having to sign anything. I was impressed. I still felt grateful to Cameron. If we allowed him to represent us in our trial he would defend us by bringing a Charter Challenge, which certainly interested me.

But Janit still does not seem satisfied with having a male lawyer represent us, or one who would like some money if we ever receive any. I

cannot convince her that the legal arguments have reached a level where we need Cameron's experience. While it is true that I usually represent myself in Court and have been representing both Janit and myself up to this point, that is, whatever I say in Court she has agreed to, but I think it might be a good idea to let Cameron try this case on its own merits. I sense some of the judges in BC are getting sick of acting as project managers for the logging companies and serving as patsies for government duplicity.

But Janit remains unconvinced. She is seeing the prison psychologist and is accusing me of being a bully. Finally, I tell her there is no such thing as an absolutely free lunch, which she takes umbrage to. The upshot of this heated discussion is that we part bad friends. After lunch we are told we must double bunk again because two new women are coming into our unit, which prompts Janit to advise the staff that she refuses to double bunk with me and to please transfer her somewhere else. They oblige her. They transfer her to Unit C.

Unit C is an intake unit. It's on the rough side. A lot of the women are fresh off the street. Dope sick and ravenous for food because without the dope they realize they haven't eaten in days, maybe weeks, even months; now they can't fill their skinny frames fast enough. Food is all they think about, how to get more of it, who has it, what's on the menu, what to trade if they have anything to trade like a couple of cigarettes, and in their pitiful condition they will steal the food off your plate if you leave it unguarded. *Janit, I think, you have no idea what you are doing.*

But the choice is hers. And she soon apparently has second thoughts herself about the entire enterprise. On July 29, two days later, she pleads guilty to the charge of contempt of Court and is given time served and released.

I was brought to Court for this hearing but not allowed into the Courtroom. Mr. Justice Dohm was presiding and made me stay in the Courtroom cells. He isn't keen on me. The first and what is apparently to be the last time I was before Mr. Justice Dohm he was very arrogant and rude to me. When I stood up and asked to be heard he said very curtly that he had already heard me, which he hadn't, and to sit down. When

THIS DANGEROUS PLACE

Mr. Justice Dohm said that he had heard me something in me snapped and I advised him that the Court had never heard me, nor the voice of the people of British Columbia who want to keep their irreplaceable, old growth forests and that he was simply colluding with the Crown to keep forestry issues out of Court. Or words to that effect. Some of our supporters were in the Courtroom at the time and applauded my chastisement of Mr. Justice Dohm. So he does not take kindly to a loud mouthed lecture from a seventy-five-year-old woman who keeps getting plucked off logging roads.

I am sure Mr. Justice Dohm would agree with my youngest daughter, Marian, who advised me in her own fit of pique that if I didn't start showing a little restraint in my old age and stop worrying them to death, the family would have to do what the Inuit are accused of historically doing with their elders in times of stress, only my family would not abandon me on an ice floe, but on a truly isolated logging road. She was only kidding. I think!

So, when I refused to plead guilty or sign an undertaking promising that I wouldn't go back into the forest on the same day that Janit pleaded guilty and was released, I was shipped back to BCCW ranch in leg irons and handcuffs.

Now I am alone with the other crazy ladies in Unit A. But again, not for long. As before, there are ladies crazier than I who need my space, so a few days later I'm shuffled over to Unit D.

Another intake unit. Actually the worst of the lot. I am sure that placing me here is a ploy on orders from the Attorney General's office. They must reason that as Janit has broken under the conditions of Unit C and pleaded guilty for release; perhaps under the horrific mess of Unit D, I will do the same. I think it is truly embarrassing for the government to have elder women in prison over their demonstrably rotten logging practices.

For starters, the unit is horribly overcrowded, thirty-odd women stuffed into a unit built for seventeen. The Campbell government has closed the Open Living Unit to save money. The Open Living unit was housed in another building. The women allowed to get into that unit were considered to be good bets for rehabilitation. But the Open Living Unit is no more and these additional thirty-odd women are now added to that

other growing female population, the newly poverty stricken women who are being cut off welfare and are finding their way into prison via prostitution and drugs.

However, if my being transferred here is a ploy to make me plead guilty and leave their establishment they are wasting their time. I have the ability to retreat from the surface of things and live within my own soul's interior.

I keep my cool as the lunch and dinner trays arrive in the unit, and the BCCW version of the New York Stock Exchange accelerates:

"A pita bread here for a chili!"

"A date square for a pita!"

"Three carrot sticks plus a cigarette for a pita and chili!"

"I'll buy a dessert! I got four sugars and two creamers!"

"Anybody need tobacco? Three cigarettes for your whole lunch ... "

The jumping up and down and bartering goes on as the trays are distributed. In this unit the guard must personally distribute the trays. She counts the trays as they are rolled in and makes sure there is a tray for each inmate, no more, no less. There have been occasions when a tray is snatched when the guard is distracted and then declared by inmates that the trays came up short. By counting and calling off each inmates name, tray theft is curtailed. Some of the women are not above stealing off each other's trays, even from the two pregnant women. They know the pregnant women will be refunded their loss and they don't give a damn about the rest of us. They probably don't give a damn about the pregnant women either. It's just part of an unwritten code: like you never go to the cops, or when you're in prison, to the guards.

But it's uncivilized to have to guard your food. Even though I know that because of my age I might fall into the same category as the pregnant women in the inmate's value system and I would probably be among the last to be stolen from. What a lousy way to live, though, to be so reduced by drugs.

I am deeply troubled by the fact that so many of them slash. The second day I'm in Unit D I accidentally overhear a conversation between two women who both bear the telltale slashing scars on their wrists. It is a whispered conversation.

I am by the magazine rack leaning down in a stooped position looking for a request form. Almost all communication that has to do with requests has to be written. I need a black ink pen. The canteen only sells blue ink pens that have very faint ink. Inferior stuff, all the way around the prison canteen, and way overpriced. Since the Campbell government has privatized everything it can in here, a lot of the items for sale cost more than on the outside.

But my two whispering unit sisters who are sitting alone on the big box chairs in front of the magazine rack aren't aware of my presence. At first I think they are talking about taking dope.

"I don't want to fucking find you dead in the morning," the one counsels the other. "You've done that too fucking much already."

"Well, so have you. I'm not going to do it much ... just enough. You know."

"You'll get sent to segregation."

"I know. I don't fucking care, I can't stand it. Just enough to make me feel better."

"You said your asshole boyfriend was coming in a few days. He'll bring you something."

"I don't care. I hate his fucking ass."

There was a small silence.

"But maybe I'll wait. Yeah, maybe I'll wait for that," the second inmate says finally. "I can always do ... the other."

They get up and move away. I let my breath out slowly and stand up. Hellfire and damnation. Am I supposed to do something here? What exactly had I heard? Could I be absolutely sure they were talking about slashing? The one woman said she would maybe wait until her asshole boyfriend came with something. Dope of one kind or another, surely. Would I be violating the code if I just asked the guard to keep an eye on the one woman? I remembered that it was permissible to advise a guard when a prisoner might be contemplating suicide. Did slashing fall into that category? What if they were talking about something else?

I decided to do nothing, but that night in bed the conversation came back to me and the issue of slashing, and the question of why so many women do it. There must be something horribly wrong with this society,

I thought, with any society that so many women feel such a need to cut into their flesh, into their veins, to make the blood come; seeking to purify the body in some way; or maybe to connect the body to the world. The menstrual blood they give monthly is not enough, nor is the childbirth blood or the blood from body blows and cuts inflicted by lovers, husbands, pimps, johns.

It isn't enough. It's as though they need to bleed to know they are alive, otherwise they might actually be dead, and in hell where female flesh is to be constantly battered and bled, and if damaged enough, then fed to pigs.

No, don't go there. I turn over in my narrow bunk. At least I have a room all to myself in this unit from hell. No, don't go to the pig farm. No woman wants to go to the pig farm even in her imagination. I will try to think of it as one of Hawking's sums-over possibilities.

Hawking claims that in his sums-over theory in his books that there isn't only the one thing happening here on earth, not just the one individual life, the one individual history, or for that matter the history of a country, the world, the universe. Instead, there are many histories of each entity that also exist in imaginary time over there at right angles to linear time that has no beginning, and no end. The pig farm is just one of many possible stories. The women who died at the hands of this mass murderer who owned a pig farm and fed his animals with the women's dead bodies still live in numerous other histories, busy doing all kinds of happier things. And the pig farm can be dismissed in the light of these other histories. Yes, the pig farm can be dismissed …

But it can't. Regardless of all these numerous other lives and histories that Hawking projects, this is the one we all live in. Accept it. Every woman alive on this earth must accept it. One man, maybe in conjunction with others, has killed approximately fifty prostitutes and fed them to his pigs.

All this while *The Province* newspaper in BC recently carried a two-page story showcasing rap music and announcing that music has changed content and instead of celebrating the dress and style of "gangsta" rap, now the big style is pimp style. Snoop Dog, perhaps the biggest pimp purveyor in today's rap game, agrees: "It's cool to look

good; it's cool to have girls on your arm and get money from them; and that's a good feeling, dig? There ain't nothing wrong with it," he said in a recent interview.

Oh, yeah. Ask some of the women in here, hopelessly addicted, their kids in custody, carrying HIV and/or other infections, who are thrown on the garbage heap of humanity. But we do the best we can in this joint, the women and I.

The weeks are flying. Soon I will be called to trial. In the meantime I write constantly, answering letters, writing endless articles that I send into an equally endless gulfstream that lands who knows where, and I'm also working on another book. I listen to the women when they want to tell me their stories.

Like the one standing in my doorway late one afternoon in early September. Actually, Green Eyes is leaning against the doorjamb. In Unit D we are not allowed to visit in each other's cells, so my visitor can't actually come into my cell. Green Eyes is tall and slender. Everything about her is slender: her long limbs and face, her long blunt cut hair. In another life she might have been a model. She seems quite stoned, and she feels stoned, she says, but it is the medication she is given by health care. While her speech and thought processes seem clear enough, her words and body movements are moving in slow motion time.

She is educating me on the difference between a crack head and a junkie. Green Eyes is a crack head and insists that crack isn't addictive, and that it doesn't make you deathly ill when you withdraw. It certainly seems addictive to me as a lot of women in here are here to support a crack habit. "It's only a physiological addiction," she insists. I can't argue. What do I know?

"I'm bipolar," she adds. "When I'm in a manic phase and not taking my medicine, I steal from department stores. I do clothes, house wares, whatever takes my fancy. And in the summer when the gardens are nice, I steal fresh food from people's gardens. It tastes so good right out of the ground like that."

"Have you ever been caught stealing from gardens?" I ask curiously, wondering what I would do if I went into my garden and found a strange woman helping herself.

"Yeah. A couple of times. I was stealing carrots in this man's yard. He had beautiful carrots, and he was right up on me before I knew he was there. So I didn't bother to run. He just looked at me and then he looked down the row where I had picked, and he saw how careful I was not trampling the rows, and leaving the tops stashed neatly, he said, "Well, you're the most responsible thief I've had yet."

"Did he let you keep the stuff?"

"Yeah. He said he had potatoes coming in, and if I just needed them for my family to come back and get some."

"How sweet!"

"Oh, yeah. It happens. Not often. Most of the people I come into contact with just try to rip you off. Like junkies. Give me a crack head over a junkie anytime. Junkies will steal you blind, even the ones you try to help. The last girl I let stay with me until she got her own place took everything from my apartment that was worth anything including … " She paused for a moment and began to count on her fingers, trying to remember.

"Let's see, she took the fucking television … " She stops, brings her hand to her mouth. "Oh, excuse me, Betty."

"It's okay," I say quickly. "I hear it all the time. Go on … "

She resumes counting with her fingers. "There was the CD player, all my videos, my new video player, toaster, microwave oven … "

"But didn't she realize that she might run into you again?" I break in.

"Oh, sure. She knew she would. I caught her in a back alley and beat the shit out of her, but that didn't get my stuff back. When you beat somebody up who owes you, the debt is considered paid because you took it out of their hide. I've been beaten myself a few times, but not for ripping somebody off. When I'm on a bipolar upswing and not careful with my medication, I get promiscuous. You know, not just with my old man, but other women's men … " She pauses and brushes a slender hand across her eyes.

"I have to go," she says. "The medication is kicking in. I can hardly keep my eyes open."

She leaves, and I resume my writing. I have to clarify my thoughts about my upcoming trial and start thinking about how much I will directly participate in it. The trial is scheduled for Monday, September 8th. I stay up late, working, thinking, and reading. It's hard to get going the next morning. I snap at people over the coffee making.

There isn't enough coffee for all of the inmates to have second cups. A lot of the women have two-cup coffee containers, which means if they are filled to the top, some women won't get any coffee at all. So, in desperation to keep some semblance of order, I have taken over the coffee making just by sheer force of will. The guards, not liking the coffee squabbles either, have agreed that I should be in charge of making the coffee in the mornings. I insist that all of the women place their cups on the counter in an orderly manner, and the two-cup people only get theirs filled halfway. This way everyone will get at least one cup of coffee.

A few of the women try to circumvent this by holding their cups directly under the coffee spout rather than letting it flow into the pot, so it takes several days of yelling and name calling to get the procedure straight. But once it's straight, the pressure on new women who come in to follow the procedure is not quite such a struggle, as the others love to yell and name call. But we manage to get along in a hit or miss fashion.

I have the drumming to look forward to in the evenings and my recreational class with Allison Granger Brown on Tuesday morning. I admire Allison Granger Brown even though she is hopelessly Pollyannaish. Tall, slender, pushing middle age, but perpetually young and encouraging in her optimism; I could dismiss her as being overwhelmed with naiveté if she weren't so funny. And because she is funny, she laughs a lot, and her laughter is infectious.

So her Tuesday morning recreational class for women inmates who don't fit into any easily recognizable category is a riot. Well, sort of. Because we are not sure why we half a dozen inmates have been called together to cook, converse, argue, laugh, and sometimes cry; we do it all without thinking of whether or not we're doing it right.

We are truly a motley crew. First there is Mary, the only Doukhobor woman left in the prison. The other two Doukhobors who were here ten years ago when I was in for blockading in Clayoquot Sound have both died. The Doukhobor women had to be isolated then because they set fire to things. I was told that for them, setting fires was like making prayers.

Mary is eighty-six, but of sound mind and memory, a small woman and somewhat enfeebled by arthritis. I want to write her story, but she says no, everything important has already been written about her and her relatives and friends and their religion. I tell her I would just like to do a human interest story and she says no, that would just be for scandalous reasons. But when it comes her turn to cook something, she cooks up a mean borscht.

She likes my cornbread. When it's my turn to cook I do southern dishes, cornbread and fried okra. Allison brings in all of the ingredients for our cooking. Once I even did a filet gumbo with real filet powder. I asked her where she got the filet powder because it isn't easy to find but she said to never mind. She is very resourceful.

The native drum master, whom I now know as Kathleen, keeper of the drums, is sometimes on hand on Tuesday mornings. Kathleen is in her early forties. I have come to value her friendship. She's an enormously strong woman, wise beyond her years, and a leader in the native community in here. She knows what it is to lose everything. But she got back up and stays up, and tries to prop others up. Her powerful singing voice and the drumming bounce off the prison walls and vibrates into the ether, winging their way toward the spirit world of the grandmothers and grandfathers.

Another prisoner in our Tuesday morning group I'll call Pepper. She is both an asset and a liability to my state of being on Tuesday mornings. Fiftyish, she uses lots of peppers and onions and garlic when it's her turn to cook, all of which I love. An Eastern European immigrant, convicted of a crime that resulted from a family struggle, she speaks with a heavy accent. She is extremely opinionated and she speaks loud and long in monologues. It takes all of Allison's Pollyanna patience to get coopera-tion from such an opinionated woman, but in the end she acquiesces,

and we usually manage some kind of conversation, be it choppy and truncated with indignant pronouncements on the immorality of the world.

We also have a large, round, beautiful young woman inmate who graces our table. Because she is very quiet except for the odd, occasional cryptic remark, I call her Cryptic. The other person who comes frequently to our gatherings is a long time inmate who is on her way out of the prison. She has many things to do before she actually gets out and Allison spends much time with her. Sometimes Allison's assistant will also dine with us, and sometimes Hank, the prison chaplain, and once or twice Julia from the Elizabeth Fry Society and several other inmates will occasionally drop in. Oh, we're a merry bunch for Tuesday brunch!

But that's only half day one day a week. The rest of the time I get to eat with my regular tablemates. Born August 4th I spent my seventy-fifth birthday in prison. I spent my sixty-fifth birthday in prison, too. What sport! Will I spend my eighty-fifth birthday in prison? My hundred-and-fifth? Good lord, have mercy on us poor sinners!

I have my books, my defenses against complete insanity. Natalie Angier and Stephen Hawking still entrance me, especially Angier. The chapter on the grandmother hypothesis is so interesting to me. It reaffirms my belief that grandmothers were not only beneficial in the past evolution of the human race, but were absolutely necessary to the human race. So I'm a believer. I was a believer before I even read Angier.

However, she leaves out one thing that still concerns elder women—sex and romance. Everybody hates to talk about grandmothers having sex, even grandmothers themselves. But let's be reasonable ... elders can't spend absolutely all of the time just thinking about how to feed and save the kids. Torrid romances certainly do occur in the elder population.

But I have to ask myself, what is the purpose of it? For a woman, sex after menopause serves no purpose of procreation, so it doesn't serve nature, that is, the propagation of the species. So it must be an adaptive thing. But why would it be adaptive for an elder woman to engage in sexual activity? If the grandmother hypothesis is true, that is, that the human race wouldn't have survived without grandmothers helping to feed their grandkids and the other kids of the group, wouldn't anything that

distracted an elder woman from her child feeding and babysitting chores be considered maladaptive? So go figure.

I leave it to Frenchy, one of my four tablemates, to bring up the issue of elder sex at the dinner table. I say dinner table for lack of another description. But then again, it is a table of sorts and it's the only dinner we get. Not that Frenchy is an elder. Or anywhere near it. She's only thirty-eight.

"How long since you had sex, Betty?" Frenchy asks bluntly. I am somewhat taken aback. None of the other prisoners has ever been so blunt. I pause in feeding my face, and look at Frenchy. She is small, attractive; her French accent is thick, loud, and staccato; and she loves to talk about sex. There is an ugly puffed scar on her forehead where she went through her truck's windshield when she drove the truck into the lobby of a small hotel. She doesn't remember the details of the accident. She was drunk and wired on coke. Several people were in the lobby when her truck came crashing through and three were injured, one seriously. She knows she is in lots of trouble. But she has mostly recovered from her own injuries, and her brown eyes at the moment are dancing with mischief.

I can ignore Frenchy's impertinent question, or be offended. I don't want to get into a scrap because the dinner is actually fairly respectable tonight: roast chicken leg and thigh, mashed potatoes, small salad, small serving of cake. I drain my glass of powdered milk slowly, stalling for time, and then set the glass down firmly on the wobbly table. The other two women at my table are attentive to my answer, although Shack, who is native and young, throws me one quick, darting glance. She has replaced Tweedle Dee at our dinner table. Tweedle Dee went home, having served her time. Until her next petty theft. Or grand. She alternates.

Shack won't be going anywhere for awhile. She is only twenty-three and has been in prison since she was seventeen. Pregnant at twelve, a mother at thirteen, she is a survivor of the street scene in Alberta. At least she survived the knife fight that killed her opponent. But she has difficulty with her survival. The inside of her left arm is criss-crossed with slashing scars almost up to her elbow. But Jingle Pot isn't as polite as Shack. She is grinning salaciously at Frenchy's question about my sex life.

"What did you say?" I ask Frenchy, although I had heard her perfectly well.

"I said, how long has it been since you had sex?" she repeats, louder, this time.

I wipe my mouth with a paper napkin, place it carefully by my paper plate and look at her across the table.

"Probably about as long as it's been for you," I answer coolly. The other two laugh. Frenchy doesn't.

"Me, I don't get enough sex, never," she says in a serious tone. "That's why I get into trouble. If I had a man who gave me sex all the time I wouldn't be out doing other stuff."

I seriously doubt that. While men are the main reason in general women are in this hole I don't think their men's lack of libido is what drove them here. At least Frenchy is full of life, and when the talk turns to her arrest she waxes indignant. She insists the police beat her after arresting her, although she also says she blacked out when she ran into the hotel lobby with her truck. Who knows the truth of it?

Jingle Pot is more interested in talking about the cake she plans to buy. This is fine with me: a safe enough topic for dinner conversation. The prison kitchen will make a fair sized cake for five dollars and a good sized one for ten. Jingle Pot wants to treat the women who work with her downstairs in building maintenance. Only Jingle Pot says she's not going to give Minnie Mouse any of the cake. She works with Minnie Mouse every day and despises her.

"I'm not going to give that bitch even a crumb of my cake," she announces firmly. "I hate that bitch. She always accuses me of stealing her mop bucket. Like a fucking mop bucket is made of fucking gold."

The prisoners use the F world as their favorite adjective. And verb. And adverb. It's used so often I scarcely hear it anymore.

"Jingle Pot, be reasonable," I say. "Even if this woman is mean to you, you can't give all of the other girls a piece of cake and exclude her. It just isn't done. It will make the other women not like you."

Jingle Pot frowns at me, but then suddenly her face clears.

"Oh, all right," she answers. "I'll just make sure she gets the smallest piece."

"Good thinking," Frenchy says approvingly. "Now tell Betty your chicken story."

I wasn't sure I wanted to hear Jingle Pot's chicken story, especially if it was one that Frenchy liked. But Jingle Pot laughed and took a deep breath.

"Well, I had this regular customer who was a nice guy, but fucking weird, you know? He liked for me to ..." She glances at me, pauses.

"Well, anyway," she continues, deciding to forego bringing her regular customer's personal sexual proclivities into the conversation, "everybody calls this guy, Chicago, because that's where he's from. He had to move and he had these two chickens he didn't know what to do with, so he brought 'em over to my house and asked me if I'd keep 'em for him. I didn't want to because one was a hen and that was okay, but the other was a full grown rooster that only had one leg. I thought, Shit, the neighbours will complain, not about the missing leg, but about the crowing in the morning. And I have this mean cat. However Chicago paid me good to take them so I did."

"Mean cat?" I ask, intrigued in spite of myself.

"Yeah, his back's been broken and he walks in this funny, straddled kind of way and he's fucking sensitive about it. He doesn't like anybody staring at him and even when he thinks I'm staring he'll spit at me. He hated the chickens right off. He got this idea that the chickens were staring at him, and he would chase 'em around the house and spit at 'em."

"Sounds like my ole lady. Are you going to drink your juice?" Shack asked, nodding at Jingle Pot's juice. Jingle Pot shoved the little cup of juice across the table to Shack. The juices were made from crystals that were carefully measured out in the kitchen, and sent up with the trays in little plastic cups that would hardly be enough for a three year old.

"Anyway," Jingle Pot continues, "the hen with good legs just up and died. I was pretty fucking sure the cat had killed it, so I kept a close eye on the rooster. Him and me got to be good buddies. I named him Noodle. He was more company than the cat and I always locked him in the house when I had to leave so the cat couldn't get at him.

"This time I forgot and when I got home I called Noodle, but he didn't come hopping to my call the way he usually did, so I rushed out into the back yard. There was Noodle on his back with his one leg pointed up to the sky and he wasn't moving. The cat ran off when he saw me so I knew the cat had done 'im in. But Noodle was still breathing, so I picked him up and pried his beak open and started giving him mouth-to-mouth artificial respiration."

Jingle Pot pauses and reaches for my cup of juice. I let her have it. The woman now has my complete attention. A storyteller has to keep her whistle wet.

"So what happened?" I ask, trying to still the bubbling laughter inside me at the image of Jingle Pot trying to give mouth-to-mouth respiration to a one-legged rooster.

"Well, my Friday regular came looking for me and walked around the house and saw me breathing down this chicken's throat and asked what the hell was I doing. I couldn't stop to answer because Noddle was still breathing, and then suddenly he stopped breathing. He just up and died.

Then I started crying and Blackie, that was my friend's name, said, 'Don't cry, I'll buy you another chicken.' I said 'No, Noodle was special, and there probably isn't another fucking one-legged rooster in town.' He said, "No worry, there are plenty roosters to be had and I can easily fix the one-legged business myself."

Frenchy and Shack burst out laughing. So did I, actually.

"Don't tell me, please don't tell me," I pleaded, "that your friend bought another rooster and cut off one of his legs ..."

"Well, what do you think you're eating for dinner tonight?" Jingle Pot asks abruptly. I give a start and without thinking quickly push my chair back, away from the chicken leg on my plate. Then it is Jingle Pot's turn to laugh. I can feel my face flush. Disconcerted at reacting to such a silly thing, I'm only too happy to retreat to my cell for lockup immediately after dinner.

I have clippings on my desk about the forest fires raging through the public forests of British Columbia up around Kelowna and Kamloops. I'll have to write an article and relate the fires to the practice of clear cutting,

and try to send it out to as many newspapers as I can. Something snappy, something that might get printed. However, when I lie down on my bunk and close my eyes, I feel an unusual fatigue in my bones, a weariness of the spirit.

What am I doing in here, I ask myself, in this place? Why do I do this? Why don't I just sign the undertaking and get out until my trial like most normal people would. Most other people don't go to these extremes. Nobody would blame me if I signed the undertaking. Or even if I pleaded guilty like Janit did and asked for time served. The authorities of all stripes would be only too happy to be rid of me."

But I would blame myself, the me I must answer to every day. Yet where am I going with this? My God, British Columbia is a huge province. It's filled with public forests, or what's left of them. The government and the logging companies and the justice system have everything on their side: they have the money, the power of the press and media, the justice system, the police and the prisons. And what do I have? At this time of my life? I'm an old woman. On the face of it I have little to recommend me. Except this… I have lived long enough to know that once a commitment is made things can begin to happen, as the seventeenth century poet Johann Wolfgang Goethe once said. And Goethe advises us from down the ages to be bold; "Whatever you do, or dream you can, begin it. Boldness has genius and power and magic in it." That's inspiring stuff. I love it. The kind of poetry I like.

* * * * * * * * * * * * * * * * * * *

Certainly that's all Daddy had, I think… he was bold. Otherwise my mother married down. She had more education than Daddy because Mama had attended college for two years before she married Daddy in preparation to become a school teacher. Mama was also fifteen years younger than Daddy. While everybody was poor back in those days, at least among the people we knew, Mama's father's family had fallen from grandiose times, relatively speaking. They were rural business people who went bust during the hard times after World War One. However,

THIS DANGEROUS PLACE

they struggled for higher education for their children. But Daddy, in spite of his lack of formal education, made a living even during the very worst times in the depression of the twenties and thirties because of his will to sell his customers sheets and bedspreads and drapes and medicines and dresses and hats was greater than their will not to buy these things when they were barely eating.

Did I inherit this kind of crazy-making will from Daddy? Am I possessed like Daddy was when he battled the ghost of Laycott? And am I to just continue to do what he was doing, battling the spirits, battling ghosts, refusing to give in, and thinking there must be some rational explanation for this dreadful situation I find myself in? If only I could divine the ghostly patterns of behavior, find a reason, find a clue ...

* * * * * * * * * * * * * * * * * * * *

Like Daddy, I wasn't frightened of Laycott Place, at least not at first, although it was enough to give anybody the willies. I was a child, then, under the protection of competent parents. At least that was my impression.

Actually, I was angrier about having to move away from my old friends than anything. And I did go to school once in a while although Mama home schooled me most of the time. I had this dyslexia thing, although it wasn't called dyslexia in those days. I don't remember it being called anything. Because many kids were needed to help work small farms at various times of the year, strict school attendance was not enforced anyway. It couldn't be strictly enforced for white kids because the majority of rural black kids didn't have schools at all or ones they could readily attend without walking half the day.

Mama explained to the school officials, such as they were, that I had problems learning to write, as I tried to write upside down and backward, so she would teach me at home. As she had more formal schooling than most of the teachers in small Louisiana country towns and districts in those days, nobody argued with her. But I did opt to attend school sometimes just to play and visit with my friends at recess. I read well and through Mama's teaching I learned to discipline myself to write right side up and

start from the left side of the page instead of vice versa. Math symbols also confused me. But as I grew older I began to feel competent in my penmanship and in managing math symbols. However, I still didn't want to go to school on a regular basis like most of the other kids because that would seriously cut into my reading time. After my lessons were done at home and a few chores tended to, Mama let me read until Daddy and Ray Allen came home and it was time to help prepare supper.

I wouldn't have liked this new school under the best of circumstances. So I was quite taken aback when Mama announced that she thought I was ready to join the regular school population as this was a new place and I was getting too old to be allowed to say home. Besides, she had every confidence that I would do well in the new school. Even though it was the last month of the spring semester I would enroll, Mama insisted, along with my big brother, Ray Allen, and my little sister, Doris, in the dreaded new school.

The school wasn't new, except to us. The building was old and weather beaten. The entire area was extremely isolated and countrified. Many of the kids were Cajun and spoke, at least on the school grounds, the peculiar half- French, half- English patois that was common in that day among backwoods Cajun families.

The countryside in general was poorer than at our old place, which was closer to Baton Rouge. Not that we had gone to the city often, but it was comforting knowing it was there. Living at Laycott Place was like moving to another planet. While the Second World War was beginning in Europe and bringing an economic quickening to much of the country, not much of it had shown up yet in this remote backwoods section of Louisiana.

Some of the kids came to school barefoot. I found that scandalous. Doris said she didn't like the new school, either. Ray Allen was noncommittal at first, but then Ray Allen never said much about anything. He wasn't a big talker like most of the Schivers. He was three and a half years older than me, and something of a brain. He was first-rate in school and liked to tinker with motors and electrical things, while I spent most of my free time outdoors or reading.

THIS DANGEROUS PLACE

When we were younger, Ray Allen liked exploring the outdoors as much as I did, but at fifteen going on sixteen he was too old now to play with me much. Doris, who was only seven, was more of a nuisance to us both than a playmate. Oh, she could be sweet at times, but she was still a nuisance. So I missed my friends acutely and grumbled and complained about living in an ole house big enough for three families when we had been so comfy in our little shotgun house with the two added lean-to bedrooms.

I didn't pay much attention to the rest of the kids at school until a couple of weeks into our new school time zone when I was accosted by Clara Nell, a big girl in the ninth grade, at afternoon recess.

I was sitting on the side porch steps of the main school building, waiting for some of the smaller kids to get off the monkey bars. I knew I was considered too old for the monkey bars, but I didn't care. All this school had in the yard were swings and monkey bars, and I loved monkey bars.

Clara Nell came and stood at the bottom of the steps. She stared up at me for a long moment. I stared back, wondering what was on her mind. She was the prettiest girl in school and when I was just watching her play around with the other kids she seemed real nice, not stuck up or anything. I was uncertain about her attention to me at the moment, so just to be on the safe side I stood up and brushed down my skirt.

"Do you really live in that haunted house?" she called up to me, smiling a little. She had deep dimples on both sides of her mouth.

"Haunted? What are you talking about?" I asked, walking briskly down to the bottom step. I didn't want to seem afraid of her.

"The ole Laycott Place," Clara Nell answered. "Do you really live there?"

I brushed my skirt down again, trying to affect a disdainful pose, and stared purposefully at her. She had thick, reddish brown hair, and while she wore homemade dresses like me, unlike me, she already had blossoming bosoms that made her dresses look different. I had overheard girlish whisperings on the school bus that her aunt had bought her some ready-made rayon panties for her birthday. Most of us wore underwear made of the same material as our dresses or blouses. They were called

step-ins. Ready-made rayon step-ins were a status symbol par excellence. I didn't own a single pair.

"What about it?" I asked, meeting her head on.

"My Uncle T Joe said Laycott Place is haunted," Clara Nell answered. Her tone wasn't mean, just sort of curious. We now had a little audience. A couple of her friends circled in a standby position and several of the little ones, including my sister Doris, deserted the monkey bars and sauntered over to listen.

"Did your uncle ever live in the house?" I asked.

"No, but ..."

"Well, if he never lived there how would he know if it's haunted or not?" I asked with a contemptuous flip of my head. But Clara Nell rose to the challenge.

"You don't have to live in a house to know it's haunted. My Uncle T Joe works at the sugar mill and he knows folks who knew the last ones who leased that place years ago and what happened to them. The man died of rabbit fever. Ask anybody about Laycott Place. Have you asked anybody?"

"No, because it ain't haunted. You're just plumb ignorant to say that, and anybody who believes Laycott Place is haunted is plumb ignorant!"

Well, that wasn't nice of me. And it didn't win me any friends the rest of the day. Everybody liked Clara Nell, not just because she was so pretty and had an aunt who bought her store bought step-ins, but because she was a motherly type girl, friendly and easy going. The little ones would run to her when there was trouble in their playground world and she'd try to fix things.

As I thought about our encounter throughout the rest of the school day, I came to the conclusion that she wasn't exactly being hateful. As if to prove it, she smiled at me when we got on the bus to go home and pushed a little white mint into my hand. I made a move to give the mint to Doris who was standing by me, but then Clara Nell gave Doris one, too. She sat across the aisle from me and Doris in the school bus, and chatted in a friendly way. Just before the bus pulled up into her laneway where she would get off with a couple of other kids, she said she and her

cousins swam in a big creek behind her house. Maybe I could come over some during the summer and swim with them.

By the time the bus driver let me, Ray Allen, and Doris off, I had almost forgotten all the ghost talk. But not quite. When the school bus rattled off into the distance and we started walking up the long, tree lined lane toward the house but then I stopped and asked Ray Allen if he had heard anything about our new house being haunted.

He stopped walking, too, and looked at me.

"Some. What did you hear?"

"That Clara Nell said our house was haunted and the last man who leased the place years ago died of rabbit fever. What did you hear?"

"Aw, I heard that, too. Lots of people get rabbit fever. It comes from skinning those wild jack rabbits. There's some kind of parasite that lives underneath the rabbit's skin that won't harm them but makes people sick. You've heard about rabbit fever before."

"I've never heard anybody die of it before."

"You've never heard of a lot of things. Come on, let's get going. Mama will wonder what's taking us so long."

"No, wait. Who told you the house was haunted?"

"Brother Guice told me he heard stuff."

"Brother who?" I asked. There were always a number of kids called Brother or Sister in backwoods families because their parents just took their time about naming them. In order to keep all the kids called Brother and Sister straight, people just tacked on their last names.

"Guice. He's the tall, skinny kid with glasses. Wears overalls."

I felt a chill of apprehension. I had never spoken to Brother Guice but I had certainly seen him around school. Brother Guice probably wasn't given to idle chitchat. He would graduate in a few weeks with only three other students. Not because the rest of his class was stupid, but because there were only three others in the eleventh grade.

At first I thought Brother Guice was one of the teachers in spite of the overalls, until one of the kids told me he wasn't exactly a teacher, but listened to older kids' lessons who needed help in the senior grades. Ray Allen had just mentioned him a couple of days before at the supper

table when Daddy asked my brother if he had met any kids at school like him. Daddy meant kids with the same interests in how things worked, like electricity and motors. Daddy sometimes seemed puzzled by Ray Allen. He didn't understand why my brother had rather stay inside and tinker with experiments than go hunting and fishing or digging in the garden. Ray Allen said he had struck up a friendship with Brother Guice based on mutual fascination with electricity.

"And Brother Guice said our house was haunted?" I wailed. "Was he funning?"

"Just don't worry about it, okay?" Ray Allen answered impatiently. "And shut up about it. You're scaring Doris. The house ain't haunted. Kids say that about any old house that ain't been lived in for awhile. Come on, we gotta get home."

But it was that very night that we received our first visit from the ghost. Not that we knew it was the ghost. Not at first. My parents had the same biological time clock as most country people, which was early to bed and early to rise, and in our house we all went to bed at roughly the same time. Except for Ray Allen and Doris. Doris always conked out earlier and Ray Allen was permitted to stay up somewhat later so he could do his mad scientist thing without interruption.

My brother did all kinds of experiments in his room with substances that more often than not were charged with electricity and buzzed, clanged, spit, and on rare occasions, exploded. He was even worse now that he had a big room just for his electrical stuff and model airplanes. The model airplanes themselves took up a lot of room. He made them out of thin strips of balsa wood and tissue paper, but they had real little motors inside. There were always airplane parts drying on newspapers on his worktable and on the floor.

When they were finished, Ray Allen hung the airplanes from the ceiling. If he wasn't satisfied with one, after awhile he'd take the motor out and rig up some apparatus inside the front of the plane with rubber bands that would take the plane up fairly high out in the field by the side of the house. Ray Allen would set the wooden plane afire just as it was

THIS DANGEROUS PLACE

taking off, and this was always a wonderful event, almost like in the war movies when a warplane was shot down in flames.

Not that we got to see many movies. But war movies were the only kind Ray Allen would consent to take me and Doris to on the rare occasions when we were all in town, so I'd seen a couple. The United States was at war now, and the newsreels were all about war.

I wasn't thinking about war the first night the ghost visited us. I wasn't thinking anything. I was sound asleep. I felt myself suddenly yanked out of that fuzzy blanket of deepest sleep just before dreaming by the sounds of loud bangings and thuddings that seemed to be coming from the direction of my brother's room. My first thought was that Ray Allen was once again in the midst of an experiment gone wrong.

I sat up in bed and rubbed my eyes. The sounds grew louder. Something that seemed to be more in the direction of the kitchen this time crashed to the floor.

I heard a voice cry out. "No!"

It seemed like a male voice, again coming from the kitchen. Ray Allen? It didn't sound like him, but it didn't sound like Daddy, either. I fairly hopped out of bed and then stood there, frozen, feet planted on the bare floor, unable to move. I wanted to go see what was happening, but my legs wouldn't work. I don't know how long I stood there, shivering in the darkness.

It was raining outside, a thick sounding blanket of rain on the copper roof, a blanket without lightning, a smothering darkness that covered the star shine and moon shine. The frogs and crickets were intimidated into silence; there was no movement, and all was dark as death. I could feel my heart pounding beneath my nightgown. I felt I was holding my breath, waiting, waiting for something, for something else to happen. And it did. Somebody suddenly turned on the lights in the hallway.

And my terror instantly vanished. The voices I heard coming from the hallway and kitchen were as familiar as my own, the voices of my parents and cousin and brother. Reassured, I stepped out in the hallway that opened into the kitchen. The kitchen door was open and the kitchen lights

were ablaze, too. Mama and Daddy and Louise were walking around the kitchen, talking in excited voices.

Louise had only been with us a couple of days when the ghost first appeared. Louise was my seventeen-year-old third or fourth cousin; Mama couldn't seem to make up her mind about exactly what degree of kin Louise was to us. Louise was definitely kin, but orphaned at birth, her mother by death, her father by desertion. Louise spent the summers with us while her Aunt Mary, who had raised her, worked as a cook in the sawmill camps. This time Louise wouldn't go back home for a whole year. Her school only went to the tenth grade and Aunt Mary wanted Louise to finish high school before she married her boyfriend Jessie, whose family farmed just across the road from Aunt Mary's house.

This was fine with all of us. Before Ray Allen and Louise got too old to play exploring in the woods, we three would spend many hours together in the swamp edges back at our old place, pretending we were finding new lands, climbing giant oaks, swinging from thick vines, watching for rattlesnakes and water moccasins, and gathering crayfish from the side ditches before returning home. If for some reason I didn't go with them on these excursions they would gig frogs, too, before returning, but when I was with them I would scream, so they wouldn't. Mama liked to cook frog legs, but I wouldn't eat them. They jumped around in the pan when frying as if the legs were still alive. It was just some kind of muscle thing in the frog's legs that contracted and then expanded with the heat in cooking. At least that's what Mama said. I still didn't like it.

Both Louise and Ray Allen were too old to do any of this stuff now, however, Louise, unlike my brother, liked to work outside. She was a tall, strong girl with a sweet bright smile and a turned up, very freckled nose. She was good natured and easy going and, looking back, I think we all loved her. Not that we kids ever told her that. At the moment, Louise seemed curious and excited about what was happening in our big ole kitchen.

Ray Allen was standing by the kitchen door. As usual, he wasn't saying much. He was wearing a pair of the short pajamas he and Daddy both wore most of the time to sleep in. Mama made them out of material

left over from her sewing for Daddy's customers, so sometimes the short pajamas Daddy and Ray Allen wore would be as colourful as our female nightgowns. This pair of short pajamas my brother was wearing had tiny rows of sunflowers on the bottoms. They were new, the material left over from some kitchen curtains Mama had made for one of Daddy's customers. I hadn't seen them before and ordinarily I would have teased him, but not now. His expression when he turned to me was like the one he wore when he was trying to figure something out that was connected with his electrical stuff, or little airplane motors: pure puzzlement. Usually, I didn't pay much attention to my brother's facial expressions, but in this instance, he wasn't at all reassuring.

But Daddy's voice was. I pushed past my brother and stepped into the kitchen.

"Aw, no use looking for a varmint in here. Something musta got underneath the house, trying to get out of the rain," Daddy was saying as he looked around the kitchen that was big enough to have accommodated Aunt Gladys' new large, bustling restaurant.

This kitchen ran the entire length of the back end of the house. Besides the wall-to-wall, floor-to-ceiling cupboards on one side of the room, there was a long island running down the middle of the kitchen with more table space than the biggest dining room tables. And there was more cupboard space underneath the island. Our little family ate in the kitchen, as the dining room was even bigger than the kitchen and was on the other side of the house.

It wasn't unusual for the dining rooms in these old plantation houses to be on the other side of, and a hallway away, from the kitchen. Sometimes the kitchens would even be completely detached from the rest of the house. In the summers the kitchens could become intolerably hot when all the cooking was done in wood stoves. But even when the kitchens weren't actually detached the masters had so many servants to do the cooking and serving in the old days they could have the cooking done in one side of the house while they ate in comfort in the other. But the dining room at Laycott was locked off because we didn't need it. We had a coal oil stove that cooked just fine without excessive heat. Mama just turned

it off when it got too hot and there was a brick or stone fireplace in every room to take the chill off any cool mornings when the weather turned. If it ever did. We were just entering the dog days of summer and mornings cool enough for a fire in one of our fireplaces seemed a long way away.

* * * * * * * * * * * * * * * * * * *

The prison bell rings and lockup is over and I am free from now until time for count which comes just before dinner. Prisoners have to be counted and if someone is missing, dinner is post phoned until all are present and accounted for. As it is Friday, those of us who want to, can gather in the Native Sisterhood trailer after count. The trailer is a doublewide, a longhouse of sorts. There is drumming and singing, prayers, smudge, socializing, and food. The elder is almost always there. She comes in from the outside; she is not a prisoner. She brings hope and good cheer and native food. Sometimes we feast on smoked salmon, blueberry jam, cakes, and cookies. The elder gives little lectures along with the prayers, before the drumming starts.

I like the elder a lot. She's a survivor of the Indian wars, and the many social ills that plague the native community. We sit in a circle around the room. Most of the prisoners who come here are native. There are a few, like me, who are non-native, but are drawn to the old native culture, which the elder so generously brings to us. Those of us seated at the drum must wear skirts because our female parts will overwhelm the drum and the grandfather spirits. Ha. I always pray to the grandmothers or the warrior women.

The elder is talking about the grandfathers, her long Indian skirts spread primly and somewhat dramatically around her, long feathered earrings swaying gently about her long, dark, graying hair. As she moves her head from side to side while speaking, she includes everyone in the room. Ah yes, the grandfathers. But tell us some more of the grandmothers, I urge silently. I want to hear of the grandmothers. I've got a grandmother hypothesis going here, lady; never mind the grandfathers ...

And now she is speaking of both grandmothers and grandfathers. The room is very silent. I sit as still as the others. I have learned how to sit still in the Courtroom, in the paddy wagon and in tiny, barred cells. I could sit on a dime for half an hour without fidgeting.

"They come for you, you know," the elder says, her dark hawk eyes sweeping the room. "The grandmothers and the grandfathers. They hear your prayers. They tell the Morning Star to send the Bald Eagle when you make your prayer ties and take them up to the Creator. You are never alone. Sometimes when you are learning the Red Path, the grandmothers and grandfathers will choose you for something special, to do some difficult task. Yes, they will. If you are ready, they will come and they will choose you."

Her compelling eyes pause, suddenly fixed on my person. Her hand is outstretched in a supplicating motion, the nostrils of her strong, Indian nose flatten with emotion, her eyes bore into mine.

"Choose you?" one of the young native prisoners asks hesitantly. Her expression is clearly perturbed. "Are you talking about death?"

"Oh, no," the elder replies, barely tearing her gaze away from my face. "It's not death. It's life. Here and now. The grandmothers and grandfathers choose somebody on the Red Path and they send messages from Morning Star and Bald Eagle and Spotted Eagle and Wolf and Bear and Windigo."

I swallow hard. Is this woman talking to me? About the Red Path? The Windigo?

"Yes," the elder continues. "When the grandmothers and the grandfathers choose there is no way out. You cannot escape them without great damage to yourself. You must go forward on the Red Path until the very end."

Okay, my hair is standing on end. I don't like this. Anyway, I'm not native, and I am not on any Red Path. I'm an old white woman. Yet, for whatever reason, I'm moved. Because, dammit, sometimes I feel like I've been chosen to protest the destruction of our forests, as though it were a demand by something outside me, a something above and beyond me. And even as I have convinced myself that I do this out of a sense of

duty there still remains a nagging feeling that there is some additional thing involved, something else besides the personal offense I take at the indecent clear cutting of an irreplaceable rainforest, this senseless liquidation of a veritable garden of Eden; this destruction of an ancient world.

"How do you know you've been chosen?" one of the other inmates asks. This one is small, dark, young, long jet-black hair, tilted eyes as black as midnight: the quintessential Indian maiden.

"You'll know," the elder says solemnly, nodding her head. "You'll know."

Awwwwww. I just want to play the drums and sing songs. I don't want to go through some mystical experience analogous to God blinding Saul when he was just minding his own business on the way to Damascus, and turning him into a woman-hating Paul. Well, I only go by what I read. Paul didn't have much use for women. Anyway, girls just want to have fun. Let's play the drums, okay?

We play on the big drum, six of us who have been practicing together. I am learning some of the songs and can sing all of the words to a few. I know that's the way a lot of the native prisoners learned the songs of their tribe; they learned them in prison. I sink into the repetition of the drum beats; they fill me up with echoes of a lost civilization that will never be fully recovered in its honesty and simplicity. The wailing chants are beautiful and I am a part of them, the sounds resonate within my soul and fill me with a terrible sadness. I am being borne upon and below a deep, deep into the heart of sadness on the wings of the drum beat and the thrilling, throaty voices of the singers.

It is always over too soon for me. Back in my cell and locked up for the night I get out my notebooks and try to make sense of my upcoming trial. Up to now, I have largely represented myself in Court. My entire mode of operation in the past has been to forget about the judge who is going to declare me guilty of Contempt of Court de facto, and not allow me to use any legal argument in my defense. I must concentrate on getting as much publicity as possible in order to raise the issue of what's happening in our public forests with the people who own them, which is the public.

However, there are a few new twists here. My lawyer will do a Charter Challenge, and I am now part of an organization that I'm responsible for

and to, namely Women in the Woods. As long as there is any chance a Charter argument might be successful then I'll forgo the theatre and play the lawyer game with Cameron. Except that I want to personally cross-examine the Hayes employees, who are the contract loggers for Weyerhaeuser. And I will speak to my sentencing, when that time comes, myself. So over the weekend I try out endless scenarios, but none can be truly comprehensive until I actually see the judge on Monday morning, September the 8th.

Sunday night I set my alarm for four-thirty and go to bed at ten. I close my eyes and try to conjure up an image of the judge. I know he will be an older man because Cameron has told me this judge has been brought out of retirement to hear my case. Perhaps he is sweet and kind and full of love for humanity, for the people of this province and for the forests and the wild creatures therein.

Please, judge of my dreams, come to me, I beg the grandmothers and grandfathers of old as I drift off into never-never land, please come to me, I have been waiting for you for so long, I have been waiting now for thirteen years.

Chapter Three

Courtroom and Ghost Talk

The following morning when I observe the judge who has been assigned to hear my case I begin to suspect before the morning session is over that I may have to wait awhile longer for the judge of my dreams. Although this elder gentleman in the black robes sitting at the judge's big desk up front of the Courtroom on a raised platform seems inoffensive enough at first meeting, it's what he doesn't do that bothers me. Mr. Justice Harvey doesn't speak loudly enough. Some of the people in the Courtroom who have come to support me are leaning forward in their seats, straining to hear. I can barely hear him myself from the prisoner's box. And Mr. Justice Harvey doesn't take kindly to being asked from some of the spectators to speak up. Instead of honouring this perfectly reasonable request he threatens to clear the Courtroom. By lunch break I know I am in deep trouble. Besides his unwillingness to speak up so all can hear, Mr. Justice Harvey admits he hasn't much experience with forestry issues or civil disobedience, so I don't see how he can understand the situation I am in. Forestry issues and civil disobedience are both enormously complex issues.

Why has the Associate Chief Justice of BC, whom I understand has some say so in assigning these cases, given me this particular judge? One he has had to drag out of retirement? I am beginning to think it was a deliberate act on Associate Chief Justice Dohm's part, to give me a

retired judge with no previous experience in cases like mine, who will probably have no new thoughts about a situation he has already admitted he knows nothing about and will simply be guided by precedence. I have been told by a reliable source that the Supreme Court judges are supposed to be picked by some kind of lottery system. Somehow where my court appearances are concerned, I doubt it. Anyway, it is perfectly clear I have lost the judge lottery.

I know what precedence for disobeying an injunction in British Columbia means. For the last fifteen years Court injunctions that lead to charges of Contempt of Court have been used extensively to scare citizens away from trying to protect public property. I'll bide my time. I'm old enough to know things are not always as they seem. Sometimes surprising things happen.

The Crown proceeds with opening statements. I listen with half an ear. I've heard it all before, this description of how I have deliberately disobeyed a Court-ordered injunction because I think I am above the law. Actually, I have stated over and over that I have never ever suggested that I should not be held accountable for my actions: that what I want is for my actions to be described accurately on arrest and charge, and then to be processed and held accountable for these actions that I have actually committed, not for the bogus, purely political charge of Contempt of Court.

Out of sheer bored frustration I find myself looking at the back of Mr. S. J. Richards' head. Mr. Richards is acting Crown Counsel. He's young but wears a sober air to match his sober robes. His dark hair is cut short, but not too short, and is neatly combed. His silky robe folds precisely around him. His briefcase sits squarely on the floor with no wayward legal papers sticking out the top; folders are arranged neatly on the desk before him. I can hardly hear him speak, either. His voice matches the judge's voice, soft and slightly hesitant. He is hitching the timbre of his voice and gestures to those of the judge. Clever boy. He will go far. But hell's bells ... the man is so boring I think I had rather stay in prison than listen to him talk for a week.

I guess in Mr. Richards' defense one could say that he and the judge both look and sound boring because the law is boring. And it is. It's

boring because it is crafted primarily to protect private interests. Private interests by their very nature must be shrouded in boring language that is precise and yet difficult for the average person to decipher. If the laws that protect private interests over public ones were written in plain language and easily understood by citizens, then the public would be readily aware that the Campbell government of British Columbia is in the process of appropriating half of the land mass of British Columbia in order to get at the enormously valuable old growth public forests, citizens might be a bit perturbed.

I glance at the opposite side of the long counsel table where Cameron sits. Cameron and Mr. Richards are about the same age, I think, or maybe Cameron is older, and he has white hair like me. Only Cameron's white hair is premature and always a bit scattered and windblown. This morning he has a fresh hair cut. The style is sort of mod with rumpled, sticky up places. I think it's kind of cute. It rather livens up the heavy atmosphere of the courtroom. However, Cameron's new haircut affords opportunities for an ingrained habit he has, which is to pick at the hair at the back of his head when he's arguing before the judge.

The habit is kind of endearing. I'm the mother and grandmother of sons as well as daughters. Guys have a hard time, too. While Cameron's books and papers are not always that neat, or his briefcase at the ready, he knows the issues, loves the issues, and isn't afraid to fight for what he thinks is right. At the same time, as a lawyer, he has the flexibility to give over to me when I express the desire to take over my own trial. Cameron doesn't always get paid for his efforts, either. The Court day drags on with technical wrangling, a couple of outbursts from supporters, and at last I'm allowed to get back into the police wagon, freshly leg ironed and handcuffed, and be driven back to the prison.

I learn that while I was away in the Courtroom I have been assigned a roommate. Oh, gods and goddesses, is there no end to this misery? Evidently not. The staff officer turns a deaf ear to my pleas for a reassessment of the issue.

"It's an older lady," she says absently, her mind obviously on the building suspense in the unit as it is approaching the dinner hour. The

inmates already know the dinner menu and the bidding has started. The excitement intensifies as the trays are pushed into the unit.

"My salad for a desert!"

"My fish for two cigarettes!"

"Soup and salad for a desert!"

"Betty, I have to go," the staff officer says hurriedly. "The trays are in. Stop worrying. Your new roommate is fifty-five and she doesn't swear. You'll like her."

Ah, yes. I do like her, actually. Very pleasant woman. She has proper table manners, asks that I excuse even the most discreet of belches and doesn't fart at all. Potty humour is big in this prison. Much merriment can be derived out of a loud fart. No, this woman is perfectly acceptable to me except that she's somewhat on the heavy side. When one is double bunking inside a tiny prison cell, one's body mass can become a political issue. But it could be a lot worse. She is off whatever it was that got her here and seems quite civilized. Until she falls asleep.

Then I realize that this woman, regardless of what else she may have been up to, has a profound sleep disorder. My new roommate is fighting dreadful demons in her sleep, demons that primarily assume the persona of her ex-husband and his suspected mistress. The lack of profanity in my roommate's speech during waking hours is recouped in her night furies, and the air is thick with her shrill profane accusations. I gently shake her shoulder, trying to wake her. She stirs but doesn't wake. I shake her harder and call her name. But she still doesn't wake, she simply incorporates my touch and the sound of my voice into her unspeakable nightmares, and when she answers it is only to address someone she knows in her hideous dreams.

I cannot sleep, at all. Nobody could sleep under these conditions. Have I died and gone to hell, I wonder? By three in the morning I give up and turn on the brighter light over my bunk. Meanwhile, my roommate lurches across the mattress on the cell floor, cursing the man and woman who haunt her dreams, punctuated by fits of strangled weeping. It's too much. I reach for the paperback copy of Stephen Hawking's *Black Holes and Baby Universes* and try to get grounded. Amazingly, I do.

THIS DANGEROUS PLACE

I don't bother with Stephen Hawking's black holes. I know I won't be able to understand them intellectually in this life. I understand them only too well emotionally. I don't like them. But I love his concept of Imaginary Time. So often I have felt that I live on at least a half a dozen levels, and here is the eminent physicist and mathematician telling me, yes ma'am, you actually do, stick with me for a little while and I will try to explain it all to you mathematically.

Never mind, Stephen, I think. *You don't have to try to prove it mathematically to me. Without my fingers and toes I couldn't figure out my pitiful little budget. However, I gravitate to the idea of your Imaginary Time like a buzzard spotting road kill.*

Talk about an elegant theory! "Imaginary Time stands at right angles to our linear time," says Stephen Hawking, "and because it has no boundaries, no beginning and no end therefore we are to think of this time zone as being round, like the earth." Hawking gives as much credence to this Imaginary Time as to the time we think we are living in now; this crazy time we know and love sometimes, but mostly hate, because it has this terrible beginning and end, both for us as individuals and for the Earth itself.

The part I like most about Hawking's Imaginary Time is where what Hawking calls the "sums over histories" live. The "sums over histories" are all the other histories we could be living at the same time we are living this one.

Is this where Simone du Falon, the bride of Mark Laycott, lives now along with her husband and sister in a happier family configuration, I wonder? But how did she (because it was a she-ghost that haunted the Laycott Place), manage to break through one history to land in another? Was it because of the strengths of her passions, her loves, her hates? Could passion itself hurtle somebody from one history to another? Certainly, the original mistress of Laycott Place had a bellyful of passion.

* * * * * * * * * * * * * * * * * * *

The day after Clara Nell first told me about Laycott Place being haunted, I decided to tell Mama. After we got off the bus that afternoon and started walking down our lane I told Ray Allen what I was going to do.

"What do you want to worry Mama for?" he demanded. Although he sounded mad he didn't try to tell me not to do it. He just grabbed Doris's hand and hurried her along. If one of us didn't do that, Doris would loiter.

Even if I didn't like the house very much, I loved walking up and down the lane that led to the old plantation. The lane was a quarter of a mile long, a straight shot to the house. Huge Live Oaks stood like sentries on both sides of the lane. They were so tall the leaves on the branches that hung with Spanish Moss caught whatever breeze was stirring and sent shivers down the long, wide, forever green branches, making them sway and swoop as though they wanted to catch us and wrap us in their arms. Their very presence thrilled me and stilled my anxieties. When we got closer to the house, I hurried up and stood for a moment, gazing anew at the enormous old plantation house gone shabby with time, with its slender, soaring columns and the wraparound veranda and stained glass windows. I acknowledged to myself, that yes, indeed, there was something decidedly kind of creepy about the place. When we got inside I asked Mama right off if she knew anything about folks saying the house was haunted. She frowned.

"Haunted? Don't be silly. Whoever put such a notion in your head?"

"Some of the kids at school. You can ask Ray Allen."

"I don't have time for such nonsense. Come straight to the kitchen after you change clothes. I need you to peel potatoes. Mind you don't bang the biscuits around; they're rising on the stove."

"Well, where's Louise?" I ask, adopting a whining tone.

Louise was supposed to help in the kitchen, too. I felt cross that Louise was outside most of the time while I was stuck inside. And I didn't like her being engaged. Things were changing too fast.

The entire family was getting geared up for an early serious start with the summer gardens. We always took our gardens seriously, especially Daddy. Mama spent a right smart amount of her time with the chickens, which of course fed us too. We had fried chicken almost every Sunday,

no matter how hot or cold the weather was. Along with the pigs, our vegetables also helped feed other people, too, aside from our immediate family. My parents always sent a lot of canned stuff back with Louise when she returned to Mississippi. They always held back a portion of everything for the Williams family, too. I had known the Williams family almost since I was born. They were black and lived on the same five acres we leased yearly in our old place. They had already raised four kids but had five more to go. In the past, the meat and vegetables Mama and Daddy gave them was in partial return for the work they did for us; now it was just from habit. And we always had more than we could eat. In the fall sometimes I would stand reverently, surveying the long rows of canned tomatoes, string beans, corn, pickles, watermelon rind jelly, blackberry jam, okra, hot peppers, lima beans, and English peas. Oh, the list was endless, and it all made me feel cared for. I could feel the love oozing out of the jars.

On that particular day when I asked Mama about hearing the house was haunted from the kids at school and she told me to hush about it, then I just wanted to go outside and help dig up the new garden.

"Louise is busy helping your daddy, and Ray Allen has to pluck some chickens. Do you want to pluck chickens?"

I did not want to pluck chickens. I hated the smell of freshly killed chickens that had to be dipped in scalding water to soften the feathers. I would do almost anything rather than pluck chickens.

Still, the resentment I felt about my cousin lingered. She was no longer really my friend. Well, maybe she was still my friend, just no longer one of my closest confidants. In her free time when she wasn't doing woman talk with Mama, she was helping Ray Allen cut and glue thin strips of balsa wood for airplane frames. I felt caught in some kind of time warp, separated from my old friends, too young for woman talk and too old for little kid talk, with both my previous playmates, Ray Allen and Louise, deserting the ranks of Explorers of the Woods. That's what we had called ourselves all the summers before when we hung out together in the lush swampy Cypress forests near our old home. Mama and Daddy let us run free as long as we were together. We played Tarzan of the Apes and

Famous Explorers and even pretended we were on other planets where dinosaurs still roamed. Now I was left with peeling potatoes and minding Doris and having to attend school every day and a country bumpkin school at that. Life was just too tedious.

But I did as I was bid. There was no alternative. And at least Doris liked books and to be read to. Still, I didn't like what the kids at school were saying about our house being haunted. It made me nervous. After that night in the kitchen when the ghost first presented itself, and I went to bed when ordered by Daddy, I found myself looking at the moonlight filtering in through the stained glass panels of our bedroom door much longer than usual and listening harder to the crickets and frogs.

When the bedrooms were being divided up I had complained at first about having to still share a bedroom with Doris. After all, there were more bedrooms than we needed just on one side of the house. But Doris didn't want her own room; she was too big to sleep in Mama and Daddy's room and she wanted to sleep in mine. Louise and Ray Allen both had their own bedrooms, and that still left two extra rooms: one next to the kitchen that Ray Allen took over for his model airplanes and radio stuff and another one up front that held Daddy's goods and Mama's sewing. Doris and I were sandwiched between Ray Allen and Louise's rooms, so it was okay. Still, I felt restless that night.

It was the middle of May, but the early summer heat had socked in. Doris and I each had a little fan by our beds, but the air still felt insufferable. It would have been a lot cooler with the doors open, but that was out of the question. The mosquitoes would have swarmed in. There were screens on the windows, but the ones on the outside doors were too far-gone to mend and we didn't have the money yet to replace them. Daddy sprayed our whole side of the house for mosquitoes every night with a handheld spray gun before we went to bed and there was mosquito netting to drape over our bedsteads if the mosquitoes were especially bad. When I slept I dreamt of mosquitoes as big as my hand, and that somehow one had gotten inside my head. At breakfast the next morning when I told my dream everybody laughed.

But the news that we lived in a haunted house spread through the school like a swamp fire. And in the next few days the three of us, me, Ray Allen and Doris, were launched on the road to ridicule and notoriety.

It was awful.

Chapter Four

The Lion Appears

The kids at school pestered me with so many ignorant questions about how many ghosts I had seen at home that I tried to stop talking to them altogether. Except for Clara Nell. She had become quite friendly. I was flattered that she found me so interesting because she was older and smarter than most of the other kids. And she liked to read, too. She read more grown up books than I did. Her aunt had given her a book by a Frenchman named Guy de Maupassant and she loaned it to me. It was all short stories, and I didn't understand some of them. I liked the story called *The Two Little Soldiers*. It was so sad. Clara Nell had so many friends, all the kids were her friends, but she seemed to want to make a special friend of me. So the other kids stopped teasing me so much.

It wasn't until the day before the very last school day that I learned of some of the particulars of the supposed ghost at Laycott Place. That Monday before school was out for the summer three of the boys cornered me at lunch recess. I was sitting on the back steps of the Home Economics Building rereading *Jane Eyre*. I loved *Jane Eyre*.

In those days Home Economics was a serious subject in country schools and deserved a building all by itself when possible. In case we didn't learn it at home, girls were taught things we needed to know like how to clean a chicken, cut it up, and fry it. We also learned how to make chicken and dumplings in case our mothers were neglectful in

that department. In those days even young girls not yet in high school cooked whole dinners complete with biscuits, cake, and cornbread, and invited the principal and teachers to feast on our accomplishments. Or rather they invited themselves which was okay because it made us feel important. So I liked sitting on the wooden steps of the Home Economics building to read.

There was a big Chinaberry tree by the building that made a comforting shade. Trouble was it was a female Chinaberry tree which dropped berries, courting flies and other buzzing insects. One had to be careful where one sat. Janice Lee, one of the girls in my class, watched me clear away a clean spot on the top step. After I settled myself Janice Lee preceded to bombard me with questions about the house. But I deflected her questions with a certain dispatch and she finally gave up and went to pester somebody else.

Then I heard this hateful boy's voice. Before looking up I knew the voice belonged to Jimmy Leblanc.

"You reading ghost stories?" he asked, sniggering. I glanced up at him. If he wasn't so hateful he would've been cute. He had sun-bleached sandy hair, even more freckles than Louise, and a quick smile. Jimmy was in my class. He sat behind me and hooked sticker balls onto the back of my blouse. The sticker balls came from a bush that grew at the rear of the schoolyard, and it took a lot of brushing to get all of the sticker balls out at night.

I didn't tell the teacher on him. I didn't even tell Mama when she yelled at me for not being careful with my clothes. Kids who told weren't necessarily liked by anybody. There was a conspiracy among kids about adults, even parents. There was a code. Girls didn't fight physically with other girls or boys, and boys didn't hit girls, but every single person on earth except teachers and parents would despise you if you told.

There were two other boys with Jimmy. One was hanging onto Jimmy's shoulder. He was called by his initials, R.L. He was in the same class as me and Jimmy and chummed with Jimmy all the time. The other boy was quite tall, although the same age as me and Jimmy and R.L., but Michel missed lots of school because he trapped with his father and

older brother. The three boys stood there leering at me, shuffling, pushing each other. I was torn between completely ignoring them by getting up and walking away or staying put and engaging in verbal combat.

"So what if I was?" I answered smartly, decided on the later tactic even though I knew my tormentors would only be encouraged by my choice. "You got anything to say about it?"

"Yeah. You run across anything about Simone du Falon and that old place you're living in?"

"No," I answered coolly.

"Then you don't know nothing," RL said, pushing in front of Jimmy. "She shot her ole man and her sister and then killed herself because ..."

"Shut up, RL," Jimmy said stoutly, shoving RL aside. "You don't have to tell her all that stuff."

"I do," Pierre said eagerly from behind Jimmy's shoulder. "Because my grandpapa was there. Well, he wasn't there, but he knew all 'bout it. The lady, her name was Simone. Her name was Simone du Falon. Before she got married to the guy from France. But she got jealous of her ole man with her sister and she killed her husband in the kitchen. Then she chased her sister outside and killed her and then she shot herself, right back of your place, back there behind the willows."

I could feel the bangs that had been just sitting on my forehead, limp with the heat, suddenly crackle and threaten to stand straight up.

" ... and she get any man who move in that house. She hate the men because of what her man did with her sister. She hate the men and she try to kill them. She killed that last man that was there, she gave him a fever that killed him..."

I jumped up, heart pounding. "Just shut up!" I yelled. "I hate you! I hate all of you!" I ran. There really wasn't any place to run to except back into my schoolroom. Only it wasn't empty. Madame Chauguex was there. She was standing by the door, writing our next lesson on the blackboard. I stood there for a moment, choking back tears. She walked toward me and when I turned to leave, she caught my arm.

"What's wrong?" she demanded. "Are you hurt?"

I shook my head. I was loath to admit that I liked any of my new teachers, but I actually didn't mind Madame so much. She taught us everything but Math and Home Ec. She was somewhere in her late fifties or early sixties, plump and motherly, with graying hair drawn up in a bun in back. She always wore white starched blouses that looked crisp even on days that would strangle anything that depended on air to breathe. .And while she could be stern she was fair, and had a funny little chuckle when anything amused her.

"Tell me, then. Are the others teasing you again about your house being haunted?" she asked, looking intently into my face.

I nodded.

She made a wide, expansive gesture with her hands that implied well, what can one expect from such ill-mannered children?

"They're awful," I said.

"Yes. Of course they are. And you mustn't pay any attention. There was a tragedy in your place a long time ago; at least that's what people say. Does that mean your house is haunted? Of course not. You know, just about all of the children in this school live in houses where someone has died. If your house is haunted, so are theirs and you can tell them I said so, okay?"

Well. That put a slightly different perspective on the thing. Madame offered me her handkerchief to wipe my eyes and then patted my shoulder.

"Don't you worry, child. By the time you come back to school next year the children will have forgotten all about what they've heard happened in your house. The girls will be asking to come spend the night with you."

I doubted that. Anyway, I didn't particularly like any of them except Clara Nell. I wasn't going to worry about it because there were only one more full day left of school.

At home that day after school, I accidentally overhead Daddy talking to Mama in a loud, aggravated tone. I had taken Doris out to the stream by the side of the house. It was only a teeny stream about two feet across and three inches deep, but occasionally little fish found a path into this impossible waterway; there was just enough running water to keep Doris occupied with fishing and paper boating. Leaving Doris outside, I went

back into the house to my room for some additional pieces of cardboard to continue building our fishing fleet. That's when I overheard Mama and Daddy talking in the kitchen.

Daddy was complaining in an agitated voice that none of the black people who lived around the area would agree to come work in our fields because they thought the entire place was haunted. None of our white neighbours were interested in extra work, either. As I listened to Daddy complain I felt a little tight ball of anxiety begin to grow around my innards.

"Well, I don't know what to make of it, Jake," Mama answered in an even tone when Daddy paused for breath. "It's peculiar. But one thing is positive, even with Louise working in the fields full-time this summer and you part-time, it won't get much land plowed under. Ray Allen can help you with your routes this summer, but he won't ever be a farmer. Maybe Willie Williams and his brother Gabe would come."

I could hear Daddy pop his hand against his head, the way he did when he had just thought of something.

"You're right. Sure. That's the solution. On Saturday when I run my routes out that way I'll stop in and see Willie. Maybe Edna would come, too, and help put up some of that sweet corn I bought yesterday."

Mama was pleased with this suggestion. So was I. We hadn't seen the Williams family since we had moved. I went back outside with the cardboard in hand, my uneasiness about the help situation temporarily allayed. But when I walked over to the stream I saw that Doris wasn't sitting on the bank with her little fishing pole, where I had left her. She had walked quite a ways upstream, about a hundred feet, and was calling softly to something half hidden in the bushes.

"Doris!" I yelled. "What are you doing?"

She turned at my voice and then pointed upstream. "Look," she said. "There's a lion. It was talking to me."

I looked. And at that moment the animal Doris was pointing to half hidden in the bushes sprang free. It stopped on the bank of the stream, and stared back at me with tawny, blazing eyes. It was indeed a lion, a female lion, the kind in the New Orleans zoo. I screamed, and screamed. The lion beat a hasty retreat. Doris, frightened by my screaming if not by

the animal itself, ran to me and wrapped herself around my legs. Mama and Daddy came running out of the house.

"There was a lion," I blubbered, pointing with shaking fingers. "Standing right there. Doris saw it too, she was talking to it."

Mama untangled Doris from around my legs and picked her up.

"Don't we have enough to worry us right now without you scaring your sister to death?" Daddy scolded. "You must have seen a bobcat. There's lots of them around here ..."

"But Daddy, this one was huge, like a lion ..."

"There's bobcats in these woods big enough to eat a lion. You're being silly, young'un."

"Yes, and I've told you not to let Doris wander by herself," Mama added in a severe tone. "Come on in the house now, both of you."

We went into the house. I was sure that had been an honest to God lion standing on the bank of our little stream and not a bobcat. Maybe Doris could make a mistake like that, but not me. After all, I was almost twelve years old and had been to the Audubon Zoo where I had seen real lions. I knew a wild bobcat when I saw one. I asked Ray Allen and Louise when they came in from behind the willows where they had been target practicing with Ray Allen's BB gun if they had ever seen a bobcat in the woods big enough to be mistaken for a lion. They laughed when I told them that Doris and I had seen one. They teased me a bit but then forgot about it as the evening was swallowed up with dinner and chores.

When it was Doris' reading time, she dug out a Sunday school book that had a picture of Daniel in the lion's den on the cover. There were two male lions with their big ruffled fur necks and manes and two smooth faced female lions. The male lions were circling around Daniel, while one of the females was in a crouching position, ready to pounce on Daniel. The other female lion stood beside the crouching one, almost as if she were simply observing the scene before her. Doris sat down beside me on my bed with the book in hand.

"I saw this one," she said emphatically, pointing to the standing female lion. "By the stream. When you came. " She looked up at me, waiting.

"It couldn't be the same one," I explained. "This is just a drawing, it's not a photograph. Anyway, Daddy says we saw a bobcat."

She didn't seem satisfied, but she didn't object when I put that book aside and reached for Dr. Dolittle. We loved Dr. Dolittle. Before bed, Daddy had told me I could go on his routes with him on Saturday. Running the routes meant collecting from the people who owed money on the sheets and bedspreads and drapes and dresses Mama made that they had bought from Daddy. He sold his materials on the basis of a dollar down and fifty cents a week. The collecting would only take three or four hours. Then we would go and see Willie and Edna Williams and I could visit their daughter Sally while the grown-ups talked.

The Williams family lived in a house not two different from the one we lived in before we moved. Both were what was called shot-gun houses that had rooms just added on one right after another in a straight row. Ours had been two rooms bigger, that was all, and boasted an indoor bathroom. Willie had helped Daddy with the garden and the pig slaughtering, and Edna did for Mama when she needed it with canning and chicken care. Sally, the youngest daughter, was my age and went to a school just for black kids but we played together a lot at home. Or had played together a lot. Until we passed some kind of magical divide in age the year before that separated us. This divide puzzled me. Mama didn't seem to like me spending so much time down at the Williams house anymore playing with Sally and her brothers. And Sally didn't come up to my house as much as she did when we were younger.

But I was anxious to see Sally and tell her all about the house the kids at school said was haunted that we had moved into and how crazy I thought the kids were. However, when Daddy pulled into the Williams place and I jumped out of the car, Edna told me that Sally was away visiting her cousins. I was disappointed and by now wished I had stayed home. I had sweltered waiting in the car for Daddy to collect money from people who owed for his goods. Usually, I got out of the car if there were kids around, black or white, and talked. But nobody was outside today who could be inside out of the sun, and the moist heat seemed to want to drag me right down into the ground.

Edna, ever cheerful, pointed out that the rain clouds were gathering over to the north, which would bring some relief to the unremitting heat. She then brought out a tall pitcher of iced tea and glasses for everybody, and we all sat out on the front porch while Daddy talked about needing people to come work at our new place. But alas, the story of Laycott Place had drifted over the swamplands and into the back roads of our old parish and come to rest in Willie and Edna's ears.

"If you can get your brother Gabe to come on Monday with you and Edna, he can drive over and back and I'll give y'all extra for gas," Daddy said confidently holding out his glass for seconds on the iced tea. Edna poured silently. Willie was silent, too. Daddy abhorred silence but for once didn't rush in to quash it, even though the silence seemed to grow and grow, gaining momentum in the sweltering heat. Finally, Daddy stirred, reaching for his handkerchief. He wiped his forehead several times; shoved the damp handkerchief back into his rear pants pocket.

Then he just sat there, twirling his glass and looking at Willie in the same unusually quiet, thoughtful manner. Edna seemed to be gazing over Daddy's shoulder way out into the back yard where the White Leghorn hens Mama had given her for doing some washing and ironing were scratching in the shade of the azalea bushes.

Then Willie cleared his throat. "I be honest with you, Mista Schiver. I ain't coming to work on that place. Neither Edna nor Gabe neither. Gabe say he ain't coming."

Daddy sat his glass down on the turned over wooden barrel that served as a porch side table with a deliberate flourish.

"Why, Willie, I can't remember you ever refusing to come work for me before this. What's the matter?"

"You knows what the matter is, Mista Schiver, that's why you bees over here to me and Edna. You knows that place you got now is hainted."

"Willie, wherever did you even hear of such a thing?"

"From folks, suh."

"Folks. I see. " Daddy's voice was faintly contemptuous. He knew Willie was talking about coloured folks.

"Well, you know, Willie, sometimes folks can be mighty superstitious," he continued, "and you're a Christian, God fearing man, Willie. You know it's a sin to believe in superstitions. There ain't no such thing as ghosts."

"Yessah."

"The only ghost, Willie, that the Bible allows, is the Holy Ghost. If the Holy Ghost is in our new place now wouldn't that be a blessing?"

"Yessah."

"Then you and Edna come work for me. You know I pay fair."

"Yessah. I do, suh. But me and Edna ain't coming."

Daddy rose to his feet, exasperated. Willie and Edna got up, too.

"We's sure sorry, Mista Schiver," Edna said. "I'm just pureintee sorry. You tell Miz Schiver I just be so sorry and we be praying for you all."

"Thank you, Edna," Daddy said stiffly and quit the Williams' front porch forthwith. I scrambled after him. In the car Daddy backed up and drove out of the Williams' lane without another word. I looked back over my shoulder and caught a glimpse of Willie staring dejectedly after us, and Edna wringing her hands. This was not good.

As soon as we arrived home Daddy took Mama into their bedroom and shut the door. We kids held our own conference out under the black walnut tree by the side of the stream. We were all getting seriously worried.

* * * * * * * * * * * * * * * * * * * *

Oh, my God, so long ago I think, suddenly realizing that my prison cell roommate with the profound sleeping disorder has quieted down except for a gentle snore. Quickly, I must take advantage. I put Stephen Hawking's book aside, turn off my overhead light, and snuggle down into the thin bedding of pitiful plastic mattress and cigarette-burned sheets. Just as soon as my bones start to soften and relax into the metal bunk, my roommate stirs and begin to relive the meeting where she went to her husband's office and found his assistant sitting on his lap.

My God have mercy on us! I can't stand it! I try to wake her, fail, try again. It's almost six. As soon as the key turns in my lock I fly out of the cell and into the staff office. I complain long, loud, and bitterly to the

officer of the day. If there is no place for me to go other than where I am then I want to go to segregation, I say, meaning every world of it.

"There isn't room for you in segregation," the staff officer says calmly, shooing me out the office door and locking it behind her. "Segregation is full."

The officer must turn her attention to the breakfast trays that have just come down for those of us going to Court this morning. Left unattended for a moment, half of them will disappear.

"How can segregation be full?" I wail. "Segregation is where you go for punishment. I don't understand this!"

"Please get your tray and take it to your table, Betty. You're holding up the line."

I don't believe this. I can't even get into segregation? Something must be done. But what? I have to think of something. Write, that's what I'll do. I'll write to the director of the prison with copies going out everywhere ... to the moon, to Mars, to all points beyond ...

But heavens to Betsy, just when I've finished dressing for Court I'm summoned to the unit office. Maybe there is a vacancy in segregation after all? No, it is much, much better. A federal inmate has just been released. I'm told that when I'm brought back to the prison from Court I can move my things into cell 14. They will try not to double bunk me again.

Oh, happy, happy, happy! I hum and sing and gurgle with joy under my breath as I'm taken downstairs, searched, handcuffed and leg-ironed and eventually moved along in a shuffling line of irritable, cursing female prisoners who are being herded into a large police crummy. There are eight of us this morning. We slide up and down the metal benches as the crummy lurches out of the prison driveway and down the road; we are handcuffed so we cannot hold on to anything to prevent us from sliding into each other. And there is again some kind of hitch in the transportation of prisoners this morning just as there was yesterday, because we are all once again dumped out at a building downtown called "pre-trial" which is some sort of holding station.

As I am the only female going to Supreme Court as I was the day before, I am separated from the other women, who seem to be headed

to a special holding area upstairs, and am unceremoniously locked into a cell on the other side of the building which contains, as far as I can tell, only men. A couple of them are shouting from their individual cells. I am so tired from lack of sleep I don't even care. I sink down on the metal bunk and close my eyes. While I can't see the men incarcerated behind their bars as I am mine, I continue to hear them. The cells are too close together. I can't lock out the sound of their voices. I sit upright on the metal bunk, clasp my hands over my ears and stare at the ceiling while I try to conjure up images of Cypress Bay.

Cypress Bay is in Clayoquot Sound on the west side of Vancouver Island. I try to bring into my inner vision the little A-frame my son Mike built fifteen years ago, with the rocks along the banks of the little cove, the smell of ancient trees lining the banks, and the sounds of the flow and ebb of the tides along the pebble beach.

"Oh, would that I had never seen the place," I think ruefully. I fell in love with Cypress Bay with all the passion of my life. Never mind that my love has been largely unrequited, but so have many of my other loves. I love because I must, or my soul will die. While these thoughts flit through my bruised brain, I notice the blood on the wall of the cell.

From the first glance I knew it was blood. It was a large smear of blood. I stand up for a better look. The blood smear was halfway up the wall. I was in this same cell yesterday and it wasn't there then. Something has happened in this cell since yesterday, something dreadful. I call the guard. He appears promptly.

"There's blood on the wall in here," I say accusingly. The guard is older, pleasant looking. He steps in for a look. And at least he doesn't try to deny that it's a smear of blood.

"Well, you know we have a shortage of cleaning staff. Sometimes they don't get in every day to clean …"

I stare at him.

"I'm upset about the blood because it's there, not because it hasn't been cleaned yet. Do prisoners habitually bleed on the walls of these cells? What happened here that there should be blood on the wall?"

The guard sighs. "Ma'am, it could be anything from a nose bleed to a guy brought in that was hard to subdue, to a self-inflicted wound, to ... look, I'll put you in the next cell, okay?"

"Okay," I say. But I'm not satisfied. I feel I should do something, say something, and demand something, but what? I am let out of my cell and locked into the next one. A fresh off the street arrestee is assigned the cell on the far side of the one I have just vacated. I see him as he passes my cell with an officer on either side. He is tall, gaunt and very verbal. He does not want to be placed inside the cell and even though he is handcuffed, there is a brief, noisy scuffle. Lots of yelling and cussing.

Being locked up in the same space with men who are in traumatic situations is a lot different than being locked up with women under roughly the same circumstances. Women also yell and curse, but it isn't the same. There isn't among women prisoners this air of constant threat of physical violence, the thinly veiled threat of slipping into utter barbarism that permeates this place of men. I wish the sheriffs would hurry up and take me to the Courthouse. The cells there are very quiet. Prisoners don't usually rant and rave just before seeing a judge who they hope will see they are innocent of the whole thing, whatever it is they are charged with, and decide they deserve a break. The new guy who has taken possession of my old room pauses to take a deep breath and then starts over with his loud complaints.

"This is a hell hole!" he thunders. "A regular hell hole!"

Then I hear some water splashing and a loud gurgling. Too much splashing and gurgling to be playing around in water from the weak-streamed water spout directly above the toilet. My God, has the man stuck his head in the toilet bowl? He sputters and splatters for moments longer and then clears his throat, laughing maniacally.

"You gotta eat a lot of cheeseburgers to get that smart," he yells to the world. "A lot of fucking cheeseburgers!"

Cheeseburgers make you smart? *Oh God, please let the sheriffs come get me soon,"* I beg of the universe at large. But the next guy to appear at my door window is another prisoner. The police officer escorting him down the hallway is shuffling some papers and is momen-

tarily distracted. This prisoner is young and healthy looking. He flattens his face against my small cell glass window and grins at me.

"You really seventy-five?" he asks.

"Yes," I answer. "But how did you know that?"

He grins again and shrugs. The officer, recognizing that his charge is trying to talk to me, which is evidently forbidden, yanks on his arm and they proceed down the hall. I hear the cell door open down the way. The guy with his head in the toilet bowl is getting a roommate. He doesn't want a roommate. There are more scuffles and shouting and another officer joins the fray. After threats of pepper spray and new charges, the new acquaintances settles in with the cheeseburger smart one and the place is reasonably quiet. But not for long. The guy in the cell on the left side of me is evidently getting ready to appear before a judge.

"You can't wear those clothes to Court," an officer says when he surveys my fellow prisoner, who is now standing just outside his cell door. "They're prison clothes. You can't appear in prison clothes before the judge. Where are your own clothes? Do you have them with you?"

"Yeah, but I can't wear them, either. They're all bloody."

"Then you have to wear something from the free box. Stand over there while I get it."

There are shufflings and mutterings and the phone begins ringing non-stop at the desk. Then I hear what sounds like the prisoner going through possible outfits to wear to Court from the free box. He isn't impressed with any of the offerings.

"I can't wear any of this shit," the prisoner pronounces after a moment.

This doesn't impress the officer. "Stop being fucking miserable and pick out something," he says in an exasperated voice. "Or we'll take you to Court dressed in a strait jacket."

"I wanna call my lawyer," the prisoner yells.

"You've already talked to your lawyer and you'll see him in the Courtroom. Get dressed. The sheriffs are already here."

Good news, that. Maybe they'll take me, too. But no. I have to wait for another half hour for the sheriffs who are going to the Supreme Court to

finally arrive. I fairly leap into the police crummy in spite of the handcuffs and leg irons.

But I don't have to wait long in the Courthouse cells before I am brought into the Courtroom and escorted to the prisoner's box. I immediately find myself sending poison-filled glances directly to the back of Mr. Richards' neck. Neatly coiffed. Sitting like a well behaved school-boy; straight spine, shoulders back. I know he will win this case and I will be led out of the Courtroom by guards and he will give me a quick, victorious smile as I pass. Even though it is a foregone conclusion I will lose, he will nevertheless feel a satisfying thrill of triumph as I am being led away. I have known a few Crown Counsel lawyers now whom, I think, must love environmental Contempt of Court cases like mine because they are so easy. They hardly have to do anything except prove that any given protester was there. As they have the protest on film, all they hve to do is show the film. Or the photos. Usually both.

And yet Crown Counsels, on simple cases like mine, carry unbelievably thick briefcases that they stuff with unbelievably thick bundles of copies of Court orders and photographs and maps and case law all of which, if we lived in an honest world, would be reduced to one line that would say:

"The Government of British Columbia and the Attorney General's Office of British Columbia and the Supreme Court of British Columbia advises you that we will not allow you to interfere with our process of turning public forests into massive public trash heaps while fattening the fortunes of a disgusting few".

But this is not likely to happen anytime soon. Or at all. So I give over to Crown Counsel this morning his legal right, but not his moral one, to his huge briefcase that is stashed just so by his side with his opening papers neatly aligned with the edges of his desk. Cameron will conclude his defense today and will start cross-examining the arresting RCMP. Tomorrow I will cross-examine the Hayes employees with whom I had personal verbal exchanges on the blockade lines.

None of this cross-examining is easy because the plaintiffs entered evidence only in written affidavits. This means their lawyers composed the

affidavits so that neither Cameron nor I can cross-examine on anything that happened that isn't precisely described in the affidavits.

It was Judge Pitfield who ordered that the evidence was to be given in this way. Why would any judge order the evidence to be given this way in a case that involves public property unless he worried that the plaintiffs might trip themselves up if they had to give oral evidence by answering real questions? Real questions like why didn't the logging companies advise the RCMP to come arrest us forthwith instead of waiting weeks for a court injunction to be issued. And why didn't the RCMP come arrest us on their own? Isn't that what the RCMP is supposed to do? Arrest law breakers? More real questions that might reveal how Hays Logging and Weyerhaeuser worked in tandem with the Attorney General's office, the RCMP and the Supreme Court of Canada to make sure that we were arrested under an injunction?

Because then we protesters are caught in a legal black hole. We will now be charged with Contempt of Court. There is no defense for Contempt of Court. And if Mr. Justice Pitfield was worried about what some real pointed questioning might reveal, wouldn't that in itself constitute judicial prejudice? It's maddening. Absolutely maddening.

The day is long and there aren't so many supporters in Court today. When I am taken back to my prison unit at Burnaby Correctional Centre for Women, I head for my new cell on the upstairs tier. This cell is physically a carbon copy of the others: the same metal bunk with the thin mattress; the same built-in desk and bulletin board with no pins; and the same ratty curtain and chair and toilet and washstand. But blissfully I am the only one in this cell. I make up the bunk with thin sheets riddled with cigarette holes and spread the equally burned blue blanket on top and then fall into my bed. It's wonderful. I pass right out and I don't wake up until our unit is locked up for the night.

No matter. I'm rested. I have a cup of coffee grown cold from my hastily consumed dinner, so it's all good. I'll get my notes written tonight and then I'll have time for a quick shower in the morning. Tomorrow I want to cross examine the communications person for Hayes Logging. She's probably the only female employee at Hayes except for the office

workers, I muse, and it kills me the way corporations and institutions that do brutal or destructive work of one kind or another try to hire or coerce females to speak for them. Somehow they find females who are not only willing but eager to spread a woman's soft, warm glow over the carnage their employers have wrought on the environment or on people or on both. It's plumb dishearting.

I also want to ask Rick Jeffery, Vice President for Corporate Development for Hayes Forest Services Limited, a few questions. The man irks me. He pretends to be understanding of the aims and dreams of our Women in the Woods group. He even lowers himself to sit down in the middle of the logging road to talk to us. In my opinion he is a big faker. It's hard to portray vulnerability when it is insincere and Mr. Jeffery doesn't even get close.

I sit up and scribble until my eyes are so heavy they threaten to close again. It's almost two o'clock in the morning. No matter, I have to get my notes straight. If I don't sleep at all, then that's what must be done.

* * * * * * * * * * * * * * * * * * *

Daddy never read the writer Henry James who said that the "mighty will" was all there was, but he would certainly have agreed if he had. If you wanted to do something badly enough you simply set about doing it. The idea that ghosts even existed was outside Daddy's belief system, and the idea that a ghost could interfere with his particular grandiose plans for a sugar cane farm was laughable to him. But the fact that others whom he needed in order to realize his dreams believed this annoyed the hell out of him.

So Daddy was at something of an impasse in the first few days following his interview with Willie and Edna. At home he wore an intense, preoccupied air. When he was worried, or puzzling something out, he had a habit of running his hand through his white hair until it literally stood on end. With startling blue eyes behind his glasses squeezed into twin pinpoints of concentration over the matter of Willie and Edna's refusal to

come work at Laycott Place, Daddy was a walking time bomb. The rest of us tiptoed on eggshells.

We all breathed a huge sigh of relief at the arrival of Aunt Mary's letter. Aunt Mary wasn't really my aunt, she was my cousin, and she wasn't Louise's aunt, either. Aunt Mary was actually Louise's oldest widowed half sister. But she was Louise's guardian, and she had just heard from their cousin Ruby. Ruby wanted to know if Aunt Mary would inquire of Mama and Daddy if they knew of any work her husband, Les, might get if they moved to our area. Times were hard in the isolated rural area where they lived, and with a two-year-old and another baby on the way they were desperate for income.

Daddy was desperate for at least one experienced farmer who wasn't female or only half- grown; in other words, he wanted a male farmer in his prime, like Les. A letter was immediately dispatched offering free housing and food, a small monthly cash remittance, and a large portion of the crop to our cousins. They accepted and promised to arrive at the end of June, which was only two weeks away. We were thrown into a flurry of preparations.

The other half of the downstairs that had been closed off was thrown open, mopped, aired, curtained, window washed, and partially furnished. We had been using the bathroom across the hall all along as a second bathroom. Neither of the bathrooms were big enough to take a shower and breathe deeply at the same time. They were originally walk in closets that somewhere along the line got turned into bathrooms. But as each had a shower, sink, and toilet it was good enough, and our cousins would have their own private indoor bathroom. In Mississippi they'd only had an outhouse. Why, we were coming up in the world and dragging our less fortunate relatives along with us!

Daddy was once again walking around with his old confident stride, making inane jokes. Mama resumed her humming and singing under her breath as she baked, fried, stewed and pureed foodstuffs, and made plans to construct a brooder for a new batch of biddies. Louise poured over a Sears Roebuck catalogue when she wasn't digging up the garden, mentally furnishing the new rooms she and Jesse would have in his

mother's house after they got married. Doris was happily engaged in the paper doll houses I had bequeathed to her as I was now too old for paper dolls, no matter that I still found them fascinating.

There was a call from Clara Nell's mother. Mama answered the old cranky phone on the wall. Half the time you couldn't hear what people said on the other end because the wire that went from the house to the main line was too old and decrepit. The inheritors of the house declined to pay for putting in a new line while there was a property dispute surrounding the place. But my folks weren't crazy about the phone anyway, so it didn't matter a lot to them about the clarity of the incoming voices. It hadn't mattered to me before, either.

This time I rushed over and hovered around the phone when it became clear to me who the call was from. Mrs. Ferguson said Clara Nell wanted to come over on Thursday and spend the afternoon. The Fergusons kept horses and would be attending an auction just over the parish line. Clara Nell's mama and daddy would drop Clara Nell off at our place and pick her up on the way back if that was all right.

Mama assured Mrs. Ferguson that would be just fine and we would all be looking forward to seeing Clara Nell. Mama smiled at me after she hung up.

"Well, it appears you've made new friends in spite of your best intentions not to," she said. "It's the girl you like, right? Clara Nell?"

I made a little face. "She's all right, I guess," I admitted grudgingly.

Mama laughed and went outside to feed the chickens. She could tell the call had actually made me very happy. Not only because I had a friend, but because the Fergusons evidently didn't believe that our house was haunted. If Clara Nell didn't believe it, then the other kids wouldn't believe it either. Most of them wouldn't, anyway. You couldn't tell about the rotten boys. But I didn't care about them at all. Thursday was two days away and I could hardly wait.

I was sitting on the veranda waiting when the Ferguson truck, pulling a horse trailer, appeared down the lane. I went out to meet them and Mama came out too, to pay her respects. She apologized that Daddy was working, but he would be home later and maybe they could stop in for a

spell when they picked Clara Nell up. I could tell right off that Clara Nell got her thick, glossy auburn hair and friendly manner from her mother. Mr. Ferguson, a big, burly man who let his wife do all the talking, nevertheless seemed pleasant enough. Clara Nell scrambled out of the truck, and the Fergusons turned around the circled driveway by the stream and headed back down the lane. I heard a horse neigh from the back of the trailer as they drove away.

"Are your folks selling the horse?" Mama asked as Clara Nell soothed down her skirt and brushed bits of hay off her bare legs.

"Yes, ma'am. Well, maybe just trading. My daddy says we need another mare. We have two colts, but he thinks we need more. Do y'all have horses?"

"No, child. We have chickens and pigs. We don't know anything about horses except maybe work horses. Let's go inside and have some iced tea and then you and Clara Nell can decide on how to spend your afternoon."

I was glad Mama took charge of the first part of Clara Nell's visit. It soothed over any awkwardness. We went into the kitchen and sat down at the built-in island with its pull out table setting. Clara Nell could see the cavernous kitchen was made homey by Mama's Swiss organdy curtains. The early scuppernong jelly liquid bubbling on the stove gave off a full bodied, luscious smell. The day's heat was mitigated by a good brisk breeze stirring around the house blowing in through the screens, and all in all, I wasn't ashamed of the house I lived in.

And I was downright proud of Mama. Clara Nell's mother was fine, but mine was better looking. And Mama had a nice way about her that most women I knew didn't have. Ray Allen and Louise were in the chicken house patching up places where the boards had come loose or disappeared altogether. I suspected they were smoking in the process, although I had never actually caught them. But Doris was hanging in the doorway. Mama poured her some iced tea, too, and motioned her to the table. I looked at Mama questioningly.

"Doris is going to help me make a rice pudding for supper," she said, thus assuring me that Doris wouldn't be allowed to tag after us for the afternoon. "It's too hot for you girls to stay indoors. Betty Jo, why don't you

take Clara Nell for a walk down by the willows? The stream gets bigger down there and you can stick your feet in, but don't get your clothes wet."

She didn't have to say it twice. We walked calmly enough out of the back yard, but when we hit the trail by the side of the stream we started running, just for the sheer joy of it. We weren't racing, just running, lost in the delirium of being young and alive. Clara Nell's long hair was flopping everywhere and we were laughing and pushing each other, just acting goofy. By the time we got to the willows where the stream widened I was wet with perspiration underneath the arms of my blouse and my head felt damp all over with sweat. Clara Nell's cheeks were bright red from the heat and exertion. We pulled off our socks and shoes and waded into the shallow gurgling stream. It was cold, cold and delicious.

"Is this stream part of the river behind your house?" I asked wondering if I sat down in the stream whether my skirt would dry before I got back home. Clara Nell splashed her burning cheeks with the cold water.

"No, you boob. This is just a brook. Just a piddling little brook." And with that she skimmed a fistful of water with her hand and splashed me. Well. Could I resist such a challenge from a visiting upstart? Apparently not. By the time the water fight was over we were both soaking wet, including our skirts and blouses and hair, but we were much, much cooler. By mutual consent we finally declared it was a draw and staggered out of the stream, still laughing, to the bank. We sank down on the mossy shore.

We sat in the shade of an old oak tree first, but then after a bit moved back out into the sunlight so we would dry out.

"I wish we could wear khaki pants like boys, don't you?" Clara Nell asked, flipping her skirt into the warm, humid air.

"Mama said I could around the house," I confided. "She said she would get me a couple pair for Christmas. But I think it's just because of Louise, my cousin. Louise has a pair of overalls. And she wears them when she's working in the fields. She doesn't ask anybody, either. She just puts them on. But then she's getting married next year."

Clara Nell ceased her skirt flipping, and propped up on one elbow, lay across a smooth mossy patch next to the rocks that bordered the stream

and looked at me. Her blouse was still damp. The outline of her developing breasts was plain to see.

"I don't have any breasts yet," I blurted.

"Oh, you will. I didn't have any last year, either. I got breasts and my first period almost at the same time. Have you got your period yet?"

I shook my head, feeling woefully inadequate.

"Well, don't worry about it. It's a real nuisance anyway. Who do you want to marry when you're grown up?"

"I don't know. Not a farmer."

"Me neither. Okay, maybe a horse breeder like my daddy. Do you think any of the boys in school are cute?"

"No."

"I know one who thinks you're cute."

"I don't care," I said off handedly. I kind of knew who she was going to name.

"His name is Jimmy LeBlanc," she went on, her brown eyes dancing. "And he told me you liked him, too."

"Oh, that big ole liar," I said, throwing a twig at her. "I don't like him."

"He's my kissing cousin, you know," she answered, brushing the twig away. "On my mother's side."

"I don't care. I don't like him. He teases me all the time about … you know. This place."

"He just wants to talk to you. He is cute, though. If he wasn't my cousin I'd like him."

"Well, who do you like?" I asked, curious now.

She hesitated for a moment.

"If I told you, you promise you won't laugh?"

"Promise. Hope to die."

"I like Ray Allen."

"My brother?" I wailed, astonished. "He's too old for you and he's …" I paused, struggling for the right word.

"He's what?" Clara Nell asked, sitting up and watching me.

"He's … all he cares about is taking things apart like old radios and making electrical models of things that never work like he wants them to,

and building model airplanes. Why do you like him? Most of the time I don't even like him."

"That's because he's your brother. I don't like my older brother, either. He thinks he's so smart just because he's at Louisiana State University. And he teases me when he's home until I want to brain him."

"Ray Allen don't tease me, he just ignores me," I said. "Is that why you wanted to come over here to visit just so you could see Ray Allen?"

The thought filled me with a kind of sadness, but Clara Nell laughed. "Maybe a bit," she said, laughing a little. "I have to admit, I really wanted to see this place, too. You know, find out first hand what all the kids are talking about."

I felt a flash of anger then, but I didn't say anything. I put on my shoes and socks silently and then stood up.

"Let's go," I said, although my skirt was still damp. Clara Nell could tell I was mad. She stood up, too.

"Don't sulk, Betty Jo. The main reason I came was to be friends with you."

I didn't believe her. But I waited until she got on her shoes and socks before I turned and began to cut through the undergrowth to reach the trail on the other side that led away from the stream toward the direction of the willows.

"Why are we going this way?" Clara Nell asked, pushing straggling tall grasses out of her face.

"It's shorter," I said abruptly. I didn't understand the feeling of anger pushing up at me that was almost a rage, a gripping sensation of betrayal. When we reached the willows I stopped for breath.

The willows covered a wide swath of land. They were reedy self-generating plants and as nobody had cut them back in years they had grown out of control and now covered land at least the size of half a football field. They were taller than my head, taller than Clara Nell's head. I could hear her breathing almost down my neck.

"I don't like this, Betty Jo," she said in a hushed voice.

The devil got into me. In my childish feelings of hurt and thirst for revenge I decided to scare her.

"Why not?" I asked. "You wanted to see this place. Well, this is where, according to Jimmy and the other kids, that the wife shot and killed her sister and then herself."

I was fudging. I had no idea where the spot was that the supposed crimes had occurred except that it was somewhere near where the willows grew. As I said the words I scared myself. My skin suddenly crawled with goose bumps. I thought I saw something in the willows, something moving, something light in color, but darker than the willow bark, something low to the ground, something monstrous, something evil ...

I screamed, and screamed. And ran. So did Clara Nell. We were still screaming and running when we got closer to home, which brought Ray Allen and Louise out of the chicken house. They hurried forward to meet us.

"For God's sake, what's the matter with you girls?" Louise asked from her superior vantage point of an engaged woman. "Are either of you hurt?"

I stopped, catching my breath. Clara Nell and I looked at each other, ashamed now of our behavior. What a couple of ninnies!

"No, we're not hurt," I said. "We just thought we saw ... a varmint or something ..."

My voice trailed away. Ray Allen and Clara Nell were looking at each other. I noticed even in my agitated state that Ray Allen was noticing Clara Nell's heaving breasts.

"It wasn't another lion, was it?" Ray Allen asked, smiling at Clara Nell.

"Lion? Are you serious?" she simpered, dimpling at my brother. "We just sort of scared ourselves. There aren't any lions around here, maybe a rabbit ..." She broke off and looked at Louise. "You must be the cousin."

Louise smiled. "Yes 'um. I'm Louise. You're the famous Clara Nell I've heard so much about. Betty Jo talks about you a right smart. Me and Ray Allen's finished here and we're hungry. Let's get to the house and see what's for supper."

The path through the garden and chicken yard area was too narrow to walk four abreast, so it just sort of fell naturally that Louise and I walked in front while Ray Allen fell in step behind with Clara Nell.

Good spirits reigned all through supper. Clara Nell was just naturally a charmer. She was bubbly and laughing and talkative, but she could listen, too. She listened attentively to Daddy's jokes and laughed heartily at the punch lines. Ray Allen couldn't keep his eyes off her. Even Doris was enthralled. She brought her paper dolls out for Clara Nell to inspect after dinner. When the Fergusons came to fetch Clara Nell they came in briefly, much enthused about their new mare they had traded at the auction and was waiting in the trailer. When they all left, Daddy pronounced them fine folks.

When I was putting away the dishes Clara Nell had obligingly dried, Mama questioned me. "Did you have a good time with your friend?" she asked.

I didn't see any point in lying. "No. She really came because she has a crush on Ray Allen."

Mama's mouth made a little 'o'. "Well, that's not uncommon, honey. Girls look over their friend's brothers all the time. It doesn't mean that Clara Nell doesn't like you. I'm sure she must."

"Okay," I said. But I didn't mean it. It wasn't okay. It was just that I didn't have any friends to call my own and had so wanted Clara Nell to like me as her friend, maybe even her best friend, and now I knew she wasn't really my friend at all. I felt like the little soldier in the book she had given me to read ... when he found out his friends were carrying on behind his back.

Du Maupassant had written in the story *The Two Little Soldiers* about how the first soldier had taken the milkmaid away from the company of both soldiers for a private relationship and how the second little soldier felt:

"He now divined why his comrades had gone out twice during the week...and he felt within him a burning grief, a kind of wound, that sense of rending which is caused by treason..."

The section had stuck in my head and I applied it to Clara Nell's behavior. "I hate her," I thought before I went to sleep. "She was just pretending. She didn't really like me at all."

My sleep was troubled, and around mid-night the kitchen ghost struck again.

Chapter Five

More Cousins Arrive

The prison guard has just passed my cell door and peeked in. They must check every hour on all the inmates all through the night. They are very quiet. In their work rounds they glide silently from cell to cell, shadowy phantoms that the prisoners get so used to we don't even notice. If the guards catch somebody smoking, or taking drugs, or having sex with another inmate, they will raise their voices, lights will go on; there will be a general hullabaloo. It usually won't last long unless there is suspicion that drugs have been distributed throughout the unit. Then we may be in for an all-nighter, accompanied by the dogs. But that's only happened a few times.

Forcing my mind back to the notes I must make for cross-examining the employees of Hayes Logging, I finally manage to concentrate. Not that it does any good. The following morning my worst fears are realized.

Judge Harvey won't allow me to ask any of the questions I wanted to ask, questions that would have, if answered, fleshed out what actually happened at the blockades. I would have been able to emphasize that I had asked Rick Jeffery many, many times to call the RCMP and have us arrested, which he refused to do, and that the money his company lost by our continued blockade was his own bloody fault. The communications officer was just so sweet on the witness stand it would gag a goat. She emphasized that I seemed to be the leader of the blockade and that the

men on our side in the blockade weren't allowed to speak when people came down to the blockade line.

She was correct in this. We made the rule before the blockade even started that the boy friends, husbands, male supporters in general who accompanied the blockades would stand behind the women's line and not speak during any exchange with loggers or other employees of Weyerhaeuser or Hays Logging Company. And if the RCMP came they weren't to speak to them, either. It was a woman's blockade. But we didn't have to worry about the RCMP. They never came except at the very end, to arrest us. Which was the very reason for our rules placing men behind the women's line. The RCMP in British Columbia often don't have the staff to attend a blockade in some remote section of public forest and if they actually do, they often don't have the inclination. There was some really nasty violence at the last blockade I became involved with in the Elaho Valley north of Vancouver. Eighty to one hundred loggers ambushed eight young people who were tenting in the area who were just keeping an eye on how the logging was being done. They were beaten, tents and belongings burned and three of the young people were sent to hospital, one a woman. The attackers were never punished by the RCMP, the Crown, or the Courts of BC. And this isn't the only example of unpunished violence against protesters in this province. And as we were in the Walbran Valley in an extremely isolated area where the RCMP wouldn't attend, I felt the absolute priority was to keep everybody physically safe. One way to do this was to keep men on opposite sides of the issue from verbally challenging one another.

But the communications officer pretended she didn't understand such a ridiculous thing as women being in charge of a potentially dangerous event when able bodied men were around. I inquired of her qualifications in psychology and communications. She did have some but I don't think her studies stuck with her. Any run of the mill psychology or communications university course would discuss the difference in how men and women communicate. And that the most danger of physical confrontation is when opposing groups of men begin verbally challenging each

THIS DANGEROUS PLACE

other over issues important to them both. But the Hayes communication officer demurred.

When I asked her if she communicated the same with men as she did with women she answered in effect, of course, there was no difference. When I pointed out that even the U.S. Army recognized the difference in how communications and information are given and received by the public, especially if it is bad news, by using a woman as their official spokesperson she said, "People are just people, and they're all the same, men and women." Funny woman. I gave up the cross examination of the communications officer for Hayes Logging.

But the judge cut me off every time I tried to ask anything, anything at all, of Rick Jeffery. *Gee, these affidavits are wonderful gadgets,* I thought, *to completely derail any possibility of justice for the public, another enabling mechanism for the corporations to rule; the Courts to dance around the issue, and the trees to fall.*

Cameron wasn't in Court, so I called him when I got back to prison. He will wrap up the arguments tomorrow. If I am convicted, which I feel I most certainly will be, then all I have left to do is compose my address to the Court before sentencing.

I fix a last cup of coffee and collect my mail before we are locked up for the night and take it all to my cell. Settling back with the mail, I open a package first. It's from a supporter. A book. A beautiful book. Full page photographs of the wild animals of British Columbia.

As I flip through the pages I pause before a stunning photo of an adult cougar. The magnificent animal has been caught by the camera just as it lowers its head to drink from a pool of water below a small rainforest waterfall. I am reminded of the similarities of this rainforest cougar and the illusive big cat that Doris and I saw when we played on the banks of the little stream at Laycott Place in the backwoods of Louisiana.

* * * * * * * * * * * * * * * * * * * *

"Don't keep your light on too long," Mama cautioned me before she left our bedroom at Laycott Place that night after Clara Nell's visit. Mama

always came in to kiss me and Doris good night. I said I wouldn't and she patted my shoulder in silent sympathy for my day's disappointments with Clara Nell and then disappeared down the hall. I always left our door open into the hallway. It was cooler left open. Louise's light was already out, but I could see Ray Allen's. He usually stayed up later.

"Fix my fan, please," Doris said sleepily. I went to her table and positioned the fan so that it would blow right on her face. That was the way she liked it. It was the way I liked mine, too.

"Is that okay?" I asked.

She nodded. "I saw the lion again today," she said in the same sleepy voice. I gave a start.

"What?"

"After I helped Mama with the pudding, she said I could play outside by the stream where the tree is, but not to go any further. And I didn't. But I saw the lion again. The lion said I shouldn't be scared."

I sank down on my knees by my sister's bed.

"Doris, listen … did you really see the lion? Are you making this up?" I asked, wanting desperately for her to admit she was only teasing.

"Yes, I saw it, I did. Just like you and me saw it. It came almost up to me and, well, it didn't exactly talk, but I knew it didn't want me to be scared, so I didn't holler for Mama."

"What did it do then?" I asked, trying not to let her see how this frightened me.

"Nothing. It just looked at me, and then went back in the trees."

"Why didn't you call Mama?"

"Cause Mama and Daddy don't believe in the lion and they'd just fuss and it didn't hurt anything. I think it wanted me to pet it."

I grabbed Doris by the shoulder. Roughly. She tried to push my hands away but I held her firmly.

"You listen to me," I said, shaking her some. "You must never, never let the lion get close to you and it don't matter that Mama fusses or that Daddy thinks it's something else. That lion could hurt you. It could kill you. And I'm going to tell Mama and Daddy the first thing in the morning. You always, always yell and tell them, you hear?"

"Let me go. You're hurting me!" Doris cried out.

I loosened my grip. "All right, but do you understand what I just said?"

"Yes, I'm not deaf and I'm going to tell Mama you shook me."

I stood up. I was shaking myself. Should I go and tell Mama and Daddy now? That Doris said she saw the lion again? But maybe she was mistaken. When Doris played in the yard by herself Mama always kept a close eye on her. Wouldn't she have seen or noticed anything peculiar happening by the stream? Doris had a big imagination. I'd better wait and tell Mama in the morning.

"I want a glass of water," Doris said. I looked at the washstand that stood between our beds that held our water pitcher and two glasses. I had neglected to fill up the water pitcher.

"I'll get some," I said. I picked up the rose patterned pitcher that Mama won as a church door prize and stepped out into the hall. Daddy wasn't a big churchgoer, so Mama didn't get to church as much as she would like, but they had a kind of agreement. Daddy would take us to church at least twice a month if he didn't have to go in himself. It seemed to work.

Ray Allen's light was still on and I could see Mama and Daddy's light down the hall. Ray Allen was at his workbench fiddling with his electrical stuff as I passed. Reassured, I went on into the kitchen and turned on the light. The water gurgled like crazy when it came out of the old pipes in the kitchen but it always tasted fresh. Daddy said it was because the well was spring fed. I filled the pitcher with the cold spring water. *If Ray Allen wasn't so snotty I'd go tell him about Doris saying she saw the lion again,* I thought. *But he would probably just laugh.* Besides, I was put out with him for trying to act so grown up around Clara Nell.

I turned out the kitchen light and returned to my bedroom. Doris drank a whole glass of water and then fell asleep without further ado. Calmed now, I climbed into my own bed. The droning of our two fans and the emotional excess of the day overcame me. I followed my little sister into dreamland only to be rudely awakened four hours later by crashings and thuddings and cries, all coming from the kitchen.

By the time I tumbled out of bed and made my legs work right, Mama and Daddy and Louise and Ray Allen were already up and the kitchen

lights were blazing into the hallway. Doris woke up, whimpering and rubbing her eyes, and followed me out of the bedroom. She held fast to the end of my nightgown until she saw Mama just inside the kitchen and then she ran to her, whimpering louder. The crashing and thudding noises had stopped, but Daddy was in the process of making some noises of his own. He was slapping the palms of his hand against the side of the kitchen wall close to the west windows.

"Jake, what are you doing?" Mama asked in a strained voice.

"Trying to find some hollows in this wall ... something the wind could get into and make a racket ..."

"But the racket wasn't the wind, it sounded like things falling. Like pots and pans falling off the shelves."

Daddy turned and gave Mama an exasperated look. "Do you see anything that has fallen, woman?" he asked.

We all looked at the kitchen arrangement of pots and pans. Most of Mama's fry pans and even the big boiler were hanging on the island's hooks made just for that purpose. The string of hooks bolted in across the top of the island was so long it could have held three times as many pots and pans. Mama's cooking utensils were just as we had left them after the supper wash-up, all hanging neatly on their hooks. Mama pushed Doris aside and opened the bottom doors of the island. Doris, unnerved, grabbed at my nightgown again. I looked where Mama was looking. No, the roasting pans and muffin tins were all neatly stacked. There was nothing amiss.

"You see?" Daddy said. "It's just a sound ... and it has to come from inside these walls. Either some varmint has got up into the walls or there's some kind of wind tunnel developed over the years that's affecting the copper roofing over part of the kitchen. Louise, you and Ray Allen slap your hands around that side of the wall and see if you can hear anything peculiar."

Ray Allen and Louise slapped along with Daddy and then they tried rapping with their knuckles. After awhile the whole exercise must have seemed kind of silly to Daddy because he told everybody to go back to bed.

"I'll look under the eaves tomorrow," he said as we all trudged out of the kitchen. "It's squirrels or maybe a raccoon has found his way into the house, raccoons ain't got a lick of sense nohow , they'll stick their heads in a milk bottle... Scoot, you kids. Back to bed with you."

We went back to bed, all right. But I couldn't fall asleep right off. Rats! That's what I thought of. What if it was rats in the walls? The very idea made me feel sick to my stomach, but then I remembered that our cousins were coming the next day and that made me feel better.

I liked our cousin Ruby a lot; she was cheery. She had a tinkling, infectious laugh and her little boy, Howie, was just the cutest thing. Her husband, Les, was nice, too. It would be good having them just across the hall, livening up those empty rooms. Then I forgot to listen for any more strange noises and drifted off to sleep.

By the next afternoon we were all ready for our new housemates. They finally came around five, just in time for dinner, their old truck trudging down the lane, puffing and wheezing, Ruby with her head stuck out the truck door, waving and smiling.

Everybody perked right up. We had a Sunday dinner for an early supper, fried chicken with all the trimmings. We ate early because our cousins hadn't had much to eat as they had driven all the way through without stopping. They were absolutely delighted with their new accommodations. Ruby kept wandering from room to room on what was now her side of the house and murmuring over and over ...

"All this space, my gosh, all these rooms ... I can't believe it," she breathed. We females followed her around, happy she was happy. She and Les may have had financial troubles, but they scarcely seemed to have damped Ruby's high spirits. She was already showing with her second pregnancy and it seemed to become her. She was even prettier than I remembered when I had seen her the year before on a little family trip to Mississippi, her fair hair glossier, her translucent skin smoother and fairer. Louise was happy too, to be with her cousins again who were really more kin to her than to the rest of us.

I gave up trying to determine what degree of kin Ruby actually was to Mama, as Mama's father had another whole family before he married

her mother. His first wife had died, but there were a half a dozen children who were half-brothers and sisters to Mama, and their offspring and their cousins and half cousins ... it just got too complicated. Mama said just think of all three of them, Ruby, Les, and Howie, as being simply cousins, like Louise.

After an initial shyness Howie warmed up to all of us but seemed to prefer Louise, as if he were gradually remembering her from his past life when she and Aunt Mary lived down the road from them in Mississippi.

In fact, Howie began to stick to Louise like one of the sticker balls Jimmy LeBlanc used to torment me. His plump little hands searched her face and pulled at her hair, laughing the whole while, his sparkling brown eyes dancing with joy. Doris looked a bit askance at Howie, obviously noting that he was a powerful attention getter, but when he made it known he wanted to go see the chickens scratching around outside she volunteered to take him.

"Betty Jo, you go with them," Mama said. "And don't let Howie play in the dirt. Let him wade in the stream. That'll cool him off, okay?" It wasn't okay with me, but I certainly didn't say so. I wanted to stay with the grownups. Daddy and Ray Allen and Les were outside looking at the fields and their voices floated down as I took the kids to the stream. *Oh, well,* I thought resignedly, *Howie is a darling baby.* I took off his sandals and held his arms while he splashed the water with his fat little feet. I also found myself looking nervously around, glancing back into the bush every little while. Doris noticed.

"Are you looking for the lion?" she asked. I jerked my head around.

"Why in the world do you ask that?" I demanded. She had her bare feet in the water, too. She had started playing at splashing Howie, which caused him to squeal with laughter, but now she was just sitting on the edge of the bank.

"I dunno. You just looked like you wuz."

"Well, I wasn't. And you haven't seen anything else that looks like a lion, have you?"

"No. I'm not going to have to take care of Howie all the time when you're helping Mama, am I?" she asked, changing the subject.

"I doubt it. I'll probably be the one. But he's so cute."
Doris' delicate, heart shaped face fell a little.
"Of course you'll have to help," I added hastily. "He seems to like you."

* * * * * * * * * * * * * * * * * * *

But I can't dwell in the past, I tell myself firmly, shutting the beautiful book of wild animals and placing it firmly on the side of my prison bunk.

As I am now convinced that I will be convicted by Judge Harvey, that I will be declared guiltier than a startled skunk, I will start on what I will say to the Court before sentencing, which could come as early as tomorrow. I pick up my writing tablet and pen and begin:

"Sir ..."

Chapter Six

Country Girls

This address to the Court has to be good. It's the only shot I'll have now to get into the Court record my own story, my own aspirations when I stood on that isolated logging road in the Walbran Valley, not once, but twice. Let's see …

"Sir," I begin again. "I would like to speak to my sentencing first from the point of view of being an elder. I turned seventy-five in prison last August 4th and decided that I really liked the term "elder." "Elder" has a ring of dignity about it. While in prison I have been learning to drum and sing native songs with the Native Sisterhood and have noted that the respect afforded elders is still alive and breathing in their society, even in prison. I think this was true in most ancient societies. Elders bridge the gap between generations. Without elders the human race would not have survived, and there was power and prestige in being an elder."

I pause with my pen and paper. But Mr. Justice Harvey is an elder too, I remember; he must be as old as or even older than I am. We have matured in totally different directions, maybe on totally different planets. Well, class and gender certainly enter into this aging thing too, I remind myself. After all, I know lots of women my age, primarily Southern women, who are products of their time and still think that politicians and preachers respect them. One's upbringing is difficult to overcome. But there is also the desire to push forward. Our DNA is trying to evolve, for God's

sake, and as Hawking says, "the universe is going somewhere and we're going with it."

"Today it's no longer true," I write, "that elders are respected in our culture. Unless the elders have lots of money. Of course then they will be respected. However, lacking lots of money, the job descriptions for elders have changed. Their knowledge is no longer considered valuable. And there are very few jobs of any kind in our culture for elders because of the computerization of economic and even social life. Because being an elder today has no power or prestige, nobody wants to be one. Hardly anybody will even admit to being one even when they are one. However, I would like to shout this to the heavens if I could …

What good are high tech computers going to be when the waters are dried up or polluted or both, when the food has become so industrialized and chemicalized that it makes people sick, when our forests are all gone and the remaining soil turned to desert … "

Okay. Maybe this is a good opening. But I have to think about it …

"Betty, you have Court in the morning," a passing guard reminds me.

"Thank you," I call out to her retreating figure. Yes, I'll have to be up by six. But there's hours yet, before I have to sleep. I continue writing …

"Elders have perspective because we were there. We were there, and while politicians may have been just as corrupt then as they are today, the wars just as brutal or more so, and greed rampant everywhere, at least the Earth itself, our very life support systems, was relatively unscathed.

That's not true today. Our life support systems are being threatened in ways that fill many members of my generation with absolute terror because we know that our generation was blessed in a way our grandchildren will never know … we were raised in an almost chemical free environment and because of this, it has been brought to my attention by science writers that my immune system along with others of my generation is stronger than that of our great-grandchildren. So I am speaking to this Court as an extremely worried elder about what my own grandchildren, along with the world's grandchildren, will inherit. But I also want to speak to my sentencing as a woman."

Okay, so far so good. I put down my writing tablet. I would really like a cup of coffee but there wasn't any left for dinner. I rummage among the pitiful little items in the basket on the bottom shelf of the sink. The basket was a gift from a departing inmate. It holds extra packets of salt and pepper along with two packets of sugar, one insignificant amount of grape jelly in a sealed plastic packet, two non-dairy creamers, and yes, oh yes, one packet of instant coffee on the very bottom of the basket. I empty the coffee, cream and sugar packets into my cup and wander out into the common area in search of the kettle.

Four of my unit mates are playing cards at the table closest to the sink. As I fill up the kettle I overhear them talking about another prisoner. Although the prisoner being talked about is quite slender I will call her "Heavy". Heavy is a prison term that denotes prisoners who are usually older, (although Heavy is only thirty) and have been in a long time (Heavy has been in over ten years) and who are known to be tough. One does not really want to mess with Heavies. However, our Heavy is quite nice, at least to me. And she is beautiful. She has long dark hair, startling white teeth, and a creamy olive skin. She holds her head high. And she has just slashed. She is in solitary confinement. Coffee heated in the microwave in hand I pause by the gossiping women's table.

"Not Heavy," I say. "She doesn't slash as a rule, does she?"

"No," the older, sicker inmate sitting at the table answers. This one has spent half her life in the care of the province, first in and out of "juvy", they call it, the prison for juveniles where she got pregnant for the first time, then prison, repeatedly in and out, more children, all of them taken away, she is HIV Positive, almost all of her teeth are gone. "Not usually. But they moved her, you know, out of her unit. She's been in the same unit for five years. I don't know why the fuck they thought they had to move her."

"They said she was a player," the big butch dyke offered. "You know … that she bossed everybody around."

"Well, fuck man, you been in one place that long it's your home, you know … what the hell is it to them, anyway? " Bunny says angrily, slamming down her cards. Bunny is a petite blond with big boobs. "I hate this fucking place. It sucks."

I took my coffee back to my cell. *Jesus,* I thought. *Heavy.* I had talked to her several times, about her life. She said she would like to talk to me some more, maybe I could write something about her. I had encouraged her to try to write about her life herself, and we had tentatively planned a time when Court was over for me, and when she felt like it, to get together so I could give her some pointers about how to begin writing.

In the meantime, she had slashed. At least she had not cut herself deeply or she would be in hospital instead of solitary. What a practice- to throw a disturbed, self-mutilating prisoner into solitary confinement. How enlightened. Yet I do know it's for the protection of the inmate, since while in confinement a close watch is kept on the inmates. But my God, there should be some mental treatment by professionals of those in solitary. As soon as Heavy is out of solitary, I'll try to talk to her, I promise the universe at large. In the meantime, I have to get on with my Court address.

But the news of Heavy's slashing has disturbed me. From what she has already told me, all Heavy ever knew before prison was violence. When she finally turned the tables she found no sympathetic ear. She was a murderer.

Oh, my God, what brings some of these women to murder? Couldn't they just leave? Was there no other way? Were their lives so tangled with others in misery that the misery itself was a death grip and the only way out was the knife or the gun?

* * * * * * * * * * * * * * * * * * *

Like Simone du Falon, I think, the ghost of Laycott. She was a double murderer, and a suicide. Was it a spur of the moment thing? The shock of finding the two people she loved most in a compromising position? Or did she already know, or at least suspect, the truth sometime before the actual violence occurred? Had she been struggling with this secret, trying not to believe it, hoping she was just imagining things until, when it became absolutely clear that she was not just imagining things, she snapped?

Or maybe Simone didn't love her husband at all. Maybe she married him because he was rich and she and her sister were poor. And after

having sacrificed herself to also insure her sister's fortune besides her own, finding her sister embroiled in such a betrayal was just too much and that pushed her over the edge. Or perhaps Simone du Falon was simply mad and there was nothing between her husband and her sister except mutual concern for Simone's unbalanced nature that was growing steadily worse ... or perhaps Simone's sister was the unbalanced one and maybe somewhat simple minded and the basis of Simone's fury was that her husband could take advantage of such a situation, and that her sister was better dead than to be the victim of such black villainy by her husband and that they were all better off dead ... Who would ever know the truth of it?

Most of the time when we lived in the house I forgot all about the stories and it seemed silly to think that a dead woman's fury could hang over a specific place and nestle in its walls, perhaps haunting the stream and the willows, but biding its time. Especially since Mama had the place all fixed up nice, now, and Ruby with her little family was all settled in. Les had brought his good carpentry skills with him and the sagging left side of the front veranda was now fixed and the screen doors were in the process of being rewired all the way around. The summer was flying by. Les was a good field worker, too. Daddy worked alongside Les when he could be home. Louise stayed out in the fields with Les, too, unless Mama needed her in the house. And Ray Allen tried his best. He just wasn't a natural farmer but he was there, doing what he was told for the family enterprise. The three worked non-stop clearing the acres of weeds and brush before turning the soil over. They worked two plow horses leased from a farmer who delivered them and checked on them on a weekly basis, along with two plows to turn over the rich bottom land. Daddy told Mama that if the weather held without too much rain they could get in a good fall crop of sugar cane on at least five acres. They would continue clearing into the winter and next spring plant fifteen or twenty acres. Maybe thirty. They would just buy the workhorses. Harvesting help might be a problem then, but it couldn't be worried about now. Spirits were high.

I had my twelfth birthday. Clara Nell and her cousin Amy rode their horses over and ate big pieces of the chocolate birthday cake Louise

and Mama had made, with heaping dishes of Mama's homemade peach ice cream we had all helped churn in the ice cream machine. I hadn't gotten much acquainted with Amy before school was out, although being only six months older and one grade higher she was closer to my own age. Tall and wiry, she had a thin, intense face and wasn't especially pretty like Clara Nell. But I liked talking to her better than Clara Nell. She wasn't boy- crazy yet, and she told me she had picked out the book she and Clara Nell brought for my present. It was a copy of Jane Austen's *Pride and Prejudice*. I knew the title from my own reading but hadn't read the book before.

After we finished cake and ice cream Mama said we could go sit on the back veranda if we wanted to because Doris would be taking Howie down for a nap and the grownups would seek the shade of the front veranda. Mama was always so tactful.

But conversation on the back veranda was embarrassingly awkward. Ray Allen and Clara Nell just acted weird. Clara Nell giggled at the antics of the Rhode Island Red hen that had new chicks. Scratching around the grass, the hen found a big bug of some kind, and eight fluffy chicks tumbled over each other to experience what mama hen had found. So it was kind of cute, but Clara Nell acted like she had never seen chickens before. Ray Allen just smiled in an idiotic way. After awhile Amy asked if I would like a ride on her horse.

"I don't know how to ride," I admitted ruefully.

"I'll teach you. Come on, you can sit in the saddle in front of me."

We beat it around to the front veranda where the adults were already sitting drinking iced tea and talking. Mama gave permission for me to ride with Amy, but only up and down the lane, which was alright with me. The horses were tethered next to the stream under the shade of an enormous oak tree.

Amy helped me into the saddle and then squeezed in behind me. She showed me how to hold the reins. I tried to do what she said, but I was stunned by how it felt to be on the back of a huge riding horse. I was used to seeing work horses, but I had never been on the back of even a work horse. This animal was breathing deeply. He snorted. I could feel the

blood coursing through his veins. He gave off a heat and energy that was scary. He tossed his head to assert his own will, and I realized that I was far off the ground. I was afraid of him.

"Don't be scared," Amy said. "We're just going to trot a little bit."

By the time we trotted down to the end of the lane I knew I would never be able to ride a horse like Amy did. Or ride a horse at all. I didn't like the sensation. Riding a horse involved being closer to a big dumb animal than I wanted to be. At the end of the lane I asked to be let down. To cool off, we washed our faces in the little stream that found its way all the way down to the end of the lane and then crossed underneath the gravel road in a cement culvert to disappear on the other side into a swamp.

"I'm glad y'all moved here," Amy said, leaning against the trunk of one of the stately Live Oaks. "My daddy said he was glad, too, that it was time somebody put a stop to all the stories about your house. My daddy's the preacher, you know. He told me to tell y'all to come to church. We just live on this side of where Clara Nell lives and the church is on the lane that runs behind our house. He told me to invite you folks to church and to tell your mama and daddy that he wants to come visit y'all."

"I reckon they'd be proud," I said. I didn't tell her that Daddy rarely set foot in a church and maybe wouldn't be so proud to receive a visit from the preacher, but I knew Mama would. "Did you read the book you gave me?" I asked.

She nodded.

"Did you like it?"

"Sorta. But all the people worried about was money and getting daughters married so they'd have some money. I like Charles Dickens better. He writes about more common people. Do you like Tom Sawyer and Huckleberry Finn?"

"Oh, yeah," I answered quickly.

"I like them, too, but I know them by heart by now. I'm going to get a new book soon. A really grown up novel. Clara Nell's aunt ... she's my mother's cousin; she works in a bookstore in Baton Rouge. She said she's going to bring me a copy of *Gone With the Wind*."

I had never heard of the book. We sat down on a grassy knoll by the stream and Amy told me what she knew of the plot of *Gone With the Wind* and then confided she wanted to be a writer. I was taken aback.

"A writer?" I asked. "What kind of a writer?"

"Oh, you know ... stories. All kinds of stories. I want to write a story about my Uncle Tim who was in the First World War and got killed in France, and how my grandpa saved a colt that was having trouble being born and all kinds of things, and I want to write about your house and the first people who lived in it."

The cool water from the stream and a faint breeze stirring through the trees offered some solace against the heat, but it wasn't enough to cause the sudden chill I felt.

"What would you write about our house? " I asked .

"Oh, just the stories that everybody knows. That the lady of the house killed her husband and her sister and herself."

"Why would you want to write about that?" I asked, picking up a strand of clovers.

"Well, just because. It's a story. I'd say that I know the girl who lives in the house now."

I threw the clovers into the stream. "We'd better get back," I said. "Mama will think I've fallen off the horse." I almost did, going home, when a large king snake unexpectedly slithered across the lane. Startled, the horse reared up, upsetting my balance and making me pitch over to the left side. I managed to hang on, and Amy pulled me back upright. She held on to the reins and settled the horse down.

But my nerves didn't settle down. I wanted to get off the horse and walk but I was ashamed to ask, so I went with the trot. When I dismounted, I decided I was finished with horses forever. I would never get on the back of another one if I could help it.

When we walked up to the house Clara Nell was out front with the others waiting for us. She said she and Amy were told to be back by four and had to leave. After Amy told Mama and Daddy what her daddy had said about coming to church and both girls thanked everybody for the cake and ice cream and I thanked them again for the book they got back

on their horses. I tried to ignore Clara Nell's flashing of dimples in Ray Allen's direction and Ray Allen's goofy returning grin just before they left. I'm sure everybody else noticed this little flirtation going on right before their eyes but nobody said anything as the girls rode away.

The men and Louise went in and changed from the town clothes they had donned in honour of my birthday guests and headed back to the fields. It was sweet of them to do that and I decided they weren't such bad kin folks to have after all. They worked late to make up for the lost time for my little party and didn't come back to the house until dusk. We ate a late supper and finished off the rest of the cake and ice cream.

After the supper dishes were put away Mama gave me my present from the family ... two brand new pairs of khaki pants, the first pants I had ever owned. I couldn't hide my delight, even though I knew I couldn't wear them to school when it started again. Girls weren't allowed to wear pants to school even in a little isolated country school like the one we went to. Girls had to do all kinds of field work and tend to animals and ride horses and climb trees and play ball and engage in rough and tumble play, all in skirts. But Mama promised I could wear the pants at home. And she told me that Aunt Gladys had a wonderful birthday surprise for me but couldn't give it to me until the following Sunday when she came for dinner. Later, just before getting ready for bed Mama privately gave me another, more meaningful present, a present that came with a little heart to heart talk. The present was a little cellophane package that held a new sanitary belt."

Mama explained what a "period" was and that I might start having them before my next birthday. I had a vague idea about periods but was shocked that Mama thought mine might be so close.

"It's nothing to be frightened of," she assured me. "You'll just see some blood in your bloomers or on you nightgown. Come tell me and I'll get some napkins and show you how to put them on the belt. You'll bleed for four or five days and then it will go away and won't come back for another month. It happens to all girls sooner or later and means that when this happens you'll be able to bring new life into the world."

Mama said some other things, too, but the bit about being able to bring new life into the world spooked me. I lay awake a long time that night, thinking about what Mama had said about this. It scared me. I didn't want that power. I didn't want to be responsible for any new life; I was still a new life myself. After awhile I ran worried hands over my chest and hips and thighs, half afraid they might have changed without my knowing. But everything seemed okay, the same as before, so I stopped worrying and went to sleep.

But two weeks later I had something new to worry about ... we were visited by invisible horses.

Chapter Seven
The Horses

It was just before midnight when the entire household was awakened by the sound of horses' hooves racing around outside on the veranda. I knew it was more than one horse because the sound was thundering as they raced around, their flying hooves threatening to gallop right into the bedroom. I sat up in bed and screamed. Doris screamed, too, and flew out of her bed into mine. The sound of galloping hooves kept on. So did my screaming. Doris was clutching at me so tightly I had to forcibly pull her arms from my neck in order to breathe.

At the same time I was trying to keep my little sister from choking me to death in her panic I was overwhelmed by the feeling that she and I were both in dire danger of being swept away by some dark, unspeakably evil force.

Suddenly, our bedroom light came on. "Stop it! Stop that yelling!" Louise said, rushing over and giving my shoulders a sound shake. Doris, after choking me half to death, decided on the spot that Louise was a better protector from whatever terror had befallen us and held up her arms. Louise picked her up and scowled at me.

"Well, what's happening?" I wailed, getting up. "What was all that racket?"

"I don't know," she said. "Les and Uncle Jake are trying to figure it out. Everybody's on the veranda. Aunt Bug sent me in to get you and Doris. Come on."

She didn't have to tell me twice. Out on the veranda Daddy and Les were walking up and down with flashlights. Ruby was standing by the railing holding Howie, who was whimpering and rubbing his eyes. Louise went over to talk to her, still carrying Doris, and I beat it over to Mama and Ray Allen who were standing by the door of Ruby and Les' bedroom. The stained glass French doors were left open. The bedroom light was streaming out and the mosquitoes were streaming in.

"What was it, Mama?" I asked, almost whispering. "It sounded like horses, didn't it?"

Mama patted my shoulder absently. "That's what it sounded like," she answered. "It sure did sound like horses."

But whatever it was had left. Daddy and Les walked back up the veranda toward us, talking.

"I never heard of anything so crazy," Les was saying to Daddy. "It do beat all. Our horses ain't stirred. They're in the barn. And no mud or muck on the floorboards. It's been raining; there should be some signs."

"Well, we'll probably see tracks in the morning," Daddy said firmly. "Somebody's horses are out. Probably belongs to the Fergusons or that preacher fella. I'd better go tell them."

"I'll go with you, Uncle Jake," Les offered.

"No need. The women folk are all of a jitter. You stay. Anyway, it's just down the road. Ray Allen, you come with me."

I personally was happy that Les was appointed to stay with us until Daddy got back instead of Ray Allen. I didn't care that it was just somebody's horses that had burst out and gone freedom berserk in the night, they had scared the bejebbers out of me. Ray Allen followed Daddy off the veranda and out to where the car was parked by an overgrown hedge. We watched the car's taillight disappear down the lane. Howie was still whimpering and Doris wouldn't let loose of Louise's neck.

"Tell you what," Mama said suddenly. "We got a barrel of lemons in there, and Les, you're going to have to spray your room again, anyway,

before you and Ruby and the baby can sleep, so we'll make a big batch of lemonade while you're doing that. Then we'll all wait up for Jake and Ray Allen to get back."

"That sounds right good, Aunt Bug," Ruby said.

"Yes'um, it do," Les agreed, obviously relieved to follow Mama's lead. He went in search of the mosquito sprayer and the rest of us trooped into the kitchen. The little kids settled right down. Mama gave Howie her oldest pot and a wooden spoon to bang, and he stopped whimpering and got down to the business of banging it in the middle of the floor. Doris got interested in rolling the lemons to soften them, Louise cut the lemons, Ruby and I squeezed them, and Mama chipped and crushed ice. Then Mama put all of the ingredients together. It tasted wonderful. Les came in after he finished spraying his and Ruby's bedroom and washed his hands at the huge sink to get rid of the chemical spray stink. Then he gratefully accepted a tall glass of refreshment. It took awhile for Daddy and Ray Allen to get back, so we made another pitcher of lemonade. It just tasted so good. It was so hot in the house, outside, everywhere. We were all sitting together around the big island table working on the second pitcher of lemonade when Daddy and Ray Allen came home.

As soon as they walked into the kitchen I knew something was wrong. Ray Allen could hide his emotions, and often did, as he was a quiet guy anyway. A lot of the time I didn't really know what Ray Allen was thinking or feeling. But anybody who knew Daddy would know immediately by just looking at his expression that something was wrong.

"So did you find whose horses they were?" Mama asked as she handed Daddy and Ray Allen glasses of lemonade.

"Naw," Daddy said, taking his glass. He drank half of it without stopping. Ray drank thirstily, too, but kept his eyes on Daddy. We all kept our eyes on Daddy, waiting for him to finish the lemonade so we could find out what happened, if anything. But he didn't say anything else about it, even when he finished his drink, except to tell us all to go to bed. It was very weird. But when Daddy said to go to bed you went to bed and didn't ask questions. The next morning Louise and I both cornered Ray Allen out

by the pig pen. Only Ray Allen didn't want to talk about what happened the night before.

The pigs were still new and I hadn't got used to them yet. They were shoats, with sleek reddish brown hides, only half grown, a male and female. They were our piggy bank. We'd get piglets in eight or ten months or so. But I knew better now than to make friends with any of them. It was too hard to eat them when they were slaughtered after you had played with them and given them names. They ran over when I came up, trying to push their snouts through the wire of the pen. I had gotten into the habit of bringing them some little treat from the table. But I didn't have a treat this time. They turned away when I told them I didn't have anything, and ran off, their curly tails vibrating in indignation.

"How come Daddy didn't say anything last night about whose horses they might be?" I asked Ray Allen, planting my feet firmly in front of him. I didn't like the way people were acting. Daddy had been upstairs all morning pulling off some of the loose boards he had found in a bedroom up there that was built the over the kitchen ceiling. Mama was very quiet, not singing or anything, and Ruby and Les and Howie were in their rooms. It was unusual for Daddy not be out on his routes selling or collecting on a weekday, or else out in the fields. "Did you talk to Clara Nell's and Amy's folks?"

"Yeah. But no. It wasn't their horses," Ray Allen said, pushing me aside. "Nobody knows whose they were. Probably weren't even horses. Just forget about it."

I turned to Louise. She had just finished pitching the last of some straw into the pen. The straw kept the pigs out of the mud, although they seemed to dearly love the mud.

"Did Daddy say anything to you?" I asked. Louise turned her back as she gathered up the stray clumps of hay that had fallen out of the old hay bucket.

"About what?" she asked over her shoulder.

"About whose horses they might be," I said impatiently. "You know … the ones that were running around our veranda last night."

Louise straightened and looked at me. Louise was fair. She always wore a straw hat to fight the sun off when she was working outside. She had more than just a casual dusting of freckles across her nose. As she looked at me I watched her freckles because they seemed to grow and swell over the fair skin of her face.

"Nobody said nothing to me about it," she said abruptly and then turned away again. I looked at Ray Allen. He turned his face, too, and started back to the house. Louise followed. I stared after them for a long moment and then, feeling abandoned with only pigs for company, hurried to catch up. In a couple of days things seemed to settle back to normal. The house and fields were bustling with activity. We didn't have as many different kinds of vegetables to can as our garden had a late start but there were plenty of tomatoes and cucumbers and okra. And we had already planted a late summer garden that would take us through the fall and early winter. Besides, there was a new thing for me to think and worry about. School would be starting again in a couple of weeks. And this time Louise would be accompanying us. I could tell she wasn't exactly eager. And Mama had emphasized that I was to accept that I would be a regular student at the school, too. This meant doing regular boring assignments and having a big whack of my reading time bitten into. But there was no sense in continuing to complain about it. Sometimes Mama could be as stubborn as a Daddy.

"The school is okay," I offered one evening when we were sitting on the back veranda steps. It was Saturday and school would start on Monday. "It's really small, and you'll be in the highest grade. Ray Allen will protect you if any of the big boys try to bother you," I said. "The boys won't bother you anyway. They're actually kind of shy. And you're already engaged."

"Oh, I'm not afraid of that," she said. "I could probably whip most of the boys in the school. Including Ray Allen."

I laughed. "You probably could, at that. Why don't you want to go, then?"

"It just seems like a waste of time. I don't know why me and Jessie can't just get married now. We're going to farm his mother's place, so it ain't like I'm going to be using another year of schooling."

"Well, you'll be eighteen next month; can't you just do whatever you want then?"

Louise sighed. "Yeah ... but no. Aunt Mary raised me. I have to do what she says, at least in this."

"It won't be so bad," I said. She sounded so forlorn I wanted to comfort her. "Besides, you won't have to work so much in the fields."

"I like field work and I hate algebra. I want to go see my fella."

"Well, maybe Jessie can come for a visit," I offered. "Ask Ruby to ask Aunt Mary if that would be okay."

She brightened. "You don't think your mama would mind?"

"No indeed. You want me to ask her for you?"

"No, I'll do it. Thanks, hon."

Well, that little exchange made me feel very grown up. Louise did ask for and receive permission for Jessie to visit. After several letter exchanges, the date set for his visit was for the last weekend in October, which was a little bit of sugar to make the medicine of school go down for Louise.

I personally was eager to get back into the school system, something I thought I would never do. But the house was oppressive and there were books at the school. Since moving to Laycott Place my library days had sorely declined; the family was too busy to go into the city or even visit the smaller towns in a casual way that would allow for exploration into other, closer libraries. We were now a lot closer to the city of New Iberia than Baton Rouge but it would still take most of a day to get there and back. Whatever was needed to work the farm or keep the household going Daddy would try to buy from the scattered smaller communities in the area on his way home from either selling or collecting from his routes. And in school there was a sympathetic teacher and principal who I thought could probably be counted on to furnish me with interesting books. Plus at least two girls I was friends with. On the first day of school Amy told me something that I didn't really believe but that still scared me. It was about the horses we heard on the veranda that night. It seems that she and Clara Nell had heard all about them, too.

"They're not real horses," Amy whispered at our first recess of the day. We were sitting on a fallen log at the back of the schoolyard. The log was

shoved up against the school side of the fence guarding the house where Mr. Foster, the principal, lived with his wife and three little boys. I wanted to sit on the steps of the Home Economics building under the shade of the Chinaberry tree, but a gang of the little kids were playing a hop skip game there. Amy had practically dragged me to the relative privacy of the log because, she said, she had something really important to tell me that I should know about.

"What?" I asked hesitantly. "What should I know about?" I had a feeling that what Amy was so anxious to tell me might not be about something good.

"The horses. The ones your daddy and brother came down looking for. I heard my Poppa talking to Mom about it...those weren't real horses y'all heard. They were ghost horses. They belonged to Simone du Falon. You know, the woman who shot herself after she killed her husband and sister...the ones who first owned Laycott Place. Simone loved horses. She raced them. So the horses y'all heard actually belonged to this wife who murdered her husband and sister and then shot herself and Poppa said he told your daddy the horses come back once in a while and that sometimes when they come Simone is riding one of them..."

I jumped up. "Shut up!" I said fiercely, turning on my erstwhile friend. "If that's all you got to talk about, then don't talk to me at all. What you're saying is stupid, and your daddy is stupid, and now all the other kids will be talking about this stupid stuff, too. I hate you! I thought you were my friend."

I stalked off. But I didn't cry. I was too hurt to cry. I was saved by the bell. Neither Amy nor Clara Nell was in my class, but Jimmy LeBlanc was, although this time he sat on the other side of the room. He seemed more subdued than before. He even offered me a brief smile when he glanced my way when I got up to read during literature class. I knew I was a good reader, so I put special expression into my voice on the poem, *The Highwayman* by Alfred Noyes. It was a beautiful poem anyway. So full of romance and drama. I loved it. I could tell Madam was not so keen on my choice of poem to read because it was full of talk of blood and a woman's breasts but she didn't say anything.

At lunch Amy came over to me and apologized for upsetting me, and I had to say sorry for calling her daddy stupid, which I did somewhat begrudgingly. Then she said she wouldn't talk about the horses anymore.

Clara Nell didn't say anything about the horses at all, although I met her twice during the day. She just smiled and said "hey", but then she was over with the big kids now on the senior side of the school. I saw her talking and laughing with Ray Allen while they were playing a game of pitch and catch.

I didn't say anything at all about what Amy had said about the horses when the four of us, me and Ray Allen and Doris and Louise, walked down the lane towards home that afternoon after school. Louise had survived her first day at a new school apparently okay, and had even made a friend, Tina Cascara, another engaged girl who sported a small diamond. Engaged girls could go to school as long as they were just engaged; when they married they had to quit no matter how close they were to finishing.

* * * * * * * * * * * * * * * * * * *

I press my aching back against the wall above my iron bunk bed. *Times have really changed,* I think, remembering. For me at least, considering the society I started from. *Where did all those people who inhabited that special time go?* I wonder. And then remind myself that most are dead. But were they? Is it possible that nothing actually dies? Stephen Hawking seems to think so. Not only possible, but that this is the way it is. I like to think so. It's comforting to think that my deceased family members are in numerous other worlds pursuing other interests. After all, Hawking's interpretation of the universe, one that he says he can prove mathematically is no different in many ways from ancient beliefs, including those of many First Nations tribes. I press my back more firmly against the wall to try to relieve some of the pressure in my spine. The pressure comes from trying to write sitting cross legged in my bunk on a notebook that is resting on my crossed legs. I think better in this position in spite of the pressure on my back. And I have to get cracking on this.

If the judge decides to give a judgment on the spot and after immediately sentences me, then I must have a statement ready. Okay. So now I want to talk about trying to be a visible old woman in a society where old women by definition have become invisible, which is no mean task.

"Daddy," I say, appealing to my dead father, "you could talk the horns off a Billy goat. Give me a little help here."

But Daddy is silent. He has no opinion about my being an old woman. He was sexist anyway, and except for Mama whom he thought was the smartest woman he'd ever met, he was ignorant, old school country. I heard him tell Mama once that there was no sense in spending so much time educating me, that I'd get married early.

Which I promptly did. Still, I was reading at university level when I married because Mama was the best teacher I could have had. And I had learned how to research what I wanted to know. *Do I regret marrying so young?* I ask myself as I struggle to find a comfortable writing position on my bunk. *No,* I decided quickly, *aside from the fact that it's a shame on general principles for a sixteen-year-old girl to marry.*

All of the experiences I've struggled through over a period of seventy-six years have led me here ... to this jail cell. And while I'm not crazy about this prison thing, the thought processes and depth of emotional commitment that paved the way to this prison are mine. They are me. I'm here because I love. I love the earth and the earth's creatures. And even that first mentally abusive, schizoid husband gave me three great, talented boy children that initiated me into little boy land, a sweet, funny place to be when it wasn't scary.

But how to express my love to a Courtroom process that is dead and incapable of emotion? This wouldn't be easy.

Chapter Eight

Becoming a Woman

I have opened my address to the Court emphasizing my credentials as an elder, and now I want to say some things from a female perspective as the mother of a dead daughter. But I don't want to speak of Barbara Ellen directly.

I will talk about the industrial use of sex hormones that I believe gave Barbara Ellen breast cancer at the age of twenty-seven. I start writing again …"

"Sir, one of the most hair-raising results of the widespread chemicalization of industry, including the tons of chemicals used in our public forests since clear cutting became standard practice, is the recent research linking herbicides and pesticides to the fifty percent decline in sperm count in human males, epidemics of breast cancer in young women and prostate cancer in young men, and the finding that is to me the most frightening of all … the poisoning of mother's breast milk.

"The practice of clear-cutting, alias retention logging, requires massive amounts of chemicals on replanting; chemicals that, according to the scientists, writers and researchers of the books, *Living Downstream*, *Our Stolen Future*, *The Feminization of Nature* and others, seep into topsoil and ground water.

"So it has seemed to me for a long time that the men in charge of the world's affairs have not been willing to approach the environment in

a respectful manner, seeing the life support systems of the earth instead primarily as 'cash cows' for themselves, just as our present Premier of British Columbia apparently views our magnificent, irreplaceable, old growth public forests as his 'cash cow.' So it was around a year and a half ago that I, along with a group of like-minded women, came together and formed a collective we called Women in the Woods."

My back is not happy pressed up against the wall of my cell. I can't find a comfortable position. *But never mind,* I tell myself. *This has to be done.*

Summon up that ole determination, that never say die tenacity you inherited from your old man. Call up Daddy's ghost ... that stubborn, stubborn man.

* * * * * * * * * * * * * * * * * * * *

Oh, yes, Daddy was the most stubborn man in southern Louisiana. Even when the horses ran around our veranda again on that Saturday night early in September, Daddy wouldn't let on anything much was wrong. Not in front of Les and Ruby, who were awakened by the horses' hooves just like we all were except for little Howie.

The next day was Sunday. When the chores were done and Ray Allen and Louise went out to target shoot with Ray Allen's pellet gun, I followed. I could tell Ray Allen didn't like me tagging along, but he didn't say anything. When we got to the edge of the willows he walked over and set an empty baking power tin on top of an upended wooden crate and then walked back to where I was watching Louise load the pellet gun.

"I'm getting scared of this place," I blurted out, apropos of nothing. Ray Allen looked at me. Louise glanced over, too.

"I'm scared the stories are true," I went on. "You know, about what the kids say at school. Ain't you scared, too?"

Ray Allen frowned. "They're just crazy stories. I don't think anybody died in the house or out here. You think a little Cajun woman could kill a man just like that?"

"Well, sure. If the Cajun woman had a gun," I answered quickly.

"It wouldn't matter. Say for instance, you had a gun and you wanted to kill me. Don't you think I could take it away from you before you could actually shoot?"

"But what if I had a pistol like the woman who...you know. Simone. And what if I knew how to shoot."

"But you don't. And not many women can shoot, even now, at least not regular type women. And especially not in those days when women had to get all wrapped up in long skirts and corset things like they used to wear ..."

"Ray Allen, you're forgetting something," Louise broke in quietly. "I'm a better shot than you are. And I'm a regular type woman. At least Jessie thinks so."

I grinned at Louise. She was defending our sex and I felt a flash of feminine solidarity. Even though I no longer felt all that close to Louise because she was such a practical person by nature and seemed, aside from occasional horse play with Ray Allen, too grown up now that she was engaged, for me to discuss girl things with.

Ray Allen made a face at our cousin.

"Well, you're different in a way. You're like a pioneer woman or something. And the only reason you're a good shot is because you're kin to me."

Louise let out a hoot and scooped up a mess of dead willow twigs and tried to stuff them down Ray Allen's shirt. Still troubled, I turned and walked back to the house. Ruby and Howie were taking a nap and Doris was nagging for Mama to make her some more paper dolls. I asked Mama if I could walk over to Amy's house and she said no, and asked if I was I suffering from heat stroke to even ask such a question that it was way too far and she wasn't about to let me walk on the road by myself anyway. Instead I got stuck with the paper doll brigade. Ordinarily I wouldn't have mind, but Mama seemed tense and the house oppressive. The day dragged on. Even at suppertime when everybody returned, the evening had a sour mood.

After we had all gone to bed, or I thought we had all gone to bed, I lay awake, unable to sleep. It was raining but not enough to sing me to sleep

by its pattering on the roof. I had a headache. I was wondering if I should get up and ask Mama for an aspirin when I heard the old rocking chair out on the veranda start creaking a little, as though someone had just sat down and started gently rocking.

"Doris," I whispered loudly, wondering if she could hear the sound, too. But she wouldn't wake up. The rocking continued. My heart began thudding in my chest. I got up slowly, not making a sound. I would run to Mama and Daddy's room and alert them. Just as I made it to the door there was a flash of lightning and as I turned I could see the silhouette of the person in the rocking chair through the window. It was Daddy! I ran to the French doors and opened them.

"Daddy?" I asked hesitantly.

The rocking chair paused. "I'm just sitting out here for a spell," Daddy answered. His tone was sharp. It was the tone that would not tolerate questions. "You go back to bed now."

There was another streak of lightning, and then two more in rapid succession, and this time I saw the outline of his shotgun laying across his lap.

"Did you hear me?" he demanded, his tone sharper this time. "Go back to bed."

"Yes, sir."

I went back to bed. But I tossed and turned, too alert now to sleep. Was Daddy waiting for somebody? Who could he be waiting for? The ghost horses? Was he was going to shoot them? Sleep was impossible. How could anybody sleep with Daddy sitting in the old rocking chair on the veranda with a shotgun on his lap waiting for God knows what?

I earnestly desired my mother's presence. Would she be irritated if I went to her room and told her I was scared? She might. Sometimes she would be annoyed if I questioned too closely some of the things Daddy did that didn't seem reasonable to me. She must already know that Daddy was out on the veranda with a shotgun. I wondered if Ray Allen was asleep. Or Louise. Maybe I could just knock softly on Louise's door. Then just as I sat up on the edge of my bed, I felt something fluid and sticky between my legs. Horrified, I got up and went to the bathroom. It was blood. My period had come. Now I had a good excuse to go to Mama's

bedroom. I fairly flew down the hall. Mama wasn't asleep either and got up right away and found me some napkins and a clean nightgown. And an aspirin. She let me stay in her room for a long time while she talked about how I was a big girl now, almost a grown woman, and how I had to start being careful around men. If any man or boy tried to get me off by himself somewhere, I was to come and tell her or Daddy or Ray Allen right off. She had already told me that before anyway, but I acted like she hadn't.

She finally told me to go back to my room. I went reluctantly. Mama had talked down my anxieties about having my first period and the aspirin was working on my headache. But I noticed Mama didn't seem to want to talk about why Daddy was sitting out on the veranda in the dark when I mentioned it. However, the unfamiliar paraphernalia of sanitary belt and napkin felt uncomfortable and that blunted my worry about Daddy sitting up with his shotgun. And I was also aware of a thrill of pride as I settled down in my bed again. I was a woman now.

As I drifted off to sleep I thought I could hear Mama out on the veranda talking to Daddy, but I had had enough excitement for one day and couldn't make my ears or my eyes stay open.

* * * * * * * * * * * * * * * * * * *

And I am having trouble keeping my eyes open right now as I sit on my prison bunk with a pen and writing tablet on my lap trying to write an address to the judge in case I get convicted and sentenced tomorrow. The rules are that prisoners get to speak their mind and heart before sentencing, so I want this to be good. So I'll tell Mr. Justice Harvey at this point about our environmentalist collective we named *Women in the Woods*.

"Sir," I begin, "It was around a year and a half ago that I, along with a group of like-minded women, came together and formed a collective we call *Women in the Woods*. If I may, I would like to read the first paragraphs of our Mission Statement:

> *We declare that women, as mothers, grandmothers, daughters, sisters, nieces, aunts and friends, have a special interest in the preservation of our life support systems. Women are, and have been, historically speaking, moderators of society and stewards of the land.*

"And it is in this role of moderators and stewards that we struggle to protect what is left of the public forests of British Columbia from privatization and devastation by provincial governments, the logging companies, and the indifference, if not actual collusion, of the Courts of British Columbia.

"Sir, our group does the usual things that most environmental groups do. We write letters, petition the government, call and visit MLAs and speak anywhere we are invited to speak.

"When we first read Gordon Campbell's *Working Forest* proposed legislation and understood the ramifications of the proposed legislation, and what this would mean for every man, woman, and child in BC and indeed, in all of Canada;

"And realized that for whatever reasons, the press seemed unable or unwilling to try to explain to the public in general just what these proposed changes would bring to us all, then Women in the Woods decided to launch our own campaign to alert the public.

And here I would like to return to Women in the Woods' Mission Statement, page 2, paragraph 2. And I quote:

> *We, Women in the Woods, do not disdain using peaceful civil disobedience as a tool to bring attention to the plight of the public forests of British Columbia. We are aware of the long and honourable history that peaceful civil disobedience has played in the evolution of law in this country and on this continent.*

THIS DANGEROUS PLACE

We recognize that peaceful civil disobedience, far from being in opposition to the law, is part and parcel of the law and we, Women in the Woods, declare our right to engage in participatory democracy.

I lay my pen down and get up to stretch. I glance at the clock on my desk. A quarter to ten. If I hurry I can get a shower before count and lockup. I grab my towel, soap, and pajamas and rush across the common room, past the TV room where the door has been left open and some late shoot 'em up movie is blaring down the short hallway. No matter, once into the shower room the sound is muffled. There are two showers, two sinks, a bathtub and a toilet. I'm in luck. The shoot 'em up has gathered most of the inmates to its bosom and I have the place to myself. So I shower leisurely and wash my hair, which may not be a good thing because my hair has grown longer and will be fly- away in the morning for Court.

The hair situation is disgusting. I have adopted a very short hairstyle that needs frequent cutting. Our regular beauty parlour, where inmates who were already beauticians or in beauty school before their arrests and incarceration, worked under an experienced motherly beautician from the outside, has been closed down by the Campbell government. For the time being there are no haircuts. The prisoners are only allowed play scissors, the kind kindergarten kids use. They won't even cut paper and they certainly won't cut hair. But Campbell is cutting every decent activity in this prison he can and his scissors are very sharp. Oh well, at least I'm clean. I beat it back to my cell one minute before count and lockup for the night.

The unit usually quiets right down after night lockup, but the movie must have been unusually exciting as the prisoners yell back and forth to each other for at least a half an hour. This is the time the guard leaves for her own supper break.

I never liked the idea of being locked into a cell with no guard on duty. This is the result of more prison staff cutbacks by the Campbell government. What if there was some kind of an emergency and we couldn't get out of the cells? Like a fire? Or an earthquake? Or even a flood. After all,

the prison sits on very low lying land right by the Fraser River and it has been raining rather steadily recently.

But I can't think about that right now. Even though I know my address to the judge will not change his judgment of me, or his sentencing, I want it to mean something. And for what it's worth, at least my address will be in the court record.

Chapter Nine

The Mighty Will

"Sir," I continue writing my speech to Mr. Justice Harvey:

"Last Valentine's Day, on February 14, in order to raise public awareness of what was actually in Gordon Campbell's proposed *Working Forest* legislation, Women in the Woods blocked the right turn lane on Government Street in Victoria that leads to the front of the Parliament Buildings.

"We chatted up the motorists with chocolate kisses and information sheets and it all went very well. Of course the police appeared shortly and told us to take our Valentine banners, our chocolate kisses and ourselves out of the middle of the road. I refused, was taken to jail, and charged with obstructing a police officer, spent two weeks in jail and that was that. Everybody, including me, felt that justice was served because I was arrested and charged as any other Canadian citizen, and BC citizen would be, under the Criminal Code.

"However, justice in the service of the Criminal Code wasn't able to penetrate the borders of Tree Farm License Number 44 in the Walbran on April 24 when Women in the Woods blockaded there. In fact, when the Criminal Code ran up against Weyerhaeuser, a powerful US based transnational logging corporation on Tree Farm License Number 44, the Criminal Code just lay down and died.

"It took almost two and a half weeks for me and Janit to be arrested on Weyerhaeuser's Tree Farm License compared to the less than thirty

minutes it took to be arrested in the streets of Victoria for essentially the same action, blocking a public thoroughfare.

"However, it took over two weeks for Weyerhaeuser and its contractors and lawyers, and the Attorney General who instructs the RCMP – over two weeks for all these corporate and legal wheels to start meshing so the entire rigmarole of herding citizen protesters into that one legal straitjacket, that one black hole of special arrest and charge category that would guarantee that worried citizens who step out peacefully on a blockade in their own public forest will be deprived of any of the protections of the Criminal Code that even the most violent murderers have access to.

"All of this legal rigmarole that took Weyerhaeuser and its contractor and the Courts over two weeks to get together was to make certain that any citizen who dares to seriously challenge the powerful logging industries will have no legal defense because they will be charged with that archaic, unreasonable, undemocratic, entirely political charge of Contempt of Court, and will be faced with financial ruin and lengthy prison sentences.

"Weyerhaeuser, a US based corporate giant, will not even have to pay for this trial because the Attorney General, in his wisdom, has seen fit to make it a Criminal Contempt matter so that the Crown steps in and the taxpayers pay the legal costs for the privilege of having a foreign company strip our old growth public forests of our most valuable trees."

Okay, enough about that, I think. I pause again, drink a glass of water, and walk around my cell. The unit seems to have quieted down. God, I would like to just close my eyes and drop on my bunk into a deep, dreamless, restful sleep. But no, I can't.

I have to be strong. And stubborn. Even if I am fighting a losing battle with ghosts as Daddy did years ago at Laycott Place.

* * * * * * * * * * * * * * * * * * * *

After Daddy's all night sentry duty out on the veranda he was cross the next morning. He hadn't slept and the horses hadn't come so he could shoot them. His stomach was upset and he couldn't eat any of

Mama's biscuits or egg gravy with bacon, but he drank three cups of strong coffee, which gave him more heart burn and indigestion.

Mama fussed at him for drinking all that coffee and we were all glad to quit the table and go our separate ways. On our walk down the lane to the road to wait for the school bus, I whispered to Louise that I had my period and she smiled, and asked if Mama knew and I told her yes. Doris, annoyed at our whispering, said to stop it, that whispering was rude. Ray Allen, who was walking ahead turned around and frowned as if he thought we were whispering something bad about him.

As we waited for the bus none of us mentioned Daddy sitting up all night on the veranda with a shotgun. Doris didn't even know as she went to sleep early. And nobody had said anything about it at breakfast. It was all just too weird to think about, much less talk about. I couldn't tell at breakfast what Ruby and Les might have thought about Daddy's actions. Maybe they didn't even know.

Once at school I forgot about it because with my sanitary belt and napkin as the secret password, I joined the sisterhood of girl-women. Word spread like wildfire among the older female students and I was treated especially nice by some of them and offered confidences about their first periods. Clara Nell even crossed the psychological divide between senior and junior girls and came over at recess to congratulate me. A strange business, all of it. I was both embarrassed and proud. When we got home from school that evening, things among the adults seemed more or less okay.

Until that night. The ghost struck again in the kitchen as usual, around midnight. The sounds of pots and pans flying all over the place, loud thuds like something heavy falling on the floor, a sound of a woman shrieking. Or was that Ruby, or even Mama? I jumped out of bed. The lights were already blazing in the hallway and kitchen. Ruby was standing at the entranceway to the kitchen, handkerchief held to her mouth. Was she crying?

Mama stood beside her. I didn't like the way Mama looked. Her face seemed pale and peaked under the high ceiling lights and she wasn't saying anything comforting to Ruby. Or to Les or Daddy, who were

standing just inside the kitchen doorway. And instead of one of her long, modest flowered nightgowns Mama was wearing a nightgown I hadn't seen before. It was shorter and off the shoulder and made of some flimsy kind of material. Mama hadn't made the nightgown she was wearing, I was sure of it. In just a few minutes Ray Allen and Louise joined the group.

Nobody was talking. The only sound now came from Ruby who was sobbing softly into the handkerchief. After a moment Les moved to her side and put his arm around her. Daddy stood, his head cocked, as if listening for the noises to return.

"It's that wall," he announced after a moment. "That wall over there. We'll start in the morning. I'll tear the entire damned wall out if I have to."

"Ruby, stop your fretting," he said, turning to her. "Your ole Uncle Jake is going to get to the bottom of this little puzzle and your ole man's gonna help me. Everybody just get back to bed, now. Hear me? I'm going to stay up awhile."

Well, Daddy was in charge, and there was nothing to do but get back to bed. I no longer felt quite so scared. Daddy was determined, and if it was a matter of a contest between Daddy's will and the ghost's, I'd put my money on Daddy. As Doris hadn't wakened during the ghost visitation I tried to get back into bed without waking her. Only she heard me, stirred, half sat up. From the light flickering in from the hallway I could see her sleepy face.

"Betty Jo..."

"Hush. Go back to sleep," I said, adjusting my fan slightly so the breeze would hit right on my face.

"The lion was here," she said.

I paused in my fan adjusting.

"What?"

"The lion. It was right here, in the room."

"Don't be silly. You were dreaming."

"No, I wasn't. It came right by the side of my bed. It wanted me to pet it."

"I'm going to tell Mama," I said.

She rubbed her eyes. "Okay."

I got up and went down the hall to Mama's bedroom. Now I was really scared, I didn't care that Daddy was standing guard in the kitchen, I didn't like this lion business.

"Mama ..."

She turned and held out her arms. I told her about Doris seeing the lion again. I was crying and shivering. She held me for a moment and then we both went and told Daddy. After that all of us went back to talk to Doris only she had already gone back to sleep. Daddy said never mind, not to wake her again, that he would talk to her in the morning and get this nonsense out of her head.

I finally went to sleep myself and dreamed of having my period, only the blood wouldn't stop coming and I was bleeding to death. When I woke up the next morning I felt sick and Mama let me stay home from school. Mama even said I could stay in bed, but it wasn't very restful. Daddy and Les spent the entire morning tearing down the south facing kitchen inside wall looking for the source of the noises. There was dust all over the kitchen and wall stuffing insulation in piles on the floor. I remember thinking that I would give anything if we could just move back to our old place where everything was so simple and good.

* * * * * * * * * * * * * * * * * * * *

And yes, I think from my prison cell in Burnaby, British Columbia, if I could just go back to Cypress Bay in Clayoquot Sound right now where my A-frame still sits jauntily on a cliff rock overlooking the water, where the tides splash gently against the rocks below, where a couple of bald eagles nest in the old cedar tree in front, and where the resident mother bear teaches her cubs how to fish in the small waterfall that empties into the ocean across the cove. There, where for me for a few years life was so simple and good, before I got drawn into the life and death struggles of the rainforests.

But I must try to finish my address to the judge.

"Sir," I continue, "There is, in my opinion, a significant body of disagreement within the British Columbia Supreme Court about how the

issue of civil disobedience should be treated. And the issue comes up often enough.

"As Canadian citizens and BC citizens we collectively own huge tracts of BC lands and forests. Our provincial government is supposed to hold our public lands and forests in trust for us, and for future generations. Instead, Gordon Campbell is seeking to divest BC citizens of our lands and forests altogether.

"In Campbell's proposed *Working Forest* legislation, he would change the very definition of our public forests by renaming them "Working Forest", and then this new description must have new directives to guide it. The *Working Forest* will include all of the public forests outside of parks and will be primarily designated as open to industrial logging so that investors will feel "safe" in investing. It seems that "risk taking," that time-honoured excuse for wealthy capitalists to make obscene profits, is a myth; what wealthy investors want is surety. And Gordon Campbell is prepared to give it to them."

"Oh God," I think, putting the writing tablet aside, *"I do go on."* But this is my chance. I didn't get to do much in this trial as Cameron didn't want to put me on the stand as my own witness. I let that pass although my instincts were against it. Who can speak better than me about my own motives, but as Cameron reminded me, motives are not important here. Not with a Contempt of Court and not concerning sentencing. Maybe I'll just skip to the sentencing.

"Sir," I begin again, "I have never suggested that I shouldn't take the responsibility for my own actions. In fact, sir, I insist on taking the responsibility for my own actions." I pause; reflecting.

But when does the determination to take responsibility for one's own actions harden into a stubbornness so pervasive that there is nothing else but the will, the mighty human will?

Like Daddy's will at Laycott Place, and the way he acted when Les told him that he and Ruby and little Howie were going back to Mississippi.

Chapter Ten

Cousins Leave; Voodoo Arrives

It was a Saturday afternoon just after four o'clock. I remember the time so well because I was in the kitchen with Mama and Ruby helping to get the supper going. I wanted to hurry and get my part done which was to wash and prepare the collard greens so I could maybe have time to read another few pages of the book Amy had recently loaned me. It was the book she had mentioned at my little birthday party, the book that she was expecting from her aunt called "Gone With the Wind." But there was a problem. Amy was afraid her preacher father would disapprove if he found the book and would take it away. So Amy's mother, who was really religious, too, but didn't like to interfere so much with Amy's education as she didn't have much herself, and had heard that "Gone With the Wind "was also about history, solved the problem. Mrs.Sharkey suggested that I keep the book and bring it to school with me every day and Amy could read it at school. But I hadn't quite finished the book and it wasn't going anywhere until I did. How could I take the book anywhere until I knew what would happen to Rhett and Scarlett with Melanie dying and all?

Still, my mind was taken off Scarlett's dilemma somewhat by the delicious smells coming from the oven. We were having two ducks stuffed with corn bread dressing and sweet potato pie. The weather hadn't

turned yet and the days were still almost as hot as they had been in July. The oven was making the kitchen hotter, but we were all preoccupied and I hardly noticed the damp bandana folded around my forehead. We females all wore bandanas when we were cooking over the stove in hot weather. I hated wearing them but Mama insisted. The people working in the fields had to wear them, too, and made to promise to keep the clothes moistened from a bucket of water that was sent with them. Mama feared heat prostration worse than a rattlesnake. Her father had almost died from a heat stroke before he died of a heart attack. Daddy had bought the ducks ready to cook earlier from a small farmer as he ran his Saturday morning routes and they had to be cooked immediately. They were big, plump birds that looked so smooth and fetching even in their raw state that I could hardly wait for supper.

I had just put a big mess of collard greens in the sink to clean when I looked out the kitchen window and saw Daddy and Les and Louise and Ray Allen coming back from the fields. I was surprised. Daddy had said they would work until around six.

"Mama, Daddy's already coming home," I said, turning off the faucet. "The others, too."

Mama came to the open window and looked.

"I don't reckon anybody's hurt," she said after a moment.

Ruby joined us at the window. "No, they're all walking on their own legs," she said, and turned back to slicing tomatoes, cucumbers and raw onion for the salad dish. Mama gave her a searching look, but Ruby kept her back turned. I wondered what Mama was finding so interesting about Ruby's back.

When the three men and Louise hit the back porch Mama was there to meet them. "You're back early," Mama said, looking at Daddy. Daddy hung his straw hat on the peg just inside the kitchen door. He didn't say anything right off. Neither did anybody else.

Mama put the pitcher of ice water out with four glasses and the people in from the fields drank thirstily. Then Daddy sat his glass down with a loud thump and looked squarely at Mama.

"You might as well know," he said loudly. "They were going to wait and tell us tonight after supper, but Les let it slip. Les and Ruby want to leave. Soon. They want to go back to Mississippi."

"Oh, no," Mama gasped, turning to Ruby. Ruby stared down at the floor for a moment, still holding the kitchen knife. Then she carefully placed the knife on the counter and turned to Mama.

"I'm so sorry, Aunt Bug," she said softly. "I'm just scared … I'm scared this house will … mark my baby."

Daddy snorted angrily. "Like there's such a thing as haints. That's nonsense and you know it. Les, you know it, too," he said looking over at Les. Les didn't return the favor. He kept his eyes on his wife. "There's a cause for all those crazy sounds," Daddy went on, "and I aim to find it. If y'all will stay just a mite longer, we'll locate that damdable noise."

Ruby faced Daddy's wrath squarely. "And the noises on the veranda too, Uncle Jake? You going to locate those too? You would have to plumb tear the whole veranda down, and the house along with it. Everybody should move out of this house, not just me and Les and Howie. There's evilness here, Uncle Jake."

Daddy's intense blue eyes crackled. "Woman, you're just in the family way and nervous. Bug got that way, too, when she was in the family way with all three of our young'uns. Ruby, there's a chance for you and your man here to get out of the backwoods of Mississippi and make enough money to get a good start for yourselves and your young'uns. If you have a lick of sense you won't let a few noises that we haven't got to yet run y'all off like whipped puppies. I want you to think about it."

There was a long pause and then Ruby faced Daddy again, her lips set in a tight line and the colour rising high in her cheeks.

"I been thinking, Uncle Jake. Me and Les both. We want to leave. By Monday if that's alright. We won't ask for anything. Just maybe a little gas money to get home on."

Daddy turned and stalked out of the kitchen without saying another word. Ruby burst into tears. Louise looked like she wanted to cry, too. Les went to his wife's side.

"I'm right sorry, Aunt Bug," he said over Ruby's heaving shoulders. His gentle brown eyes were hangdog, pleading for understanding. "If it was just me I'd stay, but it ain't just me."

"I know that, Les," Mama answered. She turned to Louise who was standing behind Ray Allen as if she would like to hide.

"Does that mean you're leaving, too?" she asked bluntly. Louise looked from Mama to Ruby.

"Yes, Louise, you better come home, too," Ruby gasped through her tears. "Aunt Mary would be worried sick if she knew what was going on here."

I'm not sure what possessed Louise to refuse the invitation. Maybe she, like Daddy, thought it would be a kind of giving up.

"I don't know, Ruby," she answered slowly. "I'm in school here. Aunt Mary don't want me to come home and get married till I get my diploma."

Ruby straightened and wiped her eyes with the back of her hand. "All right, but I'm going to tell Aunt Mary why we came back."

"I'd take it as a kindness if you wouldn't tell her that I'm worried about… you know, the noises and all." Louise said. I stared at her, surprised at her stand. "She'd just worry," Louise went on slowly. "And I feel like Uncle Jake does. I don't believe in ghosts, either."

"All right, Louise," Ruby answered, "but maybe the ghost don't care if you believe in it or not."

I felt a big wad of sorrowfulness in my stomach. Then it seemed to be in the back of my throat.

I could hear Howie's shouts of laughter from the back porch. I opened the door and joined Doris and Howie who were trying to get control of the duck feathers. Mama had set Doris to the task of sweeping up the duck feathers that remained on the porch after the plucking. Howie was helping her sweep with his own little broom, shouting as the feathers would fly. Doris wasn't shouting or laughing.

"I can't get these feathers to stay in one place," she complained crossly. "I hate these feathers. I'm never going to marry a farmer when I grow up."

"Me, either," I agreed. "And we don't have to save every little teensy feather. Let's open the screen door and sweep the rest out." Out the rest of the feathers went.

Three days later Les and Ruby and Howie went back to Mississippi. Away from Laycott Place. They left in a flood of tears. Ruby, Louise, Mama, Doris, me... we all cried as our cousins packed everything they owned back into their old truck to leave us. Little Howie was bawling, too, because everybody else was. Except for the men folk. They were stoic, with stiff upper lips.

* * * * * * * * * * * * * * * * * * * *

Let's see. Oh, yes, why I insist on taking responsibility for my own actions. I want to try to explain this to the judge.

"Sir, that's why I prefer to remain in jail after arrest rather than sign an undertaking or promise not to go back into our forests because this would take away from me the responsibility of my own decision making.

"Sir, whatever the process, I have been incarcerated continuously since June 24. That's three months where I might have been released had I signed, and three weeks without charge. Altogether, it amounts to 'dead time,' time I won't get credit for when the day of sentencing arrives.

"Just as I do not agree that I have been fairly arrested and charged, I also do not agree that I have had a fair trial in this Courtroom. As a Canadian citizen I want my arrests and charges to accurately, honestly, and correctly correspond to my actions, to have my provincial government, my RCMP, my judicial system, uphold my rights, as a citizen, to be treated fairly and equally before and under the law as any other citizen.

"I want a correct legal description and charge for what I did, which was block a public road in the Walbran Valley on Weyerhaeuser's Tree Farm License Number 44, and I will continue to press argument for the use of the Criminal Code in these circumstances.

"Sir, I refuse the charge and conviction of Criminal Contempt of Court. It is a political charge and not a true one. I do not own it, and I will never admit to it no matter how long I stay in jail."

My eyes will no longer stay open. I push the writing tablet aside and throw the ragged blanket across my legs.

My memory immediately turns, drugged and dopey with lack of sleep, back to Laycott Place. And those dreadful days right after Ruby and Les and little Howie went back to Mississippi.

* * * * * * * * * * * * * * * * * * * *

Now everybody was afraid of the house, except Daddy, and maybe Louise. I flatly refused to sleep anywhere but next to Mama and Daddy's room. Ray Allen also complained about being so close to the kitchen. So everybody moved. Mama and Daddy took Ray Allen's old work room that was directly next to the kitchen for a bedroom. Doris and I moved into Ray Allen's old bedroom next to Mama and Daddy. Ray Allen took the bedroom Doris and I vacated, and Louise moved into Mama and Daddy's old bedroom. That left an extra room in the front of the house for Ray Allen's electrical stuff.

After the dust settled from all the bed dismantling and remantling and moving chests of drawers and boxes of personal possessions around, everybody seemed reasonably satisfied with the new arrangement. Daddy was now on the front line of defense with the ghosts. He said we were all just being scaredy cats because of a few noises.

In the following days and weeks he continued to tear down walls in the kitchen and the upstairs room over the kitchen in his spare time when he wasn't furiously plowing the fields. He urged Louise and Ray Allen on in the fields, too, to the detriment of their homework. They were too tired to do homework after putting in four hours of hard farm work. Twice I thought I smelled whisky on Daddy: once when I passed his chair bringing more rice to the supper table and another time when I stepped aside in the kitchen so he could wash his hands in the sink after coming in from the fields.

Daddy could be a moderate and happy drinker, but sometimes when he drank he turned mean. I didn't like him when he drank, even when he was in a happy mood, because he could go from happy to mean in two

seconds flat. His temper was bad enough when he was cold sober. The rest of us tried to give Daddy lots of room.

I think we were all depressed. Mama did her chores silently without the usual humming and singing under her breath. Louise and Ray Allen tried to be helpful, both in the fields and in the dismantling of the kitchen, which was proceeding at an alarming rate.

I was in the school library one afternoon at recess when the principal, Mr. Foster, came in.

"Are you looking for anything in particular?" he asked, noting the pile of books on a chair where I was rifling one section of the bookshelf. The library was sparse, both in books and in space, but Mr. Foster often brought in books from the main library in Baton Rouge.

"Yes, Sir," I answered sheepishly, suddenly aware of all the books I'd pulled out of the shelf. "I was looking for something on lions."

"Lions?" he asked. "Let's see."

I waited while he thought. Mr. Foster would take any question from the students under serious consideration. All the kids liked the principal. He was short and round with graying, rumpled hair, but his eyes were a soft, warm brown that made you feel comfortable and unafraid, unlike the principal of the other school. Even though I only attended that school occasionally I kept my distance from Mrs. Harcourt because every time she saw me she would question me about what I was studying at home. None of it seemed to suit her. But at this school the little kids would run up to Mr. Foster when they were playing outside, or even in the hall, and take his hand, even the shy ones, to tell him something or ask him a question.

"There's just the encyclopedia, I'm afraid," he answered after scanning the library shelves for a few minutes. "We really should have something more on wild animals other than story books, especially for the younger ones. And our encyclopedias are old. You want something on African lions, I suppose?"

"Uh, no sir. Not exactly. I was wondering about lions around here."

His eyebrows climbed in his round moon face. "Here? In southern Louisiana?"

"Yes, sir. Has anybody around here ever seen any lions in these woods?"

He went into his thinking mode again.

"No, Betty Jo, I don't think so," he said slowly after a moment. "At least not in the last ... oh, hundred years maybe. At one time I think some variation of the mountain lion lived just about everywhere in the United States, even in Louisiana, but not in the last hundred years or so. No, I don't think so. Why do you ask?"

"Because my little sister and I saw one. By the stream that goes by our house. It was a female lion, like in the zoo. Only Daddy said it couldn't have been because there weren't no lions in Louisiana and it must have been a bobcat. But I know it was a lion. It was standing in front of me as plain as day. And Daddy didn't see it. He only came when I screamed. My sister Doris said she saw the lion again when nobody else was around."

I couldn't believe I was telling him all of this. I felt ashamed. It was like I was telling family secrets. Yet I needed to tell him, to tell somebody outside the family about the lion. I could leave the kitchen noises in the house and the sound of horses on the veranda to Daddy because he knew about them, but he wouldn't acknowledge the lion and this made me feel worried and uncertain.

"Well, let's see, Betty Jo, you say you saw the lion standing by a stream next to your house?"

"Yes, sir. I saw it plain as day. So did Doris."

"How far were you from the lion?"

"Oh, about from here to the swings over there," I said, pointing out the window to the playground where two little kids were pumping double on the swings. Two girls or two boys would stand up on the swings facing each other and then bend their knees. Another kid would give a hard push to get the swing started. The two on the swing would alternate in pushing their weight hard, back and forth, to gain momentum and sometimes the swings would go dangerously high until one of the teachers or older kids would make them stop. The smaller kids could rarely get a swing to reach a dangerous altitude, so at the moment, the schoolyard was calm.

"That's quite a long way, Betty Jo. Two hundred feet or so. And was the sun shining?"

"Yes, sir."

"Well, maybe there was some kind of reflection off the stream that distorted your vision and made the animal you were seeing seem larger."

"But Doris saw it too."

"If she was standing by you she was roughly in the same place of distance or she might simply have taken her cue from you. You said it was a lion so she thought the animal was a lion, too. I'm not saying that you didn't see a lion, Betty Jo. Just that it is highly unlikely that the animal actually was a lion. Does that make sense to you?"

"Yes, sir," I said. But it didn't. Not really.

"I'll bring a book on lions from the main library," he said, smiling now. "Next week."

Just then Brother Guice came in to talk to Mr. Foster about cleaning the school yard of brush on one side of the grounds. The older kids did most of the maintenance of the school. I busied myself with placing the books I'd piled on the chair back onto the shelves and then slipped quietly from the library. I hoped that Brother Guice hadn't heard any of the lion conversation. I would be embarrassed if he had heard and then told Ray Allen. By the time the school day was over, I was convinced there was no lion. It was probably like Daddy said, just a bobcat.

Anyway, when we got home from school there was something new to worry about. Aunt Gladys, mama's much-married younger sister, was there and she wanted to bring out a voodoo woman to chase the ghost out of the house. Daddy was raising the roof because Mama seemed interested in what Aunt Gladys was proposing.

"Have you women completely lost your minds? Don't either of you have a lick of sense? A voodoo woman in my house? Not under my roof."

"But Jake, what could it hurt? It won't hurt nothing and it might help," Aunt Gladys answered calmly, helping herself to a piece of cold cornbread sitting on the table. She was used to Daddy's outbursts. "You got any cold milk, Bug?"

Mama brought a small bowl half filled with milk and a spoon and set it in front of Aunt Gladys. Aunt Gladys carefully crumbled the corn bread into the bowl, her polished red nails and diamond rings flashing in the sunlight angling to the west through the back kitchen windows. She

owned and operated a Cajun food restaurant, but one of Aunt Gladys' favorite dishes was still a big slice of Mama's cold cornbread crumbled in a bowl of milk. Mine, too. I would have asked for a bowl, too, but the very idea of a voodoo woman actually coming to our place to exorcise was so fascinating I could hardly breathe. Daddy's short white hair was standing straight up, showing the effects of much nervous mulching with his hand.

"Gladys, you can run a restaurant business, but I wouldn't put no money on your common sense. You gonna bring out the same voodoo woman that was supposed to run off that silly woman who took your last husband?"

Aunt Gladys had really suffered through that episode and I didn't think it was fair of Daddy to bring it up. Not that I was overly fond of Aunt Gladys even though she had given me the first real pair of tap shoes I'd ever owned on my last birthday. New shiny patent leather shoes with rounded toes and real taps on the soles and heels. But I didn't like the way Aunt Gladys would take over Mama's time when she came around, it was like she wanted Mama to recognize that she was the most important person in the universe, even when Daddy was home. And it wasn't as though Aunt Gladys had just been married to the one husband; she was looking around for a fifth. But she wasn't impressed by Daddy's blustering.

"Which one?" she answered nonchalantly to Daddy's question, stirring up her bowl of milk and cornbread. "And who cares? But just for your information this is a different voodoo woman, one that is highly recommended. You don't seem to be making any headway in finding the damned ghost."

"That's because there ain't any ghost, and I'll find the noises. Since I took up a portion of the sub-flooring over there by that cupboard we haven't heard any noises, have we, Bug?"

Mama just looked at Daddy. Daddy thought he had fixed the problem several times before, but he hadn't. That very night, as if to prove to Daddy that he hadn't fixed the noises, the ghost returned. This time evidentially complete with low moans. I didn't hear the low moans. I didn't even stir. Doris and I slept through the whole thing. But Mama and Daddy and Ray

Allen and Louise didn't. Louise sat next to me on the school bus the next morning and told me all about it on the way to school in whispers.

"I wish I could leave," I whispered back. "I wouldn't stay here if I could leave. Why are you staying? Ain't you afraid?"

Louise shrugged. "Yes and no."

I nodded. That was about the way I felt. I was somewhat afraid, but not terribly. Not since that night when the horses first ran about the veranda. *Perhaps we were all just getting used to the ghost*, I thought. But the ghost made people depressed. Especially Daddy.

"Uncle Jake ain't about to give up the fight," Louise added after a moment. "And you know something, when he's riled up; he's meaner than any ghost."

I giggled, because that was about the way I felt about Daddy too. His cussedness was a comfort sometimes, at least in this situation.

"Anyway," Louise went on, "I feel bad about Ruby and Les leaving, but to tell the truth I ain't exactly crazy about moving in with Jesse's folks after we're married. I'm thinking about, just thinking, mind you, about asking Jesse if maybe we could come here and farm instead of staying with his folks. He's got another brother who could help his folks out. I'd druther live with y'all. I think Jesse would, too, after he got acquainted with Uncle Jake's ways. He's a real hard worker. And I like y'all's house; I never thought I'd live in such a fancy place."

I stared at her in amazement. But no, she wasn't funning. Her calm blue eyes were serious. Louise always sat very straight on the bus and in the mornings, at least, her short, straw blond hair was neatly combed. She took trouble with her ironing, too, and always looked neat for school in one of her three white blouses paired with one of her two blue skirts or the green and yellow plaid one. Louise had a pink flowery dress for church, but she didn't like it. I didn't like her in the dress, either. It didn't suit her strong, slender frame. Louise didn't have Ruby's pretty face, but she wasn't homely, either. She didn't freckle everywhere like some of our other relatives and she had nice, white, even teeth. Mama was going to make Louise another dress for church when she had time, out of some

plain blue cotton that would match Louise's eyes. She was talking about making Louise's wedding dress, too.

"But it's haunted," I said in a hoarse whisper. "The house is haunted."

"Shsh. Uncle Jake's going to find the trouble, and stop talking about it at school."

"I never started," I napped. How could Louise be so dumb? By the time Daddy actually found the trouble, if he ever did, the whole house would be in shambles.

Mama and Aunt Gladys prevailed on the question of the voodoo woman. The voodoo woman was booked for a gig at our house. Mama didn't want us kids to know the voodoo woman was actually coming and we might not have, except Doris overheard Mama and Daddy arguing about it the evening before when they thought we were all outside. We were, but Doris had gone back inside to our room to fetch her baby doll. She wanted the baby doll to enjoy the dollhouse we had just constructed out of a big cardboard box in the back yard under the Walnut tree. Louise and Ray Allen were in the barn. When it got really hot they would pour water over the work horses after coming in from the field to cool them down and then give them a good brushing. But when Doris came back from inside the house she didn't have her baby doll. And she was frowning.

"Mama and Daddy are fighting again," she said with a downward pull to her mouth. I turned back to the dollhouse with a sinking feeling in my stomach.

"What are they fighting about?" I asked, putting the finishing touches to the table made of carefully balanced rocks and sticks inside the box.

"About the woman coming to voodoo our house," she answered, sitting down on the grass beside me.

"Watch for the chicken poo," I warned mechanically. "When's the woman coming?"

"Tomorrow. I heard Mama say she'll come when we're in school. Daddy's yelling about it."

"Too bad," I said, sitting back on my haunches to survey my handiwork. "I'd like to see that."

"Well, I wouldn't," Doris blurted. "I hate this place. I want to move," and she burst into tears.

I stared at her for a moment, surprised. I didn't ordinarily show much physical affection for Doris because she was just my bothersome little sister, and she was spoiled anyway with all of Mama's attentions and huggings. However, she was so distressed I moved close and put my arm around her.

"It's okay," I said. "Stop bawling. Mama and Daddy won't let anything happen to you."

She wiped at her eyes fiercely, swallowing her sobs. "They just fight all the time. Why can't we just move?"

I stood up and kicked at the cardboard box I had been carefully crafting into a house. The side of the box crumpled, scattering the rock and stick furniture. Just then Ray Allen and Louise emerged from their chores in the barn and came over.

"What's the matter, Doris?" Louise asked. Doris didn't answer. She just hung her head. Ray Allen looked at me.

"She's upset because Mama and Daddy are fighting again," I said finally. "Over the voodoo woman. She's coming tomorrow."

* * * * * * * * * * * * * * * * * * *

I can't hold my eyes open any longer. I undress, brush my teeth, and turn out my light. I have learned to live with the overhead light that never turns off by wearing a black eye mask that my friend Shelly Wine had the foresight to insist I bring into prison with me. But I hardly need the mask. I am so exhausted I fall unconscious before my head hits the pillow. When I wake up the next morning I can't remember where I am for a few minutes. Until I hear the guard at my door.

"Wake up, Betty. Court this morning. You don't have much time."

And this time I am driven in the prison crummy (police wagon) straight to the Courthouse cells. There is a decent showing of supporters in the Courtroom. In case the judge passes judgment this morning and is prepared to mete out sentencing immediately I should have my Court

address to sentencing ready. But it isn't ready. I fell asleep before I could finish. I will have to ad lib.

Cameron winds up his last arguments by early afternoon and the judge not only reserves the sentencing, he reserves the judgment, which is a letdown. I know he's going to find me guilty and this pussyfooting around is maddening. Judge Harvey just doesn't want to declare me guilty in the Courtroom. It's easier to do it in his office and simply release the verdict to the lawyers. At least I can get some sleep now. I turn in early and get up early.

The next morning I'm dressed and waiting at seven for the guard to come unlock my cell, but she doesn't come. Nobody else is let out, either. Prisoners start banging on their doors. One of the guards finally comes around and tells each prisoner individually through her cell door that there is a lockdown.

This is not good. A lockdown so early in the morning means something bad happened during the night. Maybe there was an escape. I think there's only been one successful escape in this secure part of the prison, and I can't remember how that was supposed to have happened.

Coffee. I would really like a cup of coffee. I look through my tiny window into the common area. After the initial door banging, everything has quieted down. There is no movement in the hallway or the common area. I can see the guard on duty inside her glass bubble. She is talking on the phone. *Okay, come on, tell us what's happened,* I plead silently. *Or at least bring us some coffee.* I move over to the barred, narrow outside window that lets in the daylight. I can see part of the track field to the left, part of the kennel run to the right. Nothing moving there, either, which is highly unusual. The kennel women should be out with the dogs by now. Suddenly, there is a turn of the lock at my door and a covered tray is placed wordlessly on the floor. I hurry over to retrieve it.

"What's happening?" I ask, but I'm too late. The guard is already turning the lock to my door; she and her buddy are busy with other trays. I sit on the side of the bunk and take the cover off my tray. Two pieces of white bread that can't be toasted without access to the toaster, which is in the common room, two little cups of synthetic red juice, and a cup of

lukewarm coffee. Oh, well. There are two little containers of jams nestled next to the white bread that contain half a teaspoon of jam each, and I have saved a little container of peanut butter from the day before. I'm not hungry anyway. I don't like this lockdown. I'll just wait until we're unlocked and can get to the toaster. I sip on the lukewarm coffee and wait. An hour passes. I decide to do my exercises.

Without my little Walkman I wouldn't be able to go on with this show. It has a radio, and I have a choice of two music stations that play the kind of music I can dance to. One of the stations is up to the challenge this early in the morning and I'm doing a little soft shoe to a golden oldie when I see the guard at my door again. She's unlocking it. I tear the earphone off my head and rush over.

"You can come down to the common area with the others," she announces solemnly. "Hank is here. He has something to tell you."

Hank. Hank the Chaplain. Hank the bearer of bad news. I leave my cell, pause on the platform of the second tier and look below. The women are slowly gathering around Hank in front of the bubble. Nobody is talking or laughing. We know. We are awaiting the announcement of death. Who will it be? We want to know, but dread knowing, our limbs are heavy, our eyes are stricken.

* * * * * * * * * * * * * * * * * * *

When Doris told me and Ray Allen about the voodoo woman coming I tried to stay home from school the following day to experience the visit, But to no avail.

"Mama, I'm sick!" I cried through a forced raspy voice, hand to my throat. "I can't swallow!"

Mama, holding a pot of hot oatmeal in one hand walked over to where I was standing by the kitchen sink. Her hazel eyes glittered green as they bore into mine and I knew she wasn't to be messed with. I backed up against the sink.

"You get dressed and get out to that school bus or you're going to be swallowing a lot harder than you ever thought you could," she promised.

Well, some days it doesn't pay to get out of bed. I complied and the four of us trudged out to the school bus as usual.

"Nobody has to talk about this at school," Ray Allen cautioned, "about the voodoo woman coming. Okay, Doris? Will you remember not to mention it?"

Doris nodded solemnly, but I worried about it all day. Not so much about Doris telling, which would further inflame our schoolmates' curiosity, but about Mama allowing it in the first place. For Daddy having a voodoo woman come in to chase the ghosts off wouldn't make any more difference to him than if a preacher came in. But I knew it made a huge difference to Mama. She must be feeling really desperate. I knew for a fact she was feeling cross. Neither of my parents ever hit us, but I wouldn't have been stupid enough to try to push Mama any further that morning over staying at home. Doris really wasn't to be trusted. By the time we got on the school bus that afternoon for the ride home all the kids knew we were to be visited by a voodoo woman. It was awful. I wished I were dead or at least comatose for the next ten years.

Aunt Gladys had already carried the voodoo woman away by the time we arrived home, leaving behind a strange sickly sweetish smell that seemed to saturate the entire house. Two of our young fryers lay headless in the sink. Ray Allen groaned when he saw the headless fryers.

"I hate having to pluck chickens as soon as I get home," he complained.

"You don't have to pluck these," Mama said. I looked at her. There were two lines on either side of her mouth I hadn't noticed before, and her forehead was getting creased with frown marks. "I just want you to go bury these chickens as soon as you change your clothes."

"Bury them?" Ray Allen echoed. "What for?"

"Just do what I tell you. These are two chickens I don't intend for us to eat."

"Where's Daddy?" I asked. "Was he here for —?"

"No, and never mind where your Daddy is. You and Doris change, too, and get started shelling the sunflowers. Louise, you can come help me in the kitchen."

So Mama saw that we all got busy with our assigned chores, thus deflecting any questions about the voodoo ceremony. Doris and I shelled the sunflowers out on the back porch. These particular sunflowers came from our old place and the heads were too dry. They had huge seedpods. You just held the head firmly with one hand and raked your thumb across the pod with the other. The seeds came off pretty easy, but after awhile your thumbs got sore. The seeds were for the chickens. It would never have occurred to any of us, or any Southerner at that time, to eat the seeds ourselves.

As we shelled, I fought off an impulse to reach over and pinch my little sister, hard . For being a blabber mouth.

"Why did you have to tell everybody at school about the voodoo woman coming?" I demanded after awhile. Doris stopped shelling and stared at me.

"I didn't tell anybody," she said. "Ray Allen said not to."

"Then how come everybody found out?"

"I don't know. I didn't tell."

I stared at her. Sometimes Doris would do something she had said she wouldn't but I had never known her to lie after doing it.

Just then I heard Daddy's car come down the lane. A few minutes later we could hear him and Mama arguing in the kitchen. From Daddy's louder than usual voice and slurred responses I could tell he had been drinking. A lot.

Chapter Eleven
The Unraveling Begins

I walk slowly down the stairs from the upper tier of Unit D and gather around Hank in front of the guard's bubble with the others. My mouth feels weird, dry and sticky at the same time. The other prisoners and I do not look at each other. All eyes are straining forward, seizing upon Hank and the senior officer who is standing beside him.

"Hank wishes to speak to you," the senior officer says when all the prisoners in our unit have assembled. "He has something to tell you."

Obviously. Hank steps forward slightly and holds his hands before him in an encompassing gesture.

"There was a death last night," he says simply. "It was Heavy. She died in her sleep."

There are sudden cries and shrieking of disbelief from the long timers who have known Heavy well. I feel stunned myself. What a waste; what a pathetic waste of life! It was a waste of a beautiful woman whose inner anger turned deadly when she was but a young woman of twenty; now she is gone, barely thirty. The last ten years of her life had been spent in this miserable place. I turn away and race upstairs to my cell. I can't bear to look at the others who knew her even before her crimes. I can't comfort them. I can't offer soothing words.

I need soothing words myself. I lost my own daughter who was barely thirty when she died. How is it possible that beautiful, vibrant

young women can die by their thirtieth birthdays? How are such needless deaths possible?

In this moment I know both deaths were needless and that they had a common cause: a lack of respect for human beings and a favoring of industry's 'bottom line.' What is the breast cancer that took my daughter, but neglect of the health of young women by the chemicalization of industry that lowers our immune systems? And what is the social cancer that takes young First Nations women by neglecting their developmental health? If this is allowed to continue, the 'bottom line' of industry will kill us all in the end.

"Betty, do you want to talk? " A male voice asks from the top of the stairway. It's Hank voice. He is not allowed to come into the cells unless accompanied by a guard. I get up and walk out of my cell to where he is standing.

"No, thank you, Hank," I say, "tend to the others."

"I understand you had been talking to her."

"Yes. She wanted me to write her story. I told her we would start on it as soon as my trial was over. What is so maddening is that this prison tries to punish and rehabilitate at the same time and it's impossible. It's two diametrically opposed urges, don't you see?"

I'm blubbering. I sit down on the top step and blubber away. Hank pats my shoulder awkwardly and moves down the stairs to comfort another woman who is sobbing wildly in her cell. I get up and go back to my own cell. Yes. The reason the women's prison is such a dismal failure is that physical isolation inside a prison compound eventually kills the spirit because just the notion that a woman is so bad that she must be separated from the rest of society is so soul destroying to her that it's rare a woman who has enough self-esteem to fully employ any of the rehabilitation programs offered.

Every woman knows in her bones, even the most degraded of women, that it is through females that society is glued together. To be cast out by society and forced to connect only with other outcasts is to further doom a woman who has usually been sexually abused since childhood, who is hopelessly addicted, who is in essence a motherless child, and who can

see no future. What in God's name are prisons about except to further crush the life and hope out of increasingly tired and frail bodies?

What kind of a society are we that we are making so many criminals? A society has to be judged by the kind of citizens it produces. Criminals are not born. They are made. Society makes them.

My heart is sore. The little bluebirds of optimism that usually sit on my shoulder have fled. I think of Barbara Ellen. My darling daughter, where are you? Is your journey long and hard? Come to me. Hold my hand; tell me about your work in progress. Do you understand things that you didn't before?

Do you visit with Mama and Daddy and Aunt Doris, and do they tell you stories about Laycott Place and its ghost? You were fascinated by the story, more than any of the other kids, but I didn't tell you everything. Do you know it all now, how it ended?

* * * * * * * * * * * * * * * * * * * *

I didn't want to go back inside even when Doris and I finished shelling the sunflowers for the chickens. The voices inside were getting louder. Daddy was yelling at Mama and Mama was yelling back.

Then I heard Daddy yell at Louise: "Why are you even still here?" "Why didn't you go with your kinfolks? You might as well go, too. You don't have to feel sorry for me. I don't need your damned pity. I can take care of my own family. Mary wants you to come home, so go to it," he hollered. "You people can't live outside Mississippi anyway."

Then Daddy flung the screen door open and stomped across the back veranda in a fury, down the steps and then headed for the car. Mama came out after him.

"Jake, you stay out of that car!" she yelled, hurrying down the veranda steps. "You're too drunk to drive."

"I'm never too drunk to drive," he yelled back, and he beat Mama to the car. Suddenly, Mama had to jump back out of the way because Daddy didn't quite get the clutch in first and the car jerked forward. As

we watched, he got the old Chevy turned around and headed back down the lane. Mama came back to the porch.

"Where's he going?" I asked.

"Call Ray Allen," she said, ignoring my question. "It's time for supper."

I followed the stream down to the willows, calling Ray Allen's name every few minutes or so. He didn't answer. Why had he gone so far just to bury two chickens? Out of the corner of my eye I saw something slithering through the bushes across the stream. I stopped, heart pounding. The slithering stopped, and then I saw Ray Allen sitting on a stump by the stream.

"Are you deaf?" I yelled. "Didn't you hear me calling you? Mama says it's time for supper."

Ray Allen got up slowly and brushed some twigs off his pants. He picked up the shovel and came toward me.

"Why didn't you answer me?" I persisted.

"Because I didn't want to," he answered in a mean tone, and brushed past me. I hurried to catch up.

"Any particular reason you didn't want to?" I asked, trying to make my voice heavy with sarcasm. He stopped, turned, and looked at me.

"No, except that I hate this place. I wish we had never moved here. We have to try to get Mama to make Daddy leave."

"How are we going to do that? You know how stubborn Daddy is."

"Yeah, but maybe between you and me we can persuade Mama to tell Daddy we'll leave without him if he doesn't agree to come with us."

My teeth began chattering, and although the heat of the day was still heavy in the air, I felt an unfamiliar chill seeping around my body. I hugged my arms around my shoulders.

"Agree to come with us where?" I wail. "Daddy says we don't have any money to get another place."

"Well, we have to. I'll quit school and get a job. You don't want to stay here, do you?"

"No," I cried, pushing back tears. "I hate it, too. But you have to be with me to tell Mama."

"Yeah, we'll do it together."

"What about Louise?"

"I don't think Louise will reckon it's that much of her business."

"I heard Daddy yelling at her. He came home drinking. He was yelling he didn't care if she left, too."

"Hell fire," Ray Allen said. "Is he still drinking?"

"I don't know. He left in the car."

"Well, let's get home."

When we got to the house I noticed right off that Louise's eyes were red from crying, which was a surprising thing. I'd only seen her cry once before in our entire lives together and that was when she heard her father was dead. She had never known him, but I guess just knowing that she had a father somewhere and that he wasn't dead like her mother had been comforting. That had happened three summers ago when she was with us. I hadn't seen her cry before or since.

Daddy's words had wounded her deeply. I felt a rising tide of anger against my father stirring around in my gut. What right did he have to make us all so miserable, even if he was the breadwinner and the man of the house?

After supper all four of us students took our homework to the long island table in the kitchen as usual. Mama sat in a chair by the kitchen door while she basted in the sleeves to Louise's new blue church dress. I could tell she was straining to hear any sounds of Daddy's car. Mama always said sewing was soothing to her, especially sewing by hand, but she looked up every few minutes that evening, her ears cocked toward the driveway outside. But Daddy didn't show.

Homework done, quick wash ups, and Mama shooed us all to bed. My ears were straining too, for the sound of Daddy's car, and I couldn't fall right to sleep. Drunk or sober, Daddy kept the ghosts at bay, and I felt I had to stay on guard until Daddy got home. I finally did fall asleep and when I woke up the next morning I knew without asking that Daddy still hadn't come home.

Daddy sucked up a lot of energy, wherever he was. When he wasn't around, the energy fields surrounding the rest of us were in some sort of equilibrium, but as soon as Daddy entered the house, or anybody's

house for that matter, or a car, or a field, or a gathering of any sort, it was as though some kind of swirling vortex of clashing positive and negative ions engulfed everything around him, leaving the rest of us struggling to breathe.

So the house was quiet when I got up that morning, the only sounds coming from the kitchen, where, by the smell of it, Mama was frying slices of salt pork. I washed my hands and face, brushed my hair and quickly dressed. My sister, brother and cousin were all still sleeping. At least they were still in bed. But that was okay because it was Saturday.

"Where's Daddy?" I asked when I went into the kitchen and pulled out a chair. Mama set a plate of fried salt pork and scrambled eggs and two high rising baking soda biscuits before me wordlessly. Mama's baking soda biscuits were the most delicious of any in the whole state of Louisiana, Daddy often said, and I believed him. Mama only made these kinds of biscuits on weekends. I sat down and dug in, momentarily forgetting about Daddy, until I had finished off my last biscuit with a big dash of cane syrup accompanied with my last bite of crisp fried salt pork.

"Where's Daddy?" I inquired again. Just then Louise appeared in the doorway with Doris tagging behind and Mama busied herself serving up their breakfasts, too. She had no sooner put their plates before them when Ray Allen showed up. Since none of them asked about Daddy's whereabouts I began to feel weird about it and didn't inquire again. After everyone had eaten, Mama told me to clean up the kitchen while she went to her sewing room to make some drapes for one of Daddy's customers.

Doris went with Mama to the sewing room. Doris liked to sew too. Mama would give her bits of material to make doll clothes and she would sit happily with Mama this way for hours. Mama tried to interest me in sewing, but while I could read books for hours on end, I couldn't sit still for sewing lessons, or music lessons.

Mama was teaching Doris and Ray Allen both how to play on the old piano and how to read a bit of music. Mama also played the accordion. She had a guitar, too, that she had bought with egg money and was teaching Doris and Ray Allen to play it. Ray Allen could also play the harmonica, something he picked up on his own, and Doris had a lovely

singing voice. When they were playing and singing in our old place I'd usually head out for the wooded strip just in back of our house. I was allowed to go there by myself during daylight but was forbidden to cross the fence. But sometimes I stayed in to listen to Mama, Doris and Ray Allen make music and when I did they would usually play something that I could tap dance to. I tap danced the same way Ray Allen played the harmonica, by ear. Tap dancing is a percussion thing, like drums. It keeps rhythm. You don't have to know how to read music to tap dance. I didn't go much into the wooded areas close to the house by myself.

I missed the woods I had known all my life. It wasn't that I didn't like other areas of forests. I knew several different kinds of Louisiana woods like the swampy Cypress stands that you had to use a little flat bottomed boat called a perow to travel through, or forests composed mainly of oaks, or ones containing both Live Oaks and regular oak trees, or of the pine tree woods that grew in Mississippi where lots of our kin folks lived. The different woods all fascinated me. But I didn't know the Laycott woods and I hesitated to venture far into into them without Ray Allen or Louise. Somehow I just couldn't get connected with the Laycott woods. I was afraid of them.

So that morning when Mama avoided my questions of Daddy's whereabouts, I was left alone in the kitchen to clean up. Ray Allen and Louise had been dispatched to water and feed the horses and take care of the chickens and pigs. I was still wondering where Daddy was, as I looked out the window over the sink while scraping the last bits of the morning's lean salt pork that had stuck to the iron skillet. The morning was bright, already stinking hot, and it wasn't even nine o'clock.

I was holding the scraped and cleaned skillet, ready to hang it on its hook over the kitchen island, when out of the corner of my eye I saw the lion slinking across the back yard. My eyes popped open and I stared. The lion was absolutely the same one I had seen before, the adult female with a slick honey coloured coat, large and menacing. She moved slowly, deliberately, crouching low to the ground. She was stalking, heading to the back of the chicken house where the pig pen was, where Ray and Louise

probably were by now. The skillet slipped from my suddenly nerveless fingers and dropped on my foot. I screamed. Mama came running.

"The lion!" I yelled. "It's in the yard. It's going to get Ray Allen and Louise!"

"What in God's name are you talking about?" Mama asked, rushing to the window. "What? Where?"

"There's a lion in the yard. And it's going after Ray Allen and Louise, out by the pig pen …"

I have to say this for Mama. She could be decisive in an emergency and she didn't stop to ask any more questions. From my agitated state I had obviously seen something threatening and was convinced it was after Ray Allen and Louise, so to be on the safe side, she better get Daddy's shotgun. She ran to the kitchen fireplace, took the gun down off the mantel, fumbled briefly for some shells behind the loose brick where they were kept, and after telling me to stay put and keep Doris from following her, ran out into the back yard loading the gun as she went. Doris, who had trailed Mama into the kitchen and unnerved by these sudden developments, wrapped her arms around my legs.

"I don't want Mama to shoot the lion," she whimpered. "The lion is my friend."

"Hush," I said, pushing her away. I leaned over the sink, pressing my nose to the window, trying to see. Mama had disappeared around the back of the chicken house. What if the lion not only hurt Ray Allen and Louise, but Mama, too? My heart stopped at the thought. Time seemed to stand still. Everything was so silent. All I could hear was the thudding of my heart. I couldn't stand it. I had to know what was happening. I picked up Mama's sharpest and longest kitchen knife and then grabbed Doris's hand and led Doris onto the back porch.

"You stay right there," I admonished shakily. "And don't you move one inch, you hear me?"

Her eyes were as wide as her little pink rose china tea set plates. Maybe it was the fierceness of my voice, or the knife I was holding. She nodded wordlessly and I dashed wildly across the back yard brandishing Mama's carving knife: Betty Jo to the rescue.

"I'm coming, I'm coming!" I yelled. Just as I rounded the edge of the chicken house I saw Mama and Louise and Ray Allen walking down the path from the barn and pigpen toward the house. Ray Allen was swinging the bucket that had carried the corn mash for the pigs and Louise had taken charge of Daddy's rifle. I felt dizzy with relief. I ran toward them.

"Did you see it?" I cried.

"Betty Jo, you've got to stop scaring us all to death about a lion," Mama said crossly. "I almost had a heart attack, and give me that knife. Who did you think you were going to use it on, for Pete's sake? Are you losing your senses?"

I gave over the knife and then turned to Ray Allen and Louise.

"But didn't you see the lion?" I wailed. "It was going right toward the pig pen and it was crouching, like lions and cats do when they're fixing to attack. I saw it as plain as day, it was huge. It wasn't a cat or anything, it was a lion."

"We didn't see anything, Betty Jo," Louise said gently. I turned to Ray Allen. He shrugged. Mama put her hand on my shoulder.

"Honey, we're all kind of nervous right now. And we got real things to worry about, not imaginary stuff. Maybe it was some kind of varmint you saw and it heard you screaming and that scared it away," Mama said. "But please stop talking about a lion. I want you to promise me you won't talk about a lion anymore, or imagine a lion around our place. Will you promise me that?" Her voice had lost its crossness as her eyes searched my face. "Will you promise me that, Betty Jo?"

"I promise," I said. "I'm sorry I scared everybody."

Mama gave me a little smile and patted my shoulder. "Good. Where's Doris?"

"Where's Doris?" I echoed.

"I left her on the back porch."

"Well, run see about her."

I ran. Doris wasn't on the back porch. She was over by the stream.

"What are you doing over here?" I demanded, trying to push back the scalding tears of frustration forming around my eyeballs. In my anxiety I just wanted to shake her. "I told you to stay on the porch."

"I forgot. Don't be mad. The lion came. It wanted me to come out to the stream and pet it."

I stared down at her. So the lion was there after all. Doris had visited with the lion. I had seen the lion myself, yet nobody else could see it. Was I going crazy? Was my little sister crazy, too?

"Don't cry, Betty Jo," Doris said, taking my hand. "I'm sorry I went to the lion. I won't do it anymore. Please don't cry."

I gave her a little hug one with one arm hand and wiped at my tears of anger, fear, and frustration with the other hand. I wanted Daddy. I needed his assurance that there were no such things as ghosts; that the universe operated according to well-known laws; that things couldn't suddenly, or even over a long period of time, just go haywire for no reason and start doing things outside the laws of nature. Where was he? Had something horrible happened to him that nobody knew about, not even Mama?

"It's okay," I said, leading Doris back to the porch before the others arrived.

"I won't say anything about the lion," Doris said.

"Okay," I answered. It didn't matter. Nobody believed us anyway. After the gun and the shells were put away in the kitchen and the knife returned to its drawer and everyone had washed up, Mama asked us all to go sit in the front parlor. We all filed dutifully into the front room. I sat down on the old maroon horsehair sofa between Doris and Ray Allen. Louise sat on the end next to Doris. This was such an unusual request by Mama we all felt embarrassed and strange and didn't know where to look.

Mama pulled up the cane bottomed chair in front of the sofa and sat down. "Kids, I think it's time we had a talk," she said earnestly. All of us kids just stared at her. "I'm worried sick about your Daddy. Right now I don't know where he is. I thought maybe he had been in an accident, but he doesn't seem to be in any of the hospitals."

"Is he coming back?" Doris asked.

Mama stifled a sob. "Oh, honey, I hope so. Yes, he's coming back. I'm sure he's coming back."

She didn't sound sure enough to suit me. She asked all of us to hold hands and she would lead us in prayer for our Daddy. At this point I knew

we were in terribly serious trouble. Mama was religious, but not overtly so. She believed that people showed their religion by their actions, not by asking the Lord for special favours. But here she was asking the Lord for a very special favour: she was asking not only that Daddy be returned to us, but that he be freed from his obsession in trying to find the noises in the house and that he be led to know the only reasonable course of action was for us to move out of Laycott Place. And the sooner the better.

After Mama prayed she asked if any of us would like to add anything to her prayer, but we were all too shy, or too stunned by the events. We didn't know what to do or think or say. It definitely didn't seem like the time to try to persuade Mama to make Daddy move as she obviously felt helpless before the task herself and was turning to a higher power. So when she said we could be excused, we didn't tarry.

We all had chores that could have busied us, that we might have been doing while we waited for news from Daddy, but none of us, even Mama, especially Mama, seemed to be able to concentrate on anything. We all wound up out on the front veranda, where we could see immediately if Daddy's car turned into the laneway. Mama brought out iced tea and the rest of the morning's biscuits. Mama's biscuits were as good cold as hot, but I couldn't eat another single one. Just the sight of them made me feel a little sick. Nobody else seemed to want to nibble at the biscuits, either.

Then, suddenly, we heard rather than saw, at least at first, Daddy's car coming down the laneway. Everybody stood up and as the car came into view down the road we could definitely identify it as Daddy's old Chevy. There was a collective sigh of relief from our gathering.

"It's Daddy!" Doris cried, running down the steps. Doris was Daddy's favorite. He didn't like it when he occasionally heard me speak sharply to her and would go out of his way to bring back the especially good peanut brittle Doris liked when his travels took him anywhere near the little candy shop on his collection routes. Daddy stopped the car in the front driveway to the house and got out. He patted Doris' head, walked across the yard and, standing on the bottom step, addressed us all.

"Y'all might as well know," he said. "I've been in jail. I was arrested for drunk driving. I had to pay a fine, but I'm out. I'm sorry to have worried you."

We all stared at him. In truth, he looked terrible. His clothes were rumpled, his fair complexion was mottled and reddened, and his white hair was standing on end. But he was home. His eyes searched Mama's face, looking for some clue to the extent of her anger. Whatever he saw there seemed to encourage him.

"I'm tired and I need to lay down," he said. Mama stood aside as Daddy came up the steps, crossed the veranda and went inside the house. She turned and followed him in.

"In jail?" Doris asked, nonplussed. "Daddy was in jail?"

"Yes, because he was drinking," Ray Allen said. "But you don't need to talk about it at school."

Ray Allen seemed extremely anxious about what Doris told at school, and I remember thinking it was because of Clara Nell and not just because it made us all objects of such miserable attention from the other kids. He didn't want Clara Nell telling tales about our family and the house we lived in to her folks. They certainly wouldn't be impressed with the news that Daddy had been in jail for drunk driving. Maybe they would decide not to allow Clara Nell to associate with us anymore. And while Ray Allen wanted to move he obviously wanted to be able to see Clara Nell again at some point.

Later that night there was another disturbing thing ... the voodoo woman's magic didn't work, either. The ghost of Laycott Place struck again, in the kitchen. *At least it waited until Daddy got home*, I thought, when I was awakened by the sounds of pots and pans being thrown furiously around in the kitchen. *Thank goodnesss.*

Chapter Twelve

The Contest is Over

Back in Unit D in the Burnaby Correctional Centre for Women, the cellblock is still in turmoil over Heavy's unexpected death. Rumors abound. Was it an overdose? Heroin, crack, pills? The consensus was that Heavy was not a heavy-duty user. She seemed to have carved out a little niche for herself inside the prison, in her unit, in her work duties, and among the other inmates. Except for the recent slashing she seemed to be one of the more stable ones. However, she had recently been moved out of the unit where she had been living for years. Nobody seemed to know why. Had the move so destabilized her? Or was her death an accident and not an intended suicide? And who was responsible for giving her the dope?

Heavy had been there almost since the women's prison had opened. She was so beautiful and such a fixture there that her death was shocking. It left a deep hole in many of the women's psyches. The following day there is a memorial. Most of the prison population gathers in the rotunda. The drumming group sits together on the west side of the rows of chairs. While I had come to consider myself part of this group, somehow I know without asking that I shouldn't sit with them or offer to drum with them at this time of personal sorrow. Their sister had fallen. One of the stronger ones.

After everyone is seated Hank rises and speaks first of Heavy's time with us. He speaks simply and not overlong. Then the elder, dressed in full

Cree regalia, with her back straight as an arrow, eyes flashing, addresses the women, both native and non-native, who have come to remember Heavy. The elder's voice is strong, and passionate as she talks about how women must come together to help each other, to mourn together, to try to recover the most sacred possessions of their lost worlds, their families, their culture, so that women like Heavy, like all of us, would not have to eat our anger and swallow it and have it kill us. Then a sobbing prisoner I don't know gets up and plays *Amazing Grace* on the guitar and sings with an unexpectedly lovely voice that makes many of us weep. After she sits down, Hank invites the women who knew Heavy best to step forward and speak of her, so that they might share the daring or funny things Heavy had done or said.

The women begin to respond, each rising to her feet in turn to tell some story about Heavy. Several poems are read and then the sobbing begins. The women weep openly. The drumming starts, accompanied by the native singing. Wild and free, the women's voices bounce and echo around the rotunda, joyful at times, sorrowful at others, songs I had tried to learn but never could.

One must be born with some predisposition to be able to understand and mimic the cries and throbs, and wails and chants, the lovely hymns of praise of family and nature that are the basis of authentic native music. Still, I could feel the spirit of the drumming and singing surging in my veins. Then after awhile the elder gave her seat around the drum to another native woman, and began to dance, with slow graceful rhythmic steps at first, her long skirt and fringed jacket swaying with her delicate movements. Then the rhythm quickens and the elder's arms turn into a giant bird's wings, swooping low and graceful, then reaching for the sky, crouching again as she turns and twirls, dark head thrown back, her moccasined feet hardly touching the floor; I would scarcely have been surprised had she lost contact with the floor altogether and flew along the dome of the rotunda.

The drumming and singing continue for a long time. When it is over, we prisoners are strangely quiet, subdued. We trudge back to our units without incident, without horseplay or raucous laughter or loud calling to

friends. It's almost as if during the ceremonies for Heavy we have come face to face with our own deaths. It is very sobering.

But I mustn't allow anything to interfere with writing my court address to Mr. Justice Harvey, not even Heavy's death. I try to focus.

Instead I fall into reverie thinking about my own people who have passed over on that other, different journey: among them Mama, Daddy, Doris, Louise, ... and of that brief period in a decaying house with a violent history when we were all bound together in an adventure that with each passing day spiraled more wildly out of control.

* * * * * * * * * * * * * * * * * * * *

After Daddy's night in jail he was rather quiet for a couple of days. We could hear Mama's voice floating from their bedroom, from the kitchen, from the front veranda, from the yard, beseeching Daddy ever so earnestly to agree to move forthwith. Daddy was mostly silent, an unusual state of affairs for a compulsive talker.

Until the following Tuesday night when the ghost horses struck again.

What an odd and frightening thing to wake from a deep sleep to the sound of horses' hooves thundering around the veranda, galloping a million miles a minute. I screamed and jumped to my feet. Doris woke and screamed, too, and then hopped out of her bed and flew into mine. She wrapped her arms around me in a stranglehold. Petrified, I cowered, holding onto Doris. It seemed as if the horses could break through the glass doors and trample us to death in their fury.

Then suddenly a light went on in the kitchen. I got up, trembling, and went to the door carrying Doris while she hugged my neck so tightly I could scarcely see to walk. I finally pulled her arms away just in time to see Mama and Daddy struggling in the doorway, physically tussling over Daddy's shotgun. I immediately dumped Doris to the floor. She gave a piercing yell and grabbed at my nightgown. I ignored her and hurried to Mama's side.

"Jake, no!" Mama screamed. "Don't take the gun. Leave it, they'll go away."

"I know they'll go away because I'm going to shoot the sons of bitches."

"Jake, you can't shoot them, they're ghosts,–"

"The hell they are, the hell they are, get out of my way, woman."

Daddy pushed Mama so violently she fell back against the doorjamb. In his rush to shoot the ghost horses, he didn't even stop to see if he had hurt her. He just kept going through the kitchen door, rushing out onto the back veranda. Mama was making strangled sob sounds in her throat when Ray Allen and Louise, awakened by Doris's screaming, if not to the ghost's noises, suddenly appeared.

"Mama, what is it?" Ray Allen asked, taking Mama's arm.

"He's gone crazy," Mama cried. "This house has driven him plumb crazy."

Doris was still yelling. I went over and picked her up.

"Shut up!" I said fiercely. "Just shut up!" Amazingly, she did, and resumed her stranglehold around my neck.

The sudden blast of the shotgun seemed to anchor the situation. It was Daddy. He was shooting at something, something close. Mama clasped her hands over her ears and moaned, "Oh my God, oh my God, oh my God…"

"I'd better go see," Ray Allen said, pulling his shirt on over his regular pants. With others in the house besides the immediate family he would rather have been ripped to pieces by a dozen ghosts than be caught in his floral pajama bottoms, especially in front of Louise. On all ghost appearances he now appeared fully dressed except for his shoes.

Mama reached out and grasped Ray Allen's arm. "No," she cried. "He might accidentally shoot you. He'll think you're one of them."

"Mama, just let me go look. I have to see what he's doing," Ray Allen answered, pulling his arm away.

"I said no," Mama cried again, her voice louder and more desperate.

"Mama, I have to,–"

Ray Allen jerked free of Mama's hand and ran through the kitchen and out the back door. Then almost immediately my brother screamed back into the house where we females remained in a huddle of fear and apprehension.

"Mama! Come quick! Daddy's been hurt!"

We all dashed to the back veranda steps. There was no light fixture on the back porch, but the yellow light from the open kitchen door and windows allowed us to see that Daddy was half sprawled down the steps on his back, his shotgun thrown askew by the side of the steps. Mama kneeled and bent over him. The moon was full, casting bright shadows. Daddy's face was pale and twisted with pain and some substance seemed to be staining the front of his white undershirt around his lower belly, spreading as we watched. And when Mama tried to raise Daddy up to a sitting position I could see his left leg was bleeding, too, all the way from his thigh down. Louise came bounding down the steps with a flashlight. Mama and Ray Allen eased Daddy back down so his shoulders rested on the middle step and when Louise trained the flashlight glare on Daddy's belly and left leg even Doris could tell it was blood streaming from Daddy's body.

"Daddy's bleeding," she said in a shocked voice. "Daddy's bleeding—"

Ray Allen straightened from the bent over position where he had been trying to help Mama assist Daddy to sit up.

"An ambulance! Mama, call an ambulance!" he ordered excitedly.

Mama straightened. She had gotten all bloody, too, from trying to help Daddy. Blood was smeared all over her nightgown.

"An ambulance? No! It would take too long. It's the middle of the night. It's hard to find this place in the daytime. We have to drive Daddy to the hospital. Louise, get some clean towels from the linen closet and a couple of those small sheets for Doris' bed. We have to stop some of this bleeding."

Daddy opened his eyes and looked at Mama. "It was the damdest thing," he said, taking a deep breath. He was panting like he'd been running. "I just stepped off the porch and stumbled a little bit and the gun jerked out of my hand …the damn gun … went right off … "

"Hush. Don't talk. We're going to take you to the hospital."

"I'll bring the car closer," Ray Allen said. "I'll drive him."

"No, let Louise. She's had more experience and can get us there faster. I can sit in the back with Daddy. You stay here with the girls."

"We want to come, too," I said through chattering teeth. "We don't want to stay here."

Mama looked at me. Her face was like a yellowish mask, her familiar features suddenly unfamiliar, stiff, controlled.

"Hush. I'll send somebody to stay with you after we get to the hospital. In the meantime Ray Allen will look after you and your sister. Louise, where are you?"

"Right here, Aunt Bug. Here are the towels. And the sheets."

Louise and Ray Allen lifted Daddy's torso off the steps so Mama could stuff towels onto Daddy's midsection and then tightly wrapped one of the sheets all around his lower body and left leg to hold the towels in place. Then the three of them carried Daddy to the car and stretched him across the back seat. Ray Allen ran back to the house and fetched Mama's purse and housecoat and shoes along with Daddy's wallet. Then Louise got behind the wheel of the car, turned it around, and she and Mama and Daddy sped off into the night.

Traumatized, I realized that the three of us were now all alone. We didn't even know what hospital Mama and Louise were headed for with Daddy bleeding like a stuck pig or where the hospital was. I stood in the driveway with Ray Allen and Doris, watching until the car's taillights grew dim and then disappear down the lane altogether.

Doris burst into fresh tears. "Mama!" she sobbed.

"Hush that bawling," I said through clenched teeth. If I didn't clench my teeth they would chatter right through my ears. My entire body was chattering. "It's going to be all right."

But I seriously doubted that.

"Ain't it, Ray Allen?" I demanded, turning to him.

"I don't want to go back in the house," he answered, looking toward the lighted kitchen. "Let's stay out here until somebody comes."

"But there's ... you know... the horses ..."

"They've gone. Look, the sky is clear. We can just go sit in the front yard on the grass and count the stars."

We walked around to the front lawn in our bare feet, not even thinking about shoes, or anything except getting away from the house. We walked

down to the far end of the front yard next to the lane where the little creek ran. Ray Allen searched the area with the flashlight to make sure we weren't going to run across any dangerous night varmints unexpectedly. Satisfied, he told me and Doris to sit down in a soft cushion of clover. After a final sweep of the flashlight, he sat down, too.

We took up our positions. While the house was the battleground the ghost could and did take over, somehow the woods on the other side of the stream terrified me more. I was sure the wild horses had come out of the woods and had jumped the stream in order to hit our front veranda with such force. Even ghost horses couldn't just suddenly materialize out of nowhere with all that energy ... and there was the lion out there...it was a lion, I was sure, in spite of what everybody else said and not just a harmless woods varmint or even a bobcat that small animals might fear, but not humans. I knew it was a real lion that Doris and I had seen. At least, that night, I was absolutely sure it was.

So Ray Allen and I sat back to back with him facing the stream and lane and the woods beyond, monitoring any activity that might start taking place there, while I sat facing the house. It was agreed that I was to watch the thin, pale shaft of light seeping from the kitchen at the back of the house that was casting shadows across the rear driveway. Doris sat in my lap with her feet drawn up over my legs so the grass chiggers wouldn't bite her bare feet. Thank goodness we both had on long cotton nightgowns that covered our legs and most of our arms and the mosquitoes weren't droning their worst in the clover patch.

"I reckon I could go in and grab a couple of blankets," Ray Allen said after a moment.

Doris stiffened with panic at the very idea. "No, don't leave us!" she shouted right in my left ear. Her shrill voice penetrated both my eardrums and left them ringing.

"All right," Ray Allen said quickly. "Hush! I won't leave."

Doris settled down again into my lap. "Is Daddy going to die?" she asked.

"No," Ray Allen answered.

"How do you know? He was all bleeding—"

"They'll fix him up at the hospital," Ray Allen said soothingly. "They'll stop the bleeding. Look, there's the Big Dipper up there, and the Little Dipper, and over there is the Milky Way. And the moon's so bright you can see the man up there, sitting in the moon. Look…"

Doris looked. For once, Ray Allen kept up a steady stream of talk for which I was decidedly grateful. I actually hadn't realized he knew so much about the stars and the stories about some of them…how they were supposed to represent ancient gods and goddesses who got married and even had children when they weren't messing around with mortals.

Under the drone of Ray Allen's descriptions of the stars and the planets and the stories about them Doris's head lolled back against my chest and after awhile I could tell she was falling asleep. My ears stopped ringing. My teeth had stopped chattering, too. Except for swatting the mosquitoes away and my butt getting numb and feeling slightly damp from the dew speckled grass and crushed clover, I could almost have gone to sleep myself just leaning against my brother's back, but I was afraid of the horses and the lion. Mostly the horses. They might start running again. I had to stay awake to help Ray Allen chase them off. I had to keep my eyes on the house and watch the thin light coming from the back of the house where the kitchen was, to tell if there were any changes to alert Ray Allen to. But the ghost seemed to lay low. And the horses did, too.

There was a cool, sweet breeze. If I hadn't been closed in with the body heat of my brother and sister, I might even have felt chilly. The frogs were singing along with the crickets. After what seemed like forever my own eyes started to close of their own accord and I was half aware my body was crumpling, leaning sideways into the edges of sleep.

Ray Allen nudged me from time to time to stay awake and I would straighten up only to crumple again some minutes later. Once he turned the flashlight on and arched the beam over the creek, saying he thought there was a varmint out there because he saw two eyes shining. That snapped me to attention but after awhile Ray Allen turned the flashlight off, muttering that whatever it was out there had gone away. I lost consciousness into sleep again. For a time. Then I felt Ray Allen abruptly pull

his back away from mine. Still groggy, for a long moment I didn't know where I was. Then Ray Allen leaned over and gave me a hard shake.

"Wake up, Betty Jo," he said sharply. "There's a car coming down the lane …"

* * * * * * * * * * * * * * * * * * *

I have to admit I've lost interest in this blasted address to the judge. Heavy's death has discombobulated me. But there's nothing I can do about either one. Heavy is dead and I will be sentenced, whether I'm ready or not. And I am troubled by my evident fascination with reliving the Laycott Place saga at this particular time. Ordinarily I don't think about it at all. It's there, but I don't consciously go back and try to relive it. *Is there any reason I should be doing this now?* I ask the universe. *Are there lessons here in this recalling of Laycott Place, something to learn, something to know that I haven't realized before because my mind shies away from what I can't understand…*

But I must summon, I must summon, I must summon my will. I decide to take a nap instead. When I wake up the night has passed and it is Sunday, visiting day. Marian will be coming.

Marian brings me goodies; we talk for two hours. She is anxious about the sentencing. A young woman dedicated to the direct approach to life, she figures it's always better to know the worst right off. I finally waylay her worrying questions by inquiring of the others. Marian is my only child living in Vancouver, so she is able to visit the most often and always brings me the latest news of the other children and grandchildren. When visiting hours are over it's almost time for dinner.

When the trays arrive I don't feel like eating at all. There is tasteless pasta; the vegetables are overcooked and unidentifiable, accompanied by another wooden cookie. There is a can of salmon in my room. I give my dinner away and retreat to my cell and can of salmon.

Maybe fish really is brain food. After eating it, and during evening lockup, I am suddenly able to remember Daddy, to see him, to think of

him without anxiety, without rancor, without trauma, and without blame for that night of long ago.

* * * * * * * * * * * * * * * * * * * *

In my haste to get up from the bed of clover where Ray Allen, Doris and I had sought refuge from the house and the ghost horses, I inadvertently dumped Doris to the ground, and she rolled over, crying out.

"Get up!" I said, trying to brush the grass and debris from my gown. "Somebody's coming; maybe it's Mama and Louise."

We were standing by the lane when the car rolled to a stop. It wasn't Daddy's car. And Mama and Louise weren't in it. Just a man. A big hulk of a man. At first I thought it was Mr. Ferguson, Clara Nell's father. But as he walked past the headlight of his car I saw it was Amy's father, Mr. Sharkey, the preacher. He came to the school sometimes to talk to the principal.

"My goodness, what are you young'uns doing out here in the night? Well, never mind, we gotta get you somewhere safe. You're coming to my house, is that okay with y'all? I hope so, 'cause that's what your Mama wants. Come on, now, let's get everybody in the car."

"Sir, the horses, –" Ray Allen began.

"We'll talk about that in the morning, son."

"No, sir, I mean our work horses. They have to be looked after in the morning. The pigs and chickens, too."

"Oh, sure, son, we'll tend to all that in the morning. The important thing is to get you three to a proper house and beds."

I posed the question Ray Allen hadn't asked.

"Daddy?" I begged. "Is he all right?"

"As far as I know, honey. The doctors at the hospital operated on him as soon as your folks got to the hospital. The doctors took some of the shot out of his gut and leg. Your Mama will telephone you at my house later about how he is. Let's get going, now."

I wasn't even embarrassed about being in my nightgown with no shoes. I scrambled into the back seat of the car, pulling Doris in after me. I felt a sweet, wild relief that somebody had come who was an adult, who

was responsible, and who was in charge. At the Sharkey household, Doris and I were put to bed in a small guest room with a flouncy bedspread and Swiss dotted curtains.

"Where's my brother?" Doris asked sleepily as she climbed into the clean, flowery sheets.

"Don't worry about your brother," Mrs. Sharkey said soothingly. "He's sleeping on the couch downstairs."

When Doris and I got up the next morning, Ray Allen and Mr. Sharkey had already gone over to Laycott Place to see about the animals. Before we went down for breakfast Mrs. Sharkey gave me one of Amy's dresses and then cut off the bottom of one of Amy's outgrown skirts for Doris. Amy, whether under restraint from her parents or because she understood the delicacy of the situation, didn't pester me with questions. When Ray Allen came back with Mr. Sharkey he remembered to bring shoes for me and Doris as well as a few of our dresses. And then we three orphans of the storm simply held our breaths waiting for Mama to call. Around four in the afternoon, the call came through and we passed the phone around. Doris talked first and then it was my turn.

"Daddy's in a bad way, honey," Mama said to me. "He has to be operated on again tomorrow morning to take some more of the shot out of his stomach." Her voice sounded tired and far away. In my entire life, I had only spoken to my mother over the telephone three or four times. Those times I could tell it was Mama talking, but this time it didn't sound like her.

"When are you coming for us?" I blurted first thing.

"I don't know. You have to be my big, brave girl and I'll come for you as soon as I can. Right now I have to see about your father."

"Is he going to die?"

"I pray not. I need you to take care of Doris and see that you all mind your manners while you're with the Sharkey's, especially see that Doris doesn't take up too much of their time."

"I'll take care of Doris, Mama."

"Good girl. Let me speak to Ray Allen."

After Ray Allen talked to Mama he and I fitfully rehashed what she had said. While Daddy was still in danger, at least Mama was okay. And

Louise was with her. We felt better after Mama's call. We even managed to eat supper. But right after supper the Sharkey's living room started to fill up, at first just with men. Mr. Sharkey told Ray Allen to go into the living room, too, with the men. It was some kind of men's prayer group. I helped Amy and Mrs. Sharkey clean up the supper dishes. And then Doris and I were told we could take baths and put on our own clothes. I liked the Sharkey's bath tub. So did Doris. It was a treat after so many months of just taking showers. But after we were dressed we were told by Mrs. Sharkey that women were coming to the prayer meeting, too, that it was a special meeting to pray for our father's recovery.

"Our prayers will be dedicated to your father," Mrs. Sharkey explained and took me and Doris by the hand and led us into the living room where at least twenty people sat on the long couches and dining room chairs brought in for the occasion. "We're going to beg God to spare your father."

The room became very crowded and stuffy when we were all seated. When Mr. Sharkey started talking and praying it felt even stuffier. It was very odd sitting there next to Doris and Amy, hearing a man I hardly knew pray for Daddy; a man Daddy didn't know at all. Daddy probably wouldn't be interested in hearing about God and church and the devil, I thought. After awhile one of the older women with grey hair sitting next to the big fan started moaning and praising God, and a chubby little man slipped out of his chair to his knees and head thrown back and arms held high began loudly begging for forgiveness with a catching sob in his voice, and pleading that the devil be banished from Daddy's heart and body. The room began to reverberate with ever louder cries and moans and shouts of "Praise God", and "Deliver us all from hell fire".

Doris's hand sought mine. This was scaring her, I knew. It was scaring me. I looked across the room at Ray Allen. His eyes were on the floor. Suddenly, Doris burst into tears. Nobody seemed to notice but me. I stood up, and holding her hand, headed for the door.

"She's upset," I explained to Mrs. Sharkey, who rose to follow us. "Please let me take her outside for a little while."

"Of course, honey, of course. But pray for your father while you're out there, okay? It's all our prayers together that rise up and reach God's heart."

"Yes, ma'am."

Out on the brightly lit back porch, Doris and I could hear the shouts and cries of praise going on in the front room while we rocked in the wooden porch swing.

"I want Mama," Doris sobbed.

"I do, too," I wailed, trying to keep from crying myself.

But we never got Mama again, at least not the way we had her before. After hovering near death for five days and nights, weak from loss of blood and fighting infections, Daddy, bolstered by several blood transfusions and another operation on his lower abdomen and upper left thigh took a turn for the better. The prayer group along with Mr. Sharkey's entire church, accompanied by a hefty donation from Aunt Gladys, got enough money together for Mama to rent a small, three bedroom house near where we had lived before and to pay expenses for several months until Daddy got back on his feet. Not content just to help out with money, Mr. Sharkey, along with four of the men from his prayer group, braved the evils in Laycott Place and moved all our furniture and belongings over to the new place. Within three weeks we were all installed in our new home.

Louise and Mama brought Daddy home from the hospital when everything was ready. Daddy didn't look like himself. He was so thin the skin around his eyes seemed to sag and he walked slowly, moving as if he were fearful he might break something. His left leg just didn't seem to want to work right.

However, within a couple more weeks Daddy was strong enough to get up and down without help and with the assistance of a cane began walking with more confidence. At that point Louise decided to go home. She didn't want to start going to a new school and she found the house too small and the garden plot almost nonexistent, and decided we didn't need her anymore. Surprisingly Aunt Mary agreed that perhaps Louise didn't need a diploma anyway and besides, she hinted that Jessie was getting restless with his girl being gone so long. Louise announced she wanted to go back to Mississippi. She and Mama cried together the day Louise went out to catch the bus that would take her to the big bus station in town. I cried, too. So did Doris. Louise hugged us all and then

threw caution to the winds and even hugged Ray Allen. I was startled to see him hug her back. We all, even Daddy, supported by his new walking stick, stood on the side of the road to see our cousin off. We all thanked her for the hard work she had done for us and we promised to come to her and Jessie's wedding. She waved at us out of the back of the bus window until we couldn't see the bus anymore.

While I missed Louise I was happy enough at first with the situation. I was back in our old familiar rural neighbourhood with my old friends. When Ray Allen and Doris were enrolled back in the old school, I expected Mama would make me attend, too, but she didn't. However, I soon found out that staying at home wasn't going to be as much fun as it was before. There was a pile of regular books and school assignments waiting for me every morning, collected from the regular school. Along with workbooks. And because Daddy was still weak and had to be waited on, Mama spent a lot of time with him. Which meant that besides the boring old studies I also had to help with housework besides helping get supper on the table.

By the time I finished the day's school assignment and did a few chores there was only an hour or so before Ray Allen and Doris got home. But I still preferred staying home to going to school because sometimes Mama would let me spend another hour or so during the day just reading. And she was lavish in her praise for the work I did around the house and I liked being helpful to her and Daddy. I was sure we would soon start going back to our old church. But we never did.

Mama and Daddy kept in touch with the Sharkeys. Or they kept in touch with us. As Daddy slowly but surely grew stronger the Sharkeys started coming regularly to our house for visits, in spite of the distance, and then gradually started bringing some of the others from their church group. Sometimes Amy came with them but this church group didn't include Clara Nell's family, much to Ray Allen's consternation. The Fergusons went to another church. But Mama was so grateful for the Sharkey's help that she wanted to be more involved with them and the other members of that particular church. And I think she thought it was their prayers that saved Daddy from dying. But what was the surprising

thing to me was that Daddy got involved, too. In fact, he got saved in the religious sense and became a born again Christian.

When I was fourteen years old Daddy went to a religious seminar every week end over the following year and at the end of his studies, he became an evangelical minister. Shortly after that he began to serve as a revival preacher for the same fundamentalist denomination that the Sharkeys belonged to. With his loud voice Daddy could preach the house down. Or the tent. And he did. And along with his new message of absolute good versus absolute evil, and Mama with her accordion, and Doris with her guitar and lovely singing voice, they all hit the revival tent circuit.

Ray Allen abstained whenever he could. For my part, I was ambivalent about it all. I loved the music, and there's something very happy about sitting in a tent or church full of people who have come to praise the Lord.

But I could never get it straight about the Lord. It just seemed such an arbitrary thing for anyone as powerful as God was supposed to be, for him to order that the sufferings of eternal hell fire should be anyone's lot simply because they didn't believe that Jesus was God's son, or that Mary was a virgin, or that the devil was as strong, or almost as strong, as God, or that there was a devil, or for that matter, even a God.

I knew that Daddy didn't use to believe any of this, either. But faced with what he came to believe was some sort of personification of absolute evil in Laycott Place, Daddy must have come to the conclusion that the only way to fight this was to muster faith in an absolute good, in other words, in God; only religion could explain what had happened to him at Laycott Place, and therefore only religion could redeem him, and redeem us all.

Ray Allen and I weren't much up for redemption. Which caused no end of arguments in our house as we got older. I wanted it back the way it used to be when church was sweet and gentle, where you went to meet your friends, where there were often good things to eat, not this intense, passionate, raw emotional outpouring of grief and praise. There was no mind to it. It was all emotion. It scared me. I wanted out.

In looking back, I feel that Daddy was absolutely right to try to improve our economic situation by leasing a farm to grow sugar cane. We were

in sugar cane country. We would be at war soon, and prices were rising. Daddy had a plan, a workable plan. And when the ghostly things started happening in the kitchen and around the veranda of Laycott Place I think Daddy was profoundly right to declare war against the ghost at Laycott, to believe passionately that there had to be a rational explanation for the seemingly inexplicable events that happened there. I believe that Daddy was correct at first in demanding a reasonable explanation of the universe, and resisting superstitious explanations of phenomena that as yet are poorly understood, by religion or science.

I can't explain what happened at Laycott Place when we lived there. Certainly no member of our immediate family that I know of ever drove out that way again. If they did, nobody ever mentioned it to me. And Laycott Place was a forbidden subject of discussion in our immediate family after the accident. And even though I still saw Amy through church activities we never talked about Laycott Place except indirectly. I surmised that she was probably forbidden by her parents to mention it. However, almost ten years later, when we were both married and had babies we meet accidentally in downtown Baton Rouge. I lived there, Amy was just visiting friends. She lived with her husband in Brownsville, Texas.

Amy and I had an iced tea together that day in a restaurant. Neither of us had our children with us. She told me about her husband, who was an engineer and a lay preacher in their church, and about her two little girls. And she was realizing her dream of becoming a writer; she was writing children's stories for a religious magazine. And without our parents around she ventured some information we were formally forbidden to talk about. She told me that Laycott Place wasn't leased to anybody else after we left and that she had heard the ownership question of the house and land was finally settled in court and the property put up for sale after she and her husband moved to Brownsville. It was bought by a developer who promptly tore the house down and was waiting for the two smaller towns that had built up around to move closer so he could build some new houses or businesses. The developer thought the whole area would soon become very prosperous and there would be a lot of new people moving in. It was only a matter of time before the property would become

extremely valuable, he told Amy's folks. This news depressed me. With the house gone, what had happened to the ghost of Simone du Falon? And her horses? And did the lion still roam the woods across the stream from the willows?

In the end the ghost of Laycott won, I think, as I sit on my jailhouse bunk, *not just because Daddy gave up fighting the ghost, but because after the accident he lost faith in his own will.* Of course what happened at Laycott Place was enough to freak anybody out, especially after Daddy's accident. While I can't explain what happened there I have come to believe that the super natural isn't really super natural at all because nothing is supernatural. Ghosts, or the appearance of ghosts, or the suggestions of ghosts or the very idea of ghosts is simply something natural that we, as yet, don't understand. And mysteries in themselves, such as the improbable appearance of ghostly happenings, shouldn't have been an excuse in my opinion, for my father to stop questioning the universe and instead accept some readymade religious explanation that has its own history of ghosts.

Ray Allen left home as soon as he turned eighteen and joined the Air Force. He got his wish. He learned to fly. When he came back after the war ended he went to university and became an aeronautical engineer. He and I remain united in our opposition to religion. But we lost Doris as an ally. She remained firmly anchored in the church. From her earliest years she loved church music and the promise of an afterlife without pain. She became a nurse. But in the immediate years after Daddy's conversion there was only one way for me out of that house, out of that hothouse of Daddy's fanatical religion and Mama's compliance: I married at sixteen and left home.

My mother was both my anchor and a source of my despair. She taught me many things. To this day I thank the universe that I was lucky enough to have a mother as teacher who recognized that I learned differently than most and who gave me time and space to find my own direction. But our quarrels over religion left us both exhausted, even many years later. My mother desperately wanted me to be 'saved'. I told her I was already saved as much as anything else in nature was saved and if I

was going to hell then so would all of the other people in the world who believed in completely different religions. Sometimes she would be very sad in her worry for me in my unsaved state. It was only after my father died at age eighty that we came to an agreement. She would not preach religion to me if I wouldn't preach feminist politics to her.

And this worked. It worked until my mother died suddenly on my seventieth birthday. She was standing at the kitchen stove in Baton Rouge frying catfish for my sister's husband when she simply dropped to the floor. She was ninety-seven. She died being of service to her family and to her religious community. And that she went away from us while frying catfish seemed somehow to be marvelously fitting. Would that I, and others, also be so lucky.

And I've come to a place of peace. Yet this place of peace has thin spots. The problem? How to reconcile my own aversion to dogmatic religion with an equal yearning for spiritual connection and guidance. I think this question plagues a lot of people. We long to be fully developed spiritual beings. Yet I question whether this can be accomplished as long as we remain partially brain dead in the major areas of human life that is steadily and irrevocably wrenching us apart individually and collectively… the rapid rise of corporate power which has resulted in enormous environmental destruction and increasing economic and cultural disparity of all of us, as well as increasing disrespect for women.

In my opinion these two main disconnects walk hand in hand. In the early days of hunting and gathering, sexism and classism just wasn't part of humans' daily lives. Everything was shared. And yet when we read modern Pulitzer Prize winning science writers like Natalie Angier who holds the female body and brain up as nature's most marvelous combination of beauty and utility then we have to ask ourselves…were is all that female brain and beauty of being when it comes to making the decisions about whether the deforestation of the world will continue until the entire planet looks like Haiti? And we will no longer have any trees to collect the rains and hold the water that rushes down the mountainsides? No way to replenish the soils, to clean the air, to store the toxic carbons, to give us air

to breathe? Is it only the masculine brains that will make these decisions until the life giving functions of women are silenced completely?

So what am I suggesting? I am suggesting that we as women, collectively, start recognizing our own worth, as so many feminist writers past and present advise that we must do and demand equal say in what happens to the resources of this earth. If we don't, the males of our species who are charged with global decision making of serious matters like war and peace (even if a country has a female head of state she will listen to her military and spy agencies) will lean toward settling matters by the use of the sword, land mines, tanks as big as buildings, unmanned drones, guns that fire faster than the human heart beats, or the human mind thinks, and always with the specter of nuclear war not far from either. And all of these horrific activities dance around to the steady whine of the chain saw.

Wars and military expansion suck up money and goods that make certain corporations unbelievably prosperous and a lot of other people poor and dead. This lust for corporate profits in tandem with the need for guns, tanks, ships, war planes, missiles and military compound is killing our earth. None of these activities can go on without digging deep into bowels of the earth for minerals and cutting down what's left of the big trees on top. Deforestation of any large area around the world directly contributes to a carbon increase in our atmosphere. Old growth forests are the most efficient carbon sinks known to man (or woman). Yet we continue to cut down all old growth forests that can be reached. In British Columbia where the easily accessible valleys have been mostly cleaned out of old growth forests, the largely unregulated logging companies take to the air with helicopters and are now logging off the mountainsides that are inaccessible by road. I believe that collectively women can stop all of this.

While I can't explain what happened at Laycott Place, and still don't believe in ghosts or religion, I do believe in the human will. I believe in the human will because I have one. It lives with me. And it isn't inherited. The human will is made by struggle and honed sharp by refusal to give in to despair, even when faced with prison, with the death of one's children,

even when faced with one's own certain death. I also believe in evolution, in the physical and social evolution that we create ourselves in our earthly lives, and in doing so, I believe we co-create the world. The spirit we seek lies in this struggle, which takes place largely within ourselves.

* * * * * * * * * * * * * * * * * * *

Sitting here on my jailhouse bunk, I now know how I will end my address to sentencing for the judge. I begin writing anew.

"Sir," I begin again, trying to visualize Mr. Justice Harvey's face as I write. "What I want as a citizen is to have my arrests and charges accurately, honestly, and correctly correspond to my actions; to have my provincial government, my RCMP, and my judicial system uphold my rights as a citizen; to be treated fairly and equally before and under the law as any other citizen.

"I want a correct legal description and charge for what I did, which was blocking a public road in the Walbran Valley on Weyerhaeuser's Tree Farm License Number 44. I will continue to press arguments for the use of the Criminal Code in these circumstances.

Sir, I refuse the charge and conviction of Criminal Contempt of Court. It is a political charge and not a true one. I do not own it. I will never admit to it no matter how long I stay in prison. There is one thing I ask, in all due respect, sir, and that concerns any possible conditions attached to my sentencing. For me to sign such an agreement would mean for me that the Courts could command me to police myself to their requirements through my embracing an internal control that would make me lose faith in my own sense of direction. I refuse that, sir. It would take away from me the responsibility of my own decision-making.

"Freedom consists of the ability to choose freely the courses of thought and action presented to one and I exercise this freedom wherever I am. In prison I consider myself a political prisoner and conduct myself accordingly. My body is in prison, but my spirit is not. And neither, in prison, do I think of myself as separated from my children and grandchil-

dren, from my friends and colleagues, and from the old growth public forests of British Columbia.

"I carry all these things in my heart. They are part of me, and I will not bargain or condition away one iota of my freedom or theirs, or in my utter belief in democracy and the rule of law. If conditions are imposed on me by this Court, I will not feel honour bound to abide by them.

"I must repeat here what I advised Mr. Justice Parrott before he sentenced me in 2001 for blockading in the Elaho Valley: "Sir, you must lock me up or let me go. Thank you".

There. It's finished, with time to walk the track for an hour or so. I put my pen and papers away, run a comb through my hair and hurry down the stairwell, through the rotunda, and walk hurriedly across the hallway that leads to the track door. Loud rock music is coming from the adjacent gym next to the door; a sign women are using the gym equipment. I am not tempted to join them. I need fresh air.

There is a breeze coming off the Fraser River. Oh God, how I would love to start running, as fast as I can, across the road, away from the prison boundaries, past the tall trees, over the grassy banks, and plunge head first smack into the ancient, icy waters of the river. *Well, that would refresh me*, I think. But it's okay. I just feel a little light-headed from all the remembering and writing.

As I step onto the track I see that the last rays of the sun are striking the six Burnaby skyscrapers in the distance. If I am lucky, if the atmospheric conditions are just right, the building and the sunset will put on quite a show. A few moments later it happens. The optimum conditions have been reached. One building catches fire, ablaze with the flaming, bursting ingots of molten lava that ignite the other four high-rises, and all of the leaping, scalding lights that have been activated by the setting sun are performing before a soft pink and blue sky.

Within a few heartbeats, it all disappears. The sun slides behind our part of the world for the night. The six high-rise buildings are now left cold, leaden, barely perceptible in the evening dusk. The entire show has lasted thirty seconds or less.

I start my walk. An hour's walk for me is roughly a mile and a half, maybe two. I'll shoot for two. Got to keep the blood circulating and my spirits up.

THE END

L to R: Ray Allen age 21 (Home on leave from the Air Force), our Mother, Me age 18, and Doris age 14 – 1946.

Ray Allan age 22, in Air Force uniform – 1947.

Me age 19 – 1947.

Doris age 15 – 1947.

About the Author

Betty Krawczyk immigrated to Canada at the height of the Vietnam War in 1966 with a physicist husband and six disgruntled children. The children were annoyed at being uprooted and the husband was temporarily jobless. These problems righted themselves soon enough. One major problem did not. Born and raised in the southern United States, Krawczyk found she couldn't tolerate the long winters of northern Ontario where her husband had found a teaching post. Eventually the family split up and Krawczyk moved to British Columbia where the rainforests were lush and the snow was sparse. Children grown, Krawczyk retired to the stunning beauty of the forests and waters of Clayoquot Sound on the west coast of Vancouver Island to live in a rustic A-frame built by her son Mike.

By the time she discovered Clayoquot Sound Betty Krawczyk was already an experienced writer. She studied Creative Writing through the University of Oklahoma and had written primarily for women's pulp magazines. While she had also been active in human rights issues and women's issues, Krawczyk yearned to write about the natural world. Instead, she found herself writing about the destruction of the natural world by international logging companies.

In 1993 Krawczyk joined a group called "Friends of Clayoquot Sound" that blockaded logging trucks going into the Sound. And Krawczyk found herself in prison for the first time – but not the last. She was given three other more lengthy sentences for subsequent blockades and as this book goes to press is waiting to hear if the Supreme Court of Canada will hear her appeal on her last sentence for protesting at Eagleridge Bluffs in BC two years ago. "I am still on a blockade," Krawczyk says when questioned. "I will be on a blockade as long as the BC government and BC courts give out injunctions to every pillaging, polluting, privatizing international logging corporation that asks for one. These forests give life and breath to us all. It's the ancient role of elders to be stewards of the land. I'm simply trying to do my job." Her previous books include Clayoquot: The Sound of my Heart, Lock Me Up or Let Me Go and Open Living Confidential: From Inside the Joint.

Other Books By Betty Krawczyk:

CLAYOQUOT: *The Sound of My Heart*

LOCK ME UP OR LET ME GO

OPEN LIVING CONFIDENTIAL: *From Inside the Joint*

May be ordered through: betty.krawczyk@gmail.com

14041763R00143

Made in the USA
Lexington, KY
05 March 2012

Therapy

A NOVEL

HARRIE ROSE

Copyright © 2010 Harrie Rose
All rights reserved.

ISBN: 1439257205
ISBN-13: 9781439257203
LCCN: 2009909139

All characters and events in this novel are fictitious and any resemblance to a person or persons, living or dead, or to actual events, beyond the changing of the seasons, are purely coincidental.

Dedication

To my husband of 50 years who is everything Joe is not.

Many thanks and much gratitude go to the anonymous reviewers of an earlier draft of this manuscript when I posted it on eons. com in the Writer's Group. Special thanks are especially due to my friends Caredoe and Sunny, whose encouragement and praise kept me going and whose good advice I tried to follow.

I especially want to salute my editor, Terry Chase, whose complete immersion into this book and its characters helped me to make them clearer and more alive. She spoke of them as real people, forcing me to make them behave consistently with their individual personae. Once she emailed me,"Isn't it fun? We can gossip about somebody without guilt." Besides sharpening my writing, she diligently and carefully corrected all my errors intelligently, and, most of all, wouldn't let me get away with anything. She went over every word in this novel, again and again. Whatever is good and alive in this book owes a great deal to her lively discussions. Her final comment was"It makes me want to drive around the country roads in Rhode Island and find Barbara and have a cup of coffee with her." Any infelicities remaining are not her fault, but my own.

Prologue

They always called me the whiz kid, a powerhouse, a dynamo. "How do you do so much?" they asked. "I don't sleep," I'd laugh dismissively. Clearly, I was a challenge. The housewives I met at parties and meetings never invited me to their homes even after I invited them to mine and treated them to my homemade gourmet fare. Oh, they came, but they never reciprocated. I had a few friends, mostly from high school and college days, but nobody who was, well, chummy, with me. Even my colleagues at school were no more than polite to me. I made them uncomfortable, I guess, with my strong opinions, my large vocabulary. Yet, they held doctorates. They were supposedly intellectual. Of course, most of them were men, and a smart woman to them was a strange phenomenon, like a hen who crowed as my old Gramma would have said. I did try to woo them at first with dinner parties, but that backfired. Their stay-at-home wives were intimidated enough that I worked alongside their husbands at what used to be a male's school, recently changed to coed. That I could also cook was worse. That infringed on their domain, their claim to fame. Since the invitations were never returned, I stopped bothering to invite.

Actually, it was okay. I'm not complaining. I buried myself in my work just as I buried myself in books when I was a kid while all the other kids in the neighborhood were outside playing games. Perhaps *buried* is not the right word. I actually immersed myself

in books and also in writing little stories, all of which my mother threw out. She couldn't stand clutter.

As a grown-up, I still preferred to be by myself reading, correcting papers, writing, or doing research, not having to tangle with the thorns of polite interactions. Or dealing with Joe. When the kids were little, of course, I did things with them, and often just sat aside, looking at them play or talk, marveling that I had such adorable little boys. But now, a closed study door helped me insulate myself from their sullen adolescence. How did that happen? How did such loving little boys become such abrasive, know-it-all teenagers who didn't seem to want me for anything except for what my money could buy?

Joe remained Mr. Sociability. Everyone loved Joe, his good, blonde looks, his easy manner and dry humor. He was always a little rumpled looking, which added to his attraction of being someone you could be totally comfortable with. Although he was a lawyer, he never looked polished or spiffy. His ties were often askew. A shirttail might be not quite tucked in, his shoes not polished, and his jacket pockets bulging with a pipe, tobacco, and crumpled notes. Interestingly, he bought expensive, dandy clothes, but quickly made them his own. That was part of his charm. When he began to pursue me twenty years earlier, I know his friends wondered why. So did the girls who were pursuing him. One was a classmate of mine in college. She didn't even try to hide her shock that Joe chose me of all people. She just about said that if he had chosen almost anyone else over her she could've accepted it. End of that friendship, a shallow one anyway.

His parents were outraged when he told them he was marrying me. On top of my other flaws, I was used goods, having eloped when I was eighteen, and having had a baby when I was twenty. Then I got divorced. I met Joe a couple of years later. He was so obviously out of my league I didn't even try to act like a product of *Seventeen*. It was at a going-away party for Beth, the friend who had been wooing Joe unsuccessfully. I was in a corner with a couple of other girls, talking about school. I had gone back to college to prepare myself to be a teacher so I could support my little son. Another marriage never entered my head. Neither did a romance. Who would want me? When my

THERAPY, A NOVEL

mother asked her friend if she knew an eligible man for me, the friend answered, "I couldn't tell anyone to take someone else's leavings?" Mama was furious, but I understood it just fine. In any event, Joe walked over to my little corner and quickly started to engage me in conversation. When he told me he had studied philosophy at a conservative Catholic college, I witheringly gave him my opinion of Catholic philosophy, weighted as it was by the bias of its religious dogma. I had been a philosophy major during my brief sojourn at Brown where there were no such restrictions on whom to study or admire, and the professors especially singled out philosophies devised to prove religious beliefs. To my amazement, he didn't get angry. He asked if I wanted a ride home. We were married in a year, to his family's great consternation. I couldn't believe my good luck, that such an eligible man, a budding lawyer, would want me. His father actually asked him, "Why do you want her? She's not even pretty." Joe told me he answered, "To me, she's beautiful."

Because of Joe, we were invited to all sorts of parties and formal dinners. He was active in various associations as well as volunteer groups like the local fire department, and the Democratic Party. The inevitable events and parties that went with these groups were agonizing for me. Often I just sent Joe to go alone to his political gatherings, fireman's dinners, and the assorted parties he was invited to. Yes, my name was always on the invitation, but I knew it wasn't me they wanted. It was Joe.

I suspect they were relieved when I declined. I was too serious, too smart, too opinionated, and too talkative. Not that I wanted to be, but, for instance, people would ask what I taught. Then, when I told them, they'd make some really stupid comment, and as I tried to tell them they were wrong, I'd see their eyes glaze over and their fidgeting and looking around the room. They wanted to get away from me. I learned never to ask anybody questions like, "What do you do?" Women, especially, were very put off by that, since what they did was clean house and take care of kids. I took care of kids too, but I didn't clean house. I hired someone to do that out of my own salary, not that I advertised that fact, but conversations about cooking, recipes, or household products left me speechless. Actually, I did cook and bake, but talking about new recipes wasn't my idea of conversation.

xi

I once overheard a woman in the ladies' room at a Bar Association dinner complain that Joe was such a nice guy, but that wife of his is so abrasive, so intimidating. That was the last such dinner I went to. I felt the waves of dislike beating on my shore whenever I was at social gatherings, and finally decided I couldn't take it anymore. Joe himself was relieved, I'm sure, that I didn't go with him. It made him freer to shoot the breeze with all comers without having to introduce me or worry that I had nobody to talk to.

Me as intimidating was a laugh. Barely five feet tall and ninety pounds, there wasn't that much of me. The men at the parties did a lot more lecturing than I ever did. They stated their opinionated opinions loud and often, but that was okay. Women are supposed to listen to men and agree with them. If women are talking to other women, they're supposed to chitchat, but I didn't know how to chitchat. If you don't talk in a high, tinkly voice, with a questioning lilt after everything you say, and you're a woman, you're intimidating.

Well, my mother was a remarkable woman. She always spoke straight out, saying exactly what she meant. No hint of doubt there. Ever. She was always right. She was never mistaken. She brooked no dissent, except from my father. When he talked, she listened. What he said, she agreed to.

From the time I was very little, Mama told me not to talk so much. Not to tell people what I knew. That was being a showoff and nobody liked a showoff. My uncles and aunts used to tease me, calling me a little "sewing machine" because I was always making noise like a sewing machine. Nobody told my brother he was a sewing machine. When he talked, his noise was worthwhile. But female talk was meaningless like the sounds of a sewing machine. So I learned early on to keep everything inside.

When I got old enough to notice boys, I quickly realized that I'd better not let them know I was smart, that I knew anything, but, since I was a straight A student, they figured it out anyway. I was labeled 'the brain' in high school.

When I became pubescent, boys attracted me, but I didn't know how to deal with them. *Seventeen Magazine*, my teen-ager Bible, advised girls never to state an opinion or a fact without softening it, saying, "I may be wrong but ...." Or "I thought... but

THERAPY, A NOVEL

I'm probably mistaken." However, they advised, the best tack was to just listen to the guys and agree with what they said. Also, they counseled, a girl should find out what her date wanted to talk about. If he seemed to have a problem conversing, then you should ask questions until you hit on a topic he wanted to enlarge upon. Under no condition should a girl spout off about her interests to a male.

My rare dates were agony for me. I never figured out why anybody would ask me out. I looked like a troll, a red-haired troll and I never could think of anything to say that would be acceptable to *Seventeen*. Once a date asked me what I wanted from life, and I answered, "I want to be happy." He sneered, literally sneered, "What kind of an answer is that? Nobody wants to be unhappy. That is stupid." The date got cut short and he never called again, thank God. At the time, I felt deeply ashamed, but, years later, it occurred to me that I answered that way because I was so deeply unhappy.

Furthermore, what was I supposed to say, that I wanted to be a scholar? To get a doctorate? In 1954, what girl wanted that? Girls were supposed to find a man and live happily ever after serving him. Girls went to college to husband hunt. That's what made women happy. But I knew it wouldn't make me happy. I hated housework, couldn't sew or make a neat piecrust.

What else is there to tell about me except that I cried all night the day the doctor told me that I wouldn't grow anymore. I'd never have long legs like Cyd Charisse or Rita Hayworth, or my own mother, for that matter. She took delight in sidling up to me and saying when others were around, "I could eat beans off her head." And, she always excused my shortness to others as if it were a disease and my fault, to boot. "She never would drink her milk. That's why she's so short, not even five feet tall."

It finally occurred to me, three decades later, if she was so concerned with my milk drinking, why didn't she make me milk puddings or even coffee milk? That's milk with coffee syrup in it, a local specialty. It also occurred to me many years later that having two 4 foot 10 inch tall grandmothers had something to do with my being a shade under five feet. Being so short colored my whole life. I felt like a freak. I was always the shortest girl in my class, at a party, in the movie line. People loved to come up

xiii

to me and say, "I could eat peanuts off your head!" or, to be nice, "Good things come in small packages." What my mother never remarked on was my tiny waist, curvy hips, and firm, high tush. Only my short legs grabbed her notice. In reality, they were not short for my height. My legs were half my height, and, in pants, I looked proportionately long-legged. Her legs were longer than mine, but she was 6 inches taller than me. Her thighs and legs were slim and shapely, but topped by a boxy torso, no waist, and a flat ass. She looked terrible in pants. Nor did she care to compare my ninety pounds to her 160. Of course, I just assumed that I was scrawny. Someone once commented that I had an hourglass figure. I didn't know that "hour glass figure" was a compliment.

Going to school dances was a revelation when I was a teenager. Boys actually wanted me to dance with them. So dainty, so petite, so thin, how do you do it, the girls always said. I thought they were being sarcastic.

A girl who sat behind me in a college English class, meeting me years later, asked me if my hair was naturally curly. "Yes," I said. "I knew it, ´she responded. "I used to sit behind you and think, 'and I bet her hair is naturally curly, too'" I didn't do the double take until a week later. That's how long it took me to figure out that she meant I had everything.

Unfortunately, being short wasn't my first disappointment in life, but it was major. It was something I couldn't work my way up from as I did with everything else. School I was good at, so good I eventually earned a PhD while mothering four sons and playing wifey-wife, with a lot of help, of course, from Mamie, who cleaned the house, did the laundry, and looked after the kids if they weren't in daycare or school.

People used to say about my husband, "What a nice guy he is. He lets his wife go to school." Later on they'd say, "He lets his wife work." Well, Mamie was paid for by my fellowship money when I was in grad school, and Joe collected my paychecks from work, as I presumed a man should. His meals were always on time and the house in order. He didn't sacrifice anything by letting me study and teach. Unlike many men, his ego wasn't threatened by my successes. I have to hand that to him. I left everything up to him, managing the decisions about where to

live, how to spend money, and how not. Usually, and that included the years that I was earning a nice amount of money from being a professor and from my books, I was lucky to have a dollar in my wallet. Of course, if I wanted money to go shopping or to have my hair cut, all I had to do was ask and he'd give it to me. I never questioned the arrangement.

Odd, isn't it? Always opinionated about politics, flowers and how to bake bread properly, but never questioned what was due to me or what Joe assumed was due to him, and, at that point, didn't even realize it needed questioning. Or that anything was due to me. That is, until the 1970's and feminist complaints began seeping into my consciousness, which had been largely sealed off from anything that didn't concern the kids, my studies, my research, or my work. Joe, I took as he came, never inquiring, never complaining, always accepting his comings and goings, his spending, his ignoring me and the boys. Years later, when I was in therapy, I reminded him how much I had always done to make his life easier. His response rocked me, "St. Barbara, look at everything I did for everyone, and nobody else did a thing for me." Then he stomped off. Well, I was just stating facts, wasn't I? Why did he get so sarcastic?

Eventually, the boys grew up. One by one, they left home for college and then for good. Now that I had time, I felt deflated. I suddenly didn't have so much to do that I was frantically busy all the time. Strangely, I, the dynamo, wound down, sleepwalking through the days, until the day came that I couldn't get out of the bed in the morning, and then, all day, every day. I covered myself with my puffy eiderdown comforter, denting the oversized down pillow with my tangled bedhead, and cried and cried for days and days. I couldn't figure out why. Nobody cared anyhow.

Chapter One

When I first saw the diploma hanging on the far wall of the doctor's office, I couldn't read his name. I could make out a couple of letters, but the rest were fuzzy, as though in a different alphabet. Maybe this is what it felt like to be dyslexic, a strange sensation for a confirmed literate like me who could read in four different alphabets, Roman, Cyrillic, Greek, and Hebrew. His first name, was it Alberto? Alfredo? All I could make of the last name was that it looked long and vowelly. Italian probably. Not that I looked at it constantly, more like a glance here and there. I'd squint at the diploma through my haze, pretending to be deep in thought, measuring my words, slewing my eyes under my soggy eyelids. It took me three visits, each fifty minutes, before the name became clear. Suddenly it popped out at me. Alessandro. And the last name, Giangiaccomo.

Whoa. Stop while I backtrack a little. A little context. The doctor was a shrink. It was either get out of bed and at least go to a shrink or go to the mental hospital. Even Joe, who virtually never noticed anything that I did, finally noticed that I had stayed in bed for weeks. At least, the two or three waking hours a day that he was at home, he found me in bed. I think what really bothered him was that I'd stopped cooking his suppers, which was a major inconvenience. Actually, *the* major inconvenience. Alice, the housekeeper who succeeded Mamie, did the laundry and the dishes. She even watered the houseplants.

HARRIE ROSE

It took a while before Joe realized something was wrong. My eyes were slits in swollen lids from the constant crying. One day, he finally said,"Pull yourself together, goddammit! What the hell's the matter with you anyway? You don't have to do housework. You've got everything. This room..." he said, waving his right arm in a sweeping motion to indicate my bedroom—my haven. I didn't have diamonds or jewels, never bothered much with fancy clothes then, or anything for myself, except the bedroom that I shared with Joe, but that room was done by me and for me. The wallpaper with tiny indigo forget-me-nots strewn on a white background, the white scrim curtains on the double windows at the side and the front of the room. Near the front windows, on one end of the room, was the white wicker chaise with a blue and white flowered print that complemented the wallpaper. Between the chaise and the hand-painted antique blue armoire with its bucolic design of fluffy grazing sheep, was an antique mahogany table. My custom-built antique-white triple dresser was placed on the wall opposite the side windows. Instead of the expected mirror above it, there was a built-in three-shelved bookcase in a curlicued frame. Joe had an antique-white armoire made to harmonize with the dresser. Dominating the twenty-four foot long bedroom was a king-sized antique-brass bed, covered with a hand-quilted blue and white Vermont bedspread. An off-white, thick-piled rug set off all the furniture. At the foot of the bed was special frame to hang the quilt on when we were in bed. The biggest luxury of all was the eiderdown comforter, the softest, lightest, warmest of covers, coupled with king-sized down pillows, and 600 thread count Egyptian cotton sheets in an almost sheer white with white dots woven into them. The pillowcases and top sheet had beautiful lace borders. Surely a bedroom out of a Hollywood fantasy.

It's evident why this was where I chose to hide out. And why my bedroom was so important to me, when nothing else domestic was. In the crowded flat that I grew up in, the only place I could be alone was the bedroom I shared with my brother. He would go out to play, and I would lie in bed reading.

When the terrible sadness descended on me, I naturally took to my haven, my bed. I couldn't stop crying. I couldn't bring myself to talk to anybody. I had descended into a deep depression,

so deep that it felt that it would never lift. I was too weighted down even to try to climb out of it.

One day, when I was huddled in our ornate brass bed, Joe came into the bedroom. He leaned on the doorjamb, fists shoved in the pockets of his brown cords, one leg crossed over the other, his shoes scuffed and unpolished as usual. He didn't look at me. His complaint cut through the thick cover pulled over my head.

"You'd better get up," he said. "If you're too sick to get up, then go to a doctor. Go to a hospital. I'm sick of this. People are beginning to ask where you are. They haven't seen you around. What am I supposed to tell them?"

Good grief! He suddenly cared how I spent my time? It bothered him that I wasn't seen by the neighbors? When did that become an issue? Maybe he had just run out of excuses for me, especially now when there were no kids to care for.

I managed to answer, "I don't need a doctor. I just can't move."

"So, go to a shrink," he yelled.

"I don't know any. They don't know anything anyway."

"Don't you ever get out of that bed?" he demanded. "Do something? Make a meal? Anything?"

"I go out and teach my classes."

"And then you come back and crawl into bed."

I turned my head into the pillow "I can't move. Maybe I do need a doctor," I said, my voice muffled.

"So get one."

"I can't. I haven't any strength. You find me one."

Those were bold words. Joe never, but never, did anything that entailed responsibility for me. I was the doer, planner, executor, get-things-done member of the family, or was until this lead weight descended on me. Actually, I was amazed that he even noticed I had ceased to function. He lived his life. I lived mine.

"Okay." Joe answered my challenge. "I'll speak to Dom, but, if I do, you get up and get yourself to his office."

Dom was a psychiatrist whom Joe sent his divorce clients to when they needed a shrink to testify, especially in abuse cases.

"I can't go to Dom. I've met him. And he's an idiot."

I had first met Dom horseback riding in the woods behind our house. He was with a young Amazon, probably younger than

his own daughters, a real airhead who proudly claimed she was a poet. Actually, maybe it was Don who did the proud proclaiming. We all dismounted at his house, which bordered on the same belt of thousands of acres of woodland as ours. As we sat in his kitchen sipping too-strong coffee, I suffered through an interminable afternoon of his anachronistic opinions while Linda Ronstadt sang overly sentimental 1940's torch songs on the stereo.

"I'll just ask Dom for a recommendation," Joe said.

I could tell he was exasperated. Being a lawyer, he was convinced that he was a superior judge of people. He didn't like it when I didn't agree with his evaluations.

"He's a terrific psychiatrist. All my clients love him, but I'll ask him to recommend someone for you, but you're going."

He straightened his tie, turned, and walked out of the room. A couple of days later, he had made an appointment for me with Dom's new associate—his new partner, newly arrived from Los Angeles eager to try small city living and the fabled New England seafood, I guess. Or maybe some scandal brought him here, I imagined. I mean, people move from the Northeast to the West, to places where winter isn't so harsh, not usually from the West to the East unless they have to.

I had assented because depression feels awful. A leaden weight in the pit of your stomach. The world is dreary. You're sorry to be alive. Just a lump deep in the stomach and a gray haze over everything. The air drapes itself around you, holding you down, hampering your legs as you try to walk, not letting your arms or hands move when you talk, keeping your head bowed. You have no glimmer of interest in anything. Nothing entices. Nothing interests. Focusing eludes you, even on something as trivial as a sitcom or someone else's chitchat. It's a death in life. But if you have to, you force yourself to plod along and do your job.

I had been feeling nothing at all during the winter, which was just ending. My whole body felt numb. My brain too. People talked. Their mouths moved, but I couldn't quite make out their words. Everything sounded as if I had a thick rug over my head, as if the speaker were in the next room with the door closed. I would've thought I was going deaf, a family disability, only I could hear some sounds just fine, like music on my stereo and

car doors slamming. As for sight, I saw everything through a fog. Everything was blurry even with my glasses on.

I had little faith that a psychiatrist could help, but no faith at all that I could live without the relief he might be able to bring. Nowadays there are pills. The media claim they're Magic. They can make you want to live again. I wasn't sure I wanted to live, but I couldn't think of a way to kill myself without making a disgusting mess. A shotgun to the head splatters blood and brains everywhere. It would certainly ruin the wallpaper. That sounds stupid, I know, but I now realize that was a sign that I had a little hope for life.

Chapter Two

When I drove my white BMW to the address Joe had given me, I saw it was one of those old mansions that line the main streets of Providence. The once grand homes have been turned into doctors and dentists' offices with apartments on the upper floors. This one was bilious mustard yellow with the contrasting trim painted brown. I parked the car, and walked in. The receptionist asked me why I was there. "I have an appointment with the new doctor, I don't know his name." She may have considered me a weirdo, although she was probably used to strange people by now.

I plopped myself in a chair and waited, feeling dread. Most of the shrinks I had met in my life were arrogant. They presumed to know what was in your mind better than you did. I had never even dreamt of going to one. You had to talk to them. What could I say? What should I say? What would they think of me? Would they say unflattering things about me behind my back? I was a respected college professor. What would my colleagues say if they heard I was going to a psychiatrist? I present an assured in-control facade to the world, although that wasn't the case now. Thinking about it later, I recalled the one question I never asked myself was if this shrink could have any effect on me, much less the huge one he did have. Certainly, I never suspected why.

It all started inauspiciously enough when the short dark man walked into the waiting room and called my name that first time. I had read somewhere, probably in some novel, that the

7

beginning of love is an instant jolt of recognition that here is a person you're going to know, to be bound up with. That's not what happened when I first set eyes on the man I came to know as Alex. I had no feelings at all at first, just a strange, strong compulsion to make another appointment after the initial visit. But I'm getting a little ahead of myself.

My first sight of him was when he walked into the waiting room. I was slumped, disheveled, in worn jeans and a baggy gray T-shirt. He was dressed in a double-breasted suit, so you couldn't tell if he had a potbelly or not. He was the smallest man I'd ever seen, maybe 5 feet 2, but well formed, not a dwarf. His head was in proportion to his body. In one hand, he clutched a clipboard with some papers attached to it as he beckoned to me with his other hand. Like most of the short men I've ever met, he was well bearded. Maybe they're afraid that without a beard, people would think they're little boys, or maybe it juts up their feelings of masculinity a few notches.

"Barbara?" he asked.

"Yes" I said, reluctantly.

But I didn't rise. I just sat there sullenly. A burst of anger shot through me, my first real feeling in months. It makes me cringe when someone who doesn't know me calls me by my first name, like we're supposed to be friends or something.

"My office is upstairs," he continued.

He motioned with his hand that I should go ahead. Then he started towards the grand curved staircase that graced what must have once been the foyer of this old mansion now converted to doctor's offices. As I started up the stairs, I felt him behind me, imagining him eyeing my ample buttocks straining as I climbed. Left. Right. Embarrassing. I could feel every globule of fat in my rear as I moved, an almost hallucinatory feeling that my ass was not only naked but transparent. This scenario was repeated on the next two visits. On the fourth, suddenly, after meeting me in the waiting room, he said hurriedly, almost apologetically,

"I'll take the back stairs."

He scurried back to an alternate flight of stairs originally intended for servants so they wouldn't be seen by visitors sitting in the parlor. I never did find out why it took him three encounters to allow me to climb the front stairs without shame, although

THERAPY, A NOVEL

by then it had occurred to me to wear full skirts whenever I went to see him. In fact, when I got home from my second visit to his office, I took out a catalog and ordered dresses, dialing the 800 number at two in the morning while Joe snored blissfully away. Each dress had a copious skirt, the better to climb the stairs in and for posing gracefully as I sat opposite him in his office, the skirts in a swirl around my ankles that would be oh so delicately displayed.

At that first meeting, however, after we navigated the stairs to his third floor office, as he directed me into a chair and sat down opposite me, crossing one leg over the other at the knee, he did apologize after a fashion for the trip up.

"If you find the stairs too steep I can try to use a downstairs office."

"No. They're good for my weight," I said.

In an almost angry tone, he blurted out,"Then why have I gained thirty pounds since I've been here?"

Amazed at his outburst, I felt the smallest of thrills. Joe, my husband, never got excited about anything, which was the very thing that had made me want to marry him. I had had my fill of excitable, irascible men when I met Joe. So it was a surprise all those years later that the passion in the psychiatrist's voice evoked a rise in me. I had just been feeling dead for so long. No anger. No joy. No excitement. I must have looked half dead, beyond caring, sitting in the office wearing those ratty old blue jeans, scuffed dirty sneakers on my feet. No makeup on my face. I was sprawled, fat thighs stretching the limits of my pants legs. Not even mascara to make my pale red eyelashes stand out. My hair dirty, limp, straight. I, who had always been so particular about how I looked, who wore only outfits, never things that just happened to go together, whose hair was washed and carefully blown dry every day had transmogrified into a muddy puddle of a woman.

I know you're wondering how I kept my job. I missed some days of work, but I managed to drag myself out of bed on others. Nobody monitors if a professor is actually in her classes or how many she misses. There is no teacher attendance taken in college. My complexion was pasty from weeks in bed. I had gotten up only to leave the house to go teach three days a week.

9

Teaching meant listlessly running a comb through my hair, putting on a pair of slacks and a blouse, often the same one for weeks on end, driving into the city to my classes, spouting my lectures, all written years before, and then turning right around to come home to bed. Professors are supposed to be eccentric anyway, and aggressive unstylishness, even a bit of slovenliness, could be forgiven in a scholar. At least, that's how I consoled myself.

Up to then, I had always dressed as my mother had: tailored suits with proper accessories. Face made up. Hair carefully arranged. Nobody seemed to notice the change. Or at least they didn't say anything, but actually, I spoke very little to anybody at school, just showing up for classes, and leaving.

I don't know if I even made any sense in my classes that semester, my head was so foggy and the battle not to cry was so intense. At least nobody said anything—to my face, anyway. Students just take down every word you say without questioning, whether they understand it or not.

That first visit to the psychiatrist, when we got to his office door, he scurried in front of me and grabbed the door handle, a brass grip, opening the door, and ushering me in. The office itself was grand with ceilings at least twelve feet high, wide ornate moldings around each window and the door itself. The room was papered in teal brocade and the moldings were some kind of dark stained wood, probably walnut or oak. The ceiling sported a large ornately worked plaster medallion in its center and smaller ones around the perimeter. A large, mannish mahogany desk dominated one part of the room. Thank god there was no couch, only three wing chairs, one facing the two others. They were all upholstered in a cranberry red fabric and were flanked by what must have been reproduction Sheraton tables, also mahogany. Very settled looking. Very conservative, but pleasant. I wondered if it had been done by a decorator, someone who specialized in using the right colors and the right furniture to convince patients that the doctor was reliable and had good taste.

No pictures of a wife or children. No pictures at all. Nothing that looked personal, that could shed some light on what kind of man this was, except for the diplomas on the walls and I couldn't read those. There were what I guessed to be a few medical books in a small bookcase near the desk. The requisite boxes of tissues

THERAPY, A NOVEL

resided on the table in between the two wing chairs that faced the doctor's chair, handy for the ever-streaming flow of tears brought on by confessions. I wondered idly why they're called shrinks. Actually, I still do wonder. They're supposed to expand you, not shrink you. Or maybe I'm just dreaming the dream of the little, tiny person who wants to be as big as the grownups.

So, anyways, I ended up in that office with that doctor. The psychiatrist sat across from me in his navy pinstriped suit, his short legs akimbo, one hand resting on each thigh as he bent forward towards me, gaze intent on me. His interest was total, compelling. It felt as if a strong magnetic force emanated from him. I felt a strong desire to talk to him, but I as I've said, I was terrible at talking to people, never able to think of what to say, and when I attempted conversation I always, but always, said the wrong thing, offending everyone. Like the perfect professor I was, all I could do right was lecture from carefully prepared notes.

Theoretically, I shouldn't have to worry about offending a shrink. He was paid, after all, to listen. I was surprised at myself, concerned about the impression I made on this stranger. But what could I possibly say to him? I had always been devoid of small talk. I had never learned put my own life in words, didn't recount my daily doings to anybody, not even to myself. My parents never wanted to hear about me and neither did Joe. My kids certainly didn't either. All anybody was ever interested in was what I could and would do for them. That was normal to me. Sitting in this chair to talk about myself was not. But then I had already passed from the bounds of normal.

"First, I need you to answer some questions," he said, reaching for a paper on a clipboard on the table next to him.

"Feel discouraged?"

"Yes." My eyes filled with tears.

"Trouble sleeping?"

"No, I sleep all the time." Now the tears were running down my face. As he continued asking, each question brought a fresh spate. Not loud tears, silent streaming ones.

He just continued reading questions off the form which he held with his left hand, penciling in yes's and no's with his right, peering over the top of the clipboard with a look of concern, scanning my face. Did I eat? Drink? Take drugs? My interests?

11

My parents? Innocuous enough questions, but they made me cry.

I felt bewildered and unglued by my reaction. I never cried in front of others, even when I was a child, no matter what happened. In hindsight, I think that maybe I was crying because he seemed to care about me. I guess I could cry in front of him because he was the first person who seemed concerned about me as a person, not as a giver or a doer. Long after, it occurred to me that I was a payer, but his sympathy still seemed genuine.

I may never have cried, but I grew up with tears. Gramma used to sit and weep quietly without explaining and nobody ever asked her why. My mother would state scornfully in her usual"don't dare contradict me" tone of voice,

"She's only happy when she cries. That's how she enjoys herself."

Now I realized that such tears are from deep wells of sadness. I wish I had known it then when Gramma was alive so I could've been nicer to her. Another regret. She was bereft in the midst of all that family. So was I.

The doctor leaned forward, his shoulders hunched, still intently asking me questions from the form, making check marks as I answered.

"Suicidal thoughts?"

"Yes"

" Appetite?"

"Fine," I admitted, although it's not ladylike to have an appetite in our culture. How could I deny it though, fat as I felt? Surely, he'd noticed. I always looked fat to myself. When people told me that I wasn't fat, I figured they were being polite. Have you noticed that when you tell someone something negative about yourself, it embarrasses them and they'll even admonish you not to put yourself down. I've never understood why we're supposed to maintain the polite fiction that we aren't fat or our hair is not scraggly or our nose is not too large. It makes people uncomfortable when we tell the truth about ourselves. Anyway, he continued the questions.

"Hearing voices?"

"No."

If anything, my problem was not hearing voices. He continued peering over the top of the form, his dark eyes serious and concerned. His intensity was palpable. It penetrated to my core, cleared my defensive fog.

At that first visit, after the questionnaire, he asked me as I silently cried,"What can I do for you?"

I managed to reply, "I don't know. I don't think I want to talk though. I don't think talking will help. Besides I don't have anything to be depressed about. I have a wonderful husband, better than I'd ever dreamt of or even dared hoped for, much less deserve, a beautiful house, a good job, and nice kids, close family."

It was true. I had no American reason to be depressed. I had all the things that Hollywood and the media say make you happy: a handsome husband, one a lot of women envied me for, four beautiful healthy sons with white, straight teeth, and not a wrinkle on my face. Nobody guessed my age. I know everyone thinks they look younger than they are. They look at themselves in the mirror and see their younger selves staring back, but I knew I looked younger than fifty-two. After all, men in their thirties and forties found me attractive, not to mention that until recently male students had schoolboy crushes on me, following me around like puppy dogs, offering to carry my heavy brief case. One of my colleagues, Lorenzo, kept touching my hands and staring into my eyes when we spoke. Dave, in Computer Science, who so willingly helped me with my computer problems found any excuse to put an arm around my shoulder, hug me"in victory" when he managed to find a solution to whatever problem I had, but not until he called me one night, drunk, and kept saying,"Barbara, I love you" did I realize his true feelings. At a conference I was at in Washington, a scholar from Germany kept ogling me. When I displayed my left hand so he could be warned by my wedding band, he said in a disappointed tone,"Oh, don't tell me you are married. Not that that stops you Americans."

"It stops this American," I replied.

I can't really say it was my marital vows that prevented me from bed hopping like the other scholars at conferences. It was more shyness and shame. I couldn't bare my body to a strange man, and sex wasn't all that important to me anyhow.

No matter how often it happened, and it wasn't a daily or even a weekly thing, more like a semi-annual one, it was always surprising to me that reasonably good-looking men with social poise indicated they would want me, even for a one-night stand. Of course, those men only saw the outside, not the bra holding up the sagging breasts, or the cottage cheese thighs well hidden in the stylish slacks I wore. Nor did they see my inner quaking, my inner dread.

Of course, at that first meeting, I didn't tell the doctor about my chances with other men. I just answered his questions directly while he wrote down my laconic responses, hunching over the paper, scribbling furiously with a cheap blue ballpoint pen, the kind that you buy ten for a dollar.

Then he straightened up and leaned forward, putting his papers on the table next to his chair. He leaned forward again, hands pressed firmly on his thighs.

"We can do talk therapy along with medication to make you feel better," he informed me,"but you don't have to talk. Depression is largely a matter of a chemical imbalance in the brain. Even with talk therapy, we use medications to correct that. We can use Elavil or Prozac. Elavil is an older anti-depressant with more side effects. Prozac is interesting. It's only been used since 1988, but in the two years since then it's gotten a very good press. It's an SSRI, a serotonin reuptake inhibitor. It works by preventing your brain from absorbing serotonin too rapidly. Serotonin is the chemical that makes you feel happy. There are no side effects for most people, but it takes up to a month to work. Which would you prefer?"

"Well, everyone is talking about Prozac, so I guess I'll try that," I answered. "Uh, what does talking cost?" As soon as I asked, I felt astonished, like why did I ask about that. I didn't want to talk, couldn't talk, not me. Now I realize I was protesting too much to myself. I was yearning to talk to this man with his intensity and barely contained passion—not sexual passion. I didn't mean that at all.

"Therapy is one hundred and fifty dollars an hour, but only ninety dollars for half an hour and many people do very well indeed with that. You do have health insurance, don't you?"

"Yes."

THERAPY, A NOVEL

"That'll pay for it with a small co-pay, twenty sessions. But medication alone should also bring you relief."

Mundane exchange. Boring. But that's how it all began. And he really did say"indeed."

At the end of our first interview, clutching my prescription for Prozac, I left, walking down the grand staircase. Although he had made it plain that I didn't have to come back until my prescription ran out, I felt strangely compelled to walk over to the secretary's office in an alcove off the waiting room.

"I'd like an appointment for next week with doctor, uh.., the doctor I just saw, I didn't get his name."

She muttered something, probably his name, and put me down for the following Friday at two o'clock. In a daze, I left the office. As I walked down the front steps, the numbness that had gripped me for the past months began to recede. I went home and back to bed. With one difference. I started to think about what I was going to say to him. I knew, of course, that people told their psychiatrists all about their dysfunctional childhoods. I didn't think of my childhood as dysfunctional, however, mainly because I didn't think of it at all. In fact, I remembered little of it. Just reading a lot, playing with paper dolls, and roaming the streets of the city. But I had to have something to tell the doctor. I couldn't just go sit in his office for an hour and look at him, could I? Besides, I wanted him to think highly of me, as someone interesting, even fascinating. I couldn't let him know how dull I was. How ordinary. I had spent my whole life hiding out, not letting people see what I really was, and I certainly couldn't let this magnetic man in on the secret. The competent facade I presented the world was a skim coating over my incompetence.

The next morning, to my husband's surprise, I crawled out of bed at six o'clock, shrugged into sweat pants, shoved my feet in beat up old sneakers, pulled a T-shirt over my head and raced out the front door. I felt a great urge to walk. Living deep in the country, I had my choice of hacking my way through overgrown woodland trails or walking on paved roads. That morning I chose the roads, which were, as usual, quite deserted, with only the occasional car whooshing by.

It was early spring. The trees were pregnant with buds. The deep blue of the myrtle was creeping out of the woods. The

forsythias were showing off their brilliant yellow branches in the first of the real flashy spring shows. The robins were back, hopping on the lawn, cocking their heads to hear worms in the soil. Swallows scissored against the blue skies, enjoying the Mayflies no doubt, those thick swarms of nasty little flies that got into your mouth and eyes if you dallied outside in the early evening when the sun was down but it was still light. They made early morning walks and Little League games a torment. When my sons were still children, good mommy that I was, I never missed a practice or a game. I sat and watched them try to thwack the ball after the interminable waiting for their turns. My boredom was profound, my discomfort from biting bugs agonizing. Still, I never told anybody how much I hated Little League.

As I walked, barely noticing the Jack-in-the-Pulpits in bloom at the edges of the woods, and the pretty little yellow cinquefoils interspersed amongst the ground foliage, I started to think hard about the past, dredging it up, so I could be an interesting person to keep him, the doctor, interested. I agonized over what to say. I wished I knew someone who could tell me what actually transpired in psychiatric hours. I wanted to do it right, be the proper patient. No, I wanted to be a brilliant, compelling patient, telling the right kind of stories, asking the right kinds of questions. To give him clues about my ego and my id so he could have the pleasure of unraveling my life for me, if there was anything to unravel, that is. I had to become a great mystery, sprinkling bits of evidence that he could gather to make me whole.

As I've said, I wasn't used to relating my experiences to anybody. Ideas, yes. Scholarly arguments, yes. Imparting information, yes. But not my activities, my life. Even when I was a child, nobody talked much about what I did at school or out playing. Nobody inquired, "What did you learn in school today?" or "Who did you play with today and what did you play?" and it never dawned on me to bring such subjects up. My parents seemed content to be in blissful ignorance of the life I led.

Nobody else was interested either, not even Gramma. She was always kind, but she lived in her mind, taking herself to the happy life she was forced to leave and come to America. I lived in my mind, too, but mine was one of imagining a different world, a future world. We sat long hours together, her knitting

THERAPY, A NOVEL

needles clacking. If she talked at all, it was to recount tales about the Old Country, tales in which she was always the admired one. The things that were valued in Ukraine were of no value to her Americanized children or neighbors. When she wasn't in the mood to talk, I read her *The Forward*, a newspaper written with the letters of the Hebrew alphabet. However, the language that was being spelled was Yiddish, not Hebrew. Hebrew is the language of the Old Testament and is, ironically, related to Arabic. Yiddish is a form of German, a language related to English. In fact, when I had to study Old English in grad school, I was tickled by how much it resembled Yiddish. Gramma could read Yiddish, Hebrew, and Russian, but, for some strange reason, although she spoke English, she never bothered to learn to read it. I know now that was an act of rebellion. Knowing the other alphabets, she could easily have figured out the Roman one. In fact, she had. She must have, because, when she taught me the Cyrillic alphabet, she showed me what letters corresponded to English ones.

In my family, children were just expected to be and to behave and get good grades. Their lives weren't interesting to grown-ups. Childhood held no charms for them, apparently. It was something to be gotten through. Occasionally Aunty Ida would say,"Whatcha doin' today?" but she didn't count because everyone knew she was crazy and nobody liked her anyway, except me. The sharpness of her tongue was legendary. So was her sense of fun, her gift of entering into a child's world of imagination. She was my best playmate. The grownups put up with her because she was family.

Since I never had practice in telling people about my days, even after I was married, it never occurred to me to try to tell my husbands about them, and neither one of them, Hald, the first, or Joe, the second, seemed to feel it any loss, just so long as I didn't demand anything of them. Joe didn't even want to hear about our kids' days, so we never talked about them either. Hald didn't stick around long enough to hear about his kid, my eldest, Sam.

I only walked about three miles that first day. I realized that I was beginning to notice things again. The phoebes on the backyard fence, twitching their long brown tails and calling"feebee."

I felt curiously excited, bubbly under the thick blanket of depression. I was getting ready to live again. And it was meeting that doctor that did it. Not that he said or did anything remarkable to me. He was just himself and that was enough to breathe life into my moribund carcass.

In the kitchen, after the walk, as I boiled water for tea and carefully measured two teaspoons of Earl Grey for the pot, it dawned on me that the doctor would be the type to notice my disarray, my total disregard for fashion. He was as well turned out as a haberdashery salesman. He'd never be attracted to the sloppy fat lady who presented herself to him yesterday.

Where did that thought come from? He was just the doctor, for God's sake, and I sure hadn't been in the market for a man for over thirty years. I reminded myself that there could be no better natured, sweeter person than Joe, my husband. I pushed the errant thought out of my mind. Insanity. Yet, my next visit, I put on some mascara. By the fourth visit, I put on a dress and makeup. But that's getting ahead of myself. Sipping tea in the kitchen that morning, I still didn't even know his name, only that I could hardly wait to see him again.

∞

Chapter Three

At my first meeting with Alex, as I've said, I didn't care what I looked like. For the second one, I knew I looked ugly: uncombed hair, swollen face, fat thighs covered by rumpled none too clean jeans, but I still didn't care too much, which shows you how depressed I was.

My only concession to looks was a dim feeling I had when I was hauling on those old jeans before the second visit, that I'd better put some mascara on my pale red eyelashes, so I did. What was remarkable about my not caring about how ugly I looked is that I had always been so vain since I was a teenager. Normally, I wouldn't go in the back yard without a face full of makeup, my hair brushed and sprayed, my clothes clean, pressed, stylish. Before taking to my bed these past weeks, I wouldn't let my husband or kids see me unmade up, much less would I let a stranger. So coming to the doctor with a naked face and rumpled clothes wasn't me, not the me I'd so carefully constructed for years. That's how badly I was depressed. It was a major breakthrough caring enough about my looks even to put on some mascara for that second visit. That and the dresses I had ordered surreptitiously over the phone. Oh, I had teaching clothes, tailored suits and such, but I thought it would be nice to have some pretty dresses, long skirts and lacy blouses.

The second session began with the same embarrassment as last week's visit. I climbed the stairs with him behind me. Omigod, I'm repeating myself here. Sorry. Anyway, it was a

19

relief to get to the third floor, and to be able to sit in the chair opposite the doctor. He sat himself down and looked expectantly at me, but didn't say a word. He didn't even inquire about how I felt. Clearly, I had to supply all the material for his analysis. I wondered what he did with my answers to the questionnaire of our first visit.

"Where should I begin?" I asked.

"Wherever you want." He leaned forward, bent from the waist, as if in anticipation, eyes intent on my face. His legs were as wide apart as they could go. He had his hands on his thighs, elbows out, a picture of attentiveness. He reminded me of the earnest hopefulness of my puppy when he saw me picking up my keys, putting on my coat, getting ready to leave the house. Like I was all that mattered in the world at that moment.

So I started at the beginning. When I started to talk, a torrent of words welled up from inside, sentences I didn't know were in me, memories I had no memory of.

"I grew up in a large extended family. With no love. My mother and father hated me. My mother hated my father's family. My father hated his bosses and all rich people. My aunts hated everyone, even each other. They had fled to America during the Russian Revolution and the carnage it wrought in their village, but the village they loved—and missed. America was a disappointment. Its myth a gyp.

"We lived in a triple decker, the whole family, Gramma, the aunts and the uncles. There was one flat to every floor, all identical, a kitchen with a pantry off of it, a dining room and a parlor in a straight line, one opening off the other, and two bedrooms and a bathroom. One bedroom was off the dining room, and one off the kitchen. The bathroom also was off the kitchen. No hallways. The typical Providence five room flat. Gramma and my two youngest uncles who were still in high school lived on the first floor. Aunty Ida lived on the second floor along with whoever was renting out the second bedroom, which she had no other use for, since she had no children and her husband was dead. I knew he wasn't killed in the war, and it was a tragedy, his death. I didn't know what he died from. Nobody ever said. Aunty Ida was a participant in some kind of mystery. All I knew is that she still loved Uncle Izzy and cried when she sang

songs about missing someone or seeing them someday in her clear, bell-like soprano voice, her major claim to fame, that and being able to speak four languages. I thought that dead meant he could still come back and that's why she sang songs about seeing him again. Of course, he must be in heaven and maybe that's where she'd see him again. I didn't dare ask her outright. The word *Izzy* was taboo. My mother said if someone asked about him my aunt would go crazy. Again. So I didn't dare. There was only one picture of Uncle Izzy, a short, dark man with bushy hair. The features on his face weren't distinct in the picture so I couldn't see if he was handsome or not. He must have been, though. In the movies everyone in love was good looking. Nobody fell in love with ugly people.

"Izzy had been dead a long time, since before I could remember, but Aunty Ida still mourned him as if it just happened, still cried for him and talked longingly of him as the love of her life, although a new suitor named Abe had already started coming around, bringing flowers, bowing gallantly when she opened the door, commiserating with her about her lost love. He was sixteen years younger than she was, but he was faithful to her his whole life. He loved her being forlorn so that he could be her savior. He didn't pretend that he could make her happy. In fact, he didn't seem to want to. He preferred to wipe her tears away and say, 'Now, now, let's have a glass of tea, some cookies, maybe, dollink. I'm at your service.' His mission in life for the next forty years was to console her. After they were married, he waited on her, counted out her daily pills, cooked her meals, fed her, lived and breathed Aunty Ida.

"I often wondered what the attraction was. Aunty Ida was very pretty, true, but she had a severe limp, something congenital with her hip, I don't know if anyone knew what. I didn't wonder because of the limp, but why would a man want to marry a woman mourning for another man?"

The doctor raised his head and clasped his hands, fingers interlaced, across his chest as he prepared his answer. "You said it yourself. He wanted to be her savior. It made him feel manly and gallant to take care of her. Men are programmed to take care of women, and he found the perfect woman, one who needed a lot of care." When he was through delivering the explanation,

HARRIE ROSE

he leaned forward again, and nodded his head so I would
go on.

"I was sixteen before I realized that"dollink" wasn't a Yiddish
endearment. It was just"darling" with an accent. That was about
when I discovered that Americans drank hot tea from a cup, not
a glass, and they stirred sugar into the tea. They didn't hold a
sugar cube between their front teeth and sip the tea through
it. It was like I was a greenhorn, not a native born American. I
didn't know the first thing about how Americans behaved. My
speech was littered with Yiddish expressions until a group of girls
in high school, Jewish girls who I thought were my friends, one
day in unison mocked me, 'Here's Barbara, azoi shane, with a
meal gibt a gantse shpiel.."

"What does that mean?"

"Here's Barbara who is so pretty, with a meal she gives a whole
story. Actually, I spoke Yiddish before I spoke English, and would
use the Yiddish words when English ones just didn't have the
right punch, if you know what I mean."

"I do. I had Italian speaking grandparents."

"Well," I continued,"it was clear I didn't really belong. I was
too Jewish for the Jewish kids, not to mention for the Christian
ones, and the Christian kids formed their own cliques anyway.
So I tried to change. I overhauled my speech to the point where
I don't remember any Yiddish at all and feel funny even using
the words that have come into English like 'shlep' or 'kibitz'.
But, back to my family. Once Aunty Ida rented her extra bedroom to an old man and his wife, whom we called"Mr. and Mrs.
B," their last name being too complicated to pronounce. Their
main amusement seemed to be to listen to Jack Benny and
Eddie Cantor on the radio, Jewish comedy shows. Mrs. B would
glowingly say over and over in Yiddish, 'A blessing on his head'
whenever either one said something funny. I don't know why I
remember that bit of trivia. Maybe it's because I marveled that
there were people who never had a mean thing to say. People
who even blessed voices on the radio.

"I don't know what happened to Mr. and Mrs. B. They were
like white-haired shadows when they lived there and then one
day they were just gone. People just went in and out of my life
like that. Maybe Uncle Izzy was just gone one day, too.

THERAPY, A NOVEL

"By the time I was six in 1943 the extra room was rented to a sailor's wife who had come to be near her husband who was stationed in Newport. She was a revelation. Jewish, but she didn't speak Yiddish the way the rest of us did, and she drank coffee, not tea, and didn't know about keeping kosher, so she was always mixing up the plates and the flatware, putting the meat dishes with the dairy ones. It was remarkable to me that someone could be Jewish and not know such things. It was my first experience with assimilation, that it was possible. Gramma was scandalized, 'Such a nice girl, but she doesn't know you don't mix meat and milk. She never learned what is to be kosher.' And she'd shake her head in disbelief. 'America,' she'd pronounce. That explained all deviant behavior. 'Deviant' being any way we weren't, although she didn't use that word, of course. The other word she used to sum up non-Jewish behavior was 'goyim' which meant 'gentiles.'"

"I know what goyim means. I went to high school with Jewish kids. So you had to change your whole persona as you grew up," the doctor commented.

"More than that. I had to become what I wasn't, and I had to teach myself what I didn't really know. I didn't have a map. I didn't know what parts of me weren't American. But I did know I had to be more like goyim. In fact, I wished I was a shiksa, a non-Jewish female.

"It was even worse than that when I was really little, before my teens. My family hated me. They couldn't stand me. I guess I was just naturally annoying. I never knew why they didn't like me. I just never could figure out what I was doing wrong, but I did everything wrong. I was always being punished. Compared to that, becoming a Shiksa was easy."

The doctor sat up abruptly and made a dismissive motion with his hands. I noticed he didn't wear a wedding band.

"You blame yourself because your family hated you? How were you 'naturally annoying'? Parents have to correct children, but that doesn't mean the parents hate them or that they are naturally annoying."

"Trust me, they hated me. My mother used to yell at me, 'What did I ever do to be cursed with a daughter like you' and my father just walloped me if I opened my mouth, or sometimes

23

even if I didn't. No, they didn't love me. I was unlovable, I guess. They never had a good word for me or for anything I did."

"Never?" he asked incredulously.

"Yes, I mean never. I'm not exaggerating. Well, for instance, when I was six my mother worked and was never home during the day. Her birthday was in summer, and I decided, I don't know why, to bake her a cake. I had never baked a cake. In fact, I had never cooked, but I took down her Fanny Farmer Cookbook and found a recipe for chocolate cake. I gathered the flour and eggs and baking powder and everything else I needed and just followed the directions carefully. When it said to sift, I remembered my mother putting flour in a gizmo and shaking it into the bowl, so I got the gizmo, the sifter, and sifted the dry ingredients as the recipe directed. When I was through, I poured the batter in the pan, and then realized I couldn't light the oven. It was a gas stove, so I went downstairs to my grandmother's and got my uncle's girlfriend to come upstairs to light the oven. When my mother got home, I proudly presented her with a perfectly baked chocolate cake."

"That sounds pretty amazing. She must have been delighted."

"She took one look at the cake and glanced in the pantry and immediately started yelling at me about dirtying the pantry and that I was never to do such a thing again. I remember in her tirade she asked,

'What right did you have to use the eggs for a cake? Can't I trust you at all?'

"And she whacked me a couple of times and made me clean up."

"Was the cake good?"

"I have no recollection. I don't even know if she ate any of it. I just remember the punishment."

"So I guess you never baked a cake again," he said.

"Oddly enough, I did. Although not as long as I lived in her house. The only domestic thing I'm at all good at is cooking and baking. I make a wicked Devil's food cake. Figures, huh? I mean my mother always bemoaned me, found me worthless and wicked, so I make a wicked cake. God! That's an awful pun. I'm sorry.

THERAPY, A NOVEL

"I don't do pie crusts, though. My mother always made the best pies, with paper-thin crusts that melted in your mouth. Whenever we went to restaurants, she'd order pie, take one bite and then, so loudly everyone in the place could hear, say 'This doesn't hold a candle to my pie crusts' and things like that. I knew better than to try to make a pie myself. There's no way mine could be as good as hers. But, you know, come to think of it, she never baked cakes. Only pies."

"That's a pretty awful story " he said."There's nothing annoying about a child who wants to surprise her mother with a home baked cake. Only a warm and caring child would have done that. And, in those days there weren't even mixes, were there? You had to do it from scratch, and at six years old?

"There is something wrong with a mother who calls her daughter a curse, who yells at her for making her a surprise. You're blaming yourself? You believed her, that you were no good. You should be blaming your mother. You feel depressed. You don't want to get out of bed, to see people. How much of that is because you assume nobody likes you?" With that question, he stood up, walked to the door and held it open for me. As I passed, I realized I was close enough to kiss him. And I wanted to. It had never occurred to me before that I wasn't a disaster. My mother was. It also explained the rage I'd feel burning in me at times when she was criticizing me. How I hated her. Oh my God. I never thought such a thing before. The doctor gave me permission to hate.

His parting question resonated in me. Staying in bed was one way to avoid having to talk to people, which was always trying to me. Teaching didn't really involve interacting. I had a script to follow there. I knew what to say and how. I had written it all down carefully beforehand. I never spoke off the cuff. It was all the other things that left me asea, floundering in uncertainty, certain only that whatever I said would be the wrong thing.

And should I be blaming my mother and father? Was I awful for those flashes of burning hate? They were good parents, worked hard, made sure we ate good food and were clean. My father used to say of other people's misbehaving children,

"They're not being brought up. They're being dragged up."

25

Well, we weren't being dragged up. Our parents took seriously their duty to make us well-behaved, hardworking, and polite.

The doctor's question made thoughts race in my head. I could hardly wait to see him again. Things I didn't know I remembered came unbidden. Wouldn't stop. The memories flowed with no pause. I don't remember driving home. Just hearing vivid voices from long ago. Voices that kept up all night until I slept, and started again as soon as I woke up. So the summer began with a torrent of memory.

"Look how we sacrifice our lives for you!" was my parents' refrain.

Oh, they worked harder than anyone else. They had less than everyone else. They were such hardworking people. They never had the breaks. We had no phone. No refrigerator. But it wasn't because they didn't work. Work was all they did. That and beat us kids up, physically, mentally, verbally. Rip us down. Threaten to take us to Sockanosset, the gloomy stone buildings housing juvenile criminals next to the state prison.

When I was five or six, one Sunday, for what infraction I don't know or don't remember, my father actually threw my brother and me in the back seat of his 1939 wooden sided station wagon—which we called a beach wagon in those days. He drove us to that dreaded place. He was finally going to get rid of us. When we got to the main gates, my mother made a big thing about"Give them another chance" as we sobbed in the rear. So he turned the wagon around and growled at us about"The next time…"

Nobody ever touched me except to hit me when I was growing up. I never told anyone. I was so ashamed. So sure that my very soul was tainted if even my parents couldn't stand me. I carried that burden until my visits with this psychiatrist. A blessing on his head. With all that happened later, still, from the beginning, he made me see my life in a new way. That's what gave me the strength to do what I eventually did. But I'm getting ahead of myself.

Once I was grown and out of their house, my parents underwent a miraculous change. In time, they went out of their way to give me things, things they didn't have, like sterling silver flatware and designer clothes. Even a trip flying first class, no less. After talking with the doctor a few times, it occurred to me

for the first time that was because they were afraid of being abandoned by their children, and being left alone in their old age. So they did the only thing they knew of to keep us around: bought us things.

They started doing that after I eloped with my first husband and they thought they'd lost me forever. Maybe they wouldn't have cared so much but, at the same time, my brother joined the army and left home too. And him, they did care about, their blond and beautiful handsome son. He was overseas, so they couldn't entice him back, but I was only a few states away, within their reach. Or should I say, their grasp. And what havoc they caused, what misery, with that grasp.

In those first days of therapy, the doctor's words repeated themselves over and over again, that I was not to blame for being such a child. It was not that I had failed my parents. They had failed me. I was not necessarily innately obnoxious. Incorrigible, as my mother reiterated to me. What's more, the doctor seemed to like me, to be on my side. Nobody had ever been on my side before. Maybe he would be my Abe. My rescuer. Maybe that's why he became a psychiatrist, to save people. I glowed with warmth for him. I was to see him every Thursday at 5. The intervening days were spent walking or riding my horse on the woodland trails in back of my house, reliving my life, rehearsing what I would say to him, and then telling it to him. Amazing how a few words, the right words, could unleash so much. The silent Barbara sitting on her private volcano, silent no more.

Chapter Four

Pavarotti sang to celestial Aida on the stereo, filling the house with his adoration. I sliced the onions thinly and spread them over the haddock in the baking dish, drizzled extra-virgin olive oil over it, and decorated the top with capers and sliced Kalamata olives, one of my simpler dinner dishes. Joe would be surprised. I hadn't cooked a meal in so long. Now, as he was drinking his pinot grigio, the fish would be baking. I took the boiled potatoes off the stove, drained them, mashed them with their skins still on, and added my secret ingredient, horseradish. Fresh new peas from the greengrocers would round out the meal. I sang along with Aida as I popped them out of their pods. Just a few minutes in boiling water and they were ready. Dessert would be fresh fruit, the first peaches of the season, made into a peach crisp.

When I came home from my therapy visit, my head still buzzing with new possibilities, I called my mother as I did every day.

"How are you? What did you do today? What's new?" I'd ask, and she'd tell me the minutiae of her day, including a health report. I listened without comment, being a good daughter. I had devoted a good portion of my life to alleviating the curse I was to her, giving her presents that were the envy of her women friends, taking her on trips, going shopping for clothes for her even though I detested shopping. I finally figured it out. If you want your children to be good to you in your old age, just make sure you let them know what a disappointment they are to you

29

when they are little. Then they'll spend the rest of their lives trying to make you love them.

Today, for the first time, it occurred to me that she never asked me about my day, my health. If I tried to tell her about my disappointments in my boys and the distance of my relationship with them, she'd only say things like,"You have nobody to blame but yourself" without telling me what I should blame myself for.

My mind kept replaying what the doctor said. I considered the phone call from this new angle. She should be asking me about myself, not just telling me about herself. By now I had sufficiently expiated the sin of being me. Now came the subversive thought that it wasn't a sin after all, a thought that opened the floodgates of emotions I didn't know were in my being. In fact, until they were released, I didn't realize what it was like to be alive. My interior was suffocated, never feeling grief, never feeling joy.

I was never one for reminiscing, for talking about the old days, which, for me, as you can tell, held no nostalgia. Yet, it occurred to me, much of what I insisted on then, up to that summer of therapy with the doctor, was because of what had been in my parents' house.

It was very important to me, in fact essential, to live in a beautiful house with expensive English wallpapers and fine furniture. Everything just so. The latest kitchen appliances. Expensive matching gourmet pots and pans. Matching China dish sets, silver flatware, brocade tablecloths, beautiful porcelain dolls peeking out of corners, bisque angels floating down the walls, impeccably landscaped grounds.

I was always buying new chachkes for the house, remodeling, renovating, replanting. The house could never just be. It had to be perfection. Not just for me, but for my parents. They delighted in bringing their friends over to tour my house, to show it off, as if my success was to their credit. In reality, it was despite them, but they'd never see it that way, I'm sure. My obsession with that house had its roots in my childhood. It was both a rebellion against my dingy childhood flat and a way to show my parents that I turned out to be worthwhile despite their low opinion of me.

THERAPY, A NOVEL

And, of course, the house defined me to guests. See? It said. This is what I deserve, so I must be a deserving person, as well as person of taste. I wanted my children to grow up in a warm and harmonious setting.

My parents' flat was ugly and thrown together. The bookcases in the parlor were old wooden orange cartons. The sofa came of the junkman's wagon, made of horsehair, it was both ugly to look at and scratchy to sit on. For food storage, there was an icebox in the back hall. An iceman trekked up three flights of stairs every few days holding a huge block of ice on his shoulder. The stench of the melting ice stays with me to this day. Iceboxes stank. Our heat in the winter came mostly from the huge kerosene stove in the kitchen. There was a small gas stove in the pantry for cooking, especially in the summer when the kerosene stove was unlit. Kerosene also smells bad. The other rooms in the flats were heated by forced hot air blown through registers in the floor by a coal furnace. Coal has a bad smell, too, and it leaves a layer of dust all over the rooms. Add that to the hate and anger that wafted through that triple decker. No refuge in that house.

That's what I sought in my country home: a refuge. A place of beauty, which was also warm and inviting. A site to nourish the soul. A place that spoke of affection and love. I achieved the beauty, but the effect of it on the family? Apparently that didn't work. This was to be the topic of a session with the psychiatrist.

"When I was growing up," I told him,"the flat we lived in on the third floor had brittle old wallpaper flaking off the walls, ceilings with jagged cracks. The kerosene stove in the kitchen was the warmest spot in the house during the frigid winters. In the summer, the cheap fans my parents placed in the kitchen barely stirred the air on hot, muggy, days. In the evenings after a summer supper, usually consisting of cold borscht with sour cream or herring and cold boiled potatoes with pumpernickel bread, if we were lucky my father would sit in the kitchen on the settle, a kind of backless couch. Wearing only his boxer shorts and a sleeveless undershirt, playing his harmonica and singing in his surprisingly sweet baritone, he invited us all to harmonize with him. Which we did.

"Singing was the only happy time in my childhood. The whole family was musical. We knew how to harmonize, each of us

31

singing our part. When we drove to Boston to visit my mother's family on Sundays, we sang all the way up and back. There was no radio in the car. At dinners on the Sabbath and holy days, we all sang the blessings and the hymns. On Passover, my father and his brothers chanted the entire service at the Seder meal, and the whole family, grandmother, aunts, uncles, cousins, harmonized the hymns at the end of the meal.

"That was sweet and harmonious and that is what kept us bonded to each other. Well, my home in the country looked harmonious and warm, but there were no bonding activities.

"I tried to sing with my children, the only thing from my childhood I cared to repeat, but Joe refused to sing at all. He'd just walk out of the room at the first note. Of course, the kids followed him. Funny. I remember the songs so happily. My brother just remembers them interlarded with sarcasm, a smack in the face, general nastiness. Maybe that's why he went mad and I didn't.

"My brother Stan and I shared the bedroom off the dining room, a small dark room with only one window, a bed for him, a cot for me. The third floor flat was the least desirable. All those steep steps just to get to it. The paltry heat from the coal-fired furnace in the cellar barely heated the rooms in the winter, and in the summer, it was stifling. It seemed right to me that we lived in the worst flat. I expected nothing to be good for us. My mother always told me we had no luck. No *mahzel*, the Yiddish word for *luck*. She made it plain that some very worthwhile people, like her and my father, got nowhere no matter how hard they tried and some others, meaning everyone she knew who had more than she did, had luck and luck was all you needed to get ahead. I had a vague impression that the ones with luck weren't worthwhile.

"'Nobody works as hard as I do,' she'd brag. 'I scrub the clothes in the tub every morning, run down three flights to hang them on the line, get you kids off to school and go to work. I don't play mah-jongg all day like some I could name. But you, you're so lazy, you'll never do what I can do.'

"I heard it over and over, dinning in my ears. There was no way I would ever measure up to my mother. Even my hair wasn't as pretty a red as hers.

THERAPY, A NOVEL

"'Yours is orange. Ugly orange,' she'd say over and over again.

"'Her hair won't keep a banana curl,' she'd complain to the neighbors. 'Look, I spent all morning making Shirley Temple curls and now they're all out! Her hair curls all over her head every which way, but it's so fine it won't keep a neat set of Shirley Temple curls for more than an hour! My hair has a natural wave, and plenty of body. It keeps a set perfectly and it's a deep red. Brick red, would you say? Too bad she doesn't take after me.'"

"How did all this make you feel?" the doctor asked.

I had to think a while about that. How did she make me feel? Angry? No. "Hopeless," I said. "Like there was no way I could live up to what she wanted. I mean, what could I do with my hair? But I had to find some way to please her, some little bit of worth in me. And yet, I saw nothing in her life that I would want to be."

I went on. "My mother sold ladies' shoes in a downtown department store—which blessedly kept her away from me for long hours. She recounted her days like a litany of hardships. How picky the customers were. The woman who tried on ten pairs of shoes and didn't buy any. In those days, the salespeople had to put the shoes on and take them off the customers, and they were paid on commission by how many pairs they sold. Her commissions were good, the highest and all the other salesladies were jealous.

"'Well, if they'd run like me, they'd get more commissions too,' was her comment."

The doctor looked over my head at the old-fashioned clock. "So," he said, standing up, "Your mother was in competition with the people she worked with, and she was in competition with you, too. How did you feel about that? What do you think that did to you?"

I thought about it. How could I be in competition with my mother? Of course, I'd lose. She set the standard and she was the standard. Well, like her coworkers, I didn't run. While she was at work, I spent my time reading book after book, magazines, newspapers, anything with print on it. If I wasn't reading, I was cutting out paper dolls, making up convoluted stories that I had them act out. At other times, I drew pictures and made up stories

33

about them, but so many of my activities were solitary. Was that because I retired from the competition with Mama at an early age? To this day, I dislike playing games, being in competition. Can that be why I am a scholar, engaged in solitary research and writing? Is that why I chose to stay at a small teaching college even though I was offered positions at research universities? My publications merited me the better positions, but I always had excuses for staying where I was, where I was the only person teaching in my field. I had no competition at work.

Yes, the doctor was right. She did set me up as a competitor, one who could never win. She set the standard and the standard was her. I retired from all competition early on. By becoming the kind of scholar I became, I never had to compete, but I could achieve. I could be proud of one area of my life, even though I was hopeless in every other one.

Mama always harped on my getting fat. At the time of my therapy, I didn't really know if I was a fat child or not. For years, I assumed I was. "Don't eat that! You'll get fat!" "If you don't watch out you'll be fat like Gramma!" " Fat girls don't find husbands." Why would Mama keep harping on that unless I was fat?

Skinny, of course was good. No fat under the skin, hence *skinny*. I used to pinch my arms and stomach and thighs to see if just skin got pinched or if something under the skin was in the pinch. There was. What was under the skin must have been the fat. Looking back at the few snapshots of me as a little girl, I see a sturdy child with dimpled knees, but no potbelly, no rolls of fat. To this day, no matter how thin I am, I look at myself and see fat. It's funny because people comment enviously on how thin I am, how tiny. Just the other day, at a birthday party, I was eating a piece of chocolate cake, and two women separately commented,"I'm surprised you eat cake. You're so skinny." Well, I may look skinny to them, but I don't look skinny in the mirror. I can see fat globs on my body, even if nobody else can. I think there's a name for that, probably dysmorphia or something like that. Anyways, there should be a word for seeing yourself as fat when everyone says you're not. I couldn't talk about that to my therapist, though, because he had to think I was thin.

Well, anyways, back to my little girlhood. On good days, if I wasn't engrossed in a book or making up one of my stories, I

THERAPY, A NOVEL

played with the other kids on the block, a whole big gang of girls and boys together, white, colored, Catholic, Jewish, Protestant, Irish, Polish, Russian, Italian, all neighbors. Except for one big Italian area called Federal Hill, Providence's neighborhoods were mixed, racially and ethnically. In our neighborhood, the white mothers worked in stores and factories. The colored ones were domestics. Most of the kids, like Stan and me, didn't have mommies who baked cookies and served them with milk, the way mothers were presented in fifties sitcoms. We were all used to fending for ourselves while our parents were working.

The only stay-at-home mother I knew was Mrs. Reeves, our friends Derek's and Neisha's mother. They were a colored family. *Colored* was the polite term for *African-American* in those days. In general, though, not having to work, that is, having a husband who could support his wife so she could stay at home and clean and cook and play mahjong, that was the ideal, so my mother felt gypped, without mahzel, even with her good commissions.

Still, she had a husband. Someone wanted her and that was better than the fate she predicted for me. "'We'll never marry that one off," she'd say. There was that unfortunate orange hair that curled its own way, the freckled face, the snub nose, the supposedly chubby body, the clumsiness, the stubbornness, the laziness. Whatever I was defined what you shouldn't be if you hoped to be married off. I knew I was hopeless from the start.

The doors were never locked in our neighborhood. People walked into and out of each other's kitchens at will, sitting and chatting a while and then leaving, especially in my grandmother's flat. Few people ventured to the third floor. At Gramma's, my aunts would be sitting on the settle in her kitchen with the table positioned in between the two long windows overlooking the barren, dirt covered back yard, green only in one corner that was planted with Gramma's vegetable plot.

The settle is where everybody sat when they came in to talk, or complain is more like it, that's what their conversation was, one long complaint. The conversation was always the same. Oh, it had a different cast of characters, but it was still the same.

Aunty Sarah, visiting from New York where she lived now, would say,"I met Mrs. Tackicz on Camp Street when I went to Fishbein's to buy some hamburger for supper. Hoity toity.

HARRIE ROSE

On Camp Street, she's all *farputzed* with a hat on, a nice dress. A housedress isn't good enough to go buy some groceries in? And gloves she had on. White gloves." I was sixteen before I realized that *farputzed* wasn't an English word. The closest equivalent to it in English is 'decked out.

Aunty Ida would chime in,"I remember when she didn't have a pot to piss in or a window to throw it out of. She can't fool me with her sweet ways. The way she smiles and says, 'How are you, dear'?"

"Butter wouldn't melt in her mouth,"answered Aunty Sarah.

"She should have all her teeth out but one and that one should have the toothache," my grandmother would respond in Yiddish.

Or,

"Mrs. Klugman was at the trolley stop this morning. She didn't even ask me how I was."

"Well, what do you expect, a woman like that. The wife of a criminal!"

"Vy, vot did 'er 'usband do?" asked my grandmother.

"Oh, Ma, you remember. He got caught picking someone's pocket at a park. He's been in jail for years."

"You'd think they'd be ashamed, but they walk around like nothing's wrong. Barbara here plays with her daughter Leah. It's a shame. Playing with the daughter of a pickpocket."

That was how I found out my friend Leah's father was in jail, although, of course, I never told. Somehow, I sensed that I shouldn't tell anyone bad things about other people. To this day, I don't do that. So much for what children learn from their families. I guess I just learned to be the opposite of what I saw and heard.

"How do they live, the mother and the daughters," my grandmother asked.

"Oh, Mrs. Klugman works in Lane Bryant and supports them. I guess she can afford the rent because she lives in her sister's house. They must give her a break"

"I wonder why she never got a divorce from him. What kind of person stays married to a pickpocket?"

"Well, who else would have her? She's no beauty. She's fat. And with two children. And girls at that."

36

THERAPY, A NOVEL

"She couldn't have any pride, that's all I can say," concluded Aunty Sarah.

Even our next door neighbors, the Katz's weren't exempt from my aunts' sharp tongues, although they always gave me their daughter's outgrown clothes, and always brought over home baked cookies and cakes, and I was free to walk into their house any time and they'd sit and chat with me. They never said bad things about anyone.

"Oh, here comes Mrs. Katz. Doesn't she think we can bake our own cookies? What's she always being so generous for? Something's up her sleeve."

"You know, I heard that her husband tried being a bookie, but he's such a zhlob, he lost money on every bet and had to give it up."

"You got to be pretty stupid not to make money being a bookie"

"Where did they get the money to send their son to medical school? I'd like to know that. Her husband certainly never earned a living, and she wouldn't dirty her hands by working."

Recounting these kinds of conversation to the doctor at our next Thursday session, I remarked. "I learned my lessons well. No matter how nice anyone seemed, they were rotten at the core. You had to probe and pick until you found their faults. If you couldn't say anything bad about someone, you didn't say anything at all. I preferred to say nothing at all."

"That was a wise choice," the doctor said."Do you realize how many factors went into your seeking aloneness? By being alone, you didn't have to compete and you didn't have to tear people down. How do you think you came to the conclusion that you shouldn't rip people down when you had such role models?"

"I've thought about that. I think from books. Even from books like *The Bobbsey Twins*. And I devoured the Louisa May Alcott books. My mother had the whole set from *Little Women* to *Jack and Jill* and I read them over and over from the time I was four or five. I must've read *Heidi* a hundred times. Books taught me to learn how to feel about people, about loyalty and kindness. And remember, the movies back then, like the Andy Hardy and Shirley Temple ones gave powerful lessons in how to be polite, bland Americans.

37

"I think, too, my aunts weren't really role models because I didn't really love Sarah and I knew Aunty Ida wasn't quite right, although I did love her. We saw a lot of my mother's family, too, and they were totally different. Always sweet and soft spoken. Aunty Sarah was hateful to me. I'm ashamed to say it, but my parents were, too. There was nothing for me to bond with except for the singing, of course. And somehow, I always felt different inside from them. I wanted to take care of things. I loved baby dolls that I could rock and pretend to feed and bathe. I loved all the stray animals in our neighborhood, even the pigeons. We had a dog who was my loyal caretaker. You know, I'm a licensed wildlife rehabilitator now. I raise baby raccoons and foxes and birds who have lost their parents. I didn't get any joy from ripping people apart or being cruel and never understood why anybody else did, even someone I did love like Gramma and Aunty Ida.

"Whenever I walked in, Aunty Ida would cackle, 'Look what the cat dragged in.' She called me, 'Monkey Face.' I didn't know if being a Monkey Face was good or bad. Were monkeys cute or ugly?

"Once I told her I wanted the part of the Wicked Witch in a school Halloween play. How I had such a lapse, I don't know. I had already learned that you don't bleed around sharks and Aunty Ida, as much as I loved her, was a shark. She'd never forget anything you said and it all became fodder for her wit. Forever after, she'd ask me 'How's the Wicked Witch?' Or announce 'Here comes the Wicked Witch.'

"Still, Aunty Ida noticed me, even bought me books of paper dolls from time to time. They cost a dime at the Five and Ten, and dimes were precious to her. She worked in a jewelry factory doing what I thought was 'peacework.' This was, after all, wartime. Later I found out that this meant she was paid for every piece she created. She even took homework to do at night at home, gluing velvet on boxes for costume jewelry.

"'I can make one dollar do the work of two,' was her refrain. And she could. She put every cent into war bonds, which is what savings bonds were then, and died a millionaire. I sure don't take after her that way. I spend every cent I can get my hands on.

THERAPY, A NOVEL

"Aunty Ida was always joking with me, sharp, cutting jabs, letting me know what poor stuff I was, but she played games with me, too. She was my most fun grownup. My young uncles, Dave and Dan, didn't count. They weren't quite grownups yet and only sporadically noted my existence, and when they did it was only to make fun of what I couldn't do, like tie my shoelaces so they'd stay tied. At least they made a stab at being comical.

"'Oh, boy, here comes Barbara, falling apart. Hey, Barbara, did you get those spots on your face from falling in mud after you tripped on those laces?' Dave would begin.

"'Yeh, Barbara, d'ya think you'll learn to tie your shoes before you walk down the aisle? Maybe ya think Prince Charming will carry you to the altar, heh?' Dan would continue.

"Since I had been worked over by an expert, my mother, their teasing barely touched me.

"Aunty Ida and I loved to pig out with each other on Gramma's home baked cookies and apple dumplings, what she called *piroshkes*. Once we ate until we both threw up. It was fun in a weird way. My mother hated Aunty Ida though, and she hated Gramma too."

After I left his office, the reel of memories continued. Anger rushed through my childhood house like a hot wind, collecting in eddies in the corners of the rooms. Especially on the third floor. The barely suppressed rage in my father's voice, his voice low, strident, urgent, forming the deep rolling thunder of his anger as he unloaded his always miserable day to my mother. "He says... So I says..." in a never-ending litany of grievance at the world, his boss, his co-workers. They all hated him because he was Jewish, but he wouldn't let them get away with it. By God, he'd fight back; he showed them a thing or two by being so wonderful and smart at his job. Which was welding in the shipyard"for the duration." Everything in the early forties was for the duration. I supposed that meant the war. I knew the war. It was on the news on radio. "Sha! Quiet! We're listening to the news!" I knew the war from the newsreels, too, which showed us how America was fighting to keep democracy all over the world, to give everyone our way of life.

I also knew that when I grew up, I wouldn't have an angry, ugly house. Mine would be like the ones I saw in the movies, with

flowers all around, pretty furniture and happy voices that only said nice things about everyone and everything. I didn't know how I'd get it. In fact, my chances looked downright unpromising, but, looking around me now, it was clear I had fulfilled my dream.

My house was a world away from that dreary childhood flat. There was no settle for anyone to sit and complain on, only beautiful green leather overstuffed chairs in the family room and formal pale yellow velvet Hepplewhite sofas in the living room with nobody to sit on them most of the time.

Next week, when I saw the doctor again, I'd have to tell how I changed my world and the lovely house I lived in now, the house I wanted him to see. How would I manage that? It became my new obsession.

Chapter Five

It was the day for my fifth session with the doctor. My stomach jumped with nervousness. I was so giddy, I couldn't stop singing. I felt high, although it was too soon for the Prozac to have worked. I was scared, too, knowing I could be cast down again easily if he rejected me. I prepared carefully for my visit. After a luxurious bath scented with Shalimar bath oil, I carefully applied makeup: something to hide my freckles, mascara, eyeliner, blusher, lip-liner, gloss. My dress was new, one of those I ordered from the catalogue, a white ankle-length pleated skirt with a matching top that hugged my hourglass shape, showing off my tiny waist and ample bosom. Oh, I had dropped eight pounds between my walking and my obsessive internal dialogue. A pair of white three-inch heels that made my stubby legs look longer completed the outfit.

Then on to the beauty salon in the city where I had my hair cut to form a sleek, straight cap which showed off its silky texture. Finally, my nails were freshly painted. There was no trace of the slovenly Barbara of the past weeks. I hoped he wouldn't find me a pathetic middle-aged lady all gussied up like a young woman. I knew he was a lot younger than I, so that was a possibility. But then there was Abe and Aunty Ida, so maybe the doctor's being younger didn't necessarily mean anything. Moreover, as a psychiatrist, he was a self-appointed rescuer, wasn't he? I was already sure he wanted to rescue me. Boy, did I want to be rescued.

This time when I sat myself down in the waiting room, he appeared briefly at the door and told me to go on up alone while he took the back stairs. I did say before that this was considerate, but, although it was a relief not to have to be climbing stairs with him behind me, I still felt a little gypped. After all, this time I had come prepared with a skirt that wouldn't show off my buttocks. He climbed up the stairs so quickly that when I arrived, his office door was closed. When I knocked, his"Come in" was in a high, excited voice.

I opened the door slowly and walked in, giving him the full view of the transformed me. He just stared, and then grinned as he stroked his beard, gluing his eyes on me as I sidled through the door to get to the cranberry-red chair opposite his. He kept on grinning, apparently not able to take his eyes off me, his white teeth uncovered as he ogled me. Gat-toothed he was like the wife of Bath in Chaucer's tale. Nothing was said. He just smiled and tracked my progress to the chair. Even after I sat down, he kept staring and smiling, saying nothing. Waves of confusion rolled over me. I didn't know what to say, how to sit, or what to do, and still he said nothing, just ogled me in a raw, frankly sexual way.

"Stop looking at me that way," I said. "It makes me uncomfortable."

I curled up in a ball, drew my knees up and buried my face in them, so I couldn't see his face, nor could he see mine. Finally, he cleared his throat and, looked away from me momentarily, asked me something or said something. I couldn't process it. Then he turned back to me with full force. He couldn't not look at me. I know he didn't directly mention my physical transformation, but I don't remember what we talked about that session. Only that a little voice inside of me kept saying joyfully,"He's interested. He's interested." His relentless gaze was unnerving, while at the same time strangely exciting. I tingled under his shining eyes. How those expressive eyes pierced to my roots. No indifference here. Just delight.

My fog was lifting. As we were talking, my eyes turned toward the diploma. To my surprise, I finally could read it. The letters popped out at me. That was when I found out his name was Alexander, well, Alessandro actually. That's the Italian version of Alexander. From that moment on, in my mind he was Alex,

THERAPY, A NOVEL

not"the doctor." It would take a while until I got up the guts to call him that to his face aloud. For now, I repeated"Alex, Alex" to myself, like a teenager. His name was romantic, the name for a lover.

All the next week, as I roamed the curving country roads, my faithful Chow, Ruff, my only company, I forced myself to remember more of my early years and rehearsed some things to tell him. But that wasn't enough! How to let him know I would welcome his advances? For the first time in my life, I really wanted a man. Wanted him to make love to me. To seduce him. And I didn't know how to do that.

When the appointment time rolled around, the secretary told me to go on up alone as the doctor was in his office. Knocking on his door, I was startled by his voice, as high as a soprano's with excitement,"Come in!" This time he didn't stare as long when I came through the door, but he certainly took me in with his interested eyes. I returned his gaze boldly this time, but remained silent.

"Tell me more about your day to day life," he finally asked.

"Well, I live in a beautiful home. My husband designed it. Ten large rooms, but I'm there all alone most of the time. Joe leaves early and comes home late and the children are long gone. We have no visible neighbors. The house is at the end of an 1100-foot driveway surrounded by woods. Nobody can see us coming and going."

I was laying the groundwork for letting him know how easy it would be for him to come to me with nobody knowing. No nosy neighbors. No casual bystanders. Just in case he wanted to come see me.

"Sounds lonely," he remarked, but that's not what I meant to convey.

"I guess some people would think so," I answered, and then paused.

"But I never let myself think about that until you just said it. You know already that I've always been alone. I've chosen aloneness. I'm not lonely because of where the house is. It's beautiful out there. And I do have my animals to tend to. I often just look at my rooms and think how lucky I am to have such a beautiful place when I grew up in such a dreary tenement."

43

Mentioning the tenement one memory presented itself, which I recounted to him.

"I was terribly afraid of men with booming voices. One day, my father's cousin Jack came to the house, and roared a hello to me. I was playing in the yard, and Jack made a grabbing motion towards me. I got panicked and started to run and scream. There was a big rock holding the back door open and as I was running for the house, I tripped over it and gashed my forehead badly. The blood streamed down my face onto my dress and I screamed and screamed until my father came running out of the house. He grabbed my hair, pulled my head back, and smacked me in the face to stop the screaming. I had to go to the doctor's to get stitches, but when I got home, my father beat me for making a scene, for dirtying my dress, for causing him trouble, and for being unfriendly to a cousin."

"Was that usual? The beatings, I mean?" he asked.

"I was always bruised somewhere on my body from beatings, from being pinched hard, and the tenement houses were so close together that the neighbors had to have heard the yelling and crying that went on in my house, but nobody thought anything of that in those days. It was just considered discipline. In my entire childhood, not one person ever touched me except to hit or pinch me or to yank my hair."

"It was that bad?"

"It was that bad. But it was all I knew."

"Do you see any relationship between those circumstances and your depression now? Are you still convinced you have no reason to be depressed? These early experiences get buried in your psyche. They affect how you feel about yourself."

"Good grief! I know that. I've read Freud. In German. But I think I've overcome it all. Look, my parents always said I couldn't go to college. That wasn't for girls. But I went. I got a full four-year tuition scholarship, and I went all the way to my Ph.D., so I showed them. They said I'd never get married because I was too ugly and I was clumsy. I couldn't learn the things girls were supposed to do like knit and embroider, but I got married. Twice. And the second time to someone far better than my father. My father was a fruit peddler and then a welder in the shipyard. I married a lawyer, and that means a lot in a Jewish home."

THERAPY, A NOVEL

"In an Italian one, too." he added. "You must have been a smart little girl. Why wouldn't your parents want you to go to college? The Jews I know want education for their daughters as well as their sons."

"Yes, but the Jews you know aren't from the Old Country or bitter and disappointed in what they found here and what happened there. My family was sour from broken dreams. They ridiculed soft feelings like love or compassion. If you cried, you got hit, and laughed at to boot. They derided me when I took in a pigeon with a broken wing and tried to cure it. You had to be tough and cynical to survive in their world, and, above all, you had to be angry.

"They saw my being smart as a big disability, like having a hunchback or a sixth finger. There's a Yiddish word for a girl who's too verbal. You say she has a *pisk*, which is roughly a big mouth combined with being a smartass, and, in their view, I had a pisk. Worse yet, I learned how to read by the time I was three. Nobody taught me. From what I gather, I just figured it out by matching c-a-t to the picture of a cat, d-o-g to a picture of a dog and so on until I cracked the code."

"Weren't they proud of that?"

"Not that I recall. When it was mentioned, and it wasn't mentioned often, it was as a skill useless in a girl. They cluck clucked that my brother didn't do it. He had to go to school to learn to read. I figure maybe I taught myself to read out of boredom. Except for one doll carriage and one doll to put in it, I didn't have any toys at least not when I was three. Aunty Ida's paper dolls didn't start showing up until after Uncle Izzy died and World War II had already started. Of course, my parents never played games with me or my brother. We were supposed to stay out of their way and not bother them. They were too busy working to makealiving. I thought that was one word, like *swimming* or *knitting*.

"While they were hard at work to makealiving, I did everything wrong. It was a peculiar talent I had. Dishes miraculously broke, papers fell, books landed open so they broke their spines, clothes got dirty and ripped. Most of the time, I didn't know what I was being punished for."

"Why not?"

45

HARRIE ROSE

"Well, for instance, once my parents' friends came to Sunday dinner with their twin sons. My father was carving the chicken, and my brother piped up with 'I want the dark meat.' So I thought it was okay to ask for what I wanted and I said,"I want the white meat." With no warning, my father reached over to me, grabbed my hair, and pulled me across the table, dragging the tablecloth and all the dishes with me, so that they all fell on the floor. He kept pulling me by the hair even after I fell off the table and he dragged me into my bedroom, took off his belt, and beat me until the belt was bloody, all the time yelling something about me and my big mouth."

"That's a horrible memory," my Alex said. "Was he sane? Could he have been drinking?"

"I never thought of that, drinking I mean. He always had a shot glass of whiskey by his place. It could have been that, or maybe he was crazy in those years. I never knew it was possible to love a father. For instance, when I was about eight, I went to get Dotty, a girl who lived across the street. I walked up the three flights of stairs and stood outside her door. 'Dotty' I started to call, but was stopped by the sound of sobbing. 'Oh, Daddy' I thought I heard in the sobs. I listened for a few seconds and then slunk away. About a half hour later, Dotty appeared in the street.

"'I went to get you, but I heard you crying,' I said sympathetically.

"'Crying? I wasn't crying," she responded. 'I was laughing, playing with my Daddy.' I was dumbstruck. It crossed my mind that she was lying, but, truth to tell, she had no marks on her. She didn't look like she had been crying. You know, crying and laughing can sound a lot alike, but it never occurred to me that anybody would be laughing with their parents. That was a revelation too. Something to tuck away in my brain and hold onto for a future life. Daddies who played with their daughters so they laughed and laughed. Daddies who let their daughters sit in their laps, maybe even daddies who hugged their daughters and told them they were pretty. I got glimpses of how it could be from chance observations of friends. Throw in a mix of all the books I devoured and there you have my vision of the family I would have and be part of someday—if I could ever get anybody to marry anyone as ugly as I thought I was and as unworthy.

46

But hope sprang eternal! The books I read all told me that there's a true love for everyone. And that's not counting *True Romances* and *True Love* and *True Confessions*. I wonder what my life would have been if I hadn't been able to read?" I mused. "Thank God for literacy."

"Anyhow, to get back to my family, my brother wasn't nearly the walking disaster I was. Boys were better than girls, anyhow, and Stan, my brother knew how to behave. He was everyone's pet. Blonde and clear skinned, not with ugly red hair and freckles like me."

"Do you have any pictures of yourself as a little girl?"

"I think there are a couple of snapshots. Why?"

"Well, look at them carefully. I don't believe you were an ugly child, no matter what your family said. You're certainly beautiful now."

I felt as if I was hearing angels sing. He thought I was beautiful? My heart even skipped a beat.

"B-but I'm not beautiful. I've always been homely." I said. "Everyone said so."

"Who's everyone? Your aunts? Your parents? You've already said they were poisonous. Didn't any of your boyfriends or your husbands say you were beautiful? You must know you're pretty. You can see yourself in the mirror. Your chiseled features, those big green eyes and the strawberry blonde hair. How can you not know?"

Overwhelmed, I said,"I just never thought of myself as pretty with my freckles. And strawberry blonde hair, is that what my orange hair is?" These were all new thoughts for me."Pretty was never an adjective that I ever thought applied to me."

"How about good? Or warm?" He added.

"Me? I'm a royal pain in the ass to everyone. I always have been.'

"Does your husband think so?"

"I've always been careful with my husbands, both Joe and my first one, never to bother them. I just took care of what I had to and let them do what they want."

"Real pains in the ass aren't so considerate." He answered.

He added,"Don't you discuss things with your husband, like money or the children?"

47

I gave a little laugh"You don't understand about Joe. He handles everything. All the money. And he never wants to discuss anything. If I bring something up, like the kids when they were teenagers, or even when they were little if they weren't doing well in school or something, but he'd just cut me off with 'Is this what tonight is going to be like?'"

"How about with your first husband?"

"Well, there was nothing to discuss. He took charge of where we lived and what we did. Mostly I remember climbing up mountain trails with a backpack, just following him, watching him collect wild mushrooms and herbs or cleaning fish or shooting game. We lived off the land, and I sure had little to contribute to that beyond cooking what he gathered. And, of course, he wasn't around very long after Samuel, my first, was born."

"So you let your husbands do whatever they wanted and never interfered? Why?"

I had to think a while. "I guess I didn't want to lose them, although, of course, in the end I got rid of Hald even though he loved me and fell apart when I rejected him. So I'm not such a good person after all."

"There must have been a reason for you to reject him."

"Yes, I'd had the baby and Hald fell apart."

"Sounds like a topic for another session." he answered, looking at the clock on the far wall, and starting to rise.

He walked over and opened the door, standing there so close I was almost touching him. As I passed him, he looked frankly at me, from head to toe, as if he were examining me. How could I let him know I yearned for him, wanted his touch? I had to plan carefully. I got in my car, all aglow. I had a lot to think about and to rethink. Memories to resuscitate to interpret in a new light. Barbara the pretty? Barbara the nice? Was it possible?

Chapter Six

The first thing to investigate was the matter of being a pretty child. Instead of going home, I went to my mother's house and asked her if she had any pictures of me as a little girl.

"I must," she said,"although we couldn't afford to take as many as you have of your children. Let me look."

She went to the attic and rummaged through cartons of papers and pictures all in a jumble, finally coming up triumphantly with an old black and white snapshot.

"Here. You must have been about three here"

There was an image of a little round-faced girl, looking shyly at the ground, her fingers intertwined below her tummy, one knee displaying a bandage. I could see the small nose and the rosebud mouth, the wispy light hair.

"And here's another when you were seven or eight."

Again, the little girl, face not quite so round, was looking shyly at the ground, and again her fingers were again intertwined below her tummy in a clearly shy pose. No forthright staring in the camera. No confidence in how the world would accept this poor offering of a person.

My astonished ears heard her say as I peered at it,"What an adorable little girl you were."

Me? Monkey-face, adorable?

"Why didn't you ever tell me that then?"

"Oh, Barbara, you always were such an annoying child," she countered. A wave of fury rode over me. How was I annoying?

49

I always tried to be good, to make them like me, not to be ashamed of me.

"You know, Mama, you never miss a chance to criticize me. It's a talent you have."

I turned and left, leaving her flabbergasted

She ran after me. "How could you say such a thing to me?" She asked.

"How could you say such things to me? I was annoying? Why? Because I existed?"

"You talked too much?" she said. "You were a little chatterbox."

"When? When I was two or three? All little kids talk a lot then. It's cute, the things they say, the mistakes they make when they talk. It shows how their little minds are figuring out language. When my kids were little, I loved hearing them talk. Why couldn't you have loved hearing me talk? What was wrong with you as a mother, as a person, for God's sake? I was cute and smart and loving and if you couldn't love me, you were the one with a problem."

I flabbergasted her and myself with this outburst. Alex would be so proud.

"I sure never talked to you by the time I could remember, by the time I was five or have you forgotten that? Can you think of me ever telling you anything about my days as I got older? Did you share the smallest part of my life?"

She looked scared and drawn. Old.

"But I do love you Barbara. You don't know what I was going through those years. Times were hard. I was a little crazy"

"Well, I didn't make them hard for you. I was just a little kid who needed affection and love. And you're not crazy now, are you, but you gave me a gratuitous dig anyway. Maybe you'd better think about what you put me through my whole life. And that includes how you never protected me from Papa."

Anger at her mounted in me. I had deserved a nurturing mother like anyone else, but I never had one, and now she was old and wanted me so she wouldn't be alone.

Alex had asked in one of our sessions, one when I mentioned how much I wanted to die,

"Who are you angry at? Why?"

50

THERAPY, A NOVEL

At that time, I had no answer. Now I did. It was them. Ma and Pa. And, Joe, my fair-haired husband, the wonderful catch I was so lucky to have caught.

All my life, I felt afloat in the world, attached to nobody, knowing nobody really, and nobody really knowing me. In fact, making sure nobody knew me, because if they did, they'd know how awful I was.

Chapter Seven

All week long, as I roamed the country lanes, my anger grew, dispelling the depression. Memories came flooding back. I rehearsed my monologue for my next therapy visit. Early on I was apprised of the evils of being a chatterbox, a "sewing machine" talking too much, and *too much* meant whenever I said anything, but I also learned young never to show emotion, and certainly not to cry. When the broadcast came on December 7th, that the Japanese had bombed Pearl Harbor, we were all in the kitchen. The solemnity of the announcer and the gasps of the adults frightened me and I started to cry. I was barely four.

"What are you crying about?" my father shouted. "I'll give you something to cry about."

"Meyer, she's scared," my mother said, which was odd as she never intervened, never tried to save me from him. When he beat me, she just left the room, but this time she stayed. He smacked me in the face. My cheeks stung "God damned Japs!" He yelled. World War II had begun, and somehow it was my fault.

By then, I had taught myself to read, and by the time I was five, I could read anything, adult books, newspapers, even my father's old college textbooks. AS I said, my parents didn't seem particularly proud of that. After all, being able to read didn't enhance their prospects of getting me married off, the only worthwhile fate they could imagine for a girl. Who wanted a studious wife? A man wants a *balaboosta*, a wife who kept a house so clean you could eat off the floors. Even as a little child, I wondered why

53

anyone would want to eat off the floors. I certainly wasn't going to shine in that department.

At any rate, they never mentioned my precociousness except, in later years, to complain that I hadn't done my chores because I was reading again. My father constantly accused me of "being too big for my britches," of thinking I was so smart, using big words. Worse yet, I couldn't knit, sew, tat, or embroider. Did I mention you had to do those things also if you were a *balaboosta*.

On my next visit to Alex, as I told this story, pangs of misery arose when I recounted again how disvalued I was as a child and teenager. You'd think he'd be sick of hearing it. Tears began to fall. Alex leaned over and handed me some tissues. I couldn't finish the entire story in one session. The rest had to wait until the following week.

What I told him over those two sessions was that my family found me as awkward and useless as a sixth finger, and other children found me too smart, too different, a situation aggravated by the clothes I had to wear, home-made sweaters and dresses, nothing like the other girls' store bought garb.

I fit in nowhere. Nobody wanted me, but I formulated a plan. I would become a teacher and then I wouldn't need a man to support me, and I could read all I wanted. You were nothing if nobody wanted to marry you unless you were a schoolteacher. True, people even made fun of them as in the movies where they were called 'schoolmarms,' but that was better than being just an old maid working in a lowly factory job, an admission to the world that nobody wanted you, that you were terminally undesirable, with no *raison d'être*.

All my teachers were women and not married, but they were respected, looked up to by other grown-ups and they had power over children. It was my secret that I would become a teacher. I knew my family would guffaw if I told them. They'd be sure to point out how stupid an idea that was. How impossible. "Don't be silly," my mother would say."You have to be Irish to be a teacher." In truth, all the teachers in my school had last names like McGinn, Donnelly, Brady, and O'Kelley. Hope lives in young breasts, however, and everyone thought I was Irish with my red hair and freckled face, so I figured they'd make a mistake and let me be a teacher.

THERAPY, A NOVEL

The problem was college. Boys in our family could go. My uncles were both going to go, but girls? My father's favorite comment on that subject was"You don't need a college degree to change diapers." Since he also said no man would ever want to marry me, the illogic of that statement didn't occur to him. But I knew you did need a college degree to become a teacher. My uncles told me they were going to get scholarships because they were smart. Well, I was smart, too. I read a lot and that meant you were smart.

All the kids in the neighborhood and at school stood in awe of how smart I was. When new kids came on the block, I'd be pointed out with a half whispered,"She's smart." Of course, they had to whisper it because it wasn't a good thing like being able to double Dutch with jump ropes, but still smart could get me to college. And it did.

"Did you ever play with other children? Didn't you have any friends at all?" Alex asked.

"At school, not until I was in junior high. Then I met two girls who were bookworms like me and had to wear glasses. They're still my friends. In the neighborhood, all the kids on the block played together. You belonged just because you lived there. Mostly we played war all summer long. The gang of us roved from one grassless, dusty backyard to another behind the houses where we all lived. There were sixteen of us all told with a five year spread in our ages. In war, the girls could only be nurses or spies, while the boys were the soldiers and had guns. I always chose to be a spy, but it meant that I got put up against the garage wall and the soldiers shot me for being a traitor.

"'First, before we shoot you, do you have any last wish?' they'd ask.

"My last wish was 'I wish to live.' Sometimes they shot me anyway. Other times they'd say, 'Okay, you can go, but you can't spy on anyone again.' Either way, I'd then be out of the game because what good was a spy once she's been uncovered? Sometimes I was a German spy and sometimes a Japanese one, but it made no difference in the outcome. Americans didn't have spies so I couldn't get any glory, but still it was better than being a nurse and clucking over Donny, Vinny, and Hugh, three of the boys who always played American soldiers. And nurses ended up

55

HARRIE ROSE

getting killed too. Besides, I was smart so being a spy fitted me. And I loved to climb the big old maple trees that lined our sidewalks. Being a spy gave me the perfect excuse to hide out on a densely leaved branch above where the troops were plotting their next move. Come to think of it, I was a pretty good spy. I'd shinny down the tree trunk as soon as the troops left for enemy country, crouch down low and slink across an alternate route to get to the Germans or the Japanese and whisper to them, 'They'll be coming at ya through the Greenberg's yard. Head them off at the pass.'

"Since I was usually thrown out of the game by late afternoon, it gave me an excuse to go read. Reading was my real life. The public school was numbingly boring, and I never could figure out what I was supposed to be learning there, much less why. Neither could the teachers. From the first grade on, they had me listen to groups of other kids reading aloud, or even correct the spelling tests. In those days, there were thirty-five to forty kids in a classroom, what are now called"special needs" kids included. In my class, we had a girl so palsied she could barely walk, a boy who had fits, and one we were told was a"Mongolian Idiot," but he was sweet even so.

"We lived in the middle of the city, so I could walk the ten blocks to the neighborhood branch of the public library by the time I was six. My mother worked and Gramma rarely left her kitchen, so I walked alone. Often, there were grown-ups on the streets and I would walk up to them. Oddly enough, to these strangers I could talk. I'd be like the little girls I read about in books or saw in the movies. I wasn't me. I would tell them all sorts of things about myself, none of them true. 'Hello,' I started. 'My name is Barbara.' 'What grade are you in,' they'd typically counter, and a whole long conversation resulted, long enough to get me to the library. On the way back, I'd pick up another grownup. It never occurred to me to be afraid. I guess it never occurred to anyone in my family to be afraid for me either. They never said anything about me going to the library or anywhere else in the city alone, just so long as I walked and didn't spend the money for the trolley car. Of course, they didn't know about the strangers I told my stories to.

THERAPY, A NOVEL

"The library was hallowed ground. The smell of books was the sweetest perfume I knew, and the hush inside was as holy as Yom Kippur. I don't remember how many books I took out each week, but it wasn't unusual for me to read a book a day in the summer and almost that during the school year.

"Oddly enough, in our spare, unlovely flat, there was actually a family library. That was why we had to have those wooden orange crates in the parlor. There was nowhere else to keep a bunch of books. In the crates, besides grown-up books was the entire set of Louisa May Alcott's family saga. Not only *Little Women* and *Little Men*, but *Eight Cousins, Rose in Bloom, Jo's Boys, Jack and Jill, An Old-Fashioned girl, A Garland for Girls*, and *Under the Lilacs*. The volumes were very old with the illustrations picturing women with skirts down to their ankles and their hair in buns. There was also a curious volume of *Lightfoot the Leaping Goat*, although I couldn't tell you today what the attraction of that was for me, all about a goat who liked to eat paper labels off of tin cans. The story of Pinocchio, translated from the Italian, not the Walt Disney version, was also in the collection, as was *Heidi*, my all time favorite.

"I especially loved the parts where she lived with her grandfather in the country, and always read those as slowly as I could, savoring each image, racing through her terrible months with Klara in the city. I knew why Heidi felt so trapped by the houses in the city. In my real life I only knew houses lined up in rows the way she described Frankfurt, only in my city the houses were so close you could hear the neighbors talking and arguing. It seemed fitting to me that the crippled Klara began to walk when she visited Heidi and her grandfather in the country. Miraculous cures could only happen there where there was space and flowers and birdsong, things I knew about only from books then, although the day would come when I would experience all that firsthand, not the miracles, but the space and flowers and birdsong, and, for a while at least, I knew what it was to be happy, content.

"How and why these books were in our home collection, I never knew. They couldn't have been bought for me or it would have been mentioned. "Look what we bought for you? Be grateful." Every toy, every pair of shoes was remarked on again and

57

again, over and over, sometimes for years by my occasional bene-
factors. 'Remember the doll carriage?' my father asked for years.
He bought it for me when I was three and it was long gone when
I was ten, but still he asked, 'Remember the doll carriage?' and
often added, 'I didn't have a suit to wear, but I bought you that
carriage.' So I'm sure they didn't buy those books for me, and
I never saw my parents read them, either. Did my mother buy
them from the peddler who drove a horse drawn cart down our
street from time to time? Did they come from her own childhood library? Did she have such a thing? I never thought to ask,
and was never told. Unnecessary information. If it couldn't be
used to make me feel grateful, then why mention it, I guess.

"I read everything in our home library, not just the children's
books. *Gone with the Wind,* several Pearl Buck novels, and a bunch
of Fannie Hursts, among others. Once, when I was about seven,
while sitting on the parlor sofa reading Havelock Ellis' tome on
sex, I asked Aunty Rachel, my mother's fat, lumbering sister, who
lived with us for a time, 'What's syphilis?'

"She leapt from the cot she was lying on in the dining room
just opposite the parlor, the fastest movement I'd ever seen her
make, and demanded,

'What in Hell are you reading?'

"She grabbed the book from my lap where I had rested it. I
was so short that my little legs stuck out in front of me, too short
to bend at the knee while sitting on the sofa. I never saw that
book again, but the others remained. I made sure never to ask a
grownup about anything I was reading again.

"There's not too much to tell about Aunty Rachel besides
that. She lived with us during the war, working in the same shipyard my father welded in. She and my uncles played raucous
games of poker in the kitchen some nights, the few times laughter was heard in our flat. Actually, she came from California, but
couldn't find a husband there, so I guess she thought she might
find one in the shipyard, but she didn't. She finally gave up,
went home, and married 'that jerk' who had wanted to marry her
all along. Most of the time in our house, she lay on that dining
room cot, or she sat at the kitchen table eating or playing poker
with any victims she could find. She loved to suck on cooked
bones from boiled beef or chicken. The dog would sit patiently

THERAPY, A NOVEL

at her feet as she cracked them with her strong teeth. He made little whiny yelps from time to time when she wouldn't share.

"Aunty Rachel was different from my father's wiry, short sisters, towering over them by more than a head, and being about twice as wide. Her devotions to me took the form of making sure I didn't eat too many cookies so I wouldn't get fat. 'Pretend you're eating them, but don't put them in your mouth,' she would admonish. 'Men don't like fat women. You won't find a good husband if you're too fat.' She certainly had reason to know that.

"Maybe because I read so much, the world beyond the pages of a book was blurry. It seems that nobody noticed that I was nearsighted, tripping over stones in the sidewalk or shoes left in the living room. It wasn't until my third grade teacher wrote my mother a note complaining that I didn't do the exercises that were written on the blackboard, that it dawned on someone that I might not be able to see. Actually, nobody in my family had thought of that. Only the teacher did. When my parents got the note, they presumed I was misbehaving in school. Anyhow, no excuses like you're practically blind in my family. They had priorities and obeying in school—and at home—was high on their list. So was not being a bother. Getting called in to confer with a teacher was a bother. If the teacher wanted to see them, then, by God, I must have done something wrong.

'What did you do wrong?' my father demanded.

'Nothing. I don't know.'

'How can you not know what you did? You have to be good, dammit.' That was my father. My mother would never say *dammit*.

'You're a rotten kid. I ought to give you a lickin' you little troublemaker.'

"And he flexed his hand, the spanking one.

'Maybe we should first find out what it's about?' my mother suggested.

'What could it be about?' he shouted. 'The school wants to see us. They wouldn't want to see us if something wasn't wrong. Look, you brat, you'll be good. Keep your nose clean. No child of mine will be a troublemaker. Troublemakers belong in reform school, not my house. You'll behave or I'll take you to reform

59

school, to an orphanage. Look at all we do for you. New shoes every year. Food in your belly. Be grateful. We're raising you up, not dragging you up like some parents.' His face got red as he shouted and he fingered his belt and put his face so close to mine I could smell the nauseating combination of cigars and whiskey while he was working himself up into a bigger and bigger frenzy, all caused by me. I escaped a spanking that time because no concrete offense could be found although I was assured that teacher had better not reveal proof of misconduct or boy, I'd get it when I got home, but I was used to that, getting it, I mean.

"He didn't spank me after the teacher told them I just needed glasses. He wasn't a complete ogre, I guess, but I burned with hatred for him. I didn't even cry at his funeral."

"Why would you," Alex asked indignantly. "He beat you."

"True, and he always ripped me down verbally too, accused me of being a liar, a smart ass. Well, anyway, about the glasses. They were a problem. For one thing, they cost money. For another, they were another thing that ruined my chances at marriage according to my mother. The other kids called me 'Four eyes,' which confirmed my mother's dire predictions about my future, and my uncles teased me about putting me on a street corner with a cup and some pencils so I could use my blindness to advantage.

"Glasses helped me see the blackboard better but they didn't make the exercises on the board any more interesting. Most of what I had to do in school was beyond my comprehension. Well, not comprehension exactly. I just didn't see the sense to it all. Oh, I could do it, but why did I need to know that stuff or do it? But I usually did what my teachers asked anyway. Once I brought home a D in arithmetic and the bruises from the beating didn't fade for days."

I thought about my life even when I wasn't in Alex's office. I had remembered the events around my getting eyeglasses while inspecting a stand of pink wild geraniums growing by the roadside as I was hiking on Old Plainfield Pike. There on that soft blue spring day were the wild geraniums and the Great Solomon's Seal and the joy of moving my legs in rhythm down the piney smelling road. The life in a tenement on Harrison Avenue played in my memory like a half-forgotten dismal movie.

Walking and reading. My lifelong refuges. Now I wandered the roads of the country, but, oddly enough, I wasn't doing any reading. Whenever I tried, memories rushed at me, my life played out like a movie reel. The gang playing war. Getting ice cream from Frank's ice cream truck. That was the high point of every summer day. For three cents, Frank would put a slab of ice cream on a cone which we licked slowly to make it last. Years later, while he was out driving, Stan saw Frank's truck and he chased after it until it stopped. He ran up to it and bought an ice cream cone, anticipating bliss. He licked it ecstatically. It was awful. Thin, not creamy at all and with no taste. Could it have been that way when we all eagerly ingested our cones and thought they were such a treat? Could even my happiest memories have been a fake? What a dirty trick. The bad things were true and the good ones weren't real.

Sipping tea, feeling serene after walking six miles one day, I bandied with the idea of telling Alex about the mixture of shame and pride that went with being a smart girl. I knew I had to come to grips with that, but I desperately wanted him to like me, to love me. He already knew I was truly damaged goods, but apparently that was what he wanted to make better.

Would he see me as arrogant if I mentioned how smart I was, what a great scholar I was? Suppose I introduced the topic by saying,"Alex, you know being smart has always been a blessing and a curse for me. I was always the smartest kid in class as a child, and one of the top ones in college and grad school. Being so superior alienated me from my family and the kids in the neighborhood, and has even made my colleagues standoffish."

Facing those facts was difficult, but I realized now that my unwilling alienation from everyone I met had to be one cause of my depression, so I had to talk about it with him. Yet, didn't it sound stuck-up to claim, in effect, that I was too smart for any-one to like me? He had already said I must have been smart as a child, but did that mean he thought I was super smart? Would he think me benighted for thinking that I was? Maybe it wasn't my intelligence that put people off. Maybe it was just me. Maybe, deep down, I wanted to be alienated. As Alex had so insightfully noted, I learned early to shun competition and, to a degree, most social relationships involved competition.

In truth, I was afraid to bring up that subject because what I really wanted was to go to bed with him. To have him drive up my long driveway on a sunny afternoon, strip me naked at the front door and create wild passion in me. God knows he wasn't a conventional hunk. He was short. Had the smallest feet I'd ever seen in a man, but he exuded sexual energy. I fantasized about his hairy chest. I'd never seen it, but I knew he was coated in black hair. He was virile and vibrant and I wanted him.

Nobody would ever know if I had an affair with him. Joe never came home before eight or nine at night. My kids never dropped in unexpectedly. Neither did my neighbors. My gorgeous house in the woods finally had a purpose beyond being my haven from the world. It was perfect for a tryst.

And, truthfully, I didn't really want to talk to him about me anymore. He woke me up. I knew from his comments that he thought highly of me. From his gaze, I knew he found me sexy. But there were things I couldn't tell him without losing his respect. He was always saying things like,"The kind of person you are..." meaning warm and loving. If he knew, however, certain truths, he wouldn't think I was so warm and loving.

He was Italian, part of a big, loving, close family, I was sure. All the Italians I knew were. And they loved their mothers. They adored them. How could I tell him my own kids didn't love me, didn't even like me. As a mother, I was a total failure. I was an outsider, on nobody's A-list. Not to my colleagues, my neighbors. Worse, I wasn't connected in any deep way even to my own family, my own kids, to Joe.

The hardest blow was undoubtedly the kids. I should have known them so intimately. They were literally a part of me, and when they were little, I knew their every whim, every pain, every disappointment, but now their walls were erected and I had no idea what they thought, how they felt. Even with my colleagues at school, I was at a remove. I wasn't one of them. I was afloat in the world, attached to nobody, knowing nobody really, and nobody really knowing me.

Chapter Six

I had only been going to him for about six weeks when I had this conversation with myself. I wouldn't yet dare call him Alex to his face, but in my internal monologues, he was only Alex. I repeated his name over and over like a lovelorn teenager. One of my problems in talking to him is that I wanted to say,"Alex, do you think..." or"Alex, I just remembered..." but I knew he wouldn't like it. Still I longed to be able to say his name. I contented myself with writing it all pieces of paper, varying my penmanship and printing with each instance of his name. Then, of course, I tore up the papers.

He was clearly one for all proprieties, always so correct in his double-breasted suits and his wing tipped shoes. He often sat with one leg crossed over the other knee, so that one foot was high enough to be in my line of vision. He had the smallest feet I had ever seen on a man, and he wore natty silk stockings. His shoes were polished to a high gloss, a shine that up to now I'd only seen on soldiers in uniform, as shiny as patent leather.

Those shod feet were a perfect contrast to my husband, Joe's. Not only did Joe wear a size twelve, but his shoes were always scuffed and dull. The thought breezed through my mind, Joe's shoes were rather like Joe himself actually. Disheveled, tie awry, pants falling down even though he wore both a belt and suspenders. Even when Joe polished his shoes, which was rare, they were dull. I idly wondered how the doctor got such a high shine on leather.

Sitting in his office, I took a deep breath and tried to explain my isolation without damning myself in the process.

"You know, being Jewish you never really belong?"

He chuckled,"Where I come from, it seemed like the whole world is Jewish."

"Well, not in my life. Even now. The little town I live consists mostly of descendants of the original Protestant settlers of colonial New England. They're perfectly cordial until I tell them I'm Jewish, and immediately their manner changes towards me, they hold me at a remove. They think Jews are a being apart, not quite human, certainly not like them. We were clearly the interlopers. One of the curses I have is I don't look like whatever a Jew is supposed to look like and neither do my husband or kids. We're all fair. We have small noses, but sooner or later we have to admit being Jewish."

"Why?" Alex asked. "Do you feel compelled to bring it up, to announce it?

"No," it usually comes about because people ask things like 'Do you have your Christmas shopping done? Or, 'What church do you go to?' I don't know why I don't just lie and say the shopping is done or that I go to such-and-such a church. Maybe it's stubbornness. When I lived in Maine when I was young, I did go to a Protestant church and not tell people the truth about me, but those good Protestants were no different from Jews. They had the same range of personalities, the same faults, the same pettiness or generosity, and after a while I didn't see why I had to hide being Jewish like it was a dirty secret, so I went back to being Jewish, wearing a star or a mezuzah around my neck, going to Friday night services, the whole thing."

"How about now," he asked. "Do you feel isolated now because you're Jewish? You teach at a Catholic college. What effect does that have? And why did you choose to teach there?"

"Well, they never asked me my religion when I got the job there years ago, and it didn't occur to me to raise the issue, not because I was hiding anything, but they were interested in my work in grad school and what I could teach, that sort of stuff. After I was there a while, a year or two, it occurred to me that they thought I was a Catholic and then I let them know I was

THERAPY, A NOVEL

Jewish. Once I did that people changed in subtle ways. Like they would bring it up all the time. If I ordered a lobster roll for lunch, one would say 'A good Jewish girl like you shouldn't be eating lobster.' One acquaintance kept saying to me things like 'I'm Italian and the Italian's didn't do bad things to Jews the way they did in other European countries.' Well, until he brought it up, I was not in the habit of thinking about what had gone on in Europe with Christians and Jews. I certainly never mentioned it. What happened there was history. I hardly blamed modern Christians for it, so why did he keep mentioning it? Because he didn't wholly accept me as an American?"

"Remarks like that made you feel alienated?" the doctor asked.

"The fact that it kept getting mentioned made me feel like an outsider, but that wasn't all. It wasn't that they were overtly hostile or spouted racist notions. It was just the subtlety of their not letting me really belong, never inviting me to dinner, or to parties even if I invited them to my home. It was remarks made out of the blue, like the time I was walking from the cafeteria with a colleague who suddenly asked, 'Could it be that Jesus was the Messiah of the Gentiles, but that Jews don't need a Messiah to be saved?' Since we had never discussed religion, much less salvation, that was an odd query, it seemed to me. Or when, at lunch, I happened to mention that our family didn't have a telephone or a refrigerator until I was a teenager, the colleague who blurted out, 'Oh, Barbara, I thought you came from a rich family?' Being slow on the uptake, it took a while before I realized he believed the myth that all Jews are rich.

"It reminded me of the time when I was a teenager and somebody asked me if I was Catholic. When I said, 'No, I'm Jewish,' she answered, clearly startled, 'You can't be Jewish. You're nice.' Another time, an acquaintance said,"You're Jewish? But you're so friendly.' I should have answered, 'And I don't even have horns.' Of course, every time I've had to admit that I'm Jewish to strangers, a thrill of fear ripped through my stomach. For years, in my late teens and early twenties, I simply denied it by not admitting it, and nobody guessed. I think part of my feeling of being the outsider everywhere I go is that I'm Jewish."

Even as I said it, I thought, but being an outcast in your own family could do the trick too. It's just that being Jewish and having my parents was a double whammy.

"Coming from where I do, LA, I always thought Jews ran everything. They were the insiders."

"Yes, but LA has the largest population of Jews in the country, even more than New York, but Rhode Island doesn't. In Potterville, we're the only ones."

"Still, what's the conflict? Look how Jews achieve. Look how you've achieved!"

"That's not it." I tried to explain. "They achieved in Germany, too and look what happened to them. You never have had to think of what would happen if concentration camps were operating again. That your children could be murdered just because they're Jews. When I was pregnant, each time, I couldn't help thinking of what would happen to my babies in a concentration camp, if they'd be murdered or tortured, and I actually felt guilty bringing another Jewish child into the world.

"I mean, I missed dying in the Holocaust only because my grandmother left Ukraine a dozen years before I was born. Of course, if she hadn't I wouldn't even have been me because my father wouldn't have met my mother, so I guess that's a stupid reason. However, all the rest of my family there died just because they were Jewish. And knowing how hated your ancestors have been just because they were Jewish, you do get a feeling that there is something wrong with being Jewish even though intellectually you know there isn't."

My voice became high pitched and strident as I talked, positively emotional, no longer flat and low with depression. Despite the grim topic, my depression was clearly lifting. I had feelings again. The lead weight in the pit of my stomach was getting lighter and so was that malaise of not caring about anything.

"Look, I don't know about your family in Italy..."

He interrupted,"They were poor farmers. Why do you think they came here?"

"Well, my grandmother was a poor peasant, but coming here wasn't just for a higher standard of living. She was forced out by pogroms, massacres of Jews for no reason except that they

THERAPY, A NOVEL

were Jews. It's horrible to know that can happen. If it happened there, it could happen here, too."

But Alex couldn't see how I felt, the feeling that my life was based on shaky foundations in a way Christian lives weren't.

"That was then. This is now. Even the Church now says it's wrong to persecute Jews, and in America, they're just too entrenched for that to happen."

He clearly couldn't understand, so I gave up trying to explain. By this time, anyhow, I just wanted to have him make love to me. Instead, I told him about Gramma and how she came to America. I thought he'd find it amusing. In fact, I felt a little like the woman in the Arabian Nights who had to entertain a man by regaling him with stories. If I wanted to see Alex, I had to talk, and if I wanted him to love me, I couldn't be antagonizing him by disagreeing with him.

Still, I couldn't find a way to make the moves on him that I really wanted. Truth to tell, I was getting bored with the whole talking-cure thing. I wanted romance, passion, action, a secret life.

"My father came from a small town in Ukraine, not a shtetl, a place where only Jews lived. One day, in 1919, during the Russian Revolution, White army officers swooped into town Ukraine, Cossacks, the Tsar's army, dreaded by the Jews because of their brutality. Gramma told me that their horses were the most magnificent she'd ever seen. One of the Cossacks called her over to ask,

'Where are the Jews?'

Frightened to her core, she still managed to look calm. She spit on the ground and in her impeccable Ukrainian, snorted,

'Jews? There are no Jews here,' and forced herself to walk away slowly, seemingly nonchalantly, but actually to gather up her children and get them out of her house. Her Christian neighbors took them in, pretending they were their own in the ensuing pogrom. Gramma was lucky. She didn't look Jewish, whatever it means to look Jewish. And Jews didn't have to wear yellow stars for identification then. Gramma figured she might not be so lucky if another pogrom came, so she gathered up my aunts and my father, collected the few coins she possessed, and packed a tin with salamis, bread, and apples. They lived near the Rumanian

67

HARRIE ROSE

border, so she went to the river separating the two countries and bribed a boatman to row them to the opposite shore. He did, but when they got there, he demanded more money.

'I don't have any more,' Gramma insisted.

'Yes you must,' he answered. 'If you don't give me your money, I'll kill you,' he added.

'Then kill me, because I don't have any more,' she insisted.

He didn't kill her or the children, but he wouldn't go, standing guard over them all day and most of the night, intermittently demanding,

'More money. Give me your money.'

Finally, he gave up, got back into his boat, and rowed back to Ukraine. Maybe he didn't have any weapons to kill all four of them. Gramma had buried the money in with the salamis. She knew she'd need it to get to America where my grandfather had gone ten years earlier. So, the boatman deposited Gramma and her children in rural Rumania. Her coins weren't enough for train fare or even to hire a horse and wagon, so it took them two years to work their way to Bucharest where they could contact a Jewish organization that was able to locate my grandfather living a happy life in Providence. With another woman and their son. You can just imagine his chagrin when he was told his wife and three children were on their way to him. I don't know what he did with the other woman, whether or not he had actually gone through a marriage ceremony with her or not, or if she knew that my grandfather was legally married. I can only imagine the tumult when the news was broken to her, but, although my family delighted in telling every single story of treachery and malice possible, they never did elaborate on that one. In any event, my grandmother moved in with my grandfather and proceeded to have two more children with him, my uncles Dave and Dan."

Alex chuckled. "Well, that's quite a story. I can see where you get your persistence, how you've accomplished so much."

"What do you mean? My grandmother was a brave woman."

"Well, Barbara, so are you. You made your way through college and graduate school with no encouragement and in the face of your family's disapproval. You've moved up about ten social notches from your parents, and all on your own. That takes guts

THERAPY, A NOVEL

and persistence. I think you're more like your grandmother than you know."

"I always felt a strong bond with her even though my mother was always ripping her down and calling her a stupid peasant. I look like her, you know. I'm practically her clone.

"I knew she wasn't stupid. She cried a lot. She was obviously depressed all the time. Don't forget, when she left her family, she knew she'd never see them again, never hear their voices. She came from a large, close-knit family with several brothers and sisters, and both of her parents were alive when she left. That's a terrible hole that nothing could fix, and she was in a miserable marriage here, and nobody seemed to appreciate her, but in the old country, she always told me, everyone respected her for her handwork and her pickles. Don't laugh. She made superb pickles, but nobody ever thought to ask her how to do it until she was so old, she forgot exactly how to make them."

Another memory popped into my mind, something I hadn't remembered in years.

"One thing she did, now I guess it'd be funny, but it was completely humiliating to me when I was little. Growing up on a farm, Gramma had a healthy respect for the wonders of manure and whenever a horse drawn wagon clattered down the street, which still happened in the 1940's, she ran out with a dustpan and spatula to scrape the manure off the street. She used it on the tomato and cucumber plants that she grew in our otherwise grassless, dusty back yard. My brother and I were mortified. We could see the other kids laughing and pointing as she scraped up the manure. Nonchalantly, I'd climb a tree and swing on the branches, pretending it wasn't happening. And I would never eat those tomatoes.

"Now I grow my own tomatoes, and, yes, I use manure to fertilize them. 'Gramma, I'm so sorry,' I say to myself as I work my garden. I feel guilty that I was so ashamed of her. She must have felt it."

"You can't feel guilty for being a child," Alex said. "No child wants to be different or have a family that's different from their playmates. Children are the biggest conformists in the world."

69

HARRIE ROSE

His words gave me an odd comfort. The very fact that he wanted to comfort me and not heap blame made me glow. No wonder I was falling in love with him.

Our conversation made me think even more about Gramma. How she would have loved the country roads I walk on every morning, the wildflowers bordering the pavement. Like me, she liked to wander the city streets, although we rarely walked together. I went towards the library. She went, I'm not sure where, but she'd be out a couple of hours alone every day. She had no friends. I wonder what kinds of birds she knew in Ukraine. In Providence there were sparrows and pigeons, robins and goldfinches which we called canaries. Even hummingbirds came into our yard. There was an ancient stand of hollyhocks that attracted them. Dense flocks of ducks and geese flew overhead every Fall and Spring in V formations, but she never compared them to anything she'd known in the old country.

She did talk about having a cow there for milk and chickens and even geese, and how the children used to take them down to the common pasture every day in the summer and go fetch them at night. My aunt once told me that it was amazing how all the animals of the village knew which house to run back to every evening, and that the pigs were always the first ahead of all the other animals and squealed all the way home. Of course, the pigs weren't owned by the Jewish villagers. But nobody ever talked about the birds or natural beauty. Oh, once my father did remark that the water in the ponds was so clear you could see to the bottom when you went fishing.

In her village, Gramma was admired for her handwork. She specialized in embroidery, knitting, and lacework, often creating for the gentry. Besides the concoctions of cable knit sweaters and other homemade items I was forced to wear, she made herself striped sweaters from odds and ends of wool, each stripe a different color and with a different fancy stitch, and she wore these sweaters summer and winter so all the kids on the block saw them and made fun of them behind her back. Just about the time she died in the early 1970's, home crafted goods became the in thing and, to my shock, I actually saw sweaters with multi-colored stripes for sale in expensive boutiques.

THERAPY, A NOVEL

They made me think,"Oh, Gramma, if you'd only lived an-other couple of years. Your stuff would have been all the rage." Then, when I tried to find them, I discovered her children had thrown them all out when they cleaned out her apartment after she died. Nobody valued the sum of what she was. It made the void of her passing doubly deep for me.

As ashamed as I was of her in public, in private she was there, the one person who never criticized me, who never made fun of me, sitting in the kitchen, telling me stories, making the past alive, showing me I belonged to something beyond this city, wip-ing tears from her eyes as she thought of her parents, her broth-ers and sisters.

She must have known she would never hear their voices again the day she escaped into Rumania. You know, that was true for all the Jewish immigrants from Russia. Nobody ever sympathized with her lost life. They had no patience with her old world ways. When I think of it, however, she never used terms of endear-ment to me, never hugged me or kissed me, or complimented me. In that way, she was like the rest of the family. I wonder why? She seemed at least to like me. But then, who hugged or kissed her? Certainly not her children or my mother. My father did say she was different in the old country. That people there kissed and hugged each other. She must have mourned never being touched in America.

Americans pride themselves on what wonderful lives immi-grants lead here, how lucky they are to have followed the beck-oning hand of the Lady Liberty, but they never think about the peasant women who came here with a passel of skills nobody wanted in the U.S.A., women who lost all their status when they became American citizens. Well, I had status when I grew up. I made sure of that, and it didn't depend on woman things like crafts or cooking.

71

Chapter Seven

So here I was, beyond middle age or at least near the end of it. Smitten, engulfed in passion for a man younger than I, a lot younger. I figured the most he could be was in his mid forties, if that. And to be in love with your shrink, that's a cliché. Maybe it was just my imagination, and I knew how unlikely it was, but he made me think he was attracted to me, too.

That he was clearly on my side might not be proof of that. Shrinks are paid to take their patients' sides, but the way he looked at me, with eyes aglow, the way he let me stand close to him at the door for a moment before I left each time, the way his gaze lingered on me as I sidled in each time I entered, the excited way he called out,"Come in" when I knocked, his letting me know I was beautiful. True, he tried to put that objectively, but the very thought that he thought I was beautiful gave me hope.

To let him know how I felt might be to make a fool of myself. That was something I was damned sure never to do ever. I wracked my brains for strategy, for weaving into my tales of life hints of how easy it would be to have an affair with me, how much I wanted it. Would he take the bait, if I could think of bait, that is? I yearned so achingly for him, for him to touch me, hug me, kiss me, make love to me. I was beginning to think of it all the time. My desire for him suffused my days, but what if I made a move, touched his hand, put my arms around his waist, would he shove me away? Deride me for being a silly old lady? Who was I to dare to come on to him? Suppose it was just embarrassing to

73

him. Suppose his interest was truly only professional. After all, he cared professionally. He was simpatico, for sure. However, that's how he made his living. If I made a move and he rebuffed me, could I bear it?

I even wondered if my stories of my childhood were interesting to him. Certainly, my tales weren't fodder for the kinds of case histories psychiatrists publish in their journals. Where was the Oedipus complex or the Electra one? Where was fixation? A merciless superego, a ranting Id? Well, he'd have to make do with my poor past. He could always ask pointed questions to make me see those things in my pedestrian tales, I supposed, although so far he hadn't mentioned a Freudian idea even once. Isn't that what shrinks are supposed to do? To uncover the mess behind the mundane?

Of course, he knew I was married and to a lawyer, a friend of his partner's. That's how I had come to him in the first place. I figured he'd never move in on me unless he knew things weren't so good with Joe. Actually, before I started going to Alex, I always felt I was lucky to have Joe, such a handsome, successful man who had taken me on even though I was what my mother, and needless to say, his, too, called 'damaged goods', a divorcée and with a child to boot.

In the 1950's that wasn't a common occurrence, and the only man you'd hope to get then was someone who was divorced himself with a kid or two, but Joe was young and single, never married before. In fact, he was three years younger than I was, a fact his parents never let him forget, along with the fact that I was, as they put it 'somebody else's leavings.'

There was no rational reason that Joe wanted me. He could have had anybody. He didn't need a woman with baggage. Who would go looking for that? In fact, I bet if someone had tried to set him up with me and got to the "she has a kid" part, he would've said, "No, thanks." He was good-looking, a young law student with a pleasant manner, but he clearly wanted me from the time he first set eyes on me at the party. He stared at me with a blue-eyed intensity that fixated me like a pinned butterfly. I ditched my date that night and went home with Joe and neither of us ever went out on dates with anyone else ever again.

THERAPY, A NOVEL

Love at first sight. Really romantic. But I never felt for him what I felt for Alex. With Alex, I was crazy.

Joe and I were married within the year. In those days, you didn't live together first. You didn't even admit you were sleeping together and you had to do it in a car because unmarried couples couldn't get rooms in motels. We were both grateful to be out of our parents' homes, although we never articulated that to each other, or much of anything else, for that matter. I kept the house, made Samuel be quiet while Joe studied, took care of Joe's clothes and his person, just as I took care of Samuel. Naturally, I cooked gourmet meals on a budget, Joe being an ardent lover of good food. Since he was clerking for a judge at virtually no pay, I was the breadwinner.

By the time he took a job with a large trial firm, I was pregnant with my second son, soon to be followed by the third and the fourth. The *Ladies' Home Journal* made it plain that it was a wife's duty to have the children clean and quiet when her husband came home from a grueling day at the office, with dinner prepared for him, and sweetness and light reigning supreme. I even made sure I had on lipstick and mascara on before he came in the door so I'd remain desirable to him.

"My husband keeps long hours," I told Alex. "He leaves the house before eight-thirty every morning and often doesn't make it home until ten or eleven at night."

"What does he do all that time?"

"Well, if I question him, or at least in the past when I used to comment on it, he'd just snarl, 'I'm busy makingaliving.' He never tells me what he does, what kinds of cases he's working on, whom he sees, nothing. He just comes in. Eats, maybe watches some TV, and goes to bed."

"How about weekends? Vacations?"

"Y'know, we can go hours when we're together without saying a word. He never asks me about my work or my life, and he never tells me about his. He never offers opinions except to say something I've cooked tastes good and he never touches me except for sex. No hugs or kisses or caresses otherwise. He never even holds my hands."

"Have you lived this way for long," Alex asked.

"I really have to think. I've always just accepted him and the way he is, but, in the past, like when the kids were growing up and there were problems, like one wasn't doing well in school, or another was stubborn, if I tried to talk to him about it, he'd just ignore it. If I persisted, he'd say disgustedly, 'Is this what today is going to be like?' If I asked about money, like when he left the firm he'd started out with and struck out on his own, and I asked about what it would do to our finances, he just snapped at me, like it wasn't my business. I guess it actually wasn't. He doled dollars out to me as I needed them and gave me plenty of plastic. Oh, one funny thing, though. He won't let me open bills that come in the mail. Says those are his bailiwick."

Alex responded,"And you accept that, all his control of money? You do earn a salary. Why do you go along with it?"

I answered,"Because I was raised to think husbands are supposed to handle financial matters."

As I said this, it came to me in a blinding flash, that I was raised with the idea that a wife obeyed her husband. She never pried into his affairs. Husbands were supposed to control things. I lived by those dicta. A deep feeling of shame washed over me. How could I have been so stupid so long? The woman's movement was, what, twenty years old?

Alex changed the tack. "You got a Ph.D., and I presume a master's before that. Did you do that after you two were married?"

"Yes, and with children."

"How did you manage?"

"I got a fellowship that paid for a housekeeper and nanny. And I studied nights after the children were asleep."

"Sounds exhausting to me. Didn't Joe help you out at all?"

"A couple of times, and I do mean a couple of times, he did stay with them while I ran to the library on a Sunday. And he'd say to people, 'I let her go to school.' as if it was some big favor. Later on, when I was working and bringing in a good salary, he used to tell visiting friends, 'I let her work to keep her happy,' but his 'letting' me work meant I had to do a full time scholar's work and make sure the house clean and neat and do all the child rearing. A once a week cleaning woman is all I had once I got out of grad school.

"Joe certainly didn't miss out on much. I even made a lot of dinner parties for his friends, cooking everything from scratch.

THERAPY, A NOVEL

Even baking my own bread, and I never asked him to help out with anything. As the kids got older, I was the one who drove them everywhere, made sure they had music lessons, religious lessons, sports activities, the whole deal. Once I asked him to pick up Ethan after his music lesson so I could have a couple of hours to do some writing on a Saturday, and he forgot the poor kid completely. I found out hours later when my mother-in-law called to tell me Joe had forgotten to take something from her house when he visited her with Jed.

'Jed?' I asked.

'You mean Jed and Ethan.'

'No, Ethan wasn't here.' she told me.

"I realized at once that Joe had never picked Ethan up after his lesson, which was in downtown Providence, a kind of seamy place in those days, and we lived way out in the country. I hopped in my car and raced to the city, hoping a police car would stop me so I could go even faster if he'd put on his siren and escort me in, but that didn't happen. When I got to the city, there was Ethan, red-faced, crying. He'd been there for over five hours. Why he never called, I don't know."

"How did you feel about that?"

"I honestly don't know. I was so numb, I never let myself feel. I just figured it was my lot in life and I shouldn't be bothering Joe. But now, telling you about it, I feel angry, resentful. Really mad at Joe. How dare he be so irresponsible with his kids?"

"Wasn't he being irresponsible with you as well?"

"Well, he did always go out to work and make money and that's what a man is supposed to do. Or at least that's how I was raised."

"But still, you were doing the same job as a male professor."

"I know. In fact, my standing joke with my female colleagues is that I needed a wife. But, actually, there were things that Joe did, like fix things around the house, build things. He's very handy and likes to putter."

"Yes, but did he ever help you with your things? Dishes, cooking. You know men with working wives do that from time to time. You say he forgot to pick one of the boys up one time. How much help did he give you with them? Raising four boys must have been a tough job."

77

"Well, looking back on it, I was a married single parent. To tell you how little he was willing to help with the boys, one night when Jed was 9, Solomon, 7, and Ethan, 5, Joe as usual came home late for dinner. The boys were seated at the table, which I'd set prettily with fresh flowers and fan-folded napkins, me ready to start dishing out the food as soon as Daddy came in the door. When he walked in, looked at this homey scenario, he said

'Look, I'm tired of this. I've been working all day and I want to eat my supper in peace without the kids.'

" He didn't add 'without you', but he clearly meant that, too. That was the end of family dinners in our household."

"And you didn't quarrel with that?"

"It didn't occur to me to. I guess I didn't think I deserved any better. I didn't want to lose him and all the articles in magazines, even my own mother, made it clear that if women didn't do what men wanted, their men would leave them. Being dumped by my husband was unbearable to me."

"Why?"

"Cause I'd be alone."

"You could always meet someone else?"

'Yeah," I thought, 'like who?' Middle-aged women, even tall, beautiful ones, ones who didn't intimidate men, couldn't find dates, much less partners. Mama was always telling me about her friends who divorced their husbands and now said, 'If I had known how slim the pickings are, I would never have divorced the bastard.' Joe himself did a lot of divorces for women in their forties and fifties and he commented on how fast even the biggest jerks found new women, but the women couldn't even get dates. Here I was trying to start a love affair with Alex. How could I point out to him that a woman my age was surplus goods? I mean, look how many more older women there are than older men. Could Alex not know the realities of the social landscape? At least with Joe I had someone to go out with, to travel with. I should have answered Alex with something like,"Are you applying for the position?" After all, he kept telling me to dump Joe. Would he be keeping me company if I did?

Chapter Eight

As I was exercising Blaze, my old horse, riding him down a dirt road near my house, a memory popped into my head, a half forgotten incident. In fact, the trigger to my first depression. Yes, I had been depressed before. I had been depressed a lot during my life, but never as bad as this last time.

Come to think of it, I got very depressed when the boys were still in grade school. Part of it was just plain exhaustion and frustration. For one thing, I had a hard time getting to the library to prepare for my lectures, because I had to leave work so early every day to pick up the boys. Remember, this was before computers, before you could call find articles online on all kinds of subjects. So, one day, I suggested to Joe that since he worked every night, perhaps he could leave work early one day a week to pick the boys up at school. That way, I could stay at the library and get research done. He just shrugged it off and said something like 'Are you crazy?' and I shut up.

A few weeks later, we were having dinner with four or five other couples, a dinner I'd prepared single-handedly, with flowers I'd cut and arranged, at the table I had beautifully set, the whole model housewife thing. I was seated at the foot of the table, Joe at the end, and the guests at either side. As usual at such affairs, I was so exhausted I was barely following the conversation. I don't recall what led up to it, but suddenly, it seemed, Joe pointed at me, and laughing said,

"You know what she wants me to do? She wants me to leave work early one day a week to pick up the boys so she can stay at the library to work?"

Everybody got a good laugh, such a good one that he repeated this performance the next few times we had those godawful dinners. I told Alex about this.

"How did you feel about that?"

"Well, the first few times he did that at dinner parties, I just sat there burning with shame, but one day, I heard myself answer, as if the voice was from someone outside of me, floating above my head, 'and what's so terrible about that?' And that started the beginning of war."

"War?"

"Yes, after that, I found myself crying a lot, but also yelling at Joe a lot, demanding that he help me with the boys. That went on for months."

"What happened when you demanded?"

"He still didn't help with them. Worse, he just came home even less. And he stopped having sex with me. Which, at the time, I did miss. A little. I felt like a shrew. Like I couldn't stop complaining to him, yet I knew I shouldn't complain. Good wives are supposed to handle the kids by themselves. If I was sensible, I'd just accept the situation as I always had done, even if it wasn't fair. But at the same time, I was furious at how skewed things were and not in my favor. Sure, I had a career a lot of people envied me for, but I also had to do everything else a mother and wife had to do. Joe's indifference and the injustice to women like me just got to me in a big way. We fought for a whole year, and I have to admit, I was the instigator. I guess I was also foolish. Nothing was going to change. Maybe I just needed to get my rage out of my system. When I think of it, I'm surprised he didn't leave me that year. I still don't know why he didn't."

"Yet you stayed with him."

"What good would it have done not to? I'd just be another lonely divorcee. A two-time loser. And I'd still have the sole care of the kids. Remember, they weren't grown up then. Joe couldn't be trusted to take care of them at all, so what would I be gaining by divorcing him? At least he took care of stuff around

the house. I couldn't manage it there without him. And, let's face it. A married woman has more prestige than a single one."

"We'll have to take this up on our next session," he concluded.

"Dummy," I thought to myself,"Why did you say that? Why didn't you ask him to meet you for a drink. Or say something clever like, 'Well, how about you?'" I should have asked him, in fact I was on the verge of asking him, if he'd like to go out for a drink. He seemed to be sending me messages, but maybe he was just playing with me or I, in my need, was imagining his attraction to me. If I did ask him out, I could be very humiliated. Suppose he laughed at me, or gave me lecture on transference. You know, transference is when the patient falls in love with her shrink. That's all I'd need. Sessions to help me get over transference. That wouldn't solve any of my problems. Besides, I'd be a Freudian cliché.

I plainly didn't know how to go about getting this guy to meet me on a date. I mean, I let him know my relationship with Joe was nil. I lived in an isolated place where nobody would know if he came to see me. I never in my life had come on to a man and didn't have a clue how to do it, or how to be sure he'd welcome my advances. Women are always at the disadvantage. A guy can flirt with her and then, if she responds, he can always be proud that he made a conquest, but also make believe she read him wrong.

Alex seemed to be flirting with me. Looking soulfully in my eyes. When he announced he was going on vacation for a week, he looked straight at my face with a wistful expression for a good two or three minutes. It was as if he was going to say, "Come with me." I don't know why I got that impression, but I did.

At the end of our last visit, as I was walking out the door, he called me, "Barbara..." When I turned around, he was gazing away from me, his hands in his pockets, and said,

"What's it like outside today?"

I answered "Gorgeous. Sunny, but not humid."

I waited. He seemed to hesitate, but he didn't say anything else, nor did he look at me. So, I paused a minute or two, and then just left. I wanted to say, "Come with me" He seemed to be signaling that he wanted to, but I couldn't be sure.

Still and all, Alex's constant asking why I stayed with Joe made me think. Why did I stay with him? The kids had left home. They didn't need to be chauffeured places any more. I think I was just afraid.

If I left, I know that Jed, Solomon, and Ethan would all blame me. They thought Joe was the greatest. He never had tried to discipline them. He'd uncomplainingly bail them out of their teenaged scrapes, some of which involved the cops, I'm ashamed to say. Joe joked with them about everything, took nothing seriously. They definitely preferred him over me. I'd lose them completely. Sammy, on the other hand, would probably be delighted, but he was married now and had his own life. Could he fill my void? Of course not.

Another thing there was no getting away from. I enjoyed my aloneness, but if I got rid of Joe that would extend to things like having someone to go out to dinner with, to travel with, to take weekends in New York with or to go hiking in Vermont with. He did fill the role of escort and that is no small matter.

Yes, I'd long known that Joe didn't value me very much. But that's not news. Only Alex did and he was getting paid to value me. Where was Joe night after night, year after year? No other lawyer I knew worked every night and even on weekends. The answer was plain when I let myself think about it. He must have another woman or other women. We hadn't had sex in years. Except for when we were on vacations, we never talked except about mundane things. Did the house need a new roof? Stuff like that.

Oddly, we always had a good time on trips. We would talk about what we were seeing. Surprisingly, Joe knew a lot about art and architecture, so he analyzed art works and castles with me, enriching my own experiences. He was an indefatigable hiker and was delighted when we were on trails and, after, at the quaint inn we always stayed at, he ate the owner-chef's gourmet meals, analyzing what she had used in the sauces. That was enjoyable too. I wouldn't have anyone else to have those experiences with if I left Joe. I was trading a miserable everyday existence for a few highlights every year.

For my own sake, I analyzed what happened after the incidents at the dinner parties. After a while, my anger got burned

THERAPY, A NOVEL

out, but I started being depressed around that time, although I still functioned. They say depression is buried anger, and I had a lot to be angry about and a lot of people to be angry at.

Nevertheless, I just slogged along for years doing what I had to and burying myself in my writing. I wrote a book and a few articles so I could get promoted. When I wasn't taking care of the boys or cooking, I was holed up in my study. Computers came on the market about then, and I got one very early on and taught myself to use it.

Believe it or not, learning to use a computer was very exciting to me. It was the first time I'd been excited for years. It was like having a crush on someone. It was that exhilarating. I got totally involved in it, learning how to do things on it, loving the smoothness of writing with a word processor. When I started there were no good manuals and schools weren't yet offering classes in computer skills, so I had to figure it all out on my own. I plunged into it, learned operating systems, writing in a whole new way, everything I could get my hands on.

Programs weren't user friendly then. I remember my first word processing program. It came with mimeographed sheets bound in a loose-leaf notebook and could be used with a Zenith computer. The program was so primitive that if you wanted to move the cursor back, you had to key in"control d," and to move it to the right, you had to key"control a." Still I found it very exhilarating. No more writing on yellow pads, laying the pages all over the floor and literally cutting out sections and pasting them to other pages. The little diskettes only held about ten ages of writing, but you could erase, move things around, type over text, all with simple pushes of keys. I thought that computer was the most marvelous thing I'd ever seen. From then on, I became a techie and have been since then.

When I first met Alex, people thought of computers as something adolescent boys were into, not women in their 50's. What I think even the computer industry failed to anticipate was that professors would jump wholeheartedly into the new technology. After all, we had to publish or perish. Once we saw how much easier it is to write on a computer, and to save what we'd written, like our lectures, we all wanted one. I was truly bitten by the bug, spending even more hours holed up in my study, learning

83

figuring out how to do all sorts of things on the computer and, of course, writing and writing. I also met whiz kid computer jocks who troubleshooted issues for me, introduced me to even more of cyberspace. Writing became such a smooth process, from my brains to my fingertips to the keys, I poured out work. Alex was amazed when I told him how much I loved computers. Even then, this wasn't what one expected from middle-aged ladies.

Meanwhile, of course, the kids grew up, and got their licenses so I didn't have to drive them all over the place.

In our sessions, Alex kept pursuing the subject of my marriage. He didn't want to explore my feelings of self-worthlessness. In fact, he didn't want to discuss my early years at all, not even the disaster with Hald and what my parents had done to him. All those fine insights in our early sessions ceased.

Apparently, leaving Joe was the only thing Alex wanted to talk about.

I finally asked him point-blank, "How do you know I'll be any happier if I get a divorce?"

"I don't. I just know it has to be the first step."

He subjected me to a litany that went:.

"Why are you staying married? Why did you stay married in the first place?"

I realize now that this was his way of dominating me. He had to make me do what I was loathe to do. That was the point. That is so often the point with men, isn't it? They have to have power over women, especially women they perceive as intelligent. Then having power is even sweeter.

At the time, however, when I was still trying to seduce him although he was getting tiresome, I looked at him directly, tilting my head as I'd practiced in the mirror, so that my even features looked their loveliest. Yes, by now I knew I was pretty, although until this occurrence, I never traded on it, never thought of it enough to manipulate a relationship or to affect it in any way.

By this time, I knew I was pretty, even recalling an incident I had somehow just put out of my head, a chance sighting. Four incidents came to mind. The first happened when I was still in high school. Walking down the hill to the bus stop, I glimpsed in a mirrored store entryway, three girls walking abreast, and the one in the middle, a very pretty redhead. After we passed the

mirror, I realized with a shock that the pretty girl had to be me as the other two were the friends I was walking with. Strangely, I pushed this incident away and forgot about it for years, I guess because it didn't square with my self-image.

The second event is the one I already mentioned. The girl who sat behind me in college and told me she used to think, 'I bet her hair is even naturally curly."

A third involved a priest I knew. I was attending a wake for a student of mine who'd committed suicide. Crying, I involuntarily put my head on the priest's shoulder. He patted my back, then pushed me away, looked at my face, and said,"Barbara, you're still very pretty." Which was a bizarre reaction now that I think of it.

The last one was when I was talking to a colleague whose last name was Pignelli. She mentioned the first name of her sister. I had a sudden flash of recognition. Christina Pignelli. I asked,"Did your sister go to Classical High School? Is she about my age?"

"Why yes," she said.

The next time we had lunch, she said,"Christina remembered you and how pretty you were."

"Me, pretty?"

I was truly astonished.

"Come on, Barbara, you know you're pretty!" My colleague answered.

So I knew some people thought I was pretty, or had been. Well, actually I knew it intellectually, but I didn't know it emotionally. I felt ugly, just like I felt fat no matter how thin I actually was.

I'd been checking myself out in the mirror at home since Alex, and was fairly sure my face was still pretty enough, if you look at it full front. My profile reminded me of the Wicked Witch of the West. Well anyway, I stared at him full-faced for at least a minute. He locked his eyes onto mine. I took a deep breath and decided that I either had to get up and leave, or tell him why I stayed with Joe. I opted for telling. Besides I wanted to shut him up about it. I knew his insights into my motivations, my insulations, my feelings were valuable and I wanted more of those, not these dreary sessions of nagging.

"Why I stayed was that I couldn't admit to the world my hus-band was so uncaring to me. It was like when I was a kid and I never told anyone about being beaten. I couldn't admit no-body loved me. And y'know, he did do some things, things that seemed loving. It's not that I'm materialistic or anything, but Joe did give me expensive presents, presents that people take as a sign your husband loves you.

"Like he bought me this Cartier watch, this big diamond, and the BMW. He's always game for vacations, to the Caribbean, to Europe, to Alaska. He loves to eat out, go visit New York City. He delighted in buying me new cars, new furniture for the house, taking me to expensive restaurants. Even $600 for a pair of shoes from Sack's. That was our joint activity, our camaraderie. Going places. Spending money.

"When we did talk, except for vacations, that is, it was al-ways about what we were going to buy. Y'know, I find shopping exhilarating."

"That's when you're manic," Alex responded.

I looked up mania that night and was surprised to find that one manifestation of it is spending money, so I guess I was bipo-lar, not just depressed.

I continued,"I mean, our marriage hasn't been a total wash. So I get high on shopping, on getting new things. Well, he did make me high then. He never complained if I spent money on my own, either, like for clothes. And there's the trips we've taken, the places we've been. All that counts, too."

I took a deep breath, and told him straight out, "I think di-vorcing Joe would be a terrible thing for me. If I divorce Joe, I'll be alone. My kids will be loyal to him, not me. At least now I have someone to go out to dinner with and we do get invited out as a couple to a few people I do like to be with. That'd stop if we divorced. I'd just be alone. There's a surplus of middle-aged single women, but not of middle-aged men. Joe will have some-one in a New York minute, if he doesn't already have someone. Then too, Joe is a crackerjack divorce lawyer, a real high powered one"

"That I know," Alex said."He's very good at what he does."

THERAPY, A NOVEL

"Exactly. He'd leave me with nothing. He knows how to hide his assets. I'd have no way to find them. I'd lose everything, my house, everything I've worked so hard for."

"There are other sharp divorce lawyers. He's tops in his league, but there is a league."

"But I'd be alone. An unattached female in her fifties, butt of a thousand jokes. The friends we have, they're couples and if they had to choose who to invite to dinner, they'd choose Joe. He's desirable. A lawyer with a practice. Available for their single women friends. Whatever else is wrong with him, even if he's cheating, he seems to want me. He has never once mentioned leaving me."

Alex nodded his head as if in agreement,

Then he said,"Of course he wants you. The question is, why do you want him? You're unhappy at home and you have been for years. When you came, you said you had no reason to be depressed, but an unhappy marriage is certainly a cause for depression. We have to work on that."

"But I'm not sure I can ever leave Joe, or that I even want to," I repeated.

"We'll see." was his answer.

This time when the hour was up, I stood up as soon as Alex did and walked towards him, stopping just inches from him. He made no move to back away. We just stood there, looking in each other's eyes, but neither of us made a move to touch the other. The moment was suspended. Time didn't seem to move. After what must have been a few minutes, we both walked towards the door. I was elated. He didn't shrink from my nearness. He didn't touch me, either, but at least he didn't move away.

❧

87

Chapter Nine

It was sunny and warm, in the eighties. Perfect late spring weather. My stomach was giddy with joy. Between my infatuation with Alex and the daily treks, I had lost fifteen pounds, and I finally realized that I hadn't been that fat, or really fat at all, before. Joe complained that I looked like a refugee from Auschwitz. I had to buy all new clothes, size petite 0 or even 00—when I could find them. Those are the smallest sizes made anywhere.

Every day, I examined my nude body in the bathroom mirror. How much had my breasts fallen? Were they still plump enough? My waist still curved in and then out to my hips, my hourglass figure intact, although the cellulite was visible in my thighs and my butt had dropped, but not all the way. Good enough I hoped, but the thought of being naked in a bright light before Alex made me queasy. It didn't look so bad in dim light, though. It was agonizing thinking of him being disgusted by my middle-aged body, but it was a chance I was prepared to take.

I conjured up my image of him every morning as I walked, holding imaginary conversations with him, asking him about himself, how he became a psychiatrist, and why. Was he married? Had he ever been? Did he have children? I wanted to know it all, his old girlfriends, his mother, his siblings.

He was vivid in my sights even though he wasn't with me. Small, but neatly proportioned, with a thatch of dark, wavy hair, no signs of baldness yet, a few silver hairs. He had a trimmed, dark-brown beard, and mustache, of course, and wore

horn-rimmed glasses with large, dark-brown eyes peering through them. His nose was straight and chiseled, his lips full and very pink, the chin under the beard jutting out and well rounded. Despite his height, or maybe because of it, he stood erect with an almost military bearing.

But most of all, I conjured up his dark, liquid eyes looking at me at different times with admiration or with concern. As I told him the facts of my dismal life, I had basked in his concern, his interest in me. I wanted that back, and I wanted more of him, too.

I had to let him know that even though I wasn't ready to leave Joe, I was available and it would be awfully easy for us to get together. I was alone all day in the country. Joe never checked up on me. He was, in fact, rarely home until late at night, and wouldn't question me if I didn't come home late, I didn't think. Once in a while, Joe still approached me for sex, which I didn't particularly enjoy. I knew that had to end, and, when it did, I had to convey it somehow to Alex. My instinct was that he would never get involved with me if he thought I was still sleeping with my husband.

I solved that problem neatly the very next day by packing my things up from the bedroom and moving into one upstairs, the one that had been Solomon's when he was still at home. That would be my first announcement the next time I saw Alex. It took Joe two or three days to notice I had vacated our once shared bedroom, and his comment was simply,

"I'm sorry that it's come to this."

Could it be that he still placed some value on our marriage? Strange. As I told Alex the next week,

"He's never home anyways. He's involved in politics. On the weekends he plays golf, goes to Red Sox and Patriots games, and twice a week he plays drunken games of pool in two different leagues. The earliest he gets home is eight or nine at night, usually later, around midnight, even when he doesn't have a meeting. I never know where he is. He doesn't know where I am either. He presumes I'm home, but I don't have to be. He never asks me where I've been even if I come home late at night."

"Are there other women?"

"Possibly. There could be. How would I know?"

It all was true, except I wasn't so sure about the other women. I mean, if it was that, wouldn't I have some hint of it, lipstick on the collar, a credit slip from a fancy restaurant, or something? Isn't that how wives find out? A lack of sex is a sign that a guy has other women. I'd read that once in a magazine. However, I was grateful for his diminished interest in sex and I certainly hadn't been encouraging it for a long time. Now I had effectively stopped it.

All this should have shown Alex how available I actually was. It would be very easy for the two of us to sneak away, for Alex to come to my secluded house, for me to stay in the city in the evenings. As a further incentive, I gave him a catalogue of my college, and said, shyly,

"I can give you a tour of the campus if you'd like."

His head instantly whipped around as he looked at me, eyes wild, broad grin, and in his high excited voice said, "Thank you."

I thought of the catalogue because in an earlier interview, he had asked me, apropos of nothing we'd been talking about, but with his eyes glowing,

"What's it like being a college professor?"

"Umm, I never thought of it. I've just done it so long. Uh, one thing is that it's real ego-busting. You're on view and being judged every minute of every class. I guess in many ways, it's like being a stand-up comic.

"Remember how you used to mock your professors, evaluate them, notice how they moved, how they dressed? Well, that's the way students are.

"Another thing is it's hard getting ideas across that are so entrenched in your own mind. You have to remember that the students don't have, um, I guess you'd call them, the theoretical constructs you've internalized. So, they don't have all the connections to understand certain things, and you have to try to get them to organize ideas into constructs, to see how one idea flows from the other. It's hard. You've got to get into the minds of twenty to thirty kids and present stuff so they can remember it and use it. And, of course, they all have different minds and all have grasped some things but not others, so you have to rephrase, but not so much that it gets boring. It's hard. Exhausting, even.

HARRIE ROSE

"Worse, you never really know if it's going across well until you get their exams, and, of course, until you see how they evaluate you at the end of the semester. Even that is based more on how they like you as a person, if you're funny or not, sympathetic or not, and whether they're getting A's. They don't evaluate you on what they've learned or if they've picked up new skills. I'm not even sure they even know that until years later. Part of what I have to teach is analytical skills so that they can apply theory in real life situations, so how would they—or I know if I've really taught them well. Besides being hard, it's frustrating. It's like working your heart out and never knowing if it makes a difference.

"The other part of being a scholar, though, is that it's about the only way a woman can speak about what she wants to, be positive, even didactic, and it's okay. Where else could I do that? I know it's in the limited sphere of what I teach, but even so, I can freely criticize other scholars in my field, even deride them, and spout forth with my own theories.

"Another great thing is that since I'm teaching about language, and students do know how to speak, they can provide a lot of input, personal experiences, things they've noticed, so there's always an interaction about something I love, and they teach me new things too. The only downside is having to correct papers. That is so boring."

Then I returned the question to him,

"What's it like being a psychiatrist?"

He hesitated a minute and then said vehemently, pointing towards me,

"People lie. They sit in that chair and they lie. They tell you one thing and three months later you find out that's not what happened at all."

Omigod, did he think I could be lying? That I was lying? Stunned, I could only answer weakly,

"They lie? People lie? Why?"

He calmed down and shrugged his shoulders.

"I guess they want you feel sorry for them."

Touché. Is that what he thought of me, too, and of my stories? My legs felt rubbery when I rose at the end of our session.

Maybe that interest I saw in his eyes was only a cultivated professional manner.

Maybe he thought I was a liar, but what did that have to do with his pressuring me to get a divorce?

Chapter Ten

Actually, once Alex was firmly entrenched in my sights, the fog started to lift everywhere. Flowers became iridescent. Birds glittered in their fancy spring feathers. The world became sharp-edged. Like Alex. Some people might think it was the Prozac, but I don't. In fact, I stopped taking it after about a month and I was still giddy with delight, all my senses sharp, my blood effervescent as it rushed through my veins. He was in my thoughts all the time. Long, imagined conversations, manic and delighted ran through my mind as I worked in the gardens, rode Blaze, or hiked on the road.

"Do you know how besotted I am with you?" I imagined myself saying.

"And I with you," would be his response.

"You're the most unusual woman I've ever met. So kind. So warm. So loving. Run away with me."

Variations on this theme occupied my every waking hour. When I saw a scarlet tanager, I heard myself saying,

"Alex, I saw a scarlet tanager. It's bright red. So red it makes a cardinal look drab, and it has solid black wings. It looks like a flying flower."

Or I would be telling him,

"The marsh marigolds are in bloom and the globeflowers. They're such vivid yellows. The wild geraniums are flashing their pink and the toadflax is bright blue."

95

Why I even imagined he would find this conversation inter-esting, much less titillating, I don't know, but spring was explod-ing around me that spring and summer and everything I saw was tied up with my obsession for him. I never imagined that this much emotion could pierce me at this stage of my life. It was like my very first love when I was sixteen, a brief, mad summer inter-lude. A true *amour fou*. I didn't even try to hide how I felt. When I caught glimpses of myself in mirrors, I could see my cheeks were flushed, my eyes glowed, and I couldn't stop smiling. When people spoke to me, I could hear the bubbliness of my voice as I answered.

I sang arias to him when I listened to music, especially the unbridled lyricism of Puccini, the deep, yearning passion.

Se como voi piccina io fossi

O vaghi fior, sempre sempre

My heart would almost break at those *sempres*. Those 'always.'

Vicina potrei stare al mio amor

Allor, dirgli vorrei:

'io penso sempre a te!'

It was a song to a flower, small enough to be put into a lover's pocket:

'If I were tiny like you

Pretty flowers, then I could

Always, always stay close to my love.

Then I should say to him:

'I think of you all the time'

I invoked Alex in my memory every day even though I saw him only once a week. Most of all, I imagined how he'd ap-proach me to make love to me. Would he be shy? That was one scenario. Or aggressive, ripping my bodice as he made for the body underneath? Polite, but firm? God, I hoped not. Excited and overbearing? I didn't know about that either, especially the overbearing part. I wanted feeling, urgency, passion, delight and I wanted it for me, too.

The thoughts stopped only when I was in his office and I could concentrate on him in the flesh, taking in his every word, every inflection. I trotted out my meager memories. As our ses-sions progressed, however, the memories grew, and remembered

more and more, even when I wasn't with him. My past was playing in full color on the screen of my mind and I couldn't turn it off. The only thing he condemned was my decision to stay with Joe.

I was even reliving my therapy sessions. I remembered that one day, it must have been near the end of May, our talk had gone well. No wretched memories, I was sure, but I don't recall exactly what we did talk about. The Catskills, I think, and how he'd once gone there on a medical convention and that I was going there with my in-laws for a weekend.

What I did remember vividly, however, was the glow in his eyes as we chatted, and when the hour was up, how he got up and raced to the door to open it. Then, with an openmouthed smile, stared straight into my face. He was blocking the door so I couldn't get out. Meanwhile, his eyes remained fixed on my face as if he was searching for something.

I thought I knew what he was looking for. To see if I had any lines at all or any signs of sagging. I didn't. My face was as tight as a thirty-five year old's. Not because I did anything to it. Just heredity. My grandmother died at 85 and didn't have a line on her face, although, by that age, she did have pouches under her eyes and the skin at her jawbone was sagging. I could imagine Alex excitedly telling a buddy,

"You wouldn't believe it. She's fifty-two, but she hasn't got a line in her face, not a wrinkle anywhere."

To be honest, my face did have a looseness to it and around my lips, pucker lines were making their appearance. But I knew I still had a youthful face, mostly because of the involuntary start people gave when I told them my age. However, I now also know that everyone thinks they look younger than they are.

Of course, what Alex couldn't see were the ravages of age and childbearing on my body: the dropped ass, the cellulite, the varicose veins that made my legs look like a topographical map of the Mississippi River. I still worried about those things, what I could do about them if I finally managed to seduce him. I went to fancy lingerie stores and tried on negligees and lacy bras and panties, looking for ways to minimize the damage of the years.

After that day, the day his eyes shone on me and he looked so openly for lines on my face, I began experimenting at home

HARRIE ROSE

with different lighting when I was in my nightgown, looking to see which lamps and which levels of brightness camouflaged the dimpling in my thighs. I began exercising with weights to firm up my breasts. Daily hikes were firming up my derriere, so all in all by the time I seduced him, if I could, my body should look, well not thirty-five, but not so hopelessly fifty-two either.

I toyed with the idea of joining the university gym because it didn't have separate dressing stalls in the women's dressing room and I figured I'd be able to catch a glimpse of other women's bodies and see how I stacked up against women in their thirties and forties. After all, if he was to have a sexual encounter, it wouldn't necessarily be with a twenty year old, would it? I didn't quite get up the courage to join, however. Besides, I hate the very smell of gyms and formal working out.

Walking was fine because I could daydream while I was doing it and it was late spring and the countryside had come alive, a feast for the senses. Feeling the soft, balmy air, hearing the birds singing their territorial possession and their wooing of mates, smelling the earth reborn and fertile, fingering the texture of new leaves, seeing the panoply of wild flowers, new ones bursting forth each week, now the white of the wild dogwoods, the earlier flowering trees having retired in the ever-changing New England landscape.

Unexpectedly I did get a chance to see a naked woman in her young forties, two actually. One was a colleague from school. I was her roommate when we both attended a conference out of town and as we got ready for bed, avidly gossiping about our male colleagues, she undressed without covering herself, so I could compare what I had to her. Frankly, mine was as good if not better. My thighs might be rippled like cottage cheese, but her stomach and hips were as well and her tits drooped as much as mine. Actually, more so. Mine hadn't fallen all the way down yet. I was surprised that her little ones hung down, not upright at all or ending with a rounded swell as mine did. Frankly, hers looked like two drooping frankfurters. Mine were like gently bowing melons. Her upper arms had loose flesh dripping from them. And her skin was covered with purple and red discolorations. Not a pretty sight.

The second sighting wasn't any better. Or should I say 'worse'? I had invited a forty-two year old female lawyer friend of Joe's to our house on a hot day so we could go skinny dipping in my pool.

Among other things, I discovered that what I thought was her natural platinum blonde hair was given the lie by the black hair of her bush. It was rather a comical sight, actually, the pale hair on top and the dark between the legs. She also drooped all over with dimply skin.

Once I saw these two females, I was ready to make a move on Alex, assured that I could compete with any forty-year-old females, maybe even ones in their late thirties, but I still didn't know how to proceed. How do you seduce a man if he doesn't make a move toward seducing you? Oh, I was sure he wanted to. Those glowing eyes, those ogling looks, that checking me out. I was filled with excitement all the time. The depression was gone. I didn't want to stay in bed anymore and I lived for my sessions with Alex.

My mind raced between visits. How could I let him know how I felt without making a fool of myself? I had already told him that I had moved to an upstairs bedroom, leaving Joe in the Master suite downstairs. Now I had to convey that Joe and I no longer had sex. Alex had to know that, I figured, before I could seduce him. After all, he might have scruples.

I casually dropped that information on our next visit.

"I don't sleep with my Joe any more. I've told him 'no more'"

Actually, I never had to tell Joe 'no more' outright. I just had to be busy reading a book. As I said, his interest in me had waned. Now that I think of it, it waned when I started to be more independent, not cooking for him or cleaning up after him. Therapy was beginning to work, and I was not the obedient wifey-wife any more.

When I told Alex that I didn't want to be physical with Joe any more, Alex had been looking down, but his head snapped right up, although he still didn't say anything. I didn't elaborate. Let it sink in, I thought. He couldn't be dense enough not to miss my invitation.

A rare silence ensued. Finally, he broke it by saying yet again,

"You're not happy at home. Your marriage is moribund. You have a career of your own. Why do you insist on staying married? It's a charade."

"I told you. I'd be alone. All alone."

"We have to work on those issues," he said.

But something happened to shatter my complacency before the next visit. As I walked in after that incident, struggling to fight back tears, I told Alex,

"It's been a horrible week. When I told you Joe could be seeing another woman, I said it as a flip joke. I didn't think that for a minute. I never, ever cheated on him. I never thought that was a decent thing to do and somehow I never believed he would do it either. I know this sounds dumb," I said to Alex,"but it never occurred to me to suspect him, until the other night when I called him and asked him to pick up a prescription for me, something he always does, but he said he couldn't and he said it angrily. His excuse was that he had to meet someone in another lawyer's office at 8:30 P.M., so he told me to go get my own pills. Who could he meet at that hour? Surely, other lawyer's offices were closed by then."

Alex nodded yes. He didn't bother to ask why I even cared, thank heavens. I myself was amazed that I cared so much. I think that with all the negligence, all the non-caring that Joe treated me with, at least I had the dignity of believing he never cheated on me. At the very least, he kept his marriage vows.

"Could I have been so duped all these years? He wasn't working all those nights? How dumb I've been."

Alex looked at me with great, pitying eyes.

"An old story. You were always faithful and you couldn't imagine that he wasn't."

Again, the emotion in his eyes directed at me, set me aquiver. No dead depression now. My mind raced. That fiction I maintained all these years, the fiction that I had the perfect husband, would be exploded. People would see me as what I was, a reject. All the self-esteem Alex had instilled in me was shattered.

"It's worse than that," I told Alex. "I can't admit to the world that he doesn't want me. When I met Joe, it was amazing. Everyone thought he was so wonderful, so good-natured, so easy-going, such a good man. This is who had chosen me. I had pulled off the coup of the century when I landed him. For me to get him at all was a miracle, a divorcée with a baby! Now it's

common, but back then that was a scandal. When our engagement was announced, his mother kept crying,

'The whole world has to know'

"His whole family refused to come to our wedding. He even had friends who told him,

'Whaddya want someone else's kid for?'

In fact, Joe broke one guy's nose because he said,

'Look, man, she's been married. You can screw her, but why marry her?'

"Before I met Joe, my mother hammered away at me,

'You're just lucky Papa and I let you and Sammy live here and you can work in our store, so you have a roof over you and food to eat. We take care of Sammy for you and let you go to college so you can be a teacher and support him. We don't take rent from you or food money. I even buy you clothes at your age. How many parents would take in a grown girl, a girl who ran off and got married?'"

Needless to say, what she said was true—to a point—but the incessant repetition was certainly not needed. I was hardly living in the lap of luxury or in an aura of sweetness and light. Before I met Joe and I could see that liberation was over the horizon, the only sweetness in my life was Sammy, that beautiful, incredible, wonderful baby. I never knew how much I could love another human being until I had him, and I understood why mother bears try to kill anybody who comes near their cubs.

Of course, it was for Sammy that I became a prisoner in their house. My parents adored him, determined to wipe out their sins against their own children by being to kind to him. To me, their message was different. Be grateful, be grateful, and be grateful. Be grateful for the cramped, cheerless room I shared with little Sammy in my parents' cramped, cheerless house while I was going to college. At least, I had won on that point. I was going to college to become a teacher. In those days, the state school of education was free, so even though I was on Welfare, I could afford it.

My senior year was made sweeter because I had proved them wrong with Joe. Just the fact that someone worthwhile wanted me was a boost to my tattered ego. Joe was someone who in

anyone's eyes was a catch. And I truly loved him for himself. He was witty and smart and handsome. God, he was handsome with those sapphire blue eyes, hair in blond buzz cut, full lips, and the widest white-toothed smile. No edges, just an easy-going, jovial nature. Whoever you were was okay with him. He never put anyone down or dissected his or her weaknesses or faults. His generosity was exceptional, not only generosity about money or things, but also generosity of feeling for others, for excusing them, of accepting them as they were. It took many years until I realized that at its core, this acceptance was really indifference.

During those early months, indeed for many years afterwards, I felt like dancing a jig in front of Mama and Papa, and chanting,

"Nah, nah, nah, nah, nah, I got a feller and Mama, a better one than you ever did. A better one than Papa ever predicted. A better one than Papa was. Boy, were you all wrong, wrong, wrong. Someone did want me, used goods and all. And he loves me like you never liked me and he's proud of me, how smart I am and how pretty I am..."

But, of course, I never dared to say it. I just did the goddamned ironing for the family. Mama was on a rollercoaster of emotion after Joe and I started dating. She was so proud of Joe, so handsome, a professional, and Jewish, to boot. He was someone to brag to her friends about!

But she was also so jealous of me she could hardly stand it. One night, Joe and I had a date to go to a movie. We assumed that, as usual, Mama would babysit Sammy. When I told her we'd be going out as soon as I finished cleaning up after dinner, she exploded,

'You go out all the time and leave me to babysit. What do you think I am, your servant? Maybe I want to go out, too! I'm sick of this."

Well, it was hardly my fault that Papa had a Masonic meeting that evening so Mama couldn't go out with him.

Actually, it became pretty clear that it wasn't Papa she wanted to spend the evening with. Did she expect me to stay home and have Joe take her out? Apparently, she did, because she got all decked out in a new dress, made up her face with blusher, mascara, and black eyeliner, wore nylons and high-heeled shoes, put

THERAPY, A NOVEL

her hair up in a fancy do, and parked herself on a living room chair opposite the sofa.

When Joe came over, she was seated so he couldn't avoid making eye contact with her. Watching this bizarre scene as I sat next to Joe, I finally understood what the expression "batting her eyelashes" meant.

"Egads! I thought, "How Bette Davis can you get?"

At the time, I was mortified at her ludicrous attempt to seduce my fiancée, but now I see how pathetic she really was. She was never a pretty woman. Thinking about that absurd incident now, I realized that, not only did she have designs on Joe, she couldn't take how pretty I was. That is, once it penetrated my consciousness that I was pretty, thanks to Alex. That's why she was always ripping me down. Alex's insights into Mama as a competitor took the blinders off my eyes.

Even after thirty years, I never told my parents one bad thing about Joe, his neglect, nothing. Just that we were happily married. Long after the bloom had worn off the relationship, I never could bring myself to criticize Joe especially to my parents. I couldn't let them have the satisfaction that, after all, I hadn't gotten such a wonderful guy, or that maybe I deserved his indifference.

I finally told Joe about Mama's Bette Davis show, and also commented that I didn't dare tell her how bad things were with Joe because I knew she'd use it as an excuse to rip me down again.

"Isn't it time you stopped caring about your mother's tongue? It's finally occurred to you she's jealous of you. Even when you were little, she must have proud of how cute and smart you were, but she couldn't stand that either. It's evident from the pictures you showed me that you were prettier than she ever was, and as you grew up, that was even harder for her to take. Why do you think she was always bragging to you about how men flocked to her, but no man would ever want you? She was really fat and lumpy and you..." his voice trailed off as he caught himself.

"You've described yourself to me as fat, but you're not ad, from the pictures, you never were. You have—and had—body image problems. What did you weigh as a teenager? Maybe ninety pounds? You topped her in every way, even as a child. Later, in education, career, even your marriage. The pictures of

103

Hald. He was certainly very good looking. He looked like a male model. So even that undesirable marriage was to a handsome man, so you topped her there, too, didn't you? You told me yourself how when you were little she always rubbed it into you that you couldn't measure up to her, but you did, and you surpassed her. And, it's not necessarily that Joe rejected you. You've clearly rejected him, burying yourself in your own work all these years. This is not the end of the world."

"But I'll be alone." I said again. "Alone."

"How did you meet Joe, anyway?"

Alex changed the subject. He must've been sick of hearing about my aloneness.

"At one of my classmate's parties, the only one I was ever invited to actually, since I was somewhat of a pariah in college. I was older than the others were and I had a kid. You should've heard my mother when Joe brought me home from that party.

'Oh, what a gorgeous guy' she actually crowed. 'And he's in law school. But be sensible, Barbara. Don't expect anything to come of this? What does he want you for, a boy like that who could get anyone. He must figure that since you had been married, you must be easy. You know what I mean. He'll use you until he finds the right girl, so don't fall in love with him.'

"I was appalled. She was telling me he wanted only one thing and that was all I was good for. She didn't let it go, practically until we got married. At first, she'd taunt me,

'He wants you for one thing. Don't get your hopes up with that one. Maybe you'll be lucky and find a widower.' But I noticed how carefully she made herself up whenever he came to call and how often she commented on the startling blue of his eyes. And if she really thought that all he wanted was sex, then why didn't she object to my going out with him at all? I mean, was she telling me to prostitute myself because that was the best I was ever going to do?

"Anyway, he did marry me, obviously, just about a year after we met. He certainly wanted to marry me, even though he risked never seeing his family again. They just about threw him out when he told them we were engaged. His father told him not to dare to invite any of his aunts or cousins to the wedding because,

THERAPY, A NOVEL

if he did, then his father said he'd go to New York and personally tell everyone not to come to the wedding. His mother actually accused me of 'manipulating' her son because I knew 'how.' I was smart and 'knew how to trap an innocent boy like Joe.' Like I was Cleopatra, maybe.

"My parents painted me as a cast-off nobody would want and his parents saw me as a wicked seductress who preyed on innocent young men. Both sets of parents reduced our love to nothing more than lust and illicit sex. I felt baffled and ashamed, even though I hadn't done anything wrong. Joe certainly wanted me for more than sex, so far as I could see. You know, there's a snapshot of me in my robes when I got my doctorate, and Joe with his arm around me with an expression of such pride on his face. He always bragged about me to other people, about what I published or where I was invited to give a paper."

As for my suspicions that Joe was now fooling around, Alex commented,

"It could be the best thing ever to happen to you."

No, I thought to myself. If you made love to me, that would be the best thing. Funny that now I wanted to stray myself, for the first time I realized that Joe might have already done the same thing. Perhaps many times. What I said aloud was,

"I have to hire a private eye, I guess, and find out what Joe is doing in his spare time."

Inwardly, I intensified my resolve to get Alex to come to me away from these office visits. Ironically, I was doing with Alex what Joe's mother presumed I had done with Joe. I was actually trying to think of how I could seduce him. This was so unthinkably not me! I had never in my life really flirted with a male, much less tried to seduce him. Not that I was such a goody-goody. I was afraid of making a fool of myself. Was this a good thing, my coming on to Alex, or a bad thing?

With Joe, that certainly didn't happen. I never thought in those terms, and my biggest fear was that he would only want me for sex until he found himself a wife, so, if anything, I was as unsexy as possible with Joe. In those days, you couldn't go to a motel if you weren't married. We certainly couldn't have sex in my parents' house, especially with Sammy there. Joe's car was a two-seater Studebaker with an old-fashioned stick shift that came

105

right between the two front seats. Maybe the thought of having sex comfortably in our own bed hastened our getting married, but sex was not the main reason for it. We really wanted to be together.

One evening I made Joe my homemade spaghetti sauce with meatballs. I was babysitting for my nephew in my brother's flat. I had to serve it in their kitchen on a picnic table with attached benches. Actually, the table was constructed to have half a table with an attached bench on each side with latches on top holding it together. As soon as we sat down, the latches gave way and the table started to come apart, depositing us on the floor. Fortunately, Joe grabbed the platter before the spaghetti slithered out, and, laughing, we ate sitting on the linoleum.

Joe had never tasted pasta so delicious.

"You can cook for me for the rest of my life," he repeated over and over. Then came the dessert: brownie pudding, my specialty.

That elicited,"You can cook for me for eternity!"

We were both very ready to leave our parents' domiciles. That was another powerful motivator. And, we were genuinely in love with each other. We wanted to wake up together every morning. Besides, as I said, I was no seductress. I was a typical 50's virgin when I met Hald.

The whole sexual revolution of the 60's was nowhere in sight then. The thought of having sex with anybody except my husband made my stomach flutter as if it were populated by squirrels. The shame of it. It just couldn't happen.

Now, at 52, suddenly, I was released of inhibition. Maybe because of the way Alex ogled me, the lust so evident in his eyes. I really felt attractive. It wasn't something I intellectually knew. I hoped he could see the lust in my eyes, but I guess I just didn't know how to show it. I knew he thought I was pretty. He told me so. He also told me in such admiring ways "the kind of person you are..., so warm..., so bright...."

Once, as a gift I gave him one of the books I'd written, thinking he would find it interesting. He took it from my hands almost reverently. His eyes glowed as he received it. He was clearly impressed.

"'I'll start reading it tonight," he promised.

THERAPY, A NOVEL

Then he looked into my eyes, his eyes glowing with what? Love?

You know, it's funny how women are—and were—always told to be sure not to let a man know she's smart and that there's nothing more off-putting than an intelligent female. However, I've come to realize that's not quite so. Men feel honored if an intelligent woman chooses them. It's a feather in their cap. It makes them feel more intelligent.

Years after these sessions with Alex, a colleague of mine and her husband came to hang out by the pool at my house. Fred, her husband, was a military man and she held a doctorate from Yale. Fred, somewhat in his cups, said to me,

"People ask me what I saw in Isabel, but I tell them, 'I don't know what she saw in me!'"

I think that's how Joe felt and that's how Alex felt, too.

If Joe strayed finally, it was because I had begun to criticize him and our life together, and also, as the years went on, I became more and more fixated on my research and writing. Once the kids were gone, I stopped making dinner, stopped watching TV with Joe on the few nights he was home, and was generally holed up in my study, reading and writing, oblivious to the world at large. Oblivious to Joe. Consumed with my private rage. My love for him was dead, and thinking it over, it was clear that I fell out of love with Joe before he fell out of love with me. Talking with Alex, I began to let the rage against Joe surface. And began to see why I was enraged.

Chapter Eleven

In the late spring, the lady slippers came into bloom at the edges of the woods where the light is always dappled, and in the woodland glens which allowed more sun than the deeper woods. If you've never seen them, lady slippers are a wonder, although I don't know why they're called lady slipper, any more than I know why lungwort is called lungwort. It doesn't look like lungs. And lady slippers don't look like slippers. They have a bulbous flower, in shades of deep rose pink growing pendulously from a curved stem with just a few tiny leaves between the stem and the flower. They look like a floral version of a male's scrotum. Phallic flowers. The perfect gift to a psychiatrist. After whom I was lusting.

These flowers grow in groups, some with as many as fifteen flowers or even more. When I saw them I thought,"Alex probably never saw anything like this," so before my next visit, I picked three, just three as they are protected plants, on the endangered species list, or so I was told. I picked the three out of a clump of at least fifteen, wrapped the stems in soaked paper towels, then put the stems into a plastic bag, which I fixed with an elastic wrapped around the top. After that, I found a small deep red antique cranberry glass vase in my cupboard and took that, too.

After my shower, I sprayed myself with Joy perfume, hoping Alex was turned on by scent. Joe wasn't. I had bought the Joy, supposedly the most expensive perfume in the world, just for Alex. I wanted to smell nice when I got close to him at the office

109

door. I wanted him to remember my scent, be reminded of me in the future whenever he whiffed it on a woman passing by.

When I got to his office building, I filled the vase with water from the bubbler. Then when I climbed the stairs to his office, I knocked on the door. His voice as always high-pitched from the excitement of my visit, yelled "Come in." It made me tingle to hear that excitement each week. It was what gave me the courage to try to woo him. On this day, I entered the room, proffering the flowers,

"Ever see these?" I asked. "Know what they are?"

"No," he answered.

"They're lady slippers," I said.

I advanced towards the desk, which he was sitting at that day. Usually, he sat in the armchair opposite the wing chair I sat on.

I went to put the vase on his desk just as he started to get out of his chair. Accidentally, I was right on him. He pushed me away. I mean really pushed! I was humiliated. Somehow we got untangled, and I don't remember the rest of the visit, but I do remember thinking with that familiar sinking feeling,"Maybe he's not so interested in me as I thought." Now I realize he was scared.

Yet there were all those other times, when the hour was over and he rose from his chair, that I would walk right up to him, real close, with no more than an inch between us, and he never moved back. In fact, I moved within smelling distance. I couldn't stand a man who smelled or had bad breath and I wanted to be sure our olfactory senses were compatible. They obviously were. At least, he ever shrunk from me or even stepped backwards. I was also hoping he'd put his arms around me, but he never did. He just stood there with his arms held stiffly at his side until I moved away. He always kept a smile on his face when I stood close to him that way, but never spoke, never touched, never tried to widen or narrow the gap. This finally became our parting ritual at every visit. I would finally turn towards the door, he would quickly reach out to turn the knob and open it for me, and I would leave. Alone.

The next visit I noticed that both the lady slippers and the vase were gone. I was too humiliated to ask him for the vase back

THERAPY, A NOVEL

although it was quite expensive, and something that I especially liked. I still don't know what he did with it.

One time looking down as the sun beamed in from the third floor windows, I was able to see the outline of his thighs and legs encased in his summer weight suit pants. They were shapely. A woman would be proud to have such shapely legs. Of course, I imagined his to be covered with thick, dark brown hair. I love hairy men and with his Mediterranean swarthy looks, I was sure he had a pelt. After all, I saw the Italian men on the beach every summer and some of them looked as if they had to comb their body hair. The very thought excited me. I was dying to ask,"Are you hairy?" I wonder what he would have done if I had come right out with it? I also wanted to ask if he was married. He didn't wear a wedding band and didn't have pictures of a wife or kids in his office, so I figured he wasn't married, although it occurred to me that he might have a girl friend.

When I left his office after the debacle with the lady slippers I was humiliated, but angry too. If he let me get so close those other times when I walked up to him, my face starry and my eyes glowing, obviously infatuated with him, then why this time did he push me away? And why didn't he ever reach out and touch me when I walked up close to him?

Perhaps I was deluding myself. He was obviously a lot younger than I was, and there was no way of getting around that fact. I didn't yet know how much younger, but I figured he must be at least thirty-five if he was already a psychiatrist, and I was pretty sure that Dr. Aiello remarked he'd been in practice a few years before he moved to Providence. One graduates medical school at twenty-five and then does an internship and a residency. That takes until one up to thirty, doesn't it? One of Alex's diplomas, displayed prominently on the wall, declared that he had completed a residency in internal medicine, as well as one in psychiatry. If he'd practiced as an internist before going back to school to become a psychiatrist, then he must be at least thirty-five, maybe even older. If he was only thirty-five, that made him seventeen years younger than I. Everyone considers it freaky if the woman is older than the man by even a couple of years, never mind almost two decades.

111

Yet, I knew of four relationships with such age differentials, so it couldn't be all that rare a situation. To let him know that it was possible to have a love affair with someone so much older, I told him about Joe's friends Hope and Dave. She was not only twenty years older than he was, but he had lately decided to become a woman and was in the midst of changing his sex while he and Hope were rearranging their relationship to each other.

Then there was my old classmate Susan whose husband was only three years older than her oldest son was. These vignettes sparked a slightly interested expression, but no comment. Still, the seed was planted. While I was at it, I also told him about Aunty Ida who'd eventually remarried to Uncle Abe and she was, I think, sixteen years older than he was, too. Oh, and Aunty Rachel whose second husband, Edgar was twenty years younger than she was. Not all men are looking for young chicks.

Certainly younger men with older women couldn't be all that uncommon if even someone as unsocial as I knew of so many. So, why not Alex and me? The only thing I didn't figure on was professional ethics. His professional ethics, I mean. I guess I figured anyone who shone his eyes on me the way he did, who overtly ogled me, wasn't going to let himself be swayed by professional ethics.

Chapter Twelve

After spending one visit reassuring him that younger men could have love affairs with older women, I next set about making my life in the country attractive, the better to woo him there. Of course, I didn't know if he'd find the prospect of rural scenery appealing. To my knowledge, he had yet to see the winding roads and quaint old houses of the New England countryside. But I had to try. At the very least, he'd get the message that nobody would see him driving up to my house. No spying neighbors. Or even if there were, they wouldn't be able to tell whose car it was passing by or what driveway it drove up to. There were acres of woodlands opposite our drive with no houses on them, and the same held true of the land beside and behind us.

I started our next session with a description of a humming-bird whirring its wings loudly over my head as I weeded the garden, thinking it was some very insistent bee until I looked up and saw the sparkling green throat and the blaze of red just above its breast.

"It's funny," I said,"how seeing unexpected things in nature gives you a kick. I guess that's part of the charm of living out there."

Then I told him about the time I sighted a rare bird a few years ago. You never know what you're going to see next outside your window in the country. Once, in early March, I was looking idly at my bird feeders, which were set up in a clearing just in front of the deep woods. Suddenly, I noticed a falcon perching

on a low, bare branch, but a falcon of a kind I'd never seen before. Not a Peregrine, although that would have been thrilling, too. This one was gray, not brown, and it didn't have the dark feathered helmet of the Peregrine.

As I looked, it hopped off the branch and ran after the mourning doves feeding on the ground, and chased them. Excitedly, I grabbed my bird book and there I found it. A gyrfalcon, noted because of its strange habit of chasing after prey by running on the ground, not by just swooping from the air like other raptors. It belonged much further North up to the Arctic, but rare sightings occurred in New England.

I called the Audubon Society. They said the last sighting in Rhode Island reported to them was in 1928! I was buoyant the whole rest of the day and bothered everyone I knew by calling them and telling them what I had seen. Not that they were interested. They clearly weren't. Nobody shared my excitement. Why should a sight of a bird arouse such emotion in me? I wondered if Alex had any ideas about that. Maybe, it resonates with our primitive selves, when humans were more one with nature. By living so far out of the city, I had put myself in that position of harmony with wild things.

After I recounted the bird-sighting incident to Alex, he remarked,

"You're really in tune with nature," he said. "It's wonderful the way you can get so much pleasure in little things. Nobody I ever knew in LA would be so excited about such a thing, and, even after all these years, when you were telling me about it, your face was animated."

"But you don't understand," I answered. "To me, sighting a gyrfalcon isn't a little thing."

"Where do you think you got your enthusiasm for nature?"

"Well, I was raised in the city, so it wasn't that. I don't know why, but I always loved reading books about animals and farms, and I've already told you how much I loved *Heidi*, especially the scenes in the mountains."

But, I thought to myself, the person who cinched it, who awakened my desire for nature, was my first husband, Hald. The trajectory towards the life I live was really set on the day I met him, not Joe. If I hadn't met Hald and married him, I'd never

THERAPY, A NOVEL

have met Joe, but I also would never have had the chance to live in nature. That experience did influence my desire to have a home in the country, although I certainly couldn't reproduce what I had with Hal, and maybe I wouldn't have wanted that kind of life again, anyway.

"Well, it really was my first husband Hald who taught me how to live with nature."

"Tell me about Hald, and what you mean by a life in nature. How did you meet him?"

"I was waiting on tables the summer after my freshman year in college Down East in Maine, my first real foray outside of my family. I was boarding at the home of a couple who rented out their married daughter's old bedroom. These people were a revelation to me. Sure of their own skins and the rightness of their world. Proud of being Yankees, descendants of the original English settlers. Mornings, Gwen, that was her name, could be found frying homemade doughnuts for sale at the local general store. I had never seen homemade doughnuts before. Secretly, I like the boxed ones better, but I didn't tell her that, of course. They did smell good while frying, though. She provided me with meals too. Meat, potatoes, what she called honest food.

"About a week into my residence, I heard loud talking and laughing downstairs. When I walked into the kitchen, there was a whip-thin sandy haired fellow, very handsome in a Yankee way, light eyes, firm jaw, prominent nose and lips so thin they almost weren't there. It turned out that he was Gwen's daughter's brother-in-law who came to stay for a week. He had just had his appendix out, and since he lived alone in the woods, they figured he'd be better off recovering in town.

"We hit it off right away. He was the most fascinating man I'd ever met, a Maine guide, taking parties of hunters out into the woods to kill animals, often while camping out in tents for a few days. As a guide, he not only led hunters, whom he euphemistically called 'sportsmen,' to where the live meat was, but he cooked for them over a campfire. He'd go out and catch fish for breakfast, breading it and frying it, and even baking biscuits using a portable oven that could be heated by the fire.

"The guides had the principle of biscuit mix long before grocery stores stocked it. They mixed all the dry ingredients

115

HARRIE ROSE

together before leaving for their woodland camps, and just added liquids when they went to bake up a batch. This was a world I never knew existed. I never read it in books or seen it in a movie. The prospect of actually going out and killing animals didn't appeal to me at first, but as everyone said, the meat I ate had to be killed by someone, so what was the difference? The more Hald talked, the more I wanted to be in his world. Nothing could be further removed from my own."

"That must have been a powerful attraction, given your family situation," Alex commented.

"Yes, and remember, in those days, young girls didn't live alone by themselves. The only way to get out of my house was by getting married. At the time, I didn't think of it that way. I only thought of Hald and living in the woods, but since then, it has occurred to me that another reason was to get away from my hellish existence with my parents. They were always bad enough, but when I started college, they were furious. It wasn't going to cost them anything, but it meant I was on the rise. In their eyes, I guess, they would lose control of me once I got educated. I would have something they didn't. A degree, and from an Ivy League School. I just know they were making my life more miserable than ever. Besides, I loathed Brown. Funnily enough, I ended up doing grad school there, and that I loved. It was a completely different experience.

" But, forget that. Back to Hald. In the summer when hunting season hadn't yet begun, he augmented his salary by getting soil samples for the state highway department. Seems in order to build a road, you have to first find out what kind of soil and subsoil and sub-subsoil it will be laid upon. Odd what jobs there are in the modern world that you'd never dream up if you didn't happen to meet someone who did them.

"Actually, I really believe that even if I wasn't so unhappy at home, I would've been attracted to Hald. His flat Maine Yankee accent thrilled me, and the way he punctuated his statements quaintly with exclamations like. "Oh Gorry!" and"Holy Jehoshaphat!" It was so different. He was so different. A mix of reticence and irony, self-sufficiency and neediness. I can hear his drawl in my head, but I can't mimic it. I can't remember whole phrases of his, but I remember the cadence of those phrases.

THERAPY, A NOVEL

"And then, too, I had never met anybody before or since whose need for love virtually oozed out of him. All my nurturing instincts reached out to him. I loved it that he needed me, that he needed affection, hugs, holding hands, snuggling."

"You yourself must have been starved for that kind of contact," Alex pointed out.

"I'd never had it in my life. The most was holding hands with a boy I dated, or having his arm over my shoulder in a movie. Actually, I was always careful to stand far away from people, especially men. Still, I had skin hunger. I craved being touched. Yet, I didn't dare to get too close physically with anyone until I met Hald. He drew me close, and I loved it.

"Later on, it was hard to reconcile his cuddling with his love for killing creatures. He'd kill anything that moved. Once he found a huge turtle walking across the road, its shell at least three feet wide and promptly cut its head off. He wanted me to make and can turtle soup from it, which I did, gagging as I was doing it, but I refused to eat it. I must say that most of what he killed, he did dress for eating. He had grown up living off the land and still did so as much as possible. Partridge, pheasant, squirrel, deer, rabbit, catfish, eel, lake salmon, he caught and ate them all."

"Did you eat any of it?"

"Of course. In that context, it didn't seem wrong. No more wrong than buying chickens or hamburger in the market. Same principle. I thought hunting was wrong only when it was done for sport and the hunter didn't eat his kill, and Hald agreed with me on that. I know he did enjoy the hunting itself, but he never did it just to kill, and he wouldn't take out parties who refused to dress their kill and take it home to eat it. He saw that as being morally wrong. Years later, I did get into arguments with animal rights activists about hunting, about there being a morality involved."

"So, you're not a conservationist?"

"Of course, I am. But I can see hunting for food. That's the way of the world. The only real alternative is to be a strict vegetarian, and even that involves killing. The big farm machinery that reaps grain often kills ground nesting birds and small animals, and planting crops uses up animal habitats. Nobody thinks about those things when they condemn hunting."

"You said, Hald had a need for love. How so more than any-one else?"

"His mother had died when he was only eight, a tragedy still fresh in his mind. Tears of grief welled in his eyes when he spoke of her and he cried when he spoke of the day of his loss. She died in childbirth with her fourth child, who also died, leaving the other three bereft, and Hald, the eldest, with a hole in his psyche that had never been filled.

The worst thing was, his father abandoned the two older boys, taking the young sister with him, and left them to fend for themselves. I don't know how long they were alone, but eventu-ally his grandparents came down from Canada where they had retired and made a home for the boys. The grandfather was a canoe maker and a guide and it was he who taught Hald to be a guide."

"His life must have seemed exotic to you."

"Well, yes, I guess it was. But another thing that got to me, be-sides his need for love, his unusual—to me—life, was his intensity. He was intense about everything. His opinions were delivered in that flat Maine drawl, but with force and conviction. He wasn't blasé about anything, and certainly not about me. He wrote me love poems, pretty good ones too. No *roses are red* rhymes, no images of moon and June, although it was June when I met him. He told me by our third meeting that he was going to marry me. Just like that, no asking, only telling. It thrilled me, the certainty of his love, the certainty that he saw a good person in me, I who was never good in anyone else's eyes. Until the end, of course, and then he didn't think I was so good, either."

"The end? You're getting ahead of yourself. I gathered you married him."

"Definitely. In those days, a nice girl would never just live with a guy, and *nice* was the opposite of *slut*, which I wasn't. The night we eloped, we drove in silence from Providence to Maine on a bitter cold December night. I had just finished with finals. Four three-hour exams on the first two days of the exam period. I was wiped. My right arm was sore from writing. Hald had appeared outside the room of my last exam, like an angel of deliverance.

'Ready?' was all he said, and all I did was nod my head.

THERAPY, A NOVEL

"We went to my house to pick up my dog. Fortunately, when we got there, my parents were both still at work, so there was no unpleasant incident. I had warned them about how serious it was between Hald and me. My mother's response was hysteria.

'How can you do this to me? You have a full scholarship at Brown. He's a nothing. He's not even Jewish. They're different from us, those people. They're cold.'

"It was funny that my scholarship counted when they didn't want me to marry Hald, but it didn't before then. In fact, they actively denigrated it and me. My father's response to my love for Hald was insulting nastiness, and, again, suddenly my academic prowess was something to be called upon, not derided.

'That's the best you can do? A *summa cum laude* from Classical High School. A scholar at Brown no less, and all you could manage is a hick from Maine? With your fancy college you couldn't find yourself a doctor, a lawyer?"

"One afternoon, after trying to talk me out of seeing Hald again, my mother dropped herself down on her bed and started crying loudly, actually sounding like 'Boo hoo' and lamenting that I was killing her. My Aunt Miriam happened by and said to me accusingly,

'See what you're doing to your mother?' I felt like a murderer."

"So, you weren't just acting out of spite when you decided to marry Hald?"

"Why do you say that?"

"Because you felt guilt."

"No, I don't think I was acting out of spite. Rebellion perhaps. Well, almost certainly that. But I probably would have fallen in love with him no matter what. I certainly wanted to get away from my parents. They wanted to own me. My mother used me like a servant at home. At the same time, yes, I did feel guilty. Although, I was also excited to walk into a new world, a whole other life. I still cherish the beauty Hald exposed me to, the peacefulness of the wilderness, the wonder of it. I would do it again given the chance.

"Yes, it also meant I didn't have to face my parents again, or so I thought, and that was a big plus. I was on my way to this new life in Maine. Shortly after we crossed the state border, Hald

119

stopped before a snow covered cottage, set back from the road by about 100 feet. It was clear and freezing, with a purity of air that knifes into you with each breath. The winter sky, black and almost glossy, was studded with trillions of bright stars, one of the joys of a New England winter and cold, cold weather. The beauty of the snow, of icicles and stars converged to an almost mystical experience.

" I got out of the car and stood a few minutes letting the serenity and beauty in before I started to walk towards the door and my new life. No path had yet been cleared in the fresh snow. I waded into the thigh-high snow and made my way to the front door, dripping wet in the foyer while the preacher's wife brought me a towel to dry myself off with. She was a tiny, white haired woman with a seemingly unquenchable sweetness. She had even baked us a small wedding cake, which she produced after her husband, finished with the marriage ceremony, but I was too excited and tired to eat it. The ceremony itself was like all the elopements in Hollywood movies. Except for one thing. After the 'I do's', the minister concluded with"In the name of the Father, the Son, and the Holy Ghost", and that's when I realized that Protestants believed in Jesus the same way Catholics did. Rhode Island had the highest percentage of Catholics in the country, probably still does, so I never knew many Protestants when I was growing up. Only Catholics and Jews. The African Americans didn't call themselves Protestants. They were Baptists or AME. They sang and rocked in their services, clapped and raised their arms to God, nothing like the white Protestants in their silent services, so I never really connected Protestants with colored people.

"I just figured that Protestants had protested and what they protested I naively thought was the idea that Jesus was God himself. Of course, now I know better. It shocked me then that people who believe the same fundamental things about God could consider themselves separate religions and even have wars over them. Jews disagreed about points of religion all the time, but they didn't form separate religions over them. Or at least not since the rift over Jesus' being God."

I noticed Alex looking at the clock he kept opposite him on a shelf.

THERAPY, A NOVEL

"Time's up?" I asked, and, as had now virtually become a routine, I stood up as he did and walked close up to him, standing there for a minute or so before turning to go out the door.

The next week, Alex asked me to continue telling him about my life with Hald.

"We started out with a picture book wedding ceremony in a picture book house on a picture book snowy evening. It was an auspicious beginning, I thought. Now"happily ever after" was going to happen. I was reborn into a new life. Maine Yankee. No running water. No electricity. No flush toilets. No central heat. Wood stoves. Oil lamps. Nature girl. That's what I was to become. No more city girl.

"Hald drove me to his cabin on the Stillwater River in Orono that night. I was a virgin, if you can believe it. I mean, you must believe it, because it was true. We didn't have sex with our boyfriends the way girls do today. This was, after all, the 1950's and lots of girls were virgins when they got married. Nobody told me I had to be.

"My mother didn't talk about such things and neither did my grandmother, but it was in the air. They didn't have to talk about it. I knew if I had sex, I could become pregnant and then everybody would know and I couldn't bear the shame. Also if I did it with someone and then he told the other boys, I couldn't bear that shame either. My brother always warned me about that. So I was a virgin from shame. Maybe shame is the ultimate thing that keeps us in line. Although I have to admit I never had any desire to have sex with anyone, not even Hald, at least until our wedding night. He was passionate but careful that first night. He whispered to me,

'I'm going to take you.'

"And take me he did. It wasn't ecstasy that first time, but I could see it had promise. For the entire time I lived with Hald, we had sex every night that we were together until the night before Sammy was born. He, Hald, not Sammy of course, was very proud of his ability to perform. Funny how men feel about that. Like they're being judged on how long they can keep it up and how often they can get it that way.

"What did I do in Maine? It was all so long ago and I didn't keep a diary. I'll have to be impressionistic, like those French

121

painters, give you the flavor without the intricate details. I remember scenes, like in a movie. Hald chopping the wood for the stove. Me bringing in buckets of water I had pumped from the well every morning. Hald teaching me how to regulate the oven temperature on a wood stove for baking. Hald trotting off to go hunting, his rifle erect on his shoulder, like a soldier on parade. Hald teaching me how to bait a hook with live worms when we went out in the canoe to catch fish for breakfast. How to fry up eels. How to shoot a rifle. How to aim to kill, although I never could bring myself to kill little furry animals much less big ones like deer or moose. I couldn't even kill birds. Those creatures wanted so much to live. How could I take that from them?

"Most of the time I spent my days cooking and baking for Hald. When he was home for supper, I often fed him as if he were a baby, lifting forkfuls of my daily creations to his mouth."

Alex's eyes lit up and he smiled when I mentioned how I fed Hald. Maybe he was imagining himself in the same situation. Come to think of it, I would love to spoon food in Alex's mouth. No, I never did that with Joe. He would've thought I'd gone nuts.

" Ten dollars a week for food was all I had and a copy of *The Joy of Cooking*. It's hard to remember that two could eat very well on that amount of money in the fifties. I did creative things with leftovers and with bare bones. Unconstrained by the Kosher laws for the first time in my life, I learned the joys of mixing milk products with meat, of using bacon to season, and ham bones in soup. Don't get me wrong. It wasn't the Kosher laws themselves I was rebelling against. It was that I was starting a whole new life. I wasn't a Verensky anymore. I was a Whittaker. It was like being a neonate, I guess, getting a completely new identity. My life was starting over with someone who adored me, had no fault to find with me."

Later, I thought about what I'd said about religion to Alex. In truth, if Hald were a churchgoer, I'd have gone to church with him just as I'd gone to church when I was renting the room at Gwen's. Although I knew even then that if I had children, and I could hardly wait to start, they'd have to be Jewish or at least know something about my religion. Hald had no problem with that. Just so long as he could have a Christmas tree. That was

fine with me. It fit my new identity as Hal's wife. How could I be willing to go to church and celebrate Christmas and still plan to raise my kids as Jews? Well, consistency wasn't part of my persona then. I guess I wasn't too crazy, though. I meet lots of families today who celebrate both Jewish and Christian holidays, both Chanukah and Christmas, because the mother and father were born to different religions.

For the first time since Hald and I split, I began thinking back on the whole Maine experience. I guess the experience of having to come back to my parents and Hald's illness was so painful I drove all thought about deep into the recesses of my mind. The worst thing about our time together was the Maine winter, but in some ways it was the best.

There is an extraordinary beauty of deep snows that stay white, unpolluted by a world of internal combustion engines. The winter skies were often deep, deep blue and cloudless, so that the snow sparkled in the sunlight. The downside of winter was the cold, of course, and also the heaviness of the clothes and boots. This was before the days of Polar fleece and Gortex boots. Winter clothes were heavy and became weighted down with the moisture of snow. Winter boots were even heavier and awkward to walk in. When the thermometer dipped to 30 below Fahrenheit, it was actually painful to be outside. Tears froze on my cheeks.

Going to the privy, an unheated outhouse, was a torture. It felt like razors were cutting my private parts. I used to tease Hald that his pecker would freeze and fall off when he urinated. It was wonderful when we came back into the cabin, however. The wood stoves were a joy, emanating a warmth that radiators or baseboards just don't have. When we came in frozen and wet, our hands stiff with cold, we would huddle by the stove, holding our hands above the burners until they were warm throughout, rosy and flexible. There was a special kind of coziness in the contrast of the heat to the cold we'd come in from.

The rural roads were always covered with ice and snow and Hald insisted the safest way to drive on ice was to speed! Wondrously, we never had an accident.

Describing my Maine years to Alex, I said,

"I remember walking down a rural road, the world covered in sparkling snow and ice and coming upon a partially frozen brook with teal ducks swimming on it, their bright feathers glistening in the cold and snowy landscape. Since the forests up North are mostly evergreen, it wasn't barren looking like Southern New England with its wintry stands of bare leafed oaks and maples. In the Maine villages back then there were few enough cars so that the snow didn't become grimy and black, there were no snow-mobiles or off-road vehicles, and the cold was consistent enough so that the snow didn't become icy and grainy as it did further south. Surrounded by the sharp beauty of winter, I learned to ice skate on ponds and snowshoe in fields.

"The summers were idyllic. We spent them in Aroostook County on a forest ranger's fire tower on the top of Mount Daicey. The only way to get there was by canoeing down a river for eighteen miles and then backpacking our supplies up the mountain trail to the cabin. The trip down was luxuriously slow. You don't go fast in a canoe, especially one laden with provisions. All there was to see was scenery: trees and bushes, wildflowers, birds, the occasional small animal. Every so often, we'd get a glimpse of a deer or a rabbit, but mostly squirrels, just like in the city, only these squirrels were little red ones, not the big gray kind. We never saw another soul on the river, nor did we see signs of humans in the woods that the river meandered through. There were no roads, no cleared trails..

"When we got to the spot that led up to the cabin, we got out, put on our backpacks, and trudged up what must have been a trail of sorts. It wasn't very clearly beaten down. Just as wide as footsteps meandering through the brush. They may have been made by bears or moose.

"I never did figure out how Hald knew just where to beach the canoe. It all looked the same to me: woods, woods, woods. There were no signs pointing the way, unless it was a natural sign like a particular configuration of trees. At the time, it didn't dawn on me to ask how he knew he had gotten to the right place, and now it's impossible. I mean I have no way of asking him, haven't had for years. It's been over thirty years since I had any communication with him. Too bad. I'd like to know how he's

THERAPY, A NOVEL

doing and if his life turned out well. I know from Gwen that he married his psychiatrist, and had three children with her.

"Back to that summer. The first time we were hiking up the trail, I was startled by a dark whirlwind that jumped out of the bush and moved jerkily across my path. Hald laughed and scooped his hand down near the bush, coming up with a fluffy chick in the palm of his broad sun browned hand, saying,"Here you are milady," as if he were bestowing a prize on me. The brown whirlwind had been a mother partridge feigning a broken wing as we got near to her nest in the undergrowth.

"The only real danger going up the trails, Hald said, was meeting a moose. They're huge and nearsighted and if they come down a path, you have to get out of their way or they're likely to just trample you down. Cheering thought! Fortunately, they usually made a racket blundering their way through the brush so you could get out of the way. Of course, there were bears, but somehow Hald didn't think they posed any danger. I did wonder what would happen if I accidentally got between a mother bear and her cubs. Somewhere I'd read that could be fatal. I could imagine her charging with a loud growl and ripping me open with her claws. Thank God, it never happened. In fact, I hardly ever saw a bear, and if I did it was always at a distance. We had a couple of dogs, a Dalmatian and a mutt who patrolled the area around our cabin and barked insanely at the wildlife who ventured near. Hald assured me,

'No bear will come where there's a dog.'

'But the bears are so much bigger than dogs,' I fretted.

'Ayuh,' he'd agree in his Maine drawl. 'But they know the dogs mean humans are around and guns, too.'

"Well, it didn't make much sense to me, especially in this Edenic spot where there were no humans for miles and miles around. How would the bears here know about guns? Maybe some brave, woods-savvy hunters made it into these woods during the season, but surely not many. Most hunters stayed where you could get to by car, not venturing into the Maine wilds where you had to lug your gear on your back, climbing up steep, brambly, rocky mountain trails. The only reason there was a cabin here was the fire observation tower.

"But as I said, we never were troubled by the bears, although I saw them, peacefully gathering berries or just lumbering through the trees. There were no wolves left in Maine even back then, forty years ago, so I didn't have to worry about them. The other animals, skunks, porcupines, foxes, minks, and beavers shunned mankind, although I got to see them occasionally, and of course you don't count rabbits, little red squirrels, and deer, of which there was an abundance. And, of course, the birds, brilliant red tanagers, bright blue buntings, bright yellow and black gros-beaks. I always thought birds with colors like that were only in the tropics, not in the New England woods. I get to see them now all the time in my own backyard. Anyway, Hald took the job of provisioning us seriously, sometimes to my distress.

'But you should try squirrel stew,' Hald would insist. 'Forget that it's squirrel. Just call it meat.'

"As much as I wanted to be a true Yankee living off the land, I couldn't manage it. Fortunately, Hald was a wonder at knowing which plants were edible cooked or raw, which nuts and berries to collect, and where the wild strawberries were. The taste of wild strawberries warm from the sun is totally different from the big ones you get in the supermarket. Hald was also an expert on wild mushrooms. Those he wouldn't let me pick as there were plenty of poisonous ones that looked almost like non-poisonous ones. It took years of experience to learn to discriminate be-tween mushrooms. Hald would come in, his hat full of them, which he'd picked on the way down the trail.

'Looky here! The bounty of the land,' he'd announce.

Often there were wild greens.

'I feel as if I'm competing with the bears for food,' I'd say.

'Don't worry,' was his reply. 'There's plenty for everyone. This is God's country'.

I always wondered what that sentence is supposed to mean. How is it more God's country than any other place in His Creation? I mean, if He created the whole world, why did He pick out one spot and consider it His? It doesn't make sense to me, except that the people who say it usually seem to think that since they belong to that land, they are His darlings. What a presumption!"

In our next session, I told Alex how I'd been thinking over my Maine days and how, actually, I had been very happy there in the wilderness.

"You really became a nature lover, didn't you. Very few people today have had such experiences," Alex commented.

"Yes. The cabin we stayed in on Mount Daicey was a two roomer. One room for sleeping and one for cooking, eating, and relaxing. In a funny way, it reminded me of the flat I grew up in. A stove dominated the kitchen. An old couch and a rocking chair were opposite the kitchen table. The difference was that this was quiet, not filled with incessant talking and arguing over politics or anything else.

"In fact, there was little talking in anybody's kitchens in Maine, at least not the incessant chatter that filled all the silences in the kitchens I grew up in. Hald never criticized me or made fun of me. He also didn't overtly say bad things about other people, only sly understatements or subtle irony. It was a revelation to me even when I boarded at Gwen's that these people were as critical of others as my family was, but they never came right out and said anything. They implied. They used razor sharp wit, and were masters of understatement. I was so used to hearing people come flat out with what they meant, that it was like learning a new language for me. Sometimes I couldn't tell if they really were ripping someone apart or were being admiring.

"After a while I did learn that they scorned everyone who wasn't them: city slickers, Catholics, New York Jews. They had an inbred sense of superiority that nothing could shake. They never bragged because they didn't have to. They knew they were who the rest of the world should be measuring themselves against. They were very polite, though. I never did learn to talk in indirection the way they did, though. Now that I live in a rural area dominated by people like the Whitakers, I see they are the same way. Little small talk. A deep conviction that they are the best, and they are the way that everyone else should be. I don't think it's really conceit, but more a very strong confidence in themselves, a confidence that comes from knowing their forebears fought for this country and set it up and made it great.

'My little Barbara,' Hald would croon. 'How I love you Barbara. Don't do me wrong sweetheart,' as he sang Hank Williams songs of loving and yearning to me.

"He often confessed to me, tears in his eyes, how the girls before me had betrayed him, cast him out, left him bereft, and made me promise I wouldn't ever let him go. To this day, I shudder when I think of how I did do just that. Only I didn't leave him for another man. I left him for a baby, our son Samuel.

"What did we do all day and night out there in the wilderness? No TV, not that that was such a big deal in the fifties, at least not to us. Television didn't hit America until 1948, but my folks didn't have one until my senior year in high school. My days then were full of schoolwork, cleaning the house, ironing shirts for my father and brother, and working in the little store my parents had opened after World War II. The store was open sixteen hours a day, seven days a week, no vacations, so the whole family had to work in it. There would have been no time to watch television, even if we had a set, which we didn't. The few times I saw it at my friends' homes, the programs seemed silly, inane. And now they say that was the golden age of television.

Living in the woods as he did, Hald had never gotten the habit either. In any event, even without the so-called amenities of modern life, we lived peacefully and almost lazily. There were loads of books to read. I had packed a bunch for the summer and, surprise! There was a bookcase loaded with novels and history books, all old, but still worth reading. Hald spent long hours manning the fire tower, making sure no suspicious tendrils of smoke were announcing a forest fire. I would walk up the trail from the cabin to bring him the hot lunch I'd prepared. I learned to bake bread in the oven of the wood stove.

"Funny where life takes you. When I was little, all I wanted was store bought bread, but now, like my grandmother, I was baking my own bread. I delighted in the brown loaves cooling in the window, radiating their yeasty fragrance.

"When you were up on the tower, you could see for miles. Verdant mountains folding into each other. It was so clear that you could see a mountaintop lake three mountains over, and the moose in it diving for vegetation and coming up with its antlers covered with green. Not a house or phone line or electric

THERAPY, A NOVEL

wire marred the beauty. You almost wouldn't know that man existed."

I told Alex how isolated Hald and I were,

"We often made love outside on the little meadows of wild grasses that dotted the mountainside. There was nobody to see. We could walk around nude outside with no fear of being caught. There weren't even any planes that flew overhead. The silence was amazing. One afternoon as we were having sex, I, being on the bottom, opened my eyes and to my horror saw a human face peering over a bush. He had short gray curly hair and a round red face.

'Aaa!' I screamed, as I pushed Hald off me. 'Who are you?'

"I didn't even have a towel to cover myself with. Both of us were as Hald put it, 'Nekked as jaybirds.' I remember my heart racing furiously. I couldn't even wait for an answer. I just ran for the cabin, crashing through brush. Boy, did I get twig cuts on places you usually think of as being inaccessible parts of your body. I must have broken the world's record for getting dressed in a hurry. I actually grabbed a gun, me the kid from Providence, and I ran back to the trail with some pants for Hald. You can't be very brave when you're unclothed.

"Hald, sitting naked on the hilly meadow, talking peacefully with the man. Turned out he was part of a team of naturalists from Bulgaria who were studying bears. The Bulgarian looked at me. I was feeling foolish, brandishing the rifle but all he said was, 'Remarkable country, America, You still have bears.'"

"You do a foreign accent well," Alex laughed.

"Well, I had all those years with Gramma. I think I internalized her accent as if it was another language, and the Bulgarian sounded just like her. In any event, we never saw him or his compatriots again. It was as if they were swallowed up by the wilderness. Remember, this was during the height of the Iron Curtain and the Cold War, but apparently the Communists thought it worth risking a Comrade defecting if only he found out information about bears."

"What else did you do to keep busy all day out there?" Alex asked. My stories were clearly a welcome break from the dismal tales most of his clients recounted.

"I would go down to the brook. It actually gurgled its way down the mountainside, and I'd catch trout for lunch, cleaning them the way Hald had taught me. The water was so shallow that I could reach in and grab the trout by the gills, but they were slippery and often just wriggled away. I had good luck with a rod and reel, however, so mountain trout were a big part of our diet. It was more palatable than eating squirrel or rabbit, at least to me.

'You don't know what you're missing' Hald would complain. 'That's okay. I don't miss it.' was my reply.

"I did eat the venison and the wild birds he shot. He regularly brought home ducks, geese, pheasant, and partridge. We didn't need much at the supermarket. Once, on a rare trip to town to stock up on staples like flour, I called my mother. Her voice was tinny and far away, but I could make out her lament,

'How can you live like that?' she asked, 'In the middle of nowhere. No electricity, no running water. Are you crazy? Come home.'

"I wasn't crazy. I stayed. I have never had such an idyllic time as those years in Maine without modern conveniences. I never once missed having running water from a faucet. I never once missed the need to compete, to prove my worth."

"So your mother did care that you were gone?"

"Oh, yes, and that was a big surprise. One day when we happened to be in town, the mailman delivered a letter from her. 'Dear Barbara,' it started. 'I feel that you're a thousand miles away from me in Maine and can't imagine where you live and how. You have left a void in our lives. We miss the music you brought into the house, the happy sound of your voice...'

"A strange feeling flooded me. This was from the woman who used to lament,"What did I ever do to deserve a daughter like you?" I didn't know what to feel or how. Never once in my life had my mother —or anyone else—ever said I was a nice person or that they desired my company. Except for Hald, of course. He wanted me around and made that plain. I was his world. My mother always took pride that she was better than me, that I'd never be half the woman she was. Why did she miss me? It made no sense. Stan was gone, in the army in Korea. I was gone. She and my father were alone with each other. They had no children to bully. Maybe that's why she missed me. It didn't occur to me

that she loved me in her own way. One thing I knew. I never wanted to go back to her. She could play her own music."

"That's quite a story, living in the wilderness. But besides nature, another reason why you loved it so was probably that you felt you were being loved unconditionally and, you said it, you didn't have to compete for anything. That's the kind of love you should get from your parents. It's good that you got it finally from Hald. I'm surprised you ever left, or did he leave you?"

"We'll have to talk about that next time. It didn't end happily at all."

Chapter Thirteen

By June, all I could think of was Alex. He was my obsession. Now I was walking eight miles a day. On those long walks, I deliberately remembered and cast some of the memories into narratives to regale Alex with during our next session. I worried about what Alex would think of me when I told him the end of the story. The narratives about Hald had been especially effective. They made Alex's eyes shine, as he listened, stroking his beard and smiling. They also let me think of those days again, days I had buried completely, experiences I thought I had lost. Finding them brought me a deep peace, connecting me again with animals and birds and peace, sharpening my eyes to my own woodlands.

One day, I came to my therapy session enraged at some hunters who had invaded the woods behind our house, looking for deer, although it was out of season. I heatedly started to tell him about that.

"You have hunters?" he asked.

Yes, why does that surprise you?"

"Well, Rhode Island is so small." He made a squaring motion with his two hands. "I didn't think it was large enough for hunters."

"Oh, you should drive out my way," I invited. "It's nothing like this, the city. It's all woods. Miles of woods. Acres of them. We even have coyotes and bears. Just come straight out Route 12 and you'll find yourself more and more in the country."

His face never changed expression as I gave him these explicit directions, but still, I fervently hoped he'd be inspired to drive out for a look. That thought filled my daydreams every day. I actually found myself looking for his car driving down the Pike while I was walking. I made sure he knew exactly when and where he could find me.

"I walk every morning for two or three hours," I informed him. "I just go down my road to Old Plainfield Pike, that's Route 14, up to Route 122 and back. Most days I don't see another person, and there aren't even many cars. Our house is set way back in the woods. You can't see it from the road." He never took the bait. I watched in vain for his car.

Often, however, I'd come to my therapy session describing the flowers and birds I'd seen on my walk. That really must have bored him. He was from Los Angeles and the joys of rural New England seemed to hold no attractions for him as far as I could tell. I didn't know if he'd even followed up on my suggestions that he drive to the rural areas of the state to see how different it was from Providence or even the suburbs.

I was really getting low on possible things to say to him, especially now that he wasn't interested in my benighted childhood. The thing that bothered me the most, the thing I had most to say about, I couldn't talk to him about. That was about my children. Someone, Jackie Kennedy, I think it was once said words to the effect that if you bungled raising your children, you've bungled everything in your life, and I bungled raising my children. To admit this to him, to anyone, would be humiliating. Now many of our hour sessions were spent in silence with me trying to think of something to say. I couldn't just keep complaining about Joe. There was just so much I could say about my life with Hald. When Alex spoke, it was usually to exhort me to leave my husband. As I've complained, he brought it up at every session. In fact, he became downright insistent. It was like his mantra:

"You're depressed because you're not happy at home."

My answer was boringly the same as I countered that I'd just have more problems if I left Joe.

I finally asked him point-blank,

"What would I do without a husband? Without my home? Why do you think I'll be happier?"

THERAPY, A NOVEL

"I'm not saying you will be happier. I 'm saying that your marriage is making you unhappy. You'll have to start a new life, but you have a chance of that being happier. I can't guarantee anything more."

And so it went. Our therapy sessions had stagnated, degenerated into his demands and my refusal. I went only to see Alex, hoping he'd forget his nonsense and come to me.

On my morning walks, now I fantasized even more about Alex's driving up the road, parking his car and joining me. As I've said, I told him exactly where I walked each morning so he could surprise me if he had a mind to, which he didn't seem to, since he never did come by while I was on one of my treks. Of course, he might have driven those roads when I wasn't out walking, but he never let on if he did.

My next ploy was to offer him a travelogue of western Rhode Island, laying out for him the sights he might take in, the colonial inn now a residence, the dairy farms, the clambake hall, the old one-room schoolhouses in each village kept as monuments to a simpler time. His face remained impassive, but I kept hoping he got the message. I didn't realize that he had his own ideas about crossing the boundary of our relationship from a doctor/patient one to that of lovers.

The best word to describe how I felt is *intoxicated*. I was intoxicated with Alex. Even thinking about him now makes me feel slightly drunk. As I picked the giant iris in my gardens to make stupendous purple and white and pink floral arrangements, I spoke to Alex in my head. I watched hummingbirds flitting to the red flowers, hovering while they got their drinks of nectar, their green and ruby throats sparkling in the spring sun, and thought of Alex. The phoebes were teaching their young to fly, and I reveled in how the little ones fluttered their wings so fast to stay in the air, like a child floundering in water as he or she tried to swim. Precious sights were more so when I imagined Alex seeing them with me, although I didn't know if he'd find them of interest. I really knew nothing about him, my love was baseless, an *amour fou*. I despaired.

One morning, as I sipped my morning coffee while sitting at the kitchen table, I looked out and noticed a dead tree at the edge of the woods. A male woodpecker was assiduously pecking

135

out a perfectly round hole in the trunk, the bright red marking on the back of his head flashing as it bobbed up and down. A female woodpecker was at his side clinging to a branch, intently inspecting the progress of the hole. Even birds want a man who can supply them with a good home. This lady woodpecker clearly wasn't about to mate with someone who couldn't supply her with a good nesting hole, perhaps an excellent one. Maybe good wasn't good enough.

It was a glorious spring and summer that year. My gardens were beautiful. Each flower announces its color differently. Some have points of color against a background of green, like the coral bells, which, despite their name, are actually either white with deep purply red leaves, or orangey red rising from green leaves. Others have bright blazes of larger colors, like the iridescent pinkish purple of my Simone de Jeune tall phlox or the prodigious plumes of white and coral colored astilbe. The wondrous thing about perennial gardens is their ever-changing palette. Plants bloom at different times during the summer, each blaze or point of color giving way to others in successive waves. Each had its moment of glory, so to speak. The gardens look different, too, depending on whether you view them from the front or the back, the bottom or the top. Walking around them every day was a ritual.

The only thing I miss about that house is the gardens. And those I miss terribly. Those gardens kept me from killing myself when I was in my deepest depression. Since you never know from year to year which plants are going to double themselves in size and which may decide not to come back at all, there is always some suspense involved in gardening. There have been times the only reason I didn't kill myself was the stray thought popping into my mind,"I wonder how many delphiniums I'll lose this year," delphiniums being notorious for giving a splendid show one year and giving up the ghost by the next spring, or by wondering how the monarda would do the next summer or how much bigger the giant hosta would be the next season.

The month of March always had me out looking for the first delphinium leaves to see which ones made it. For the most part, the other plants are more reliable. Well, actually, the mums aren't either. The lilies can suddenly disappear from your

THERAPY, A NOVEL

garden, too. To be honest, only some perennials are perennial, but that's part of the fun and the challenge. The question with most of them, however, is more of how much they'd spread since the previous year and if they would have a good bloom. I don't know why gardens mean so much to me. Maybe it's because they are the only things of beauty I've ever managed to create. I managed to mangle everything else I was supposed to create, like knitting sweaters or embroidering tablecloths, which enraged my mother who called me every kind of dolt as an incentive, I guess, to do better at the handicraft lessons she insisted on giving me. My parents never gardened.

"Grow flowers? Are you crazy? We have to makealiving. When you work as hard as we do, who has time for flowers?"

Where my passion for flowers came from, I don't know. When I was growing up, I saw flowering bushes like rhododendron and azaleas, but I rarely saw any other plantings except for stiff arrangements of annuals like marigolds or petunias. One exception was the stand of yellow and pink hollyhocks in my grandmother's back yard, which were locked in my memory. Maybe there were pictures of gardens in books that influenced me, or else there are gardening genes in one's DNA.

I took to describing to Alex the details of each of my several gardens. My mind raced feverishly, trying to figure out ways to let Alex know I wanted to know him better. That I wished he would come to see my gardens. I was consumed with curiosity about him. Why did he become a psychiatrist? Whom had he ever been in love with? What was his mother like? Was she proud of her son the doctor? What was he doing on Sunday afternoons? Where did he live? Did he have children? Had he ever been married? What did he look like when he was a baby?

Besides wondering about him, I continued unraveling my life. On my walks, I picked at my memory, grabbing a thread and teasing it until a past event loosened and floated up to my consciousness, events I didn't know I remembered. I evaluated each one.

"Should I tell Alex this or not?"

Mostly, I decided against it, since I saw how uninterested he was in my childhood, which was a funny thing for a psychiatrist, it seemed to me, so I concentrated on some current pleasantry

137

to share with him, hoping he wouldn't start pressuring me again to leave Joe. It struck me as odd that he expected me to make such a major change in my life when I was so little in command of myself. Why did he want me to leave Joe? Why did he keep harping on it? Was it that he wanted me? Then why didn't he say so. All he had to say was,"Don't be afraid of being lonely. I'll be there for you," and I would have packed my bags.

It occurred to me that therapy was a lot like teaching. I spent hours figuring out what to say in the days before my visits, just as I did before my classes, and often the only response I got, from Alex and the students, was blank stares, leaving me with a knot in my stomach, the knot of dread, of boring my listeners.

When I described my gardens to him, he was clearly bored, so I started to tell him about the birds and small animals I rescued and nursed to health.

"I'm a wild animal rehabilitator," I told him."People shoot raccoons in the spring, leaving the babies orphaned and if they or someone else bring me the young, I bottle feed them and take care of them until they're old enough to fend for themselves."

He sat up alert, hands on thighs, leaning towards me, wanting to know the particulars,

"What do you feed them?"

"Formula. You make up a formula as you do for a human baby, and you use little bottles with rubber nipples. They suck the same way babies do."

"How do you make the formula? What goes into it? Do you have to sterilize the bottles the way you do for a baby?"

"Well, you use different concentrations of milk and sugars for different animals, but I never sterilize the bottles, although, of course, they have to be scrubbed clean."

"Do you keep them in cages?"

"The older ones, the ones that can run around have to be caged, but the neonates are just in a box with old blankets for a nest. You have to rub their little tummies after they eat so they can urinate and defecate. In the wild, their mothers lick their stomachs for that reason."

"How old are they when you get them?"

THERAPY, A NOVEL

"Anywhere from a few days to a few weeks. Some don't even have their eyes open yet and have to be fed around the clock every couple of hours."

"How do you handle that?"

"Actually, I've never slept the night through since my oldest, Samuel, was born. He didn't stop waking me up until he was around seven, and then my other three started to come along. I do with the animals what I did with my own babies. I get up and feed them and go back to sleep. The only difference is that with the babies, since I nursed them, I'd just take them into bed with me and let them fall asleep curled up next to me."

He became the stern doctor then. "That's not a good idea, letting children sleep with adults."

"So I understand. Messes up their Oedipal fixations or gives them Oedipal fixations, but I don't believe it. In primitive tribes, I bet babies sleep with their mothers all the time, not lonely in a crib. Anyway, my boys sure ended up as independent children and adults even if they did sleep in my bed when they were little."

Dryly, he responded, "The danger isn't psychological. It's physical. Adults roll over on babies and smother them. I can get you the statistics on how many babies a year die that way, but back to animal babies."

"Do you keep all these little animals? You must have a veritable zoo," he said.

"Rehabilitators have to let the young go back to the wild as soon as they're mature enough to. That's a condition of your license. You don't let people come in to pet them or play with them, and you don't touch them any more than you have to keep them fed, clean, and functioning."

He was especially amused when I demonstrated for him how I taught baby birds to fly, standing on my tiptoes, hands cupped as if a nestling was in them, and then throwing my arms upwards as I uncupped my hands. He laughed. Although he never showed any interest when I talked about birds I sighted, he was excited by my stories of saving them. Maybe that was the doctor in him.

"Typically, the bird flaps its wings very fast and goes just a few feet until it falls. So I pick it up and do it again. I always do it

139

near a tree with a low limb and aim for the tree when I thrust upwards. They usually get the hang of it in just three or four tries.
And by the next day, they're gone."

His eyes glowed as I described the scenario.

"What an unusual person you are," he said. "So warm. So
caring."

I basked in the warmth of his words. But I always remembered that he was being paid to be nice to me.

Meanwhile, I hadn't given up on the gardens.

"Let me tell you about my garden," I started one day. "They
are the most soul satisfying things I have. The only thing I've
ever created—except for academic stuff, of course, but that's not
really creating. It's more assembling facts and coming to conclu-
sions from them."

I tried to catalog their beauty, but it was plain he wasn't interested in the details. He didn't care about the lady mantle with
its lacy green florets, the stands of purple monkshood in the fall
or the brilliant reds and yellows of the lilies in June and July.
I longed to invite him, to say,"Come look at my gardens some
sunny day," but I didn't dare. Suppose he refused. That would
make it so final. This way, there was always hope.

On my next visit, as I was talking, I forget about what, I noticed
that he was sitting back in his chair, his eyes almost closed, just
open enough to form two slits. I mentally followed the trajectory
of what he must be looking at so intently through those almost
closed eyes, and I realized he was staring at my ankles, which were
peeking out from under my long, white, pleated skirt. I knew he
was wondering about my legs, what they looked like. He wanted
me. I knew he did. I never wore shorts or even short skirts, so he
hadn't ever really seen my legs. And he would never unless he
came to me in my house—or his—or even a hotel room.

Something had to happen soon. I could feel Alex's curiosity,
perhaps even his fantasy. How to bring matters to a head? Was
this the time? Dare I come on to him? Suppose he shoved me
away again as he had when I brought him the lady slippers. My
ego couldn't withstand a second rebuff.

In the middle of the next session, I was talking, looking down
at the carpet, but then, in the middle of a sentence, looked up at
him. He had dressed as usual in one of his double breasted suits,

THERAPY, A NOVEL

but this day, undoubtedly when I was looking away from him, he had unbuttoned his jacket and was standing facing me, with his arms to his side, hands palm up, displaying his slender form. There was no trace of a potbelly. He must have lost the thirty pounds he had claimed that he gained the day I mentioned that walking up stairs was good for weight.

Now he had a look of inquiry on his face that seemed to say,"You like? You approve?" I'd never seen anybody do that before. No man at least. Preening, showing off his body to me. The first time Joe took off his clothes with me, he did hesitate a minute as if asking me to approve of his nude body, but that's the closest I've ever come before to having a man inviting me to inspect him for my approval as Alex was now doing. Would he make a show of his body when he was nude before me, too? If he would do this while he was clothed in his office, surely he was thinking of sex with me. I was thrilled.

As the summer progressed, each week between visits went by in frenzied thinking. During my daily hikes, he was my companion, imaginary, of course. I visualized him driving down the road I was walking on, stopping, inviting me in his car. I'd refuse. He'd get out of his car. We would go off into the woods. I'd lead him to one of the sunny dells with stands of low growing juniper amid grassy knolls. We'd make hot, sweaty, lustful sex.

I'm not sure it was the sex I was most after, although just imagining it was orgasmic. It was the look in his eyes, the glowing when he gazed at me. The lovelorn expression on his face I'd glimpsed briefly on a recent visit when he told me he was going away for a week. I knew how much excitement he could evince by his shrill pitch when he told me to come in as I knocked on the door to his office each week. In ordinary conversation, his voice was quite deep. I savored his keen"Come in!" My excitement was aroused by his excitement. His frank admiration of me, his chorus of"The kind of person you are..." when I told him how cold Joe was or how controlling my mother was or my baby animals were. He clearly meant I was special. Devoted. Loving. I wanted to show him just how devoted and loving I could be. Like the way I was with Hald. My tales of my first marriage were meant to show Alex just how wonderful I would be with him. He got the point, I'm sure.

141

One day, while walking down the road with my furry Chow dog Ruff, I heard a crashing sound in the woods to my left. A deer came bounding out in front of me, so close my hand brushed its fur. It was so fast that Ruff barely had time to bark as the deer thundered across the road into the woods on the other side. It could have killed me. One more step and I'd have been a goner, or worse, injured, perhaps for life, invalided. The tenuousness of life hit me. One second. One bizarre accident and it could be all over. After the years of depression, of wanting to commit suicide, of imagining myself dead in the woods, my head blown apart by a gun, or wrists slit bleeding bright red on dazzling white snow, the perfect opportunity presented itself. That deer could have done the job for me.

Death became an obsession. For three days, I imagined myself dead. Nothingness. Spiraling in space. Whatever it would be. I wasn't ready yet. That deer really shook me up. Made me want not to waste the here and now. Made me more determined to get Alex. To that end, I called him up and told him I had to see him. He could see me at five o'clock. When I got to his office, I told him about the deer and how I couldn't loosen death from my mind after it.

"Do you want to die?" he asked.

"I'm not sure," I lied.

It was the only lie I ever told him, one of the few I've ever told in my life. My problem isn't lying. It's telling the truth when I should have lied. That's why so many people can't stand me.

"If you think you're going to lose it, call me at this number," he said, handing me a sheet of paper.

"Why?" I asked, "What are you going to do? How will you stop it?"

"Just call me," he repeated.

It was a beautiful evening. Perfect for a rendezvous, and here we were talking death and suicide. The irony was that I would have still wanted to kill myself if I hadn't met Alex. The feelings he aroused in me were feelings of life, and the anticipation of what could transpire between us made me want to live. A summer ago, had that deer trampled me, my dying thoughts would have been of gratitude.

Chapter Fourteen

"Perhaps the most intense experiences of my life was having my babies," I told Alex on a visit shortly after I'd told him about my being a wildlife rehabber.

"I got pregnant when I was only nineteen. I was delighted from the first moment I realized I was pregnant. Finally, I was having a baby. I had always wanted a baby. When I was a little girl, all I wanted to play with were dolls. Real baby dolls, not the bride kind. There were no Barbies in those days, but if there were, I wouldn't have been interested. I always wanted a real baby of my own to hug and cradle and sing to and bathe.

"I never wanted to be a wife like my mother was, just a teacher, but I did want to be a mother, a contradictory situation. Teachers in Providence when I was a little girl were all old maids, maids meaning 'virgins' of course, and that obviated children. Still, I daydreamt that I could find a man to father a child for me, but instead of marrying him, I would tell everyone he died before the baby was born. I figured maybe they'd let widows be teachers even if they did have a child. It wasn't sex I was interested in. That was just a means to an end. I envisioned getting pregnant on the first and only try. But as it happened, I did get married, and it took a year and a half of daily sex before I got pregnant.

"My mother used to brag that she got pregnant when my father hung up his pants, a statement that mystified me all through my childhood. She had my brother nine months after she and my father married and me eleven months later. I had

143

expected to repeat her success, not that she seemed to think having us was any kind of success.

"Because of my condition—I was due the end of August—we didn't do Mount Daicey that summer. Instead, we moved to Bangor. It was a trial for Hald to have to be in the city at any time, but especially so in the summer. Yet, he was the one who suggested the move so we could be near a hospital. I was so taken with natural childbirth, having read a book on it, that I was willing to stay in the woods and cut the baby's umbilical cord with my teeth if necessary. Labor didn't scare me. Unfortunately, the last woman Hald knew who gave birth in the wilderness was his mother, and she died in the process.

"The apartment we rented was just a three-room place, nothing fancy, but pleasant to us. It was in an ell, an attachment to the main house. There was a public library nearby and I was soon its most frequent patron. I loved the feel of the baby inside me. I could feel his little hands push out like little knobs in my belly. At that point, of course, I didn't know for sure if it was a he or a she, but I couldn't call it an *it*, and *he* sounded more natural to me than *she*. Of course, now I realize that's because our language is so sexist."

"It is?" Alex asked.

"Yes, but that's another story. We'll have to discuss that later. Anyway, his legs could be felt just under my ribs. The doctor said it was a big baby, maybe going to be eight or nine pounds.

"I played classical music a lot and it alternately soothed and excited him. That's how I learned that babies can hear *in utero*. He would kick to the rhythm of Tchaikovsky's *Marche Slav* and be placated by Debussy's *La Mer*. The table in the apartment had a metal top and when I dropped silverware on it, the ping would make the baby jump visibly.

"I loved the feel of this little life inside of me. I felt like more than just me. For the first time in my life, I felt special. Sure, I was so huge I had to walk leaning backwards with my legs far apart. Sitting was almost impossible and the only position I could lie down in was on my side. My brother came to Maine to visit me, the first Verensky I'd seen since I'd eloped with Hald. He, my brother that is, not Hald, kept looking at me and giggling at the comical sight I made. But I didn't care.

"The early pregnancy puking and queasiness hadn't been too bad and was long over by the summer. Once you feel life it goes away is the old wives' tale and, in my case, it was true. The morning of the first fluttering in my stomach was the last time nausea plagued me. Being pregnant as an ecstatic time for me. Reading. Listening to music. Making a baby. For me, an idyllic life.

"I was fascinated as my body changed like it was in service to this little one. You know, first your breasts swell, the your nipples darken, and your tummy expands preposterously and then your belly-button pops inside out. It was all wonderful to me, and reinforced my faith that there had to be a God or some Divine Planner, but I've lost that faith somewhere along the way."

The memory of that summer came flooding back to me. I got really awkward, to the point of being ungainly. Actually, being ungainly didn't bother me. After all, I never thought of myself as a beauty anyway."

To myself, I thought that I didn't realize then that after the baby came, for the rest of my life, the skin on my stomach would be ruined, a mesh of stretch marks and a pocket of loose stretched out skin. Nobody ever told me about that, and I wasn't about to tell Alex that.

I continued telling Alex,"Hald was funny that summer, funny peculiar that is. He took on a few jobs guiding anglers up to Moosehead Lake, his ancestral home, but for the most part, he was in the city all summer. He never told me what was on his mind, except once. Out of the blue, as we were taking an early evening walk, he said,

'This is the last baby we'll ever have.' Astonished, I asked"Why?"

'Because there's a fifty percent chance that this one'll be a boy.'

'So what?' I asked.

"He pursed his thin lips, set his firm jaw, and refused to discuss it further. I still don't know for sure why he didn't want a boy. That was Hald. Not given to too much talk or any explanations at all.

"Somehow, I wasn't afraid of childbirth. All I'd really heard about it was what Gramma once told me while she was remarking

145

on how funny it was that Americans went to the hospital to have their babies,

'I just had a few pains and then there was a baby.' She told me.

"I went into labor a couple of weeks early, probably because the baby was so big. The doctor told me not to go to the hospital yet, to wait until the pains were a few minutes apart or my water broke. I didn't even know what that meant until it happened several hours later. For a second there, looking at the puddle on the floor, I thought I'd peed and never felt it.

"I went to the hospital after that, and was put in a labor room for twenty-four hours. Hald wasn't allowed to see me, and I don't think they kept him very well informed, so he was imagining all sorts of horrible things happening to me. At one point, the doctor told me, Hald had collared him and demanded 'If it's between my wife or the baby, I want my wife. Don't let her die.'

"Meanwhile, I wasn't suffering at all. Fortunately, I had brought along a novel, Louis Bromfield's *The Rains Came,* and I set about reading it. There I was in labor, sitting cross-legged, lost in the book, letting nature take its course. The pains weren't that bad, more like bad menstrual cramps, that's all. The only annoyance, well, really embarrassment, was the nurses coming in every so often, sticking their fingers up me and announcing 'One finger.' Finally, I asked what that was all about, and they said it's how they measure how much you've dilated so the baby could come out. I wasn't dilating very much, that was the problem. After a day of this, with no progress in the dilation, they took an X-Ray and the doctor said,

'Head's too big. It's not even engaged, down where it has to be for us to reach it with a forceps. You can't deliver it. You need a Caesarean.'

"Shocked, I asked, 'Why? My grandmother practically had hers in the field. What would she have done?'

'She would've died,' was the answer.

"Hald was still sitting in the waiting room, apparently not having slept or eaten the whole time. The first he knew that I'd had a C-section was when the nurse came out to announce

'It's a boy, eight pounds, eleven ounces.'

THERAPY, A NOVEL

"By that time, I was sound asleep from the anesthesia. It was a great disappointment to me after that I hadn't seen him born. They had knocked me out as soon as I hit the operating room.

"When I awoke, I was in a ward with eighteen beds, all filled with new mothers.

'Do you want to see your baby?' a nurse asked.

"When she brought him to me, I was blown away. Everyone had told me how homely newborns are, but this one wasn't. He had fat, round cheeks, long, black eyelashes, dark curls plastered to his perfectly shaped head. So perfect. With all the right parts. Ten fingers. Ten toes. Fat, dimpled hands, just like a doll's. Tiny perfect nails complete with miniscule half moons at the base. A rosebud mouth. And clear white skin, not the red wrinkled face everyone told me to expect. He was like a big porcelain doll. I felt ecstatic, touching his satiny, firm cheeks. He was a wonder to me. My own baby.

"Finally, two days after it all began, they let Hald in to see me. He sat by my side holding my hand, crying. Really crying. Drugged as I was, my stomach clenched in fear. I had never seen a man cry and didn't know what to do.

"What's the matter sweetheart?" I asked. "Have you seen the baby? He's so beautiful." He didn't mention the baby.

"I thought you'd die," he said, tears streaming down his face.

"Then he started to shout. "Those bastards. They wouldn't let me see you. They wouldn't tell me anything. I knew you couldn't be all right..."

"I started to shake. What could I do? Who would help me? How should I deal with this? My usual mode, of just ignoring what someone was saying wouldn't work in this situation. And I felt so weak, so helpless. I mustered up enough strength to answer in as firm a voice as I could manage,

"I'm not going to die, silly. It's all over and I just have to heal."

"But he kept on yelling until the nurses came into the ward and told him he'd have to leave. He'd become totally upset, his legs jerking spasmodically as he sat, his hands clawing at his face and hair, tears flowing down his face. Appalled, I thought, "Omigod, he's become unglued!" I was scared. What would I do? There was a baby to take care of, a daunting prospect. I'd

never even changed a diaper. I felt weak and it hurt so much where they'd cut me open.

"Hald was older, stronger, or so I thought, but his distraught, shaking man wasn't the in-charge man I thought I was married to. For almost two years, I'd relied on him to take care of me in the woods. He was the provider. The one who knew how to survive, but now he certainly couldn't take care of the baby and me. What could I do? Where could I turn to?

"The nurses managed to get Hald to stand up and walk out of the ward and I didn't see him again until day I left the hospital seven days later. What he did during that week, I never found out. I also never found out if he'd even had the curiosity to go see the baby at all before then. In those days, babies were kept safely in the nursery when fathers visited, so they could only see them through a glass window, not able to touch them until they left the hospital. I don't know if that was a good thing or a bad in this case. I mean I don't know if Hald would have been less bummed out if he could've picked the baby up or if he might have hurt him had he been able to pick him up.

"The day I was supposed to go home found me alone and frightened. Then, almost like magic, my mother appeared at my side,

'What a gorgeous baby! Just like Stan was.'

"Even when she was being an angel of mercy, she had to get in a zinger. My homeliness as a newborn was the stuff of family legend, just as Stan's beauty was. I was confused. How did she get there? How did she know where I was and that I'd had the baby? Did Hald call her? Did my doctor?

"We forget now what a big deal long distance calls were even in the fifties and there were no phones by the beds in the ward, so I had had no warning that my parents were coming.

"I finally pieced together how they knew to come. When I first went to the obstetrician, I had to fill out a form that included my maiden name, and I had told him I came from Providence. As I recall, he asked where my accent was from. It was definitely not Maine. When he witnessed Hald's breakdown, the doctor decided it wasn't safe to send such a young girl and a baby back to live with Hald. I definitely needed care, and Hald clearly wouldn't provide that, so he had his nurse call my parents. With a last

name like Verensky, it wasn't hard finding them in the phone-book. My mother apparently called the hospital and found out when I was to be discharged and talked my father into driving up to Maine to take me home, even though he'd formally disowned me when I got married.

"I resisted going with them. I knew that if I did, I'd never get back with Hald, and I was sure that once he calmed down, we could continue our idyllic life in the wilderness. My parents actually went to our apartment in Bangor and were dismayed by my cats sleeping in the crib that was to be Sammy's. You'd think they were rescuing me to come back to a life of comfort, but the truth was that, in their house, my bedroom was in the unheated, uninsulated second floor of their bungalow.

"There was no bathroom on that floor either. The house downstairs was cramped and there was no room to put a baby's crib. They solved that problem by putting the crib in my grand-mother's bedroom, through which one had to walk to get to the flight of stairs to my room. Gramma was dispossessed, deprived of all privacy, all dignity. Worse yet, they had talked her into sell-ing her tenement house and giving them the money to buy the bungalow in which they then lived. Certainly not good karma to bring home a new baby to, but what could I do?

'We're going to take you home and give you a nice rest,' my mother announced to the eighteen bed maternity ward. They had come well prepared with gifts. Clothes for the baby. A car bed. Blankets. Deli food like I hadn't seen for two years. Potato knishes, kosher salami, corned beef, bulkie rolls, and yellow mus-tard. Russian tea cakes for dessert.

'Home?" I asked. "Do you mean your home?'

'Of course. We'll take care of you. You've just had major surgery and carried that baby for nine months. You need rest.'

"It didn't dawn on them that when I left their home I meant it. I had a new home. Wherever Hald was, that was my home.

"No," I protested. 'I want to stay in Maine. I've got every-thing ready for the baby in the apartment.'

"Hald walked in just then, the first time in a week.

"I turned to him gratefully, 'Honey, tell them we're going home together, just you and me.

"To my discomfort, to my shock actually, he refused and stammered that I should go home with them. That I was sick. He didn't know how to take care of me or the baby. I felt a cold chill. For a moment, everything went black and I had trouble breathing. Hald kept insisting that I go with them. I begged him, pleaded with him, not to make me go, but he wouldn't relent. Me he wanted. The baby he didn't.

"I finally grabbed Hald's arm and drew him towards me, whispering to him frantically,

'If they take me back, they'll never let me go. Please, don't make me go there.'

"I don't know why I thought that, but somehow deep down I knew they wanted me back. There was, after all, that strange letter my mother had written about missing me and my music. I was afraid also that they wanted my baby. A second chance of child raising, but this time they wouldn't screw it up. My brother had suddenly had a complete psychotic breakdown when he was fourteen, and they'd had to face their part in that. When I abandoned them, it must have occurred to them their treatment of me had made them lose me, too. They sure hadn't done it right. They needed vindication and they were facing a lonely old age.

"Hald was red faced and strange and he seemed curiously detached. He had but one answer to my pleading.

'We have to go with them,' was his repeated response. When pressed, he just started muttering about 'them.' It was hard to distinguish words as he rambled on.

"Then the nurse brought the baby in and my mother picked him up and dressed him in the clothes she'd brought. She had crocheted a light blue bonnet and sweater for him in the week I'd been hospitalized. I was too weak to protest any more.

"So that's how I ended up back in my parents' house, a place I'd sworn never to set foot in again. My idyllic Maine life was over. Never to be restored. My mother wove her web and told me it was a home. I was stuck in it, and this time there was no easy getaway. There was little Sammy to think of and Hald had ceased to be my protector.

All these years later, after telling Alex about how I got back to Providence, walking down the road and remembering even more, I finally realized how furious I was at Hald for delivering

me back to my folks. For failing to take care of me and Sammy. There was never anyone in my life who protected me. Who took care of me just because I was me. Even now, it wasn't me my parents wanted. It was Sammy. My mother walked out of the hospital carrying him, a harbinger for the rest of his childhood. At the time, I hid my anguish under a thick blanket of numbness. For years after, until I met Joe, I felt nothing except my passion for my little boy. With him, I was besotted.

But I didn't have the last word in anything to do with him. My parents used me as his nursemaid. They made all the decisions. They decided how he should be dressed, how fed, and how disciplined, when he should go to bed, what books he should be read. They even judged my adequacy at my job being Sammy's nursemaid. To this day, Sammy idolizes them, goes to the cemetery to visit their burial sites, and lets me know what a poor excuse for a mother I was. He never forgave me for marrying Joe. My parents' told him over and over that he was the center of their world, and he thought he should be the center of mine as well.

The way Sammy got back at me for my perfidy as a mother was perfect. He refused to go to college. That brilliant, brilliant mind focused on carpentry. Eventually, however, he became devoted to creating works of art so dazzling they took my breath away, works of art he just piled in an attic and never showed anybody. The absence of his father was a gaping hole in his psyche. He felt permanently rejected by his real father. I tried to explain why Hald never came to see him, but Sammy wouldn't hear of my parents' perfidy. He just wouldn't believe that they could be so selfish and cruel. Or maybe he couldn't stand to, as it would have shaken his foundations in his world.

Chapter Fifteen

That was an old grief by now, a grief to which I had to add my other sons' lack of love for me. One way or another, I had bungled them all, although God knows I tried to give them all everything they wanted, to immerse them in kindness, to expect nothing from them, to let them grow and bloom like the flowers in my gardens. I made sure I never laid any guilt trips on them, determined never to make them feel grateful.

Once I was talking to Jed on the phone. I had called him. He never called me. As usual, this time he said, "Can't talk now, Mom, I'm busy."

So I answered,"You're always too busy to talk to me."

To my horror, I heard his voice in falsetto,

"Poor me, I always did everything for you and now you won't even take a minute to talk to your poor old Mom."

I slammed the phone down. So, that's the gratitude I got. In the process of being so good to them, I actually taught them they had everything coming to them, and I had nothing coming to me. I was reminded of the day Joe called me"St. Barbara." Had Jed heard that? I couldn't remember if he was in the room that day, but Joe had definitely taught the boys to disrespect me. He didn't have to say anything outright. The example of his behavior towards me was enough.

Well, about childrearing I always said,

"Whatever was done to me, I'd do the opposite to them." So I did. It worked out well enough for them, but not for me.

Enough of the self-pity. Joe's refusal to help me to raise the boys didn't help. He never participated except to slip them money and, later in their teens, to give them credit cards so they could do whatever they wanted. This wasn't out of generosity, but to keep them off his back. Just give them what they want. Avoid confrontation.

"But that's not good, Joe," I would protest. "They have to learn to earn their money, and to budget and save it. They can't just tootle all over the country following rock bands, treating their friends to restaurants and tickets and pot. You have to take a stand with them."

"Is this what we're going to talk about tonight?" was his standard response. That, and telling the boys, "Don't tell your mother I gave you those Visa cards." So. I was the heavy. The killjoy. What stood in the way of them and their fun, and, of course, if Joe needed to keep it a secret from me, then I must be trying to pussywhip him. No wonder my sons thought I was a bitch.

My response to the nightmare of what the boys had become was to stay in my study and write, day and night. I couldn't fight them all.

Chapter Sixteen

One fine June evening, I'd had a 5:30 appointment with Alex. Just as I started walking out the door at the end of the session, I heard Alex's"Uhh..." I wheeled back through the door to find him in the middle of the room, looking upward at the ceiling, hands deep in his pants pockets.

"What's it like outside?" He asked.

"Gorgeous," I responded. "Balmy."

I was so excited I could hardly get the words out. I started to walk out again, felt that I had found my voice and turned back again. My chest was being thumped by my heartbeat and felt ready to burst. Did I dare? I dared.

"Come with me," I said, my voice barely above a whisper.

His face lit up with joy. I don't think I'd ever seen such naked joy on anyone's face in my life. As he came through the door, I grabbed his hand. He didn't pull back. I half dragged him down the stairs.

"You car or mine," I whispered.

I don't know why I whispered, but the occasion seemed to call for it. "Uhh..." He clearly hadn't thought about it, so I propelled him to mine which was parked in the front of the building. I unlocked the passenger door first and he slid in the seat, giving that jerk to his trouser legs that men give when they sit down. As I got in, I reached for my car phone.

"What's that for?" He asked with a tinge of panic in his voice.

155

"Well, I have to call Joe and make an excuse. He's expecting me to meet him at a restaurant on the Hill."

"Oh, no-o-o. That's a problem."

"Don't be silly." I said. "I'll tell him I'm too distraught from stuff we were discussing in therapy and I want to drive around by myself for a while. He'll never suspect. And what if he does? Our marriage is dead."

"I could lose my license if he does. Look, let me out. I shouldn't be doing this. With any patient, but especially with you."

"Why not especially me?"

"Because he's a friend of Dom's and he's a good lawyer. Dom would fire me even if I didn't lose my license over the whole thing."

His cowardice was beginning to make me feel disgusted. This wasn't going the way it did in my reveries. This side of him had never been revealed in the therapeutic situation. God knows he was firm enough about my dumping Joe. He didn't bother hiding how attracted he was to me.

"Please. Don't worry," I said. Just let me call him while he's still in his car. I know it'll be okay. He know load of people on the Hill and he'll just sit with drinking buddies and gossip about other lawyers. I wouldn't do anything to hurt you, and Joe isn't the type to go suing out of vengeance. Trust me. I know him. If I want to leave him, he'll just let me go. I know it's funny, a trial lawyer who hates confrontation, but that's what he's like. I've been trying to tell you that. I'm completely in love with you. I've never felt such love for anyone. I'm crazy with it. The attraction we have, it comes once in a lifetime if you're lucky. We're lucky. Why shouldn't we be happy?"

So I called. Joe didn't even sound disappointed. He just gave a noncommittal,

"Okay, I'll go to Angelo's for dinner."

"See, I told you he wouldn't care. He didn't even ask me where I was going or when I'd be home. Look, you've gotta trust me. You can't lose your license unless I say something happened between us, and I'd never say anything. It's not a capital offense to go out to have a drink with someone, is it?"

THERAPY, A NOVEL

"The APA guidelines state that you never see a patient out of the clinical setting for any reason."

"Well, then," I said,"they'll never have to know. I won't tell. You won't tell. Joe will never know, so he won't tell. Look, you initiated this tonight. Not me. If you want out, just get out. If you want to be with me, I know a great place where we can sit and talk this over. L'Elizabeth's, it's near here."

He made no move to leave.

"Where's L'Elizabeth's?" he asked. "I can't be seen with you in a public place."

I laughed. "It's a rendezvous kind of place, and it's the most private public place you ever saw. Besides I go there all the time with colleagues and visiting professors. I go out to eat with colleagues, too. In this day and age, people don't think anything of a professional woman having a drink with a man who's not her husband. They don't think it's necessarily an affair."

Of course, I was reckoning without the intimate looks, the lovelorn expression on our faces, gazing into each other's eyes, the things that tell everybody you're in love. You don't do that with colleagues and visiting professors. Besides, the colleague I rendezvoused with most often was a priest, but Alex didn't have to know that.

L'Elizabeth's decor was straight out of the local antique stores with the walls papered in a design of roses on a white background, the moldings all dark stained wood. Besides the large wood-surfaced bar, most of the space was taken up with motley upholstered and plain wood chairs, grouped in twos, fours and sixes around tables, some marble topped and some wood, some round, some square, all different sizes and styles. The effect was both cozy and sophisticated. Since almost all of the chairs were high backed and a few were winged, when people came in they couldn't see at a glance who was there. The chairs and tables were arranged so that it was hard to scope the place out and see who was buried in what chair. We sat in the back under an oil painting of a blue and white vase and a matching bowl that had tipped, so that its apples were strewn in front of the vase. It was neither hideous nor beautiful, typical of the artwork on all the walls. A tall, wholly elegant African American waiter with a

157

HARRIE ROSE

shaved head brought us menus, which listed fine wines and spirits, but had no prices. I ordered some twenty-year-old tawny port and Alex selected a fifteen-year-old single malt Scotch, which was served in a heated glass without ice.

"You shouldn't be drinking alcohol with Prozac,"

"Oh God, Alex, I haven't needed Prozac for weeks. I couldn't see where it did anything for me, so I've just stopped taking it. You're my Prozac."

I hoped he wouldn't be mad. Spurning his medications.

"Thanks for telling me. Did your doctorate cover the pharmacopeia?"

I held my hand up, palm outward in a Stop motion.

"Hey, this isn't an office visit. Let's forget the medical advice. I haven't been depressed for a few weeks. I feel fantastic. Let that be enough."

"I'll let it ride now." He looked around. "Not to change the subject, but this is the kind of place you'd expect in L.A., not in stodgy old Providence."

"It's been here for years," I said,"This is a surprisingly sophisticated city. Not so stodgy as you think. I'm so excited to be able to show it to you. You don't really know the city yet, do you? Or the countryside. Wait till you see where I live. You won't believe that either."

"You've let me in on that secret already," he answered dryly, clearly referencing all the seductive descriptions I'd regaled him with during our therapy sessions. So he did take notice.

"Barbara, understand me please," he continued. "Tonight is as far as this can go. I'm not going to your house and we can't see each other out of the office. The APA rules are very clear about that, no socializing with patients. I meant it when I said I could lose my license to practice and then where would I be?"

Despite his words, I didn't believe him. Plenty of people had affairs with their therapists. My first husband married his, for God's sake. So how strict could they really be. I could tell he felt about me the way I felt about him and the AMA be damned. Excitement gripped me. I could barely sit still in my chair, squirming like a little kid. We stopped talking, listening to Julio Iglesias serenade us about love in Spanish which I don't speak, but, I soon found out, Alex did. Seemed he went to medical school in

THERAPY, A NOVEL

Spain. He translated the words of the songs, saying them softly in a deep, husky voice, while he looked into my eyes and held my hands.

He wasn't just showing off his Spanish. He was making love to me. He looked at me adoringly. We finished our drinks and went out into the soft June night. The port made me aglow, and I was filled with emotion just being with Alex. We walked to the car.

"Dinner?" I asked. He hesitated a few seconds.

"All right. What do you suggest?

"Ordinarily, I'd suggest the Hill for Italian food, but Joe is going to a restaurant there tonight."

"Oh, the one place I've been to in Providence is the Hill. Practically the first thing anybody said to me was 'You've got to go to the Hill. It's so Italian.'"

"Oh, you don't like it?"

No, no. I do. It's fine, but it's so crowded. And the way everybody greets everyone else in the restaurants I get the feeling everyone in Rhode Island knows each other. It's just as well we stay away from there. Is there any place quieter, more out of the way?"

"Sure, we can stay right here on the East Side or Fox Point. Or, of course, we can drive out of town, Newport, Narragansett, but it's already pretty late. Joe won't notice if I get in before midnight, but I think I'd have a hard time explaining the morning hours to him."

Wanting to impress him with another sophisticated choice, I took him to a tiny restaurant nearby. The walls of the restaurant, Chez Pat's, were dark green, and the tables covered with starched white cloths. Bare branches decorated with twinkling lights adorned the ceiling. We sat at a table for two by the window.

The place specialized in what they billed as American Bistro cuisine, with each food having its own distinct taste of herbs, spices and vinegars, artistically arranged plates with barely cooked vegetables, beans, and meat in separate heaps, decorated with fresh mint or sprigs of rosemary. The wait staff described the day's offerings using words like *confit, remoulade* and *tournedo*. They offered"Tapenade, pistore, and anchoiade with garlic croutons" and"Tatale with jicama, mango, papaya slaw and spiced

159

Brazil nuts" and"Mediterranean pan seared tuna with gremolata white bean ragu." An entirely new vocabulary of foods. It fit our mood. Like L'Elizabeth's, it was cozy but sophisticated, with the wait staff in black trousers, white aprons tucked into the waistbands hanging to their knees. Nobody seemed to be looking at us and, fortunately, I didn't know anybody there that evening.

"I like your taste in restaurants," he remarked."I can't get over that there are places like this here. It's what you'd expect in L.A., not in a small city like this."

"Why did you come here if you expected nothing in the way of restaurants or things to do? Did you think this was a backwater? If you did, why did you come?"

"Because I was hoping it still had old-fashioned family values, and there wouldn't be as much crime or the same insistence on money. When I came here to visit, I noticed that you don't see Mercedes and Rollses everywhere. The people here are more grounded."

"Maybe so. Or they just might be poorer. The population isn't as transient as LA's. Most people who live here grew up here. But we have a lot of good restaurants. Eating out is the local pastime."

"I've been noticing that."

I continued,"I want to know all about you. Where you went to school. How you came to be a psychiatrist. What your mother is like? Do you have brothers and sisters? What are your favorite foods? Do you like movies? I want to know everything."

"Whoa! I'm the psychiatrist. I ask the questions," he laughed.

"No. Here you're not my psychiatrist. Erase that from your memory bank. It's an accident that we met that way. I'd have been drawn to you wherever I met you. Let's forget that this started with my being a patient. My attraction to you was so strong, right from the start, it was just meant to be. And it was for you too, wasn't it?"

"That's for sure."

I could barely believe my ears. "You felt the same way about me? When did you feel it? The first time you saw me? The second? When?"

"I don't know exactly. Not that first time. You looked so miserable that all I felt was that I hoped I could make you feel better. I felt empathy for you. By the end of that first visit, I knew I was looking forward to seeing you a second time—and then a third. When you came into my office all dressed up I was knocked out. Partly because it looked as if you were getting out of your depression and I helped make that possible, and partly because you were such a knockout. God, you are the sexiest female I've ever met, sexy and smart and warm, not just a pretty face. But I didn't know you were attracted to me. I thought it was my psychiatry and Prozac."

"Why did you become a shrink?"

"Actually, I was an internist. Very busy one, too. But the patients were like so much meat. I'd only have ten to fifteen minutes for each one. I couldn't get to know them and it was like a rat race with me rushing from one examining room to another. I figured in psychiatry, I'd really get to know patients and each case would be unique, and it is."

So we talked and sparred as lovers do, trying to discover each other, or, mostly, me trying to discover him. After all, he already knew a lot about me. I did find out that, as I had suspected, he wasn't married, but he was divorced and had two daughters in their early teens

"Driving me crazy. My ex-wife, too," he reported.

He told me that when he finished his psychiatric residency, a cousin of his mentioned that he knew of an opening here from a friend of the friend of Dr. Aiello. They got along over the phone, so Alex came to visit, liked what he saw, and decided to try it out.

I hadn't yet asked him where he was living now, and he didn't volunteer the information. I guessed he first had to learn to trust me and to get over his fear of our being found out. Deep inside I felt some regret about his attitude. His fear disappointed me, that's the word, disappointed. At heart he was a wimp. I wanted someone who could take our joy with wild abandon and screw the consequences.

Thinking back on it, though, I realize he was the one who had the most to lose, not me. After Joe, I wanted someone with authority. Alex was an authority to me by the virtue of his role.

He was someone I was supposed to be guided by, although I now see I was doing the guiding, begging him, in effect, to be my lover, not my shrink.

He brought up the matter of the impropriety of seeing me again the second time we met at L'Elizabeth's. I wanted so badly to have a love affair with him that I responded with an actual plea.

"Please don't, Alex. Don't be afraid. How often in your life can you meet someone so right for you. Someone who's so magically taken by you? Why shouldn't we be lovers and friends? You only live once so far as we know. Please don't spoil this. I've waited my whole life for it. Please don't keep acting afraid.

"It's like you don't trust me. If you don't, then leave now. I yearn for you, but, if it's really too dangerous for you, go now. Don't draw it out. You know about me by now. More than most lovers do. I've been spilling my soul out to you. How can you think I'd betray you? Nobody can do anything to you unless I say we were lovers and I'd never say that."

He didn't answer, but he dropped the subject and didn' t bring it up again for a long time.

I never went to his office again after that night.

"One thing," he had told me after we left the restaurant that first night. "If we're going to meet, I can't keep on with you as a patient."

"Fine, good. I've said enough, dredged up a lot, and understand myself much better, thanks to you."

He beamed, "That means the world to me. It's what every psychiatrist hopes for, but doesn't always get."

So it was settled.

We met three or four week nights after he was through with patients. He even gave me his private phone number. I'd pick him up at the office. Actually, he'd sneak out, make sure nobody was around, turn his head quickly this way and that, then duck into my car. I never picked him up until his secretary had left for the day and he was the last to leave the office building.

We'd tryst at L'Elizabeth's and then go out to eat, a new restaurant almost every night. Yes, I saw people I knew and occasionally he saw someone he knew, but he didn't panic. Taking advantage of the long summer twilight, we'd walk hands

THERAPY, A NOVEL

entwined through the hilly, windy streets of the historical district, the streets that rise up from Benefit Street, enjoying the scents of honeysuckle, roses and the myriad other flowers in the gardens of the old houses we passed.

"Walking with you like this is like a dream. It's like another country from California," he once remarked. "These hills remind me of 'Frisco, but the houses! There are Victorians in Frisco, but all these other kinds of old houses. It's like being transported back in time. And it's not fake like Disney or even Sturbridge or Williamsburg. These have been her for what, almost 300 years some of them, and they're lived in, not showpieces. This has got to be the best kept secret in America."

"Some of the people living in these houses come from the descendants of the original builders, although all aren't. Oh, and wait'll you see Newport or even towns like Little Compton! There are these old houses all over the state, and old churches and courthouses. Even banks."

"How come so many of the old houses have no lawns, no shrubs?"

"Well, the earliest settlers built the fronts of their houses right to the pavement, but they have lovely gardens in back. What's funny is that the triple deckers that were built for the immigrants flooding into the city to work in the factories were also built with no front plantings, like the one I was raised in. But, even those houses with some shrubs in front have secret gardens. Let's sneak around some of these houses and I'll show you. When I first went to England, a woman told me her biggest disappointment in America was that there were no gardens. I told her we have them, but they're not in the front of houses like in England, but in the back yards. Have you been to England? All the houses, even row houses have big gardens in front where we have lawns, but a lot of the towns, like in the Cotswolds, have streets like this with rows of houses built right to the pavement, so the colonists must have been used to that look when they built here."

The plaques on the houses proudly announced their age and the name of their first owners. Samuel Staples 1760. Joseph Jenckes 1774. Jabez Gorham 1793. Sullivan Dorr 1809. Elisha Angell 1810. Whole blocks of 18th and 19th century houses. A few blocks further and the dates were later. Earle Pierce 1827.

163

Albyn Dike 1831. Isaac Hale 1846. Just looking at the plaques revealed where the city began and how it fanned out.

"Notice how insignificant the women were!" I remarked.

"How so?"

"There isn't one female name on those plaques. Surely these houses weren't inhabited by bachelors."

"Well, if you put the women's names in then you should put the children in too, shouldn't you?" Alex responded laughing.

"Oh, come on. The children didn't own the houses. If the man died, I presume the house went to the wife. Joe once told me that the old deeds had the man's name on it followed by *et ux.*"

"What's that?"

"It's Latin for 'and spouse,' so if the wife died and the man remarried, he never had to change his deed. Women were like interchangeable parts."

"You mean, they're not?" He joked.

I made my hand into a gun, "Pow. Death to misogynists!"

A few blocks more and we were in the twentieth century, 1901, 1910. The plaques still only had the husband's name on them although the enormous late Victorians had hardly been built for single men. I wondered how much input wives were given as to how their homes were designed. I pointed out to Alex the architectural details, and how they changed in each era.

"When I lived in the city, I used to walk these streets all the time. It was amazing to me that I never got tired of looking at the old houses. There was always some bit of molding, some window treatment, some doorway, some carving I had never noticed before." I said. "Even where I live now, there are houses built in the 1700's, but not so many of them. Of course, the original houses there were on farms, so they were always far apart. Nobody lived in the country just to have solitude before there were cars to drive around in."

"Before I met you, all I registered in my mind was 'old fashioned houses' and here you have me thinking of quoins and pediments. It's like, well, you've enlarged my experience.

"What I love about you Barbara is the way you notice everything, take pleasure in it. How many people who grew up here know so much about it? Dom never mentioned it as an

attraction, but things like old houses are attractions in other places. People go to San Francisco to see the Victorian houses, or buildings from 1910 or so. History is an attraction. This should be a major tourist destination. Why isn't it promoted?"

'Oh, Yankee modesty. Yankee reserve. I mean, these old places are people's homes and maybe they don't want hordes of tourists gaping at their quoins.

"But you know, there are other things. That beautiful old white church on the hill. That's the first Baptist Church ever in America. And Newport has the first synagogue. And the library I go to, The Athenaeum is the third oldest in America and it still functions as a full library.

"But you're right. Most Rhode Islanders don't know about it or just take it for granted. People here have a huge inferiority complex. They think this is a place to leave. It's just old. They don't think of it as quaint or as something tourists would like to see. We lived in LA for a short time when I was a kid, and, even then, what bothered me was that the streets were so straight and wide and all the houses were pretty new. I didn't know the word to describe it then, but I guess you'd say it has no character. This has character."

"And cold winters," he added.

"Spoken like a true Californian!"

I still longed to get him out to the country and enlarge his experience there as well, to teach him wildflowers, birds, me. Teaching is potent. I wasn't so aware of it then, but I am now.

For two weeks, I walked with Alex four evenings a week, clasping his hand, woozy with joy. Ecstatic. How I wanted him. To really have him. Sexually, of course. It must seem odd in this day and age that we didn't consummate our affair for over two weeks. All we did was hold hands and kiss.

My days also seemed enchanted. I woke up with joy. Thinking of Alex. Wondering when and how we'd finally make love. The tension was almost unbearable. So far, he hadn't made a move. Just kissing. Stroking. Like kids. In fact, I felt about fifteen only I didn't feel this good when I was fifteen. Before I trekked into the city in the late afternoons, I spent hours in my gardens with opera wafting from the family room through the open French doors. Its beauty counterbalanced by my aching for Alex.

I wanted him here with me, swooning to the greatest love songs of the Western world. But anticipation was also delicious. A few hours more and we'd be together.

I had already started paving the way for Alex coming to the house. I assured him that nobody could possibly see him coming, that our driveway was 1100 feet long, carved out of woods that hid it from any vantage point on the road. Besides my neighbors were out to work all day. Since Alex didn't object to evening appointments with patients, he could easily get afternoons off or even mornings.

By about our ninth date, when he kissed me, a long, lingering kiss, our tongues tasting each other, he said, his voice thick with desire,

"Let's go to the Biltmore."

"No," I gasped. "Let's not cheapen this. Come to my house. Please. After that, in the winter, or nights we can go to the Biltmore or wherever, but first come to my house."

"Cheapen?" He asked. "I said the Biltmore Hotel, not some sleazy motel room. I don't know how much longer I can take this. I'm not fourteen after all."

"Come to my house. Please. Joe is gone from eight or so in the morning to at least seven or eight at night, when he comes home at all. I promise nobody will see you. It's totally isolated. You'll be amazed at how uninhabited the country is here."

I know I'd made this point before, many times, but still he reacted with disbelief,

"In this state? It's so..." and he made that small squared off motion with his hands to indicate its small size, as he had done when I told him there was hunting here.

"Trust me," I answered—and then was immediately aware that that was an infelicitous expression. Whenever anybody had ever said,"trust me" to me, it was a warning not to. You know that old joke,"How do you say 'f— you in business? 'Trust me.'"

But I would never betray Alex and my house was less public than the Biltmore, and told him so. I was determined that our love be consummated in my house on my big brass bed, that we'd bathe in my deep steeping tub and swim naked in my pool. I still don't know why that was so important to me, but it's the scenario I'd dreamt up, and it had to be that way. It was almost as if I had

envisioned the setting for a torrid love affair when I decorated the house and was just waiting for an Alex to come along. It took a lot of convincing him, and strong sexual longing, but finally he said he'd come.

Chapter Seventeen

I was out of my head with joy and anticipation. I even went to Victoria's Secret and bought an emerald green satin Teddy decorated with black lace on each leg and at the bosom. I gave Alex detailed directions of how to get to the country, to ensure that he wouldn't get lost. After dressing in the Teddy, covering it with an innocent looking flowered robe and pretty pink slippers, I waited. Would he come? Would he chicken out? Would he abandon me?

By the time the dogs began to announce a visitor, I was miserable with the certainty that our affair would be over before it began. I flew to the door, and there he was. God he looked good. For once, he wasn't wearing a suit. In deference to the rural setting, I guess, he had on neatly pressed jeans, a red plaid short-sleeved shirt, with a button-down collar, and highly polished brown moccasins.

When I opened the door, he whispered,"Where can I stash my car?"

"It's okay where it is under the trees," I assured him."Nobody can see it after all. And you don't have to whisper."

"God, you weren't kidding when you said this was the wilderness. Does anyone else live around here?"

"Only through the woods a good quarter mile away. But if you shout, they can hear. My son Ethan had a terrible chain saw accident, we yelled, and our neighbor came running. He's a rescue worker for the local fire department, which is strictly volunteer,

only staffed by volunteers, I mean. Anyway, he saved Ethan's life. Put a tourniquet on his arm and stopped the spurting blood."

"What do you mean, 'a chain saw accident'?"

"Ethan was cutting wood with a friend and they went to cut a dead tree leaning against another tree. The dead one buckled so the friend lost control of his saw and whipped around. Ethan was standing too close and the saw sliced his arm. It was a miracle that he didn't lose it altogether. Or worse, he could have had his head cut off."

"Cutting wood?" He paused, and then asked,"Is that the smell in this house? Wood burning. It smells like bacon."

"Really? I hardly notice it anymore unless I've been away on a long trip, but we do use wood heat. I mean, we do have oil, but there are wood stoves in the kitchen, the family room, the living room and our bedroom, attached to the fireplaces. Of course, it means we can't ever look at logs burning in an open hearth, but the wood stoves are warmer. They give a special quality of warmth I can't explain. They throw off more heat than fireplaces, although I miss the look of open flames. But the stoves are still better. And the smell of burnt wood. That's good, too." I was babbling on out of nervousness.

He looked around as we walked from the large foyer into the family room and then to the kitchen. I was trembling, afraid my knees would buckle, but the familiar routine of showing off the house helped calm me. The living and dining rooms were to the right off the foyer, and the family room was straight ahead across the hallway that led leftwards to the master bedroom suite and my study. You could see the living and dining rooms from the foyer.

Alex looked carefully at each piece of furniture in the living room, while I felt foolish standing there in my bathrobe. Twin sofas with carved wood frames upholstered in light yellow velvet flanked the fireplace in the living room, an intricately carved round rosewood Indonesian antique table with its top protected by glass stood between them. A hand carved Chinese screen telling the story of the Buddha stood in one corner, opposite it, were hung three Chinese silk scrolls with scenes of mountains and waterfalls painted on them. On other walls, with mahogany tables under them were original oil paintings that we had bought at

THERAPY, A NOVEL

an art gallery in San Francisco, a game table inlaid with mother-of-pearl used to keep liquor and liqueurs placed on a wall near the dining room entrance, two velvet striped benches with carved legs sat in front of the bay window which looked out to the front of the house and a border of tall cedars bordering the woods.

"I like what you've done with colors in this room," he commented. The touches of red and the yellows working off the dark woods. Nice. Did you do it all yourself?"

"Of course I did it all myself. Who else would do it?"

'Well, in LA, you'd have to have a decorator. Nobody does their own house, unless maybe the poor people. I thought you said you had no talent. It certainly takes talent to make a large room like this so harmonious, so elegant and yet so inviting. What kind of sofas are these?"

I was embarrassed by his flattery.

"Uhh, what do you mean what kind of sofas? They're sofas to sit on and have conversations on"

"Well, I can see they belong to some kind of period, but I don't know the names of these things. Are they Chippendale?"

"Oh, no. They're Hepplewhite. Cleaner lines than Chippendale. See? Notice the straight legs. No ball and claw. Those two benches under the window. You can see the legs are identical. I don't mean to brag, but I thought they were so elegant the first time I saw them. That pale yellow velvet. I don't know why I chose that, but it just seemed to fit. I think it gives an air of, I don't know, contentment? They stay clean since we don't sit in here much. Only when there's company, and even then people end up congregating in the kitchen, I don't know why. The table under the painting on the left here is Sheraton, I think. Of course the pieces are just reproductions, not the original stuff like what we saw at the John Brown House when we took the tour. "

I realized that I was babbling, ruining any chances of seduction, of ardor. I led him towards the family room.

"Listen to me," I said. "I sound like a docent leading a house tour. You're supposed to be seeing me, not the stupid house. Actually, everyone who comes here wants a tour of the house. Joe is so proud of it and makes sure they know he designed it

171

himself, but I've done all the decorating. I really loved doing it."

He didn't answer. As he stood admiring the family room and its view of the gardens, he finally seemed to remember me. He turned to me, took my hands in his, and raised them over my head, pushing me into the door in one smooth movement. He leant his head down, feeling for my lips with his, first brushing his dry lips to mine, moving his head side to side in small movements, then opening his mouth wider, his tongue seeking mine, and at the same time pressing his body into mine, gifting me with a deep soul kiss.

"Where?" he queried, his voice thick with passion.

I grabbed him around his waist, and like drunken Siamese twins, we staggered out of the family room, down the hallway to the bedroom and fell on the bed. His hands began roaming over my body, insistent, kneading, as he kissed my neck, my face, my cheeks, my nose, my forehead. He loosened the satin sash of my robe and when it fell open, he kissed my shoulders, then my breasts. "Wow" he said breathlessly when the lace trimmed Teddy was revealed and he slowly started to peel it off my shoulders, down past my hips and off. I was naked. He inspected my body with his eyes, then his hands. He didn't seem to mind the cellulite and the drooping the breasts.

Actually, they didn't sag much yet. The nipples still pointed forward. But I was self-conscious about even the slightest drop. They had always been so high. I remember my cousin complaining when she saw me undressed,"It's not fair. They're big and high."

Now, of course, ten years later, my nipples point at the floor. It doesn't bother me now, however.

Anyways, back to then. I thought, "Thank God the bedroom shades are drawn and the light is dim. That didn't hide the breasts, but at least the rest wouldn't be so visible. Or maybe his amorousness would blind him. Fortunately, the general outlines of my body were still good. Flat stomach, hourglass shape. Yes, there was the Cesarean scar and the damaged skin, but he couldn't expect the flawless skin of a teenager.

"God, you have the sexiest body. I'm going to fuck you so hard." His voice was a husky moan.

THERAPY, A NOVEL

That shocked me!" I hate the f-word. It revulses me, but strangely now it caused a thrill of arousal.

I had once tried to wear something sexy for Joe, an old-fashioned pink satin corset. To spice up our marriage. I wore it under a silk robe while I was serving him dinner in the dimly lit kitchen. As I placed a steak in front of him, I undid the sash of the robe I had on, but when he saw the corset, all he did was giggle and continue eating the steak. Well, Alex didn't giggle. He took the Teddy seriously. Of course, I wasn't serving him steak at the time.

I've never been that much for sex. Oh, it was pleasant enough, a nice tickly relief, but I had never lusted for anyone, and I never thought sex lived up to its hype, even in the idyllic days with Hald in the Maine woods. Now I almost didn't know what to do with the intensity of feeling Alex aroused in me with his talented fingers.

"God, you feel good," he moaned as he massaged me all over, covering me with kisses, kissing everywhere he touched. The feeling of his dexterous fingers carried me to heights I'd never felt in foreplay or during the act itself, so far as that's concerned. From his first kiss, I felt myself get wet, my genitalia tingling insistently. As his hands and lips moved over my body, the tingling spread. I felt weightless, like a cloud.

I reached up to unbutton his shirt, unbuckle his belt. He tried to yank his clothes off himself, but I begged,"Let me. Let me. You undressed me." So he closed his eyes and let me. When I finished, he drew back and let me inspect his body as he had done mine. Just as I had thought and hoped, his chest was a solid mat of black fur. A true Mediterranean type. His stomach was flat and his buttocks well shaped and high. I hadn't had such a beautiful male body since Hald, but Hald didn't have chest hair, and Alex did.

Joe had hair, blond but plenty of it, but also a huge potbelly, so large it sagged. I caressed Alex's chest with broad circular motions, then stroked his legs, turned him over and kissed every knot on his spine. As I rubbed his buttocks gently, he moaned and turned and again began to stroke me all over, grabbing my flesh between his forefingers and thumbs, working his way all over my body as he continued to kiss me. He sucked on my toes,

my fingers, tickled my inner upper arms lightly. What he did to one side of me, he did to another. I was in total ecstasy. I didn't think I could go much higher. I was vibrating with a fluttery sensation that engulfed my entire body.

Then, finally, he entered me, and started to move rhythmically up and down. I matched his rhythm, pressing myself up to him in cadence. I felt an even more overwhelming sensation, like none I'd ever had before, as if I were melting, and I realized that at fifty-two I was having my first real orgasm. When he was through, we rested awhile, dozing off for a few minutes. Then I took his penis and stroked it, leaned down and kissed it, feeling it get hard again. Me, who was bored when novels described multiple orgasms, who found porno flicks excruciatingly dull, who always considered the sex act over when I reached one climax, and, I now realize, not much of a climax at that, I was ready for an encore. And he gave me one, two, three. The morning turned into afternoon and still we were in bed, still making love. For this wasn't sex. It was love. It was unity. It was the heights of union between two people.

Finally, around three, when we were both spent, we took a shower together, and walked out through the French doors in the master bathroom to the pool, naked. We jumped into the warm, clear water. He had never been skinny dipping before in his life, even in his backyard pool in L.A. I guess the houses are too close together there. When you're nude, the water feels like silken threads gliding in between your legs, caressing your naked body. It's the only way I care to swim now. Bathing suits feel heavy and awkward, not allowing the sensuousness of gliding through water and having it enclose your skin directly.

"Suppose somebody drives up?" Alex worried.

"Don't worry, the dogs will bark and make a fuss. We'll hear them and besides strangers are usually afraid to get out of their cars."

The dogs were a large, black mongrel, a fluffy red Chow, and a black mastiff.

"What dogs? I didn't see them when I drove up. I did hear barking, though. Was that them?"

"Oh, I locked them in the garage. One moment. I'll let them out." I scrambled out of the pool, and ran naked into the house

THERAPY, A NOVEL

to get my garage door opener. Once the door groaned its way upward and the dogs could run out to their usual guard post by the front, Alex was reassured. Then I ran back to the water and dove in. The pool was at the back of the house so the dogs didn't menace him. Good thing, too, I discovered. He'd never had a dog and didn't like them. This trio surely would have scared him off. They scared the mail carriers, deliverymen, and door-to-door salespeople. The only people they didn't scare were the Christian missionaries who came to the door regularly to give their Good Word and Bibles.

After the swim, we dried off and went back into the bedroom, still naked. Alex scanned the room, then walked over to the dressing room and bath.

"Do you realize your closet is as big as my bedroom? And is that a Jacuzzi?" He asked, pointing to the tub.

"Do you know how many people make that same comment about the closet?" I answered. "And that is a Jacuzzi. Wanna try it? The tub is big enough for two."

I filled the tub and we got in. We were seated opposite each other, so I could put my feet on his chest and rub his wet hair with my toes, at total peace with the world. My life could end then, I thought as I soaked, and I'd be happy because of the experiences of that day. When I said that to Alex, he agreed.

A thought intruded in my mind. Joe and I had never shared the tub. We had never really made love. We'd only had sex. Pretty poor sex at that, at least for me. He never complained.

Alex and I were still buoyant from lovemaking, swimming, and bathing, but also very tired and hungry, so we went back to the bedroom. Alex picked his clothes off the bed and floor where they'd fallen.

I got some slacks and a blouse from my closet and dressed respectably. Then, we went to the kitchen to get some food. Alex's eyes were drawn to the raised hearth fireplace made of antique bricks that graced one wall. A chair upholstered in deep orange velvet faced it.

"I've never seen a fireplace in a kitchen before," Alex remarked.

"I got the idea from some of the old houses I've visited, eighteenth century ones. It's wonderful sitting there on a cold

winter's day, drinking cocoa and reading. But once I had a scary experience with it. I was standing by it with my son Jed and his friend watching a fierce thunderstorm through the window. We could see lightning splitting oak trees right through to the ground. It was awesome, in the original sense of that word, but then a bolt of lightning crashed through the glass and bounced off the floors zigzagged the width of the room, ending at the fireplace, inches from my right side. Maybe the floors being tiled allowed the lightning to travel that way. I don't understand much about such things, though."

"The perils of country living! First, your son almost gets his arm cut off and then you almost get zapped by lightning. We'd better eat before any more disasters befall you." He said.

I set the table in the dining area which the fireplace was part of. The round oak table was in front of a large picture window overlooking some back gardens. As the food was warming, I laid out blue and white Spode china on a white lace tablecloth. We sat at the round oak table while I fed him some coq au vin and a chocolate soufflé I had prepared before he came. I literally fed him. Sat him down, and picked up chunks of chicken with my fingers, delicately placing them in his mouth. When he was through, he licked my fingers one by one. I laughed, tickled through and through. Then I spoon-fed him the soufflé. He laughed and grabbed me and hugged me and savored every bit.

At six, he looked at his watch and said,"I'd better be out of here. Your hubby is likely to come home and how will you explain this?"

"He won't be home for hours," I insisted, but to no avail. He kissed me lightly on the lips, and then said,"See ya Wednesday?" But before he left, he told me where his apartment was, and gave me the key to it. It was on one of the streets we had walked on. In fact, we'd passed it several times. Although he had admitted he had an apartment on the East Side, before now, he was loathe to say exactly where he lived probably because he was afraid I'd camp out on his doorstep. He was right. When I did find out, I did camp out on his doorstep, so to speak, waiting for him when he didn't expect me so I could cook him dinner, feed him, and make passionate love after. But by then he didn't mind. In fact, I

think he loved the seeing me on his front stoop. He'd drive past the house, looking excitedly towards the front, and when he saw me, honk the horn, quickly go his parking spot, scurry towards me, and wrap me in a powerful hug.

Then he'd unlock the door, and pick up the bag of groceries I always brought, stuff I needed to make him a delicious supper. However, often they'd just spill on the floor of the foyer as he started unbuttoning my coat with one hand, still holding on to me with the other as he systematically unpeeled my garments. For just such occasions, I had bought several sets of matching lacy thongs and bras from the best lingerie shop in town. I imagined the owner knew what I was up to. Why would a woman my age need such underwear? She knew I had been married for a long time.

But I digress. When I was stripped down to my undies, Alex gently pushed me towards the sofa, laying me down and unwrapping my feet from my thigh-high stockings. I had already kicked off my shoes when he first started unpeeling me. Sometimes he'd still be kissing me deeply while unwrapping me as if I were a Christmas gift.

Other times, he just held me slightly away from him and drank his fill, so to speak, by looking at me. He didn't seem to notice the stretch marks, the blue rivers of varicose veins, but I had already noticed that women twenty years or so younger than I had far worse markings, bulgier veins, even splotches of red or blue on their skins. Pimples on their backs. Rolls of fat garnishing their torsos. Not such pretty sights. At 52, my body probably looked no worse than a lot of 35 and 40-year-old women, women of the age Alex usually bedded. Come to think of it, one day as I was dressing at home, I complained to Joe about my middle-aged body, and he retorted,"A lot of 35 year old women would kill to have a body like yours!" At the time, I didn't think to ask how he knew.

I tried not to think about the women still in their twenties that Alex might go to bed with, especially those who had not been pregnant with big babies four times, as I had been. Nobody warns you when you're young and eager that having babies leaves indelible marks on your body. Or that those babies are a lifetime sentence. Not just what it does to once firm, smooth skin, but

to your brain. Their problems are yours for as long as you live. Here I go, babbling on. Sorry.

In any event, Alex certainly didn't seem to be put off by what had to offer. He ogled it, kissed it passionately, kneaded my body, and just reveled in it.

Oh, so you're thinking I must have been deluding myself, that he wanted sex and to Hell with a youthful body. Either that or I had some sort of charm that kept me young. No charm, and no plastic surgery either if you thought of that. Probably there were two reasons I hadn't aged so badly.

One was that, despite my feeling fat all my life, in truth I actually never had been, so the only stretch marks I had came from pregnancy, and that was long enough ago so that the redness of the marks had faded. Also, my skin hadn't become wrinkled from losing fat and redepositing it in a cycle of repeated weight gain and loss. After your youth, your skin isn't elastic enough to spring back from weight loss and become taut again during thin spells. The only times my skin had stretched and retightened were when I was young enough so that its elasticity did the job.

The other was that I had never spent my days basking in sun getting a good tan. Being a freckled redhead, I didn't get brown; I only burned painfully, and became even more covered with freckles. The freckles popped up even in the bright New England winter sun. Beachgoing was a nightmare to me, but when my kids were young, I felt I had to give them the joy of ocean, sand, and sun. Joy for them, that is. I hated everything about it: grit in our sandwiches, the feel of sand-covered hands and feet, and all that hauling of umbrellas, chairs, and coolers from and to the car parked in a baking asphalt lot.

The sunburns I did suffer at the beach were so painful, the blistering so unsightly, that I was always careful to keep myself covered at the beach or when skiing. SPF sun lotions didn't become available until I was in my late twenties, but once they did, I slathered them on my face every day and practically poured them all over my body when we went to the shore.

When Alex came to my house, I missed him as soon as he left, but I showered again to make sure no remnant of his scent remained on me, hid the sexy Teddy, if that was what I had put on in anticipation of his visit, or took off the matching thong

THERAPY, A NOVEL

and bra, not that Joe would've noticed that I wore them. I could shave my head and he wouldn't notice.

After our trysts, Alex's and mine that is, I had to consciously try to stop smiling at the memory of these most perfect hours. Not just because of the sex, but also because of just being with Alex, schmoozing or cuddling silently, or listening to opera together. Joe hated opera so much I couldn't listen to it all in the family room when he was home. But after Alex left, I could revel in *Tosca* or *Lucia* until the dogs announced that Joe's car was coming up the driveway.

Chapter Eighteen

My upbringing was good basic training for being Joe's wife. I didn't bother him the way I never bothered my parents, and he didn't bother with me the way they didn't bother with me. I had just had a day of love with Alex, and Joe never even suspected, but that could work two ways. Suppose he was with other women instead of working? How would I know? I was still suspicious of his activities, but I hadn't summoned up the energy to delve into it further. Also, after the incident with his refusal to go to the pharmacy for me, which pretty much convinced me he was playing around, I was afraid of hidden emotions ungluing me as they had that night. Somehow, I did care. Maybe it was ego or pride, or maybe it was the ultimate betrayal, the final proof that my whole life with him had been a sham. Now that I had Alex, I didn't want to come undone over Joe. So I put off investigating.

Still, as the summer progressed, I began thinking. He had long forbidden me to open bills. They were his bailiwick, he said. My job was to use the charge cards. Maybe I should start looking at the mail. I could steam open the envelopes and he'd never know. So I did.

To my amazement, all the bills had boldfaced"Have you forgotten your payment" or"Overdue" one them. The bank statements showed returned check penalties and almost a zero balance. The largest deposit each month was my paycheck. I could hear Joe's voice jokingly saying to friends,"It costs me money to have her work, but I try to keep her happy." It cost him

181

money? My paycheck was keeping us afloat. Barely. Where was Joe's money? What did he do with his time?

It was time I found out what was going on with him. I got the Yellow Pages out and looked up names under"Private Investigators."

Chapter Nineteen

Alex was so different from Joe. Not just physically. Like he talked. Once he got going, he talked a lot. We had real conversations. All about his predictably bossy Italian mother and his predictably cold, bitchy ex- wife. Isn't the divorced wife always bitchy and aren't mothers always bossy? He talked about his friends in high school and college and what it was like living in Pasadena with its beautiful rose bushes and about Loyola where he'd gone to college. He told me again and again how wonderful I was. Intelligent was what most people said about me, and they said it as if they were, well, scared is the only word I can think of, scared of me and my supposed intellect. But he said more: warm, affectionate, honest, direct, no pretense, good-humored, a heart as big as all outdoors, even artistic and creative.

"Don't be silly," I said at that. "I don't have an artistic bone in my body. I've always been a total klutz."

"What do you call those gardens?" he asked."They're a form of art. And the way you've decorated every room of this house. That's a gift."

I loved his praise, but wondered if a man would be considered artistic because of his home decorating talents. To me artistic meant being a sculptor or a poet or a painter. I mean, did Van Gogh have a particularly well designed home? Still Alex's praise made me feel warm and glowing, although it made me nervous. I didn't know how to answer it. Disclaimers sound so

coy, and acceptance is like bragging. But I did have to put it in perspective.

I told Alex that I really couldn't claim credit for the house itself. The basic design was Joe's. I had no say in that. Although I did end up having to carry it out.

"What do you mean?" Alex asked. "You mean you did all the decorating."

"That, too, and I'm flattered you like it so much, but actually the house almost didn't get built. If I hadn't stepped in, it wouldn't have."

"Didn't you have an architect?" Alex asked.

"No. Joe designed it himself, not deigning the help of an architect. 'What do I need an architect for? I know where to put windows and doors,' he said. He also did not deign to use a contractor. 'I know carpenters and plumbers,' he boasted. 'Why do I have to jack up the price by having a contractor? I'll do the contracting.' I should mention this was when I was working on my doctoral dissertation and building a house was not on my mind. My days were saturated, what with studying and caring for the kids. So anyways, Joe hired a carpenter, gave him a floor plan and let him set to work.

"'Wooh, I thought you wanted to build a house,' Clarence the carpenter said, 'not a motel.' Joe's plans called for a two story, eighty- foot- long house, ten large rooms and five bathrooms, this house. The perfect house for a large and loving family. Yeah, but who was going to clean such a place? Me? I felt trapped before the first stud was put up. Clarence labored mightily for a few weeks, then walked off the job and disappeared, a fact we discovered a week or more afterwards since we still lived in the city and nobody was supervising Clarence. It sort of never dawned on Joe that he should keep an eye on things. All Clarence had done was frame the outside and partition some of the rooms. When he left, he took most of the remaining lumber with him.

"'What are we going to do?' I panicked. 'We've sold our house in the city and we'll have no place to live come September.'

"'Well, I'm jammed up with court cases,' was Joe's reply. 'You deal with it.'

"I had to put my studies on hold while I sought out builders, none of whom would touch a partially started house, or would

THERAPY, A NOVEL

do so only for far more money than we had. Joe had never really considered the true cost of such a house, grossly underestimating what it would cost. I finally found a country carpenter who said he'd finish the job, but I had to spend hours scouting out materials in lumberyards, ordering what the builder wanted, so as to save money. Had the builder gone to order the lumber and moldings himself, it would have cost thousands more. He wanted to get the job done fast because he had other houses to build and he was doing me a favor by taking this one on. In effect, I became the contractor.

"The three youngest boys were only seven, five, and three then, and I had to tote them along on these shopping expeditions, three or four times a week, trying to amuse them as I pored over catalogs of moldings or flooring—whatever I was after that day—looking at samples and just waiting to be waited on, sometimes for two or three hours. Jed and Solomon whined,

"Oh, no, not again. Do we have to go to Harris Lumber? We wanna stay home. Mommy, it's boring."

"Ethan didn't talk. He would just throw himself on the ground and start kicking and screaming. Why is it we get so embarrassed when our kids make a fuss in public? After all, they are just kids. But it brings on waves of humiliation and chagrin. Must be because other people will think we're bad parents or we don't know enough to teach our kids how to behave. So much of what bothers us is really our ego, our sense of self-esteem. Losing face is the worst shame.

"At the time, I was engaged in getting this house finished, my doctoral dissertation was hanging heavily over my head. I had also lucked into a job teaching at a local college, the same college I'm still at. Preparing courses for the first time drains time alarmingly. Often I was up working through the night. The days flew by in a haze of worry and work. Every second was taken with demands. I even had to work with the bank to get financing to finish the mess that Joe had started by building this house. Where was he now? Once he hired the carpenter and helped clear a site in the woods, he just disappeared. Oh, not from my life, but from everything else.

"Since we had sold our house in the city in anticipation of Joe's estimate when the new house would be done, I had to find

185

a temporary place to live, get our stuff moved there, and get the kids into new schools as we were now in a new neighborhood. Joe didn't so much as unpack one carton. He just showed up at the address I had given him the morning before the move. He just wasn't available to help in any of the decisions. Where he was day and night, I had no clue. I mean I did know that he belonged to various organizations and he shot pool twice a week, but beyond that, all he said was that he was makingaliving when I asked for help with anything like problems with the boys, problems with getting the house built, problems with moving, anything related to family or hearth. I would've pleaded or begged or demanded if it would've made a difference, but it was clear that it wouldn't, so I just did it all."

"It's a wonder you didn't crack," Alex said. "How can anybody do so much? Did you ever sleep? Relax? Did it ever occur to you that he got into that mess and he should be helping to get out of it? I've never heard of such blatant irresponsibility"

"Not that year, I didn't rest. I felt I was wandering in another world, one with no moorings, no guidelines, and I was totally alone, with these four kids relying on me, my doctorate in the balance, a nightmare I couldn't wake up from. It was like a horrible maze with who-knows what at the end of it, if I could even ever find the end. If I slept four hours a night, it was something, and the days were go, go, go, go.

"Since Joe wouldn't check up on the construction at all, two or three times a week I had to drive from city to the country just to make sure things were being done, and also to find out what materials the contractor wanted me to get. To make matters worse, the contractor didn't consider females competent enough to make decisions. With no man to deal with, he felt like he could do as he pleased when he pleased.

"Of course, I didn't know if he was doing a good job. Neither, it turned out, did Joe. A few years after we moved in, the floors began to tilt, one upstairs bedroom began leaning. Meanwhile, Joe used to brag about how solidly the house was built. I would look at the kitchen cabinets aslant over the stove and wonder if he didn't see straight. I know I did, because once when we tried to sell the house, nobody would buy it because it was listing. Seems like the builder hadn't placed studs or something

as closely as they should be and it eventually cost us a fortune to have the place shored up. It's fine now, though.

"You'd be amazed what you have to choose for a new house. Light fixtures. Light switches. Doorknobs. Hooks to hang jackets on. I logged over 30,000 miles on my car that year—in a state that is only 30 miles wide and 40 miles long, half the size of the city of Los Angeles. And the boys were miserable. They couldn't care less about a house. They wanted to stay in the city where their friends were.

"In fact, Samuel wouldn't come out to the new house at all. I really lost him then. He elected to go live with my parents, and he never came back to me, ever. He never forgave me for marrying Joe nor for moving to the country. That pain I could discuss with nobody. I tried once to tell Joe of my anguish, and he got mad and said, 'Is that what we're going to talk about tonight?' How could I admit to anyone that I was such a lousy mother that my son cut me out of his life? It still feels like a knife slit through my stomach. I'll never get over it.

"What really got to me was that when the house was done, Joe proudly took guests around. His dream house. Made into reality by his wife, but he never acknowledged that. He never once credited that I'd gotten it built, got the necessary mortgages and the very materials that went into it. It was all his once it was done. A monument to his artistry. He made sure everyone knew he designed it. It was also a monument to his earning ability. After all, if you're a good lawyer, you make money and a big house like this looked like money. Nobody could know the financial machinations that went into the building of it. Or Joe's ineptness in pulling it off. That was my secret. In fact, you're the first person I've ever told about that."

"Seems like a lot of secrets you've been hiding. And also why have you always protected him so? Why didn't you just say, 'hey, you got us into this, you get us out?'"

"Because I had visions of our being on the street, homeless."

"Why didn't you tell people about how you got the place built?"

"I don't know. I couldn't embarrass Joe that way. He was my husband and wives shouldn't embarrass husbands. Truthfully, I didn't want to embarrass myself. "

"Do you think it may be because it reflects on you if you admit your husband is a jerk?"

I had to think that one over. "Well, there certainly is some of that. Also, I couldn't let myself admit that Joe was so shiftless. That he couldn't take care of us. It made me feel adrift. So I kept up the fiction that he was really capable and that I was just helping because he was so busy. You know, it just occurred to me, I've never been taken care of in my life. My parents never took care of me. Hald couldn't, not once he got sick, and Joe didn't."

"What happened with Hald? Why did you split from him?"

"That's a sad story. You remember I told you he broke down when I had Samuel. Then my parents came and took me home with them. Hald was so obviously out of it, and I was so weak from the Caesarean section, that I really couldn't stay in Maine. Well, to make a long story short, Hald came down to Providence and became psychotic, actually running into the streets crying and hiding under bushes, so my parents had him committed to a mental hospital.

"Actually, my parents had a hand in his going crazy. He was fragile enough, on the edge. I don't know what things my father said to him, but he admitted to telling Hald that if he converted to Judaism, they would help take care of the baby and me. He must have hammered in to Hal that he was in no condition to take care of Sammy and me. Of course, I didn't give a rat's ass if Hald converted. What difference did it make? Clearly, the conversion was bothering him. I begged Hald not to go through with it. I begged him to go back to Maine with me.

"It was clear why my parents came to get me at the hospital. They wanted Sammy. My mother kept whispering to me that she saw Hald bang the baby's head on the doorjambs, but I didn't see any bruises so I knew she was lying. And the whole idea of making a grown man, a fragile, mentally distressed man, convert to another religion when he didn't even practice his own, was too much pressure. He couldn't handle all the stuff you have to wrap your mind around, and the rabbi my father chose was very strict. No matter how much I pleaded with him, he insisted on going through with it. I don't know why. But the conversion is what pushed him over the edge.

THERAPY, A NOVEL

"Ironically, I wasn't of age yet. Then you had to be twenty-one. So, when my parents committed him, I had no power to sign him out. Then, my parents decreed that it wasn't safe to have Hald around the baby, so when he got out of the hospital, they wouldn't let him come back to me. The only thing Hald could do was go stay with a cousin in Maine while he recuperated. So, my parents punished Hald for marrying me, got rid of him, and got the baby and me. They warned me that if I went back to Maine with him, they'd never rescue me again. I didn't give a damn for their rescue, but I didn't even have the price of a bus ticket, and even if I got to Maine, Hald wasn't working. What would we live on? For myself I didn't care, but suppose something happened to Samuel. Hald still took no interest in him, never picked him up, and ignored him when he cried. It was as if the baby didn't exist for him, so in the end, although I wanted to go back to Maine, I stayed with my parents. I felt guilty about that for years."

"Why?"

"Because Hald did want me back. He felt I abandoned him, and I had promised him many times I wouldn't do that."

"Well, Barbara, you shouldn't beat yourself up over things you can't help. Your first responsibility at that point was your baby. You couldn't help it if Hald was sick. It's not safe to have a baby in a house with someone who's psychotic and hostile to the baby."

Then he asked the question I most dreaded,"You never talked about your sons. They're grown now. How have they turned out? Knowing how much of a nurturer you are, you must have been a very involved Mom."

Involved? That I was. And am. Children are a life sentence. You're never free of them, even when they're grown. Their problems are yours, so are their successes, and the way they are to you colors everything. The worst thing a woman can be is a bad mother. I couldn't admit what a lousy mother I really was, so lousy my kids didn't even like me, much less love me. On the surface, they're all right. Samuel is married with two little boys. He's making custom-built furniture, but getting heavier into his art. The others are all in school. They never call to ask how I am or what I'm doing. I'm afraid to call them too often. I can imagine them rolling their eyes at the other end of the line, impatient

with my intrusions, resistant to my suggestions, and believe me I don't give many of those and those I do give I give hesitantly. The boys seem to think I have no right to comment on any part of their lives. My own mother never hesitated to tell me in detail how to run mine and how foolish I was in all matters. That I didn't do to my boys. I never criticized them. I never pried.

"Well, Alex. I don't know what to say. My boys don't like me, much less love me. They think I'm some sort of an intrusion in their lives, and I don't know why. My whole philosophy of child rearing was that I would do the opposite of whatever my parents did, but for some reason, it hasn't made them my friends."

"What do you mean? Do you talk to them on the phone regularly?"

"Well, not so regularly. Because they don't seem to welcome my calls. For instance, I'll call Ethan, 'Hello, Ethan. It's just me, Mom. How ya doing?'

"'Fine,' he'll answer. 'Look this is a bad time. Catch ya later. Okay?'

"And that'll be the end of that conversation. Then I call Solomon.

"'Solomon, dear. This is your mother'

"'I know your voice, Mom. Is this one of your digs that I don't call you enough?'

"Comments like that make me feel both wronged and wrong."

"What do you say when he says things like that?"

I say,"No, I was just wondering how things were going. If you had any interesting cases. Is it so terrible of me to call you?"

"His response is invariably something like, 'Mom, I talk to you all I can. I know you speak to your mother every day, but I'm not a girl. I can't be your best friend.'

"'I'm not asking you to be my best friend. I'm not Mrs. Bates and you aren't Norman Bates. You're not going to have to stuff me in the cellar. I was just being friendly. There's a difference.'"

"What's the allusion to Mrs. Bates?"

"Oh, that's *Psycho*. One thing I used to do with the kids is watch old movies. Remember, Norman said that a boy's best friend is his mother. So anyway, I'll call Jed and ask him how things are going. Invariably, he says he's busy studying. "One odd

THERAPY, A NOVEL

thing. The last time, he complained that he had no time to talk because he found school hard and had to study a lot. Then he added that he didn't find school easy the way I did. Where did he ever get such notion? Of course, I found school hard. I had to study all the time to get good grades. Nothing came easy for me. I don't know if it does for very many people."

"Maybe he feels he can't live up to your accomplishments. It must be hard for kids to have a mother who has achieved a lot and they probably overestimate your abilities. I don't mean that the way it sounds. I mean they assume you're so smart that it was all easy for you. That you didn't have to work hard. It's really a kind of compliment to you. They feel you're much smarter than they are."

"But I never held myself up as an example to them or said anything about how they did in school."

"Well, maybe the very fact that you didn't insist on their getting top grades was a way of telling them you didn't expect it from them because they weren't as good as you. Either that or they thought that what they did wasn't important to you."

Bingo! His words hit me like a thunderbolt! I was trying so hard not to make them feel they had to be honor students that I actually made them feel they weren't the stuff honor students were made of, and since I was a teacher, I would know. I felt wretched. I thought I was making them easy in their own skins, approving of them no matter what, giving them unconditional love. Instead, I made them feel inferior to me. No wonder they didn't want to talk to me.

All I said to him, though, was, "I never put my work before them. I worked after they went to bed and on weekends when they were doing other things. It wasn't until they were teenagers that I'd go into my study and leave them to their own devices and by then, they didn't want me bothering them. Teenagers want to talk to their friends and listen to their music, and I let them. After all the hard work of raising them, putting their wants and needs before my own, now all I see them is at holidays.

"I will say they're pleasant enough then. They tell jokes. All four are proud of their skill in wine and food, so they get into long discussions about vintage years and gourmet restaurants. Their talk isn't particularly aimed at me. They talk sports with

191

Joe, of course, and watch Thanksgiving football with him. One thing they do is compliment my cooking a lot, and they all want doggie bags of the leftovers to take home. I always feel vacant when they leave. They're like polite strangers"

"It could be a lot worse. They could fight with you or with each other. It sounds as if they are civil and pleasant at least. I don't see why you think you've bungled being a mother."

He was right, I guess. The thorny paths of adolescence have long disappeared. I adored them when they were babies. My memory still holds the feel of them when they were babies, the rounded firm bottoms, the collagen packed cheeks, so soft but so tight. It's like a lost love, remembering your babies when they're already grown men with beards. Babies, for me, were the good part, maybe even the best part, watching them develop, learn to speak, I loved that. They were all impeccable little boys. Just a delight. Oh, they never picked up after themselves or anything like that, but I never bothered them with chores, never made them do anything, just so long as they fed the dogs and cats and groomed their horses properly."

"Besides your horse, there were more?"

"Yes, the three younger boys and I all had horses. We rode together all the time until they were teen-agers. The horror years. The way they spoke to me when they were teenagers still haunts the hallways of my mind. Those years were dreadful to me. I was consumed with pain, with shame that my boys loved me so little, that they hated me so much that they couldn't be even passingly civil to me. So I studied. I wrote scholarly papers. I prepared lectures. I read avidly. I talked to nobody. My excuse was that I was so busy." That was about as explicit as I could get with Alex. Everything else about the boys was private. Only I knew the full extent of how out of bounds they were.

To be fair, Samuel never spoke to me as rudely as the others did, mainly because he never spoke to me. He just disappeared. The first time he took off, we thought he must have been kidnapped or murdered. I was frantic, my stomach tied in knots, feelings of dread consumed me. The police found him in Hartford within twenty-four hours. Why Hartford? He never could or would explain. The second time he took off,

precipitated by my trying to enforce a midnight curfew, he stayed away for three years, living God knows where and with God knows whom.

Whenever people asked about Samuel, I cringed inside. How do you tell someone you've been such a miserable failure as a parent that your son left your home when he was only fourteen, preferring to live in slums or on the streets to living with you? You know, he never lived in this house with us. He just refused to move here. How could I tell anyone how nasty the other boys were to me? That's all my secret. Nobody knows, except Joe and he just ignored the whole business. Even when they were little boys, he never paid them any attention, no disciplining for misbehavior.

I still remember with shame and anger sitting at the dinner table and Jed, in answer to something I said, I forget what, yelling, "What do you know, bitch? Hiding away in that study of yours, writing something that nobody needs. That's all that your precious scholarship is."

Joe just sat there, munching away, and I couldn't refrain from crying. As the tears flowed, I finally complained,

"Joe, do you hear how he's talking to me?"

So he threw down the paper he was reading, got up, and smacked Jed on the head. Then Jed looked at me and began to yell, 'See what you did, bitch!' I never pointed out their behavior to Joe again.

When I told Alex an abbreviated story of that miserable incident, he responded, nodding his head in disbelief, "Well, Barbara, he taught your sons to disrespect you. Do you wonder they have such scorn for you? And what Jed said. Do you think he resented your work? That he thought it was more important to you than they were. Children are very self-centered. They want all of your attention. They don't notice what you are doing for them. They take it for granted, but the minute it seems as if something else is important to you, that they notice, and they don't like it. "

"Once they were teenagers, I never chatted with my kids. Never tried to ask about their days. To me, that was dangerously close to prying. Or, God forbid, giving advice. Even when they were little, I never asked them"What did you do in school today?" I just thought they'd tell me what they wanted to know. Now I know that was stupid. They must have gotten the impression

that I just didn't care. Certainly, my own childhood should have made that clear, but my rationalization was that I didn't want to appear as the classic Jewish mother of stand-up comics and hurtful jokes. My kids would welcome my company, never find me annoying or controlling.

"I did try to make them do chores or even do their homework. But I gave up easily. I never, but never, criticized them or told them they had shortcomings. They wouldn't have to remember a nagging mother. I would be The Bobbsey Twin's mother, the mother of my fantasy, who never got angry, never yelled. Always cheery. Sunny. My boys wouldn't have to build battlements around their souls the way I did with my mother. They'd never have to rebel against me. I was going to be the perfect mother. If they tore their clothes, I'd say, 'That should be the worst thing that ever happens to you.'

"If they ruined their books, I'd say, 'With money you can replace it. At least it's not a living creature.' If they got poor grades, and they did, all of them, I said nothing.

"There was no punishment in my house. No blame. If they wanted anything, a new toy, a new game, I ran to get it for them, and while I was at it, I'd get them things they hadn't thought to ask for. Thank God for Visa. No need for Santa Claus in our house. Christmas was every day. Or at least what I imagined Christmas to be, since it was never celebrated in my life.

"What a tally. Counting up my years of slavish devotion to each of them and matching it against their years of stomping on me, I was definitely the loser. Picking them up at school so they wouldn't have to come home to an empty house, playing with them, planning rich, meaningful experiences, taking them to music lessons, art lessons, swimming lessons, tennis lessons, no opportunity for enrichment overlooked, model train stores, coin collector's shops, whatever their current passions were. It seems to me that, between the younger three at least, they had every interest a boy could possibly have, and I tried to satisfy them all. Fully. Buying them all their heart's desires, toys, books, clothes. Their wishes were definitely my command.

"Then, they became teenagers. One called me a *bitch* and a *cunt*. One glared at me and said, 'I hate you. I hate you,' and one just never talked. None of them did well in school. All of them

THERAPY, A NOVEL

totaled cars before they were eighteen. Two did drugs. One did alcohol. One overate.

"To give you one common scenario. I would say something to Jed, like maybe ask him in a mild almost offhand way how he dented a fender on my car or if he could please cut some wood for the Jötul stove, and he'd snarl, 'Get off my back.'"

"Or Solomon would grumble, 'Just leave me the hell alone!' Ethan's favorite epithet for me was 'Bitch!' I often felt as if my chest was crushing under the weight of their words.

"Joe would sit there just reading the paper while his sons spouted off nastiness as if it were a fountain of plenty.

"After that one time he hit Jed because of my complaint, I was afraid to say anything about how the boys were talking to me.

"If I whispered to Joe, 'Do you hear that?' he'd give me that 'not again' look and clench his fists, like I had a nerve interrupting him.

"Once, Joe did whack Solomon for calling me a bitch at the dinner table. Solomon countered by whirling around to face Joe and smacked him back, then started running up the stairs to his bedroom. Joe ran after him, enraged, and grabbed him by the neck on the landing. Solomon fought back, smashing Joe's head into the wall so hard, it began to bleed. Appalled, I was speechless. I couldn't move.

"The upshot was that Solomon drove Joe to the emergency room to get stitches. He and Joe laughed about the incident many times, although I failed t see what was so funny about it. Certainly, it didn't teach Solomon to speak more politely to me. And how Joe was a good guy even though he smacked Solomon, and Ethan was okay with Joe even though he attacked him, well, it's all beyond me. I was the bitch, but I never smacked anybody. Joe's take on Solomon's fighting back was that it was my fault. I shouldn't have said anything about his epithets. After all, boys will be boys.

"The boys had testosterone poisoning," Alex joked. "Not all teenagers speak to their mothers that way, and it's not because they fear punishment. The problem is yourself. Inadvertently, you were aloof from them. Yes, you did everything for them. However, you didn't discipline them at all. You didn't make rules

195

and boundaries when they were children, so when they got to be teenagers, they felt free to vent at you.

"No matter what they did or didn't do, they got everything except grief from you. So they acted out all those raging hormones at you. And I think also that far from feeling that you were just minding your own business by letting them do what they wanted without having to account for anything to you, they thought your working in your study all the time was more important to you than they were. So they resented your career."

"That's funny. They were very proud of my getting things published and used to bring their friends into my study to show off my computer and my book-lined walls. That's one thing, they did brag about me."

"That doesn't mean they didn't feel left out of your life."

His words were like a sledgehammer. He was right. Very right. I saw my scholarly writing as a refuge. As a way of not tangling with their teen-aged unpleasantness, to be honest about it. That backfired. They misunderstood it as my ignoring them and all my gifts to them as so much appeasement to keep them out of my hair while I got on with my real work. How blind of me. How inept. I yearned for some intimate conversation with them, for the kinds of camaraderie we had while we watched movies or listened to music as when they were small. I comforted myself by saying that boys didn't talk to their mothers as girls did. Speaking of self-deception! No wonder they raged at me with epithets. Words, the essence of my studies were their weapons of choice. How very fitting.

"Did they act out in public?'""

"No. Everybody always told me what lovely boys they were. And I would think 'Thank God they don't know the truth.' I loved them intensely. Still do. Until now, their dislike for me was my secret, just like when I was a little girl, my parents' dislike for me was my secret. I never told anyone."

"Did you try to discuss it with Joe?"

"I told you. He refused to talk about them in any way."

"But the boys are okay now. Even Samuel, the runaway Oh, he's a proper businessman, is stable, a wonderful husband and father. He apprenticed as a carpenter when he was a teenager, then started his own business making custom-built rustic

THERAPY, A NOVEL

furniture. When he has the chance, he also does other artwork, like lithographs and calligraphy, and he's starting to learn glass-blowing, of all things. He has two little boys, five and three, and is involved with every aspect of their lives. His wife is the quintessential Italian mother, always hovering over the boys and telling them how marvelous they are, and I think Sammy has learned from her. From me he's learned how not to be. He's the father that nobody was to him. Once he found Marie, the love of his life, he started coming round, bringing her to the house, and later, of course, bringing his children.

"He still isn't much of a talker, a real taciturn Yankee, both in looks and temperament. That just shows that nature can triumph nurture. He's like his biological father's family in his mannerisms and his personality, even in his button-down shirts with ties and tweed jackets, but he's never met any of that family.

"He was raised in a Jewish home where three conversations at least would be going on at the same time, everyone breaking in on everyone else, but he isn't like that at all. His response has always been to observe quietly while everyone else is talking with their hands, pointing their fingers and arguing some stance or other on some issue or other. In a rare moment of silence, he'll offer his considered judgment of the issues at hand.

"Actually, there's a codicil to his story. When I was helping my mother pack to move to Florida, I came across a box of old letters and pictures. I found in it a letter addressed to me with a Maine postmark. I opened it. It was from Hald, dated about the time Samuel was two. He had written it to tell me he was coming to see Samuel and me. My mother clearly had intercepted it and somehow gotten me out of the house on the day that Hald was supposed to come. That would not have posed a problem. They just had to tell me I had to work in their store. I read the letter with a sinking feeling of sorrow and regret for what could have been, especially for Sammy. Maybe Hald would've made Sammy a part of his life. Sammy must have felt that his father didn't care for him at all. That he was abandoned by him. When he was a teenager, I told him how to go about finding his father, but he refused, and wouldn't let me talk about it. I think he was afraid if he did contact Hald, and Hald didn't welcome the contact, Sammy couldn't bear the pain of rejection.

197

"Then again, I thought of how awful it must have been for Hald to make that long trip and then come to an empty house. How different it would have been for Samuel and maybe even for me if I had gotten that letter."

"That's a pretty devastating story. Your mother was a piece of work, all right. Yet, still, you call her every day. You do her bidding. You're too good. Most people would have cut all ties to someone like that."

"Well, she does give me things. Once I was married to Joe, she and my father got generous and started plying me with money and gifts, even jewelry. And she can be very good to talk to. Surprisingly very wise. She's a complicated woman, as well as a manipulative one."

"You say they got generous. Did they suddenly come into some money?"

"No. Just their savings I guess. They both lived through the Depression and had a horror of not having any money, but I think they felt they could buy my love or that buying me things would keep me from shutting them out. That's my theory anyway. Actually, my father once said something like 'I'd rather see you enjoy your inheritance while I'm alive.' Another time he said proudly, criticizing Joe's parents for never even giving us a small wedding present, 'Well, we give our children all we can, so we have our children.'"

"Well, do you stay close to your parents because of money?"

"Good grief, no. Actually, they have very little. We have a much grander house, travel like they never could afford to. My salary alone must be more than double what my parents ever earned. Furthermore, my gifts to them surpass anything they could ever give me. I think I have spent my life trying to get them to say I'm a nice person. All I ever get or got from them was criticism. All I ever wanted from them was love."

"Do you know that all abused children take that road?"

"I've wondered about that. I think it's because they try all their lives to get their parents to love them, and if they do get them to, they can take secret satisfaction that their parents were wrong about them when they were little. Certainly, I've done everything they said I'd never do or could do. All their predictions were wrong."

THERAPY, A NOVEL

"Exactly," Alex agreed.

Once I ceased being his patient, Alex actually gave me more insight into myself than he did when I was still in therapy, especially during the last few weeks in his office. Certainly, he showed me why my boys gave me such a hard time. If he showed me my role in that, he also helped me realize how I was a victim of my upbringing and, in turn, I made my children victims of it.

One afternoon, Alex remarked,"You always say that Joe ignored the kids, but that they love him. Why is that, do you think? Just giving kids money and credit cards doesn't buy love."

"Well, he could be wonderful, making up droll stories, joking with them, being a Little League coach, but most of the time he just wasn't available. One thing he did was take them to court so they could see him try cases. That really impressed them. That and the way the other lawyers admired him, so all in all, they really respect him, and I wouldn't say anything to counter that. They shouldn't feel ashamed of him."

"Besides being good dinner guests, what are they like now?"

"Well, they all work hard and do well at what they do. They're all involved with nice, intelligent good women. None of them does drugs and alcohol any more, at least so far as I can see."

"Well, Barbara, in this day and age to raise four independent, hardworking sons who can remain in committed relations is an accomplishment. You said it's surprising that Sam takes an active role in raising their kids even though they had no role model. But he did have a role model as a caregiver. His mother."

"But you just laid out for me how I failed as a mother."

"Yes, in some ways you did, but in others you didn't. They had affection, a mother who was alert to their needs, and a mother who never criticized who they were as people. You gave them unconditional love. If you dissect any parenting, you'll find flaws. What's harder than raising kids?"

So, Alex knocked me down, then raised me up. Still he didn't think any the less of me because of my lack of mothering skills. I still think I bungled with the kids. They're never going to love me the way I love them.

Chapter Twenty

How much happiness had this house created for me? Over cheese and crackers, Alex and I discussed that one afternoon while sitting in the shade of a crabapple tree.

"Mostly when I think of the years in this beautiful house that everyone envies me for, I think of myself working madly, putting in gardens, decorating the house, cooking and baking entire Saturdays or Sundays, and juggling the kids and my job. Relaxation was not an option.

"Except for the blizzard of 1978. We were completely snowbound. The fence around the pool couldn't be seen, and you can see it's at least 5 feet high. The snow cover was so deep, it just looked like a plain out there. Even if we could have gotten our cars out the driveway, which we couldn't, we couldn't go anywhere. The long driveway to our house was clogged with almost six feet of snow and the roads throughout remained impassible for days. The day after the blizzard, as my mother was wailing at me over the phone, 'How can you stand it, being isolated out there. It's dangerous...' I heard a strong buzzing sound, almost like a chainsaw, but nobody could be cutting wood that morning. I looked out the window and saw a man in a snowmobile, standing waist deep in the snow, waving his arms.

"'Everything all right?' He was shouting. 'Need bread or milk?'

"Seems all the snowmobilers in town were acting as emergency providers, driving to the general store, which managed to stay open, and then bringing necessities to the townspeople.

"My heart glowed towards them, to think they cared. Anyway, the week we were snowbound was halcyon. Since we couldn't get to work, we did no work at home, just watched television. I saw my first talk show that week, Donahue it was. We played Monopoly and Scrabble, something I hadn't done in years. I baked cookies, cupcakes, and bread. The house was redolent with the smell of yeast and baking chocolate.

"When our driveway was finally plowed out, we walked, met neighbors on the road, and chatted lazily and cheerfully. The world looked gorgeous. Sparkling white. The sun shone brilliantly, and the sky was a cloudless blue the day after the blizzard, and stayed that way for weeks. The beauty of winterscapes is rarely appreciated nowadays. People just think of the cold, of cars getting stuck in snow or skidding on ice, but for that week, cars were useless. The roads to the city were not open. Time became honeyed. I rested. I napped. I slept. I ate. I bundled up in hats and mittens and swished through the woods on cross-country skis. There was no being rushed. No angry words exchanged. No tantrums. No misbehaving. My soul was warmed. As I looked at my boys, I could feel my waves of love beating against them, but there was no turbulence. It was tranquil and carefree. I felt love and affection from the boys. It was the most blissful time of my life. Except for the early days with Hald."

"And that's your happiest memory of living in this house? That's sad."

Chapter Twenty-One

"I know why you married Joe, but tell me again what led up to it," Alex asked one afternoon after our usual lovemaking and eating.

"I met Joe at a crazy party, a party I didn't want to go to. Oddly, my mother never gave up hope that I'd meet some nice man who'd take me and Samuel on, marry me and adopt Samuel. Funny stance for her to take, considering that she always told me no man would ever want the likes of me or the only reason they would date me after my divorce was to have sex. Still and all, she also urged me to go where there might be single men. I don't think it was so much my happiness she was after. It was so she could hold her head up in front of her friends and have the last laugh. See, my daughter's not just someone else's leavings.

"So I got invited to this party by a girl I knew from school. When the day came, my mother insisted,

'Get dressed up. Do your hair. Go!'

'I don't want to go. I'd rather read a novel.'

'You'll meet someone.'

'I know every jerk around here. Who am I going to meet and if I do they won't want me.'

"After all, the only person who'd wanted me was Martin in the past four years and he just wanted to torture me. Did I tell you about Martin?"

"No."

"He was a clinical psychologist. One of my college mates fixed me up with him. He had been married for a brief time, and was divorced. All he used to do was criticize me. Insult me. Tell me I thought I was so smart, so superior. I was so starved for social interactions that I kept going out with him anyway. Then one day, he told me he had a job offer in New York and he wanted to know if I thought he should take it. I thought that was pretty strange since he never had a good word to say about me. I told him to take it if he wanted to, and then he let loose with a real barrage of what a snotty, terrible person I was, and I realized that all along he was in love with me, but didn't think I was in love with him and that's why he was so nasty. Bizarre how some people are. Anyways, he took the job and I lost my Saturday night date. This party was the first social event I'd been invited to since he left.

"Well, my mother won. I went to the party. Actually, I had a date for it, a kid I'd known since high school, but I'd called him and told him I wasn't going to go. That was before my mother intervened. When I walked in to the party, my ex-date just looked at me and said, 'Barbara, you're a shit.'"

"Later, I was standing by the buffet table, laid out with pans of hot food like lasagnas and sliced brisket and gravy, and baskets of breads and plates of deli meats. Sort of like Jewish cooking meets the Italians. As I stood there, figuring out how I could take my leave and sneak into the house so my mother wouldn't know I'd left early, defined as 'without meeting someone,' a tall, blond handsome man walked up to the table and began contemplating the offerings. I had heard my hostess introduce him as Joe Miller, and I knew Pat Miller from school. This must be her brother. Pat couldn't stand me. It was that obvious. Her distaste for me took the form of barely responding when I spoke to her, although with everyone else she was very polite and friendly. Furthermore, I stuck out at school because I was five years older than my classmates were and had been married and had a baby. Pat Miller was one of the virgin coeds and a total conformist to boot. She would never be friendly with the likes of me, a divorced woman.

"I've never figured out why I did what I did when Joe came up to the table, except maybe I was just bored and I didn't think it would matter anyhow. I turned to him as he was filling his plate intently, and ventured,

THERAPY, A NOVEL

'Hi, I'm Barbara. We've never met but I'm an acquaintance of your sister Pat.'

He turned and stared, training his large blue eyes on me. 'Well hello. I'm Joe. Do you go to Rhode Island College?'

And so it began. We swapped school stories. He was in graduate school and waiting for his semester grades to see if he would be going back the next year. He mentioned his strict Roman Catholic undergraduate training at the very school I teach at now. We got into that crazy discussion about Catholic philosophy I told you about, and it just progressed from there. He found me different, and, later, found I was a good cook, and that, along with my getting a teaching job a year after we started dating, led to the inevitable.

"Since we both wanted out of our homes, and I had a teaching job lined up which would pay for an apartment and food for us and Sammy, we got engaged, planning to marry the first possible day after I got my first monthly paycheck.

"It was like a miracle to me. I wouldn't have to strike out on my own. I'd have someone to live with, who had promised to adopt Sammy, and I'd still be independent of my parents. How exciting and so unexpected. I hadn't dared to dream such a dream. I wanted him, those blue eyes shining approval of the me-ness of me, so we got married on a hot Friday afternoon in August in a rabbi's study. Joe's parents wouldn't come to the ceremony. Beforehand, the rabbi wrote to his parents and offered to meet with them about the situation. Joe's parents told him not to waste their time. Nice people, huh?

"Earlier, when my mother had called to invite them to dinner thinking they should be friends, Joe's mother answered, 'No thank you, I'd rather stay home'

"I was used to feeling belittled. I said I didn't care. I ignored them, but it did hurt. They never forgave us for getting married and when our sons were born, they never even came to see them. Maybe they figured the babies would be blighted by my genes.

"The early years were so busy between Joe getting his degree, me getting mine and having three more babies, that I never had time to think of not being happy. It would've been nice having one girl, but somehow I wasn't surprised that I didn't.'

205

"'It won't be any good for you having a daughter,' my mother assured me when my fourth son was born. Any more than it was for me.'

"I thought to myself when she said that, it wasn't good for her to have me. Was I so terrible then? I cooked her and my father's meals, had parties for them on their birthdays and anniversaries, showered them with beautiful gifts, visited them three or four times a week, spoke to my mother on the phone every day, first thing, before I even rolled out of bed. And it wasn't good having me? I redoubled my efforts towards her. Still the years when the boys were young and I had the excitement of discovering a new body of knowledge in grad school were good years. More than good. Exhilarating.

"Life isn't fair. You give up so much to have and raise kids, and then one day they can drive, and they go away to college and they're gone from your lives and you go from being busy every minute with kids and their needs to zero. A big emptiness. I once asked Joe, after Ethan left and we were alone,

"'Don't you miss the sounds of the kids in the house?'

"He answered, 'Are you crazy?'

"I guess I was. Especially given the rudeness I put up with from them. I missed them terribly. At least by the time they left home, they weren't swearing at me and yelling at me. All that seemed to have burned out, like it never happened. I guess getting away from me was all they needed.

"Yeah, I have always had some friends, but I've never been on anyone's A-list. Even in the Ivory Tower I settled in, I never got invited to the parties. I was never even asked to serve on committees, although everyone was polite enough at the lunch table.

"I always thought the one place I'd be valued was in a university setting, but even there, I really didn't quite belong. From little hints that people have dropped, I gather I'm considered outspoken and even blunt, but I don't know why. I think I'm careful in my pronouncements, much more so than most people especially at school. Professors are an outspoken lot. Supposedly, they love to argue, to tease out the truth, to quash fallacies. That was basic training in my childhood home.

"However, at school, I quickly learned that in that all male bastion, or almost all-male, not to enter into political or

academic arguments, pretending I had no opinions to voice. It was up to the men to have opinions, not the women. At the lunch table, the men talked and talked and the few female faculty sat quietly eating their lunches. The only speaking the women did was to agree with the men.

"When I started teaching there, most of the men were married to women who didn't even have undergraduate degrees. They were homemakers who took *Good Housekeeping* seriously. Obviously, I was not. That was strike one.

"My house was too nice. That was strike two. Seriously, I used to invite colleagues to dinner and all they did when they saw my house was ooh and aah about my beautiful house. One of my colleagues even used to ask me at school whenever he saw me, 'How's your mansion?' I even had male colleagues who said things like, 'How would you like to have to live on our salaries,' meaning that it was unfair somehow that my salary, pretty much the same as theirs, was added to my husband's, so I was rich. As if it was my fault they were married to women who didn't bring home good paychecks."

"They were jealous, Barbara. They saw you as having everything they wanted. You also published a lot, more than they did, I bet."

"Yes."

"So you aced them on all counts. Most people are jealous."

"I've never been jealous of people who had more than I. Even when I was a kid and was so poor and went to school with kids from wealthier families it didn't occur to me to be jealous."

"That's you. Everyone's not you. You have to understand the baser emotions and not beat yourself up because of other people's failings."

Chapter Twenty-Two

Waiting for Alex one day, I looked around the house, trying to see it through his eyes, wondering if he'd ever want to make a home with me. Even before Martha Stewart, I bought into the whole house beautiful deal. My inspiration was the country houses in old movies. You know, Bette Davis' cottage in *Dark Victory*. I made sure I had pretty china, nice cutlery, and sparkling crystal goblets. There were always fresh flowers in the rooms, a habit I'd picked up from Hollywood movies, I think.

When my boys sat down to eat, the table was always neatly and prettily set. Only the finest prepared food was set before them. I spent entire weekends making them homemade pastas, Mexican food from scratch, French dishes to cultivate their young palates. Their cookies and pies were always home made. Even the ice cream.

Their hair was always combed, their nails clean, and shirts tucked in. No spots. No dirt. Cloth napkins on the lap as soon as they sat own, their manners impeccable. No arguments at our dinner table. At least that was my goal, not that the goal was always realized. No icky talk. Nothing but sweetness and light. Mrs. Bobbsey had nothing on me. I lived the dream life of the magazines for women that I'd devoured since my childhood

There was a strange problem with our house in the country, the house I had labored to bring to fruition. The bedroom especially was my haven, but even so, it never felt like I belonged in that perfect *House Beautiful*. I felt a disconnect between it and

209

me, even though I had done all the decorating, chosen all the wallpapers, all the furniture, even designed all the gardens. We had over an acre cleared in the woods surrounding our house, and gardens were everywhere on that acre. There was an 80 foot shade planting at the border between the woods and the clearing, a large round garden in full sun in the middle of the lawn, another sunny space just outside the kitchen window, and opposite that down about five wide stairs were a half dozen peonies against a large boulder. Around the pool, of course, there were shrubs and flowers, as there were all along the back of the house. Then there was a rock garden and other decorative plantings in the front.

I often thought as I surveyed my domain, either inside or out,"What am I doing here? How do I own such a place?" I wasn't tall enough or glamorous enough or poised enough to live in such a place. It didn't fit me. I don't know what would fit me, but it certainly wasn't a 5,000 square foot manse.

Even when I was skinny-dipping in the pool or cutting flowers, I felt like a stranger who happened upon that place. When the boys were still at home, at least it contained life and noise, but once they left, the silence was crushing. I was so lonely there, so alone. Weeks could go by without a visitor, not even my sons or their families. It was like we had this place just made for people and no people came. Or almost no people. Of course, now I had Alex to come.

It finally occurred to me that it was time to find out why Joe was never home for dinner. Well, I knew he was playing pool because the members of the group alternated houses, so that everyone hosted them at least every couple of months. But the working late seemed suspicious. Working late year after year without any substantial income resulting from it?

When I hired a private eye, I did so with some trepidation. Suppose that I inadvertently hired the one Joe used in his practice to spy on mates being accused of adultery. I couldn't very well ask him out of the blue what detective agency he dealt with, so I decided to take my chances and just pick a name from the yellow pages.

Chapter Twenty-Three

I finally got the report from the Private Eye, with pictures and notes. Joe's visits to his girl friend every evening. His poker and craps games in an illegal gambling joint. It was all there. He did go to court. He did see clients, but in the morning and afternoons. Whatever money he earned got spent on one Kathleen O'Dowell or blown away in gaming. That was his "makingaliving."

Okay now I knew about him. But he still didn't suspect about me. I bet he figured no man would ever want me now. In his practice, he saw plenty of middle-aged women like me being dumped for a younger model. Probably he thought that I didn't have the guts to be carrying on with anyone else. Good old faithful Barbara. Always the perfect wife. Never pried. Always did what she was told. And supported him in the bargain.

Chapter Twenty-Four

The American Medical Association specifically forbids sex or romance as an ingredient in a cure, but I'm not so sure that they're right in all cases. Romance is a wonderful cure for depression. Works better than Prozac. I found that out. My cure began in earnest the day I lured Alex to L'Elizabeth's. The first day that Alex came to my house, my depression was completely cured. I felt like a worthy person, someone who could be loved, be cherished. The care he took to give me pleasure was a revelation.

"School will start soon," I told him on a late afternoon tryst. "I'll be in the city every day, and Joe expects me to work late in the library nights. I know it's nervy, but if I had a key to your apartment, I could cook supper for you, and we could spend the evening together."

He hesitated. "Well, I don't know. Suppose my partner sees you. Sometimes he stops by the apartment to talk over cases. And there's the other tenants. This is fire we're playing with."

Afraid to let him talk himself into dumping me out of his fear of being found out, I put my hand over his mouth and said,

"Shhh. I told you I'd never admit, even under oath, that we slept together, and if I say we haven't, nobody has a case against you. As for Dom, he's not so innocent himself. When I met him the first time, he was living with a girl the same age as his oldest daughter. He had cast off his wife for this airhead, and I wouldn't be surprised if she had been his patient first. How else could he have met her? Unless he went to high school dances. Please

213

don't take this away from me. You're the most happiness I've ever had except for when my kids were babies."

So he gave me a key. Two or three times a week I would leave school around four or five, go to Bread and Circus, and buy their overpriced, but wonderful naturally raised meat, and all the other ingredients for a marvelous dinner. Steak au poivre, blanquette de veau, osso bucco Milanese, filet of sole Francese, every night a different meal. I often camped outside his door when the weather was nice. But New England is New England weather-wise. As fall progressed into winter, it became colder outside, so I let myself in. He could tell I was there by the light in the kitchen. Often, he'd come in while I was intent on measuring or chopping. My first sense that he'd tiptoed in was the smell of cold emanating from him.

He'd kiss the back of my neck, gently bite my ear, and stroke his hands down my sides from under my arms to my thighs. I'd arrange the flowers I bought, set the table while the meal finished cooking, and we'd eat, feeling so passionate that we could hardly wait to finish the meal before we started to make love.

One such night, with the remains of the meal on the table, and our clothes strewn all over the floor of the living room, where we had disrobed each other on our way to the bedroom, the doorbell rang. We were still entwined.

"Don't answer it," I pleaded.

"I've got to," he answered. "My car is parked outside and anyone who would come would see that."

He quickly grabbed a robe, covered himself, and went to answer the door. It was his mother. She had had to fly to New York City to see her ancient mother who was ailing. After the visit, she rented a car and decided to come on to Providence to surprise Alex.

"What? You're already getting ready for bed?" she asked. "It's only, what? Nine-thirty, ten o'clock?"

"Um, Mom. I have a guest," he explained.

I could hear them from the bedroom. "A guest? A woman? Well it's okay. I'm a modern person. I understand."

Alex came to get me. "I can't get rid of her. You'll have to come out to get home, so you might as well meet her." So I showered quickly, put my clothes back on and braved the meeting.

THERAPY, A NOVEL

She looked me over carefully. She could see I was older than Alex. I could see it in her face.

"Miller?" she asked. "I guess you're not Italian. Are you an English Miller or a German one? I've met Millers who are either one."

"Jewish," I admitted.

"Jewish," she repeated, clearly disapproving.

She noticed the wedding band on my left hand. "You're married?"

"Well, at the moment, but it's a temporary condition."

"I see."

Dying inside of embarrassment, I said,"Well, I have to get home. Sorry to leave you with such a mess Alex." And I left.

The next time we met, Alex said,"See, we're being found out."

"I know," I answered. "Your license. You could lose your license. Alex, I know I'm being selfish, but when was the last time you heard about a doctor losing his license over an affair, and plenty of them have them. So do professors and lawyers, and nothing happens to them. You've told me yourself you've never had such a wonderful relationship. I never have either. How can we give this up and why should we? Nothing is going to happen to you and the worst that can happen to me is Joe's divorcing me and I'm going to divorce him anyways".

"Have you even started to do that?"

"No, I haven't bothered, but if it'll ease your mind any, I'll do it this week. I just have to find a lawyer that Joe isn't friendly with. That could be hard, but I'm sure I'll find one."

So I set about asking my colleagues who were divorced whom they had used. I finally settled on a female, Patricia Evans, who had a reputation for being tough which was important because Joe is a first-rate divorce lawyer. He knows all the tricks. I thought he'd be fair with me, but everyone says you never know until you start proceedings. Spouses suddenly get difficult. They both insist that they deserve the salad spinner and get into screaming battles about sofas, not to mention the bitter arguments about money, who should get how much and why.

I made it my business to go home the day I hired the attorney. Joe walked in the house at eight-thirty, took off his coat, and

215

draped it on the back of a chair. I took it, as usual, and hung it in the hall closet. He sat down and I gave him a plate of hamburgers, mashed potatoes and peas that I'd prepared for him. He picked up the newspaper to read while we ate. I took it out of his hands.

"Joe, we have to talk. Our marriage is moribund, and it has been for years."

"Is this how we're going to spend this evening? Talking about our marriage?"

For once, for the first time, actually, this question didn't shut me up.

"Yes, that is how we're going to spend this evening. I've hired a lawyer and you'll be served with divorce papers next week. Irreconcilable differences. We've grown so far apart that you'll hardly notice I'm not your wife, but I want to discuss how we'll divide everything. I don't want a fight. Just split everything fifty-fifty, as close as we can."

"Don't worry," he said grimly. "If you want a divorce, you'll get a divorce. You get 50% of the marital assets, everything we've amassed since we got married. We split your retirement funds down the middle, and any other cash."

That gave me pause. All the retirement funds, every cent, was what my school had paid in plus extra that I had deducted from my paycheck. Joe always said it was foolish to save money. Lawyers never retired. If you hit on hard times, you could never have enough saved to get you through, so you might as well go on welfare right away instead of going through your savings first. Well, nice for him, but not for me. He'd be getting half of my money, but I swallowed it. It was worth it for Alex.

"We'll get the house appraised and divide whatever we get when it's sold," he continued. "The furniture and the art work, we can each take what we want, and if we both want the same thing, we can draw straws."

I was astonished that he agreed with alacrity. In fact, it sounded like he'd rehearsed this little speech. He didn't even ask if we could work it out or if I'd reconsider or what made me suddenly go to a lawyer. He didn't ask if I had found anyone else. It was as if he didn't even care. He just wasn't interested. It was just a business transaction to him. I was crushed. All those years. All that

work. All that aggravation and poof! It was over. Oh, come on, I thought to myself. You asked for the divorce first. Still, there was a twinge of what? Resentment that it was so easy?

After Joe went to his bedroom, I called Alex from mine.

"He's amenable to a divorce and I've already hired an attorney."

"Oh."

"What do you mean, 'Oh', I asked. "Don't you have any other comment?"

"Well," he hesitated. "What then? What do you expect?"

Suddenly I understood what he meant. He was afraid I'd want to marry him and he didn't want to marry me. Although he'd asked me about getting a divorce, in a way he didn't want me to. My being married was insurance to him.

"Don't worry," I said dryly. "I don't expect any commitment from you and I've been married twice. A third time doesn't interest me. We can just continue as we have been. I'll probably buy another house in the country, a smaller one, and maybe I'll even get a small apartment in the city."

But I couldn't sleep all that night. Fear gripped me. Alex didn't really want me. Or, rather, he did want me, but he was afraid of our relationship. It was the only thing about him that disturbed me, even faintly disgusted me. Was he a coward, or did he have actual scruples? If he did, why did he come with me that first evening? He initiated it when he called me back. I was just leaving the office.

Chapter Twenty-Five

It was sleeting out. The frozen raindrops pinged at the windows. Alex and I were spooned on his bed, his right arm leaning askance over my stomach, his sharp chin nestling into my neck. I lifted his arm off me, and started out of bed.

"I have to get going Alex. It's almost midnight, and God knows what the roads will be like."

"Good God," he exploded as he sat up. "Why don't you just tell him the truth? He's got to have figured out that you have someone new. I mean, where does he think you are every night so late?"

"Well, we're just starting the divorce negotiations and I don't want him to sue me for adultery. It could affect the settlement."

"You think he doesn't suspect? Is he a fool? He'd have to be. Has he even asked you?"

"No."

"Believe me, he knows. Besides, you shouldn't be driving in on those narrow, twisting roads in this weather. It's dangerous."

"You sound like my mother."

"Well, for once your mother's right"

"She wouldn't think this is so right, believe me."

"Do you?" I guess he couldn't resist playing the shrink.

"It's the rightest thing I ever did." And I meant it.

I thought,"To Hell with Joe. I owe him nothing," and went back to sleep. Alex and I had our first breakfast together the next morning. He went to the French bakery for croissants while

219

I made a pot of strong, black coffee. We spread strawberry preserves on the croissants and licked our buttery fingers when we were through.

"I could spend the rest of my life like this," Alex said, surprisingly.

"So could I."

Was that an invitation to move in? He had always been so certain that our relationship couldn't progress to that point. Was he changing his mind? Oh, ecstasy. Of course, it was impossible. His partner would find out and Alex would be in trouble.

The divorce was perfunctory. My attorney assured me that Joe had no hidden assets and, true to his promise, we split everything down the middle. There was a little squabbling over who would get what painting and who would get the Chinese game table, but most of it went smoothly.

I found an old farmhouse, built around 1790, with a wonderful stone barn on five acres of meadow with a brook running through the property and threw myself into refurbishing it. The stalls in the barn were in good enough condition so I could keep my horse in it. I toyed with the idea of buying another one for Alex so we could ride in the woods together, but I was afraid to bring that up with him, for fear he'd start thinking about commitments and how we shouldn't be having this affair. Quietly, I began to search the classifieds for horses for sale.

I was in my element, researching architectural books to make sure that I was restoring the house to its original state, running around buying materials and furniture. Most of the stuff Joe and I had in the big house didn't fit this old one, except for the brass bed, but somehow Joe got that. Actually, a wooden one would be more appropriate for a house of this vintage. I researched furniture as well, so it could all be authentic. Buying new stuff is always fun, at least for me. I was probably the happiest woman getting a divorce in history. I even reveled in living in the house while the contractor exposed ceiling beams, ripped up modern flooring to get at the original wide planked pine floorboards. I tiptoed my way around buckets of paint and new plumbing fixtures, imagining the finished rooms. It was almost worth getting a divorce to be able to do this renovation. Between my trysts with

Alex and fixing up the house, I had reached a new plane of happiness. I began to understand about Nirvana.

A gentle Chestnut gelding came up for sale at a farm just down the road. Perfect for Alex. I bought him. The day finally came when it was warm enough for the last of the winter snow and ice to have melted so we could take a woodland ride.

Alex approved of the horse as soon as he met him. We mounted and started towards the woods behind the house. He hadn't ridden much before, but at least he knew the basics and the trails I took him on didn't involve jumping or moving at more than a steady, slow pace. I had already scouted out old carriage trails that were still visible and not overgrown. As we were riding in the chill of that early spring day, my horse suddenly shied. I managed to keep my seat, and shouted to Alex to stop. Before us was a pair of snarling dogs, undoubtedly dogs that had been simply abandoned in the woods by their former owners. That deplorable practice was and is very common. Most such dogs usually simply starve, but a few manage to survive a short time.

Many people think the dogs form packs and hunt, but dogs are scavengers, not hunters. They don't know how to hunt cooperatively with each other the way wolves do. What really happens is that hunters illegally shoot and injure a deer, not bothering to go find it to finish it off. The dog smells blood, and finds the deer and rips meat off it.

The other thing that happens is that a dog will chase a deer until the deer collapses, often dying from a heart attack and the dog manages to get chunks of meat that way. I never saw any packs of dogs in my woods, and, certainly, if I saw an occasional dog with the even more occasional deer, I never saw that dog again. The killing of deer was too sporadic to keep abandoned dogs alive very long. These two dogs were feasting on the carcass. Their snouts were covered in blood.

I almost fainted. The memory came back vividly. Blood everywhere. All over the bathroom. We were sitting in Gramma's kitchen. Aunty Ida, me, and my mother were all on the settle. Opposite the bathroom door. Gramma was stirring something on the stove and Uncle Izzy went into the bathroom. He had been in the hospital and was on a home visit.

When I was much older, I found out that he had been in a mental hospital as he'd run out in the street naked one night. But I didn't know that this particular day. So anyways, Uncle Izzy was in the bathroom which was right off the kitchen, as I've said. He was there a long time. Aunty Ida finally went to the door and rapped on it.

"Izzy, what's the matter? What's taking so long?"

No answer.

After about an hour, my father and uncles came into the kitchen. Aunty Ida was shaking with nerves.

"Izzy went into the bathroom an hour ago and he doesn't answer and won't come out."

So the men ran at the door, butting it with their shoulders until it crashed open. That's when I saw the blood. It was splattered everywhere, all over the walls, the floor, the windowsills, the mirror, the sink, all over Izzy, streaks of blood. The straight razor was in his out flung hand. He had cut his throat.

Aunty Ida's wailing came back to me as I looked at the deer and so did the awful fear I had felt on that day with no one to comfort me or to explain what he had done. I was too young to know about dying, but I did know about getting a cut and bleeding. Maybe there was no explanation, but everyone ignored me until I started to cry and my father yelled,

"You want to cry, I'll give you something to cry about!"

Since that meant a beating, I stifled the tears and I also stifled the memory. I was only three when it happened.

Noticing how pale my face had become, Alex asked,"What's the matter? Those dogs surely won't bother us if we turn back."

"It's not the dogs. It's a memory," I answered, and I told him about Uncle Izzy.

He dismounted, helped me gently from my horse, and held me closely while I sobbed and sobbed, finally grieving after all these years.

We turned the horses back and rode home on the paved roads.

Chapter Twenty-Six

Finally, we were going away for a weekend, Alex and I. The sky was deeply, uniformly blue as the ferry left Galilee for Block Island, a dream of a day to start a romantic weekend. Alex told his partner that he'd heard about Block Island and thought he'd explore it. Dom approved.

"Great idea. It's totally unspoiled. Like Martha's Vineyard, but not as built up. Thinking of getting over there myself one of these days."

Why Alex had to tell Dom where he was going, I don't know. It must have been some kind of death wish.

We hit the island about five and walked to the Atlantic Inn, a charming Victorian hotel complete with wraparound porches filled with rocking chairs, and, inside, glorious heavy wooden moldings and paneling, antique furniture and gorgeous views of the Atlantic on all sides. Our room was quaint and charming. Typically New England inn with flowered wallpaper, four posted bed, and old furniture. No phone. No television. But there was a bookcase filled with old volumes of John Marquand novels.

Our idyll had begun. The weather forecast was for 70-degree sun filled cloudless days for the whole weekend. The sea looked deep blue from our windows. We said nothing. Alex undressed me. We made love. We went out to eat in a noisy seafood place where everyone wore blue jeans and plaid shirts, walked back to the inn, hand in hand, not talking, sated, and went to sleep. The morning brought gourmet homemade granola, home baked

223

chocolate croissants, and the usual assortment of egg and meat dishes at the breakfast buffet in a room with windowed walls on three sides.

"I've never seen anything like this," Alex exclaimed. "Do you know what a place like this would cost in California? At least triple the tariff here and it wouldn't be so genuine."

"Well, this is pretty typically New England. The Vermont inns Joe and I used to go to are like this, but with mountain views instead of the ocean, of course."

I guess it wasn't very politic to mention my inn going with Joe to Alex, especially when he was so nervous about Joe. So sure Joe would make special trouble for him. He didn't need to be reminded of that entanglement. We spent the day biking all over the island, past stands of beach plums and wildflowers with glimpses of sandy beaches and rolling waves beyond them. The smell of ocean salt permeated the air the way it does at New England beaches. It was one thing I'd noticed about California beaches. The air there doesn't smell of sea.

It was all too perfect. I felt warm and glowy. But a hint of fear kept lurking deep inside, a premonition I think. We didn't talk much. Just biked and watched and ate clamcakes at a seaside shack. Went back to the inn. Made love again. And again. We showered, huddled together in the narrow stall, letting the warm water run over our bodies as we soaped each other down to our toes. We had to dress up for dinner in the hotel dining room. I felt special and pretty in my long, flowered dress. Sage green with cabbage roses, buttons down the front, the dress hugging the curves around my waist, flowing in soft folds to my ankles. Alex was natty in a navy blazer and white turtleneck that contrasted handsomely with his swarthy skin.

Sitting down to dinner, I noticed Alex's face blanch, his eyes widened, and a sick smile form. I looked up. Dom was there, walking in with who, I guess, was his latest girlfriend. They stopped at our table. Somehow, I managed to croak out a hello.

"This is Anne-Marie," he said, his hand on her shoulder. "This is the real Rhode Island experience." He laughed.

"Yeah," I responded. "You can't go anywhere without seeing someone you know." And that was true. Still is. It's the one thing visitors always comment on, the way people greet each

THERAPY, A NOVEL

other in restaurants, hail acquaintances across the rooms, say"That's Buddy over there" or"Oh, there's John Doe. I went to high school with him." The whole state is like a village. Alex looked devastated even when Dom and Anne-Marie moved on to their own table.

"What's he doing here? Spying on me?"

"Alex. It happens. It's a small place. You told him you were coming to the island for the weekend. It sounded good to him, so he came, too. Did you tell him you were staying at this hotel?"

"No, just that I was going to the island."

"Well, then, it's just a coincidence. Come on, let's look at this menu. It looks fabulous."

He fidgeted. His hand holding the menu trembled.

"I can't eat," he said. "Let's go."

"Go where?"

"Out of here. Off this damned island. This damned claustrophobic place."

"We can't get off the island until tomorrow morning," I reminded him. "There's no ferry. And he's already seen us. He knows. So what?"

"So what? Are you an idiot? This could cost me my license. The taboo of taboos. First and foremost, you don't screw your patients."

"Look, he's not going to squeal on you, and if he does, I'll deny it. Don't worry. Besides, you can always say I came onto you." As soon as I said that, I thought to myself that he had come on to me. Why did he, if he was so afraid?

"And you think of me as someone you screw? You shit. You were privileged to make love to me." I felt outraged.

"God I'm sorry. You're right, but it makes no difference who came on to whom and how we feel. I'm guilty anyway. I can't keep this up. It's too dangerous. I must have been out of my mind starting this whole thing with you. I was crazy. Insane. I don't know what came over me. But it has to stop and stop now."

"Alex, darling. Our kind of love is rare. Most people don't have it even once in a lifetime. We were lucky. It was just too bad we had to meet as doctor and patient, but we did. So what?

Please, let's have our dinner and enjoy ourselves. I'll talk to Dom. Anything. Don't panic."

But he panicked. He put the menu down and all but ran out of the dining room and out of the hotel. It was still light. I followed him, pleading. He shook me off when I tried to take his hand.

Defeated, I walked alone back to the room. A lead weight in my stomach. The crowds on the dock were like distant blobs of color and noise. My head was light. Thinking was impossible. Where Alex spent the night, I don't know.

It occurred to me finally. This was why he left California. He must have had an affair with a patient. Twice might guarantee his losing his license. The next morning he showed up to pack his things. He still wouldn't speak to me, except to say,"It's over. No more talk. It's over. Kaput. Now. No more. Don't get close to me. You're like a drug. You're dangerous."

So even he turned on me. Our love was my fault. But no, I won't think like that. Everyone is always looking for someone else to blame for their own doings. I wouldn't let anyone do that to me ever again.

I finally realized that I am a worthy, competent human being who has been awfully nice to everyone around her. Alex himself had certainly let me know that, and examining my life, I could see it. I cleaned house and cooked and ironed for my mother. Except for Hald I was a dutiful daughter who got good grades and prizes, I never gossiped about anyone or did mean, spiteful things to them. No, if Alex was afraid for his license, once he felt the attraction to me, he could have excused himself from my case and referred me to someone else. He got into this with both eyes wide open.

We walked separately to the ferry, sat apart on the voyage back to the mainland, and drove home in silence. I got out of the car, said goodbye to him, and never saw him again. Ironically, the divorce proceedings against Joe were set for Monday morning. Alex and I parted on Sunday evening. Irreconcilable differences.

Both with Joe and Alex.

Chapter Twenty-Seven

I love this house. It's little. Cozy. Old. Built in the eighteenth century as the plaque on the outside says. The ceilings are low with exposed chestnut beams. Every room has a fireplace. The one in the kitchen has a bread oven in it. The house smells like bacon. The walls must be saturated with that smell from hundreds of years of wood fires in the hearths.

The divorce proceedings went smoothly. Joe behaved gracefully, as, I hope, did I. He seemed as eager for it as I was. The day it was granted, I followed him out of the courthouse and saw him get into a waiting car. The driver was, tritely enough, blonde and probably no older than twenty-five. Whether she was around before we split, I don't know. I couldn't see if she was the Kathy O'Dowell the private eye showed me the picture of, the picture being too blurry. It made no difference anyway.

I sit in my smoky-scented living room curled up with a novel, patting the dogs, the cat purring in my lap, occasionally thinking of Alex, what he's doing. And with whom. But it's okay. I've been over him for years. I do miss the excitement, though, the manic high of love.

I've been doing some of my best research these past few years, but no more sixteen-hour days of writing, seven days a week, madly working to get yet one more paper published. Just enough to pass the days until I die. I write some. I've found old friends and new ones. The people who I assumed came to visit because of

Joe, not me, have shown me it is me they like. Or they like both of us, which is fine. I wish Joe well.

The biggest surprises are the young—to me—people who seek out my company, marveling at my wisdom, my open-mindedness, my humor. Omigod, that sounds so self-aggrandizing, so egocentric, like I'm a braggart. But it's not, and I'm not.

It came as a revelation to me that people in their 40's could be interested in someone in her 60's. It took me a long time to figure out why they wanted to go places with me or come to visit me. I was dumfounded for a long time, astonished, bewildered by the invitations to dinner, the movies, a concert. When my age came up in conversation, I was amazed to hear friends say things like, "You give me hope about getting older," and "You're my role model." Things like that. A couple of them have even said, "You're hot." Me, Barbara Verensky, hot?"

How could an ugly duckling whom people never liked suddenly become in old age someone to be sought out? In a youth-besotted culture like ours, how can an old woman be hot? If it didn't happen to me, I'd say it's bizarre.

I think my appeal is that, despite my age, I haven't become rigid. Partially, it's because I read. A lot. I love learning new things. I don't judge anyone's lifestyles, barring, of course, any that involve cruelty to others. I listen raptly to others, and don't talk about myself and my opinions, life in the good old days, or how terrible the world has become.

Actually, I love the new technology. Computers, hi-def TV's, movies on demand, even things young people take for granted like dishwashers, washing machines, and dryers. I grew up without those things and know the tedium of hanging clothes on a line outdoors or spending hours a week washing and drying dishes by hand. I love plastic money. I remember when if you didn't have cash in hand, you couldn't buy anything, even things you needed like new shoes. If it weren't for all the wars and corrupt dictatorships, the 21st century would be heaven to me. Though there have always been wars and corrupt governments. That's not new. Nor is the hand of man in causing the extinction of species.

That has been going on since man evolved. Now, extinction is speedier, but that's because there are so many people. I

THERAPY, A NOVEL

donate money to all the organizations fighting to preserve the environment, to relieve the suffering of animals, and to feed the hungry. I refuse to allow the bad things make me bitter or miserable. I fully agree that I have been lucky to be set on this earth at this time and in this place. I'm sorry the entire world can't live as I do, but there's no sense in making myself sick over that impossibility.

As it is, in America in the 21st century, most of us live better than the fabled emperors of old did. If we want music, we put a disc in the CD player or the computer or take out our MP3 player. If we want to see a drama or a comedy, we flick on the TV or put in a disk. If we need light, we just flick a switch. If we want to go a long distance, we get into our cars. No, I'm not a fuddy-duddy yearning for the days of cloth diapers and no air-conditioning.

Also, I know I don't know it all just because I've lived to be in my 60's and I don't delude myself that my own life decisions have been wise or should be emulated. I value other people's ideas. Of course, I don't dress like an old woman, nor do I try to look like a teenager. I stand erect, walk with pep, and bake delicious goodies.

I have a wonderful therapist, named Lee. He's overtly gay. No danger of a sexual liaison there, although that's not why I chose him. I know that he wouldn't be such a help if Alex hadn't liberated me first. Made me feel love. Made me feel I could be loved, desired madly, lustfully. The animality, the keenness of all my senses during that time. Certainly, I miss them. I'll never feel them again. That's okay, because now I have contentment and quiet joy.

As for my boys? Sammy is an almost full time artist. His stuff sells and he displays at art festivals all over the Northeast. For Mother's Day one year, he made me a proclamation declaring my love, devotion, intelligence, beauty, and bravery—a merit badge after all these years. The others are all right, too. We have fun times and laughter together. Their adolescent resentment seems to be spent. Their children are wonderful, of course.

It's a relief living in this old country house. Nothing grand to live up to. How can you be grand when you're not even five feet tall? And I love the spirit of generations who have lived in this house. The low ceilings, the wood paneling on the walls, the

molded chair railings, the brick oven in the kitchen, cozy, warm, they fit me perfectly.

The aloneness of my young years has come back, full circle, but for one thing. It is punctuated by friends. Still, I have hours to myself. To live in my own imagination, ponder my own thoughts. I love it. I don't want sleepovers, except for my visiting grandchildren.

My friends invite me out and stop by, friends whom I cook fancy dinners for. Strangely, when I want men, they still want me. That's a surprise, isn't it? In fact, I'm fatally attractive to little, dark men like Alex. I read the would-be lovers' ads and wonder why people need to advertise. Maybe it's the academic environment I am part of. There's always some man in the faculty lounge or the computer lab looking for conversation or a laugh or two. Some of them are fun or interesting to be with over drinks or food, and some of them even have free time to indulge themselves with me.

I know now that men aren't doing me a favor by showering me with attention. I'm worth their while. I'm funny, have interesting things to talk about, and am good natured and kind. I've learned my own value, which is the nicest thing about getting old, but I'm careful not to let myself be smug. I know I'm lucky and that people better than I are having tough times, are lonely and alone. I can't say I've earned the life I have now or that it was due to me because I did this or that. Ultimately, it's luck and I am grateful to whatever the power may be for letting me have this life now.

Age? Well, I'm in my early 60's now as I said, and if you live long enough you get old. Growing old gracefully is a laugh. There's nothing physically graceful about that decline: the sagging, the wrinkling, the aches and pains of aging. Yet, men come on to me. They find me attractive still, gracious and interesting and fun. I have gained in assurance, and that is a big draw to men.

There is emotional gracefulness: the wonderful calmness with which you greet the days and nights, the equanimity in the face of others' foibles, the sense which keeps internal turmoil at bay, the tolerance for the way others choose to spend their lives.

THERAPY, A NOVEL

Most of all, there is the immunity to the elation of being in lust or, worse, love. Because then when it ends, the raw bleeding begins. Time has soothed my old wounds. Those caused by Joe and by Alex, and before them my crazy parents. Old treacheries have lost their sting. I know people too well now to be dismayed by new ones. Let me get my joys from the hummingbirds and the little red foxes running though the woods.

When I moved to this house, the gardens were all tangled. So I spent my first winter here with catalogs, diagramming where the foxglove would go, the phlox, and the mums. Planning gardens is like solving complex math problems. You have to consider what will be in bloom and when, so that the right colors and shapes are making a show at the same time: the balls of pink and white peonies nestling near flashy red and orange Oriental poppies, the flamboyant Dresden blue hydrangeas and the yellow lilies trembling at each other.

Dreaming of gardens thriving and spreading so colors and forms grow into each other, leaving no spaces, that's what fills me with delight. Maybe rain or wind breaks the stalks of the most majestic six foot delphinium, the one you should have staked and didn't. Even if you did, no matter what, the garden is never perfect all spring, summer, and fall. Something refuses to show its head at the appointed time. Something else invades another's space. So you make notes and next season make adjustments, all in the quest for the perfect garden–which you know will never come, but the quest itself is the joy, and enough is always beautiful so moments of exquisite joy keep bursting in you for all three seasons. You wish those days of iridescent pink phlox contrasting with the black-eyed Susans could last longer, but if they did, if every flower was always in bloom, you'd forget to seek them out, to view them from every angle.

It's the same with the unpredictable weather here in New England. The sunny, brilliant blue-skied days are so magnificent because they may be followed by gray-clouded misty ones. Oddly, the flowers often seem more iridescent on those gray days. And the cold winters with everything asleep in their beds, busily spreading roots for the unfrozen days, are respite from weeding and deadheading, but also delicious with anticipation of the gentler seasons to come.

Even after eight years, I'm still poring over catalogs looking for new things to plant, new looks to try. Of course, some of the perennials aren't so perennial. Like electronic gadgets, "lifetime" means maybe four years, so you have to replace them. Then, when you choose one new plant, you realize you need another to go with it. There's no end to gardens, no point at which you can say, "It's complete. I never have to do another thing with it, just keep it fertilized, watered, and make sure spent blooms are deadheaded." Every year you have to add and subtract, change or plant more of something. Sammy paints with acrylics and watercolors. I paint, so to speak, with flowers.

I see my boys frequently, and rather enjoy conversing with them. They stop by for my lasagna or chocolate rum cake, bringing their babies with them. My older grandchildren are coming into their teens and it's wonderful. There's no baggage with them, so we can talk and discuss everything and wonder of wonders, to me they listen, take in every word. Oh, they do disagree with many points I make, but they do so nicely, giving me their reasons for objections and you know what? Sometimes they're even right. Sometimes I am.

I'm content with my work, my gardens, my tiny, fluffball pups. Little, white packets of intelligent, rascally love. My golden-red chow, Ming Li successor to Ruff, patrols the grounds faithfully, checking the perimeter every hour, beating a path from the back of the house to the front on her regular rounds. She'll keep the deer from my gardens next summer and the coyotes away from the pups. She welcomes nobody, letting a person come up to the door only if I tell her it's okay.

So I'm safe. Physically, at least. But emotionally too, I think. Nobody hurts me anymore. I only let myself care for people who care for me, really care, not people who want to use me. It's easy to achieve that, by the way. Just don't do anything for anyone unless you feel like it, and don't let anybody, anybody at all, let you think you owe them a damned thing.

Even so, in the summer, when the honeysuckle and wild roses permeate the humid air with their fragrance, and the brown bats are clearing the mosquitoes from the air, I feel a pang in my stomach. Nostalgia. And I wonder where he is, what he's smelling, what he's doing. If he's thinking of me. But I wonder for

only a moment, and then I start setting the table for Phil, or Tom, or Carl, whoever's night it's going to be. Yes, some of them are younger than I am, although that's not the criterion for being my lover. There is no one criterion. There are criteria. They have to be funny like Phil, or insightful and intellectually exciting like Tom, or gentle and handy about the house like Carl. No one is allowed to stay until breakfast. Not one is allowed to be jealous, to think of me as his alone, and I don't care if he has someone else. I just don't want to talk about it, just as I don't talk about any of them to each other.

Things last as long as they last, and then, without regrets, goodbye. My passion is learning. My friends are women. My men are lovers who don't mind a little sagging here and there. In addition, they're also good at lifting heavy objects.

THE END